THE STORIES THAT MUST BE TOLD

Also by Debby Meltzer Quick

McKinney Class of 1986
May I Have Your Attention Please
I Just Can't Say I Love You
Absolutely and Totally Smitten

Anomaly
Don't Say a Word

THE STORIES THAT MUST BE TOLD

McKinney High Class of 1986
Book 5

Debby Meltzer Quick

Trigger Warning
This text includes references to mental illness, substance abuse,
descriptions of sexual assault, verbal and psychological abuse.

ISBN: 979-8-9871874-3-2
Cover design by: Jai Design
Author photograph: Milana Gilligan Photography
Copyediting & Typesetting by: Nicole Frail Edits
Printed in the United States of America

PART ONE

DARLENE: THE BEGINNING

Chapter 1

FRIENDS FOR LIFE

BARBARA FEINMAN PICKED UP A magazine from the waiting room table and flipped through it, looking at pictures of skinny women in maternity clothes. She made a face. These women hadn't spent a minute pregnant in their whole brief lives. They should hire real pregnant models, with swollen feet, and puffy faces. That would be an ad campaign Barbara could get behind. She checked the clock. Ten after ten. The obstetrician must be running late. That was the risk at these appointments. An unexpected delivery. She sighed, shifting in her chair to get more comfortable. She might be there a while.

The door to the doctor's office opened, and a young, very pregnant woman walked in. She signed in at the front desk, took off her coat, and then sat down in a seat facing Barbara. She looked at Barbara and smiled, and then picked up a magazine.

She looked like a child. A beautiful child. She had long, straight, thick dark hair held back with a wide bright green fabric headband. Her skin was clear and rosy. She was wearing a long-sleeved dress that ended just above her knees and was covered with a bright floral pattern. And go-go boots. She wore false eyelashes and thick blue eye shadow. Barbara stared. This child looked like a pregnant brunette Nancy Sinatra.

The girl looked up and caught Barbara staring. She smiled again. "Hi," she said.

Barbara smiled back. "Hi," she said. "When is your baby due?"

"March first," was her answer. "It's a leap year this year, so if she comes one day early, she'll only have a birthday every four years." She laughed. "How about you?"

Barbara's hand shot to her belly. "May 15," she said. "So you don't have much longer to go. Are you ready?"

The girl nodded. "I guess as ready as I can be," she said. "I'm pretty excited. Is this your first baby?"

"Yes," Barbara replied, rubbing the space over her navel. "My husband and I have been trying to start our family since we got married three years ago. We finally got lucky. I was worried we would end up old and childless."

The girl looked at her skeptically. "May I ask how old you are?" she inquired.

"Twenty-three," Barbara answered. "I know that doesn't sound old, but we only have so much time, and I don't think I would want to have a baby after twenty-eight. I think that would just be so hard on the body. And how old are you?"

"Nineteen," the girl answered. "I guess I have a lot of time to have more babies." Now she started rubbing her belly. "The baby must have woken up. She's kicking like a Rockette!"

Barbara smiled. "You want a girl?"

"I do," the girl answered. "I would be okay with a boy, but it would be so wonderful to have a little girl, with the cute clothes and all. And I could teach her how to cook, and sew, and all the things that my mother taught me."

"Does your husband want a boy?" Barbara asked.

The girl looked down at her boots. "I don't have a husband." She looked up at Barbara. "I had a boyfriend, but when I told him I was pregnant, his first response was to tell me to make it go away. When I said no, he picked up a glass vase from my parents' counter and threw it at the wall. There was glass, water, and bits of flowers everywhere. It was scary. Some glass even landed on my foot, but luckily, I didn't get cut. My father came running in and kicked him out of the house. I haven't seen him since. I hope I never do. If he showed his face at our house again, I think my father would punch his lights out. He never liked him anyways." She sighed. "No, I'm in this all by myself. My parents will help some, but I'm gonna be the mom. I'm gonna to take the best care of my baby."

Barbara looked at her. She felt a wave of sympathy. Just earlier, she was feeling sorry for herself because her husband, Reggie, wasn't able to accompany her to this appointment due to work, even though she had given him a lot of notice. Now, comparing her situation to this young girl's, she felt relief and affection toward Reggie. Reggie wanted this baby. This baby had been planned.

Barbara stuck her hand out toward the girl. "My name is Barbara," she said. "Barbara Feinman."

The girl took her hand and shook it lightly. "I'm Victoria Lester," she said.

"Nice to meet you, Victoria," Barbara said. "Do people call you Vicky?"

Victoria shook her head. "Oh, no," she said. "Not if they don't want an earful from me. It's Victoria. Not Vicky, not Tory. Some of my friends call me Vee, and that's okay."

"Are your friends excited about your baby?" Barbara wondered.

Victoria frowned. "A lot of my friends have gone to college. I was going to junior college, but now I'm taking time off. I'm just going to focus on getting my real estate license so I can work and support me and the baby, and get our own place someday. But my other friends, some are okay, but some have really shied away from me. I don't think their parents really approve of them being friends with an unwed teen mother. It's hard to believe people still feel that way in 1968, what with all the peace and love stuff going on, and all the boys dying in Vietnam, but they still do. So I basically just hang around with my mom and dad most of the time."

Barbara thought about it. "Do you live in Eastboro?" she asked.

"Yes," Victoria answered. "We live on the east side of Carson Lake. My father's a product manager at Aries Corps."

Barbara smiled. "We live over by the lake, too," she said. "Reggie's an underwriter at an investment company that's affiliated with Aries. Small world! I bet our babies will end up in school together someday. Maybe we can get together after the babies come and have them play together."

Victoria looked at Barbara hopefully. "Really? I would love that! But your husband won't mind, what with me being unmarried?"

Barbara waved that off with a laugh. "No, Reggie won't care about that at all. And he's at work all day anyway, so he won't even be around."

She struggled to her feet and walked over to the reception area to request a piece of paper and a pencil. She wrote her name and telephone number on the top half, then tore the paper in two.

"Victoria," she said, "what's your parent's phone number?"

Victoria had a girl on February 28. She named her Kim. Not Kimberly, but Kim, because that's what she wanted to call her. Barbara came to visit her in the hospital and met Victoria's mother, Susan Lester. She held baby Kim and longed for her own baby to arrive.

Barbara had her baby on May 18, and she and Reggie named her Darlene Renee Feinman. Victoria came to see her in the hospital along with baby Kim, and Barbara marveled at how large the two-and-a-half-month-old baby looked beside her tiny newborn. They took their first photos together and deemed their daughters best friends.

Chapter 2

CHALLENGES

REGGIE WAS DIFFERENT AFTER THE baby arrived. He had been so anxious to start their family, but now he seemed disinterested in doing anything to participate in her care. Barbara had imagined them learning to care for their daughter together: giving Darlene her first bath, taking her on carriage rides to Twin Bridges Park, changing her into her puffy pink dress with a white collar to go visit her grandparents . . . but Reggie declined. He was either too tired from work, or too busy reading his newspaper or watching the news. He did not get up at night to get the baby so Barbara could nurse her, so Barbara spent her nights and days in an exhausted fog.

Her friends told her that their husbands were useless at helping with their babies, too, but at least they seemed interested. Reggie acted like the baby had disrupted his routine, and he resented it. It was as if he had liked the idea of a baby, but when a real one arrived, it wasn't at all what he thought he had ordered. Barbara had thought that they would start to work on conceiving baby number two soon after Darlene was born, but Reggie didn't seem very interested in that either. It was like he didn't find her attractive anymore, and he would leave the room when she was nursing. Some days passed when the only human contact Barbara experienced was holding and feeding her infant. She felt isolated, and worried. But she was afraid to bring it up to Reggie.

She called Victoria more, and Victoria welcomed her calls. Victoria was feeling overwhelmed herself. Kim was a sweet and cuddly baby, but she had a scream that could pierce her mother's eardrums. And she just wouldn't go to sleep! Victoria was tired and worn out, but she didn't want to complain. Many people had thought she couldn't raise a child on her own, but she was showing them that she could. And she was taking classes to get her real estate license. Her mother watched the baby when she went to class. Sometimes, she felt herself drifting off to sleep during class time, and she had to rouse herself and try twice as hard to listen. Some nights, while Kim finally slept, Victoria would cry herself to sleep.

Barbara and Victoria found solace in each other. Visiting one another gave them reasons to shower, get dressed, and put on makeup, even on days when they didn't need to. They would take the babies to the park, or to the diner for lunch, or just sit on the floor in each other's living rooms with the babies and talk. Sometimes, they would talk about their problems, but mostly, they gossiped about celebrities and other mothers.

"Did you see that hat that Carla was wearing at the park yesterday?" Barbara said to Victoria as they both dangled squeaky toys over the faces of their infants. "I think she's trying to look like Jackie Kennedy, but she really doesn't."

Victoria laughed. "No, she looked more like Jackie Gleason!" she said, and Barbara almost spit out her gum laughing.

The two mothers watched each other's babies for short periods of time so they could get their hair done or do other small chores. One afternoon in August, Victoria kept Darlene so Barbara could get her hair styled into a fancy beehive and buy a new dress. Her mother would be taking Darlene for the night so Barbara could cook dinner for Reggie and hopefully have a night of romance without the wails of a three-month-old baby as their background music. When Barbara came back to the Lester home, Victoria raved about her hair and gave her some makeup tips. Barbara modeled her new dress.

"Oh, Barbara," Victoria said, clapping her hands together and entwining her fingers. "You look like a movie star! Your figure is so lovely! No one would even know to look at you that you just had a baby! Reggie will find you stunning!"

Barbara blushed. "Do you really think so?" she asked, looking at herself from every possible angle in the mirror. "I always feel so awkward in my own body with nursing and just not having time to take care of myself. But maybe now Reggie will see I'm still the woman he married, and I still take care in how I look for him."

Victoria smiled at her friend. "Barb, any man would be lucky to have you for his wife. I hope Reggie knows he won the jackpot when he married you. He's a lucky man!"

Later that night, Barbara fussed over the stove making homemade mashed potatoes to go with the steak she was waiting to put under the broiler. She had cut the ends off fresh string beans and had a pot of water on the burner waiting to boil. Once almost everything was ready to go, she went to her bedroom and put on her new dress. She sat at her vanity and applied her makeup carefully, just as Victoria had shown her. At a quarter to six, she went back to the kitchen and turned on the broiler. Then she put the steak in the oven. Reggie would be home soon.

At six thirty, the potatoes were getting cold and the beans soggy. Barbara sighed and stood up to address the food. She heard the door open, and Reggie came into the kitchen.

"What's for dinner?" he asked by way of a greeting. He took off his suit coat and threw it on the back of a chair and then loosened his tie.

Barbara attempted to smile. "Remember, Reggie?" she told him. "I made a special dinner for us tonight, but it was ready at six, so it might not be quite as fresh. Why are you late?"

Reggie shot her a look. "Late? It's six thirty. That's hardly late." He looked around. "Where's the baby?"

"She's at my mother's house for the night, remember?" Barbara said through partially gritted teeth. "So we could have some time to ourselves."

"Oh," Reggie said, turning back to look at her. "Well good. It will be nice to get a good night's sleep for once without all of that hollering at two in the morning. Who can sleep through all that crying?"

He sat down, waiting for her to serve him.

"Mr. Finch wanted me to have a glass of scotch with him in his office before I left tonight, so I stayed behind for a few minutes. That's how you know they're looking at you for a promotion over there, when they start to take an interest in you after hours. I couldn't say no."

He looked up at Barbara as she placed a plate of food in front of him. "What's that all over your face?" he said with a scowl.

Barbara's hand went to her cheek. "Did I get some mashed potatoes on me?"

"No," Reggie said, squinting at her. "It looks like some kind of makeup, but it looks like you did it wrong."

Barbara raised a brow. "What?" she asked.

"And you got a new dress. How much did that set me back?"

Barbara took a deep breath. "I bought it with money I saved from my grocery allowance," she told him. "And it was on sale. What do you think?" She did a twirl for him.

Reggie shrugged. "It's a nice dress, but don't you think you should wait until you lose the pregnancy weight before you wear something like that? It's not very flattering. It's like putting a tutu on a hippopotamus." Reggie started laughing and went back to his steak.

Barbara felt like she had been hit by a truck. She was about to say something in her defense when Reggie spoke again. "This steak is dry and cold, and the potatoes are lumpy."

Tears and anger rose up in her chest. She looked at Reggie, and then turned on her heels, ran to her bedroom, and slammed the door. She threw herself down on the bed and sobbed. Reggie had never spoken to her like this before the baby, even when he did have a bit to drink. His words were hurtful and stabbing. And why? He thought he knew what it was like to be awakened every night to a hungry, crying baby? Who did Reggie think got up every night to attend to that baby, to quiet her so he could sleep, only to return later to his loud snores in their bed? Barbara was exhausted, and yet she still made an effort for them, for their marriage. But Reggie was changing.

She remembered the loving, amicable, adventurous Reggie she had met at a party at a mutual friend's house four years earlier. That Reggie had been up for anything. He liked to hike, cross-country ski, and take long rides in the country where all they did was talk. And he had loved to take her to bed, to please her, and show her how special she was to him. They had talked of having children, of going on epic journeys across the country in a recreational vehicle, seeing the Grand Canyon and Old Faithful. But now their first child had arrived, and Reggie was preoccupied with his work and ignoring his wife and daughter. And tonight, he was downright rude and insulting.

Barbara sat up and dabbed her eyes with a tissue. She would go back out there. She would eat her dinner with dignity, and Reggie would apologize for the way he spoke to her. Then they would talk and figure out what was going on. And everything would be okay again.

She went to the bathroom and washed the tears off her face, and with it, her carefully applied makeup. She patted her skin dry, smiled at the mirror, and then made her way to the kitchen. Reggie had already left the room to watch the news. He had left his empty plate on the table for her to clean up.

Barbara fixed a plate for herself, and then sat down to eat. Reggie came into the room, and Barbara waited for him to speak.

He looked at her. "Oh good. You took off that awful makeup. So you could see how it made you look like a clown, too."

He went to the refrigerator, grabbed a bottle of beer, and walked back out of the room.

Barbara sat in a stunned silence. Then, she calmly ate the rest of her dinner, cleaned the kitchen, and went to her room. She came out with an overnight bag. She approached Reggie in front of the TV. "I'm going to my mother's house," she told him. "I need to be with Darlene. I'll be back in the morning with the baby."

"Now you made me miss the end of that story," Reggie complained, trying to look around her. He sighed. "I'm playing golf with Mr. Finch tomorrow morning at City Club. Then we're having lunch. I may not be home until late."

"Good night, Reggie," Barbara said. She was going to kiss him on the cheek and then thought better of it.

He didn't look up as she walked toward the door, left the house, and drove off in her car to her mother's house.

Chapter 3

SOUR MILK

THE APOLOGY NEVER CAME. THE behavior didn't change. Barbara stopped trying to get Reggie's attention. Reggie stayed at work later, and as he predicted, he got promoted with a significant pay raise soon after. Then he made more trips to the City Club with his cronies to play golf, eat endless lunches, and smoke cigars while drinking scotch. Reggie didn't even like Scotch.

Barbara decided to spend her time and energy focusing on other things. She attended to Darlene and brought her to a play group of babies her own age. She encouraged Victoria to come with Kim when she was not in class. She volunteered to assist with neighborhood events and activities and became treasurer of the Aries Corps Wives Charity Club. She and Victoria spent more time together with their daughters, walking through department stores, going to parks, or just playing in their homes when the weather got colder. They focused on talking about the unfortunate clothing choices of the other women they knew and stories they had overheard. Barbara rarely spoke about Reggie.

Soon, it was Christmastime, and Aries was having its annual Christmas banquet. It was on the same evening as the Lester family's holiday extravaganza, and Barbara wanted to go to that instead. Reggie didn't want to show up at his work function without his wife, as it just didn't fit the image of the family man he was trying to portray to his superiors. Barbara refused to go.

"It's that Lester girl, isn't it?" Reggie hissed at her. "She's putting all these hippie ideas and notions in your head. For God's sake, you're even trying to look like her now. Take that ridiculous headband out of your hair, would you? You're not a beatnik! You're a twenty-four-year-old mother, not a nineteen-year-old slut with a bastard baby!"

Barbara recoiled as though she had been slapped. "You take that back, Reginald Feinman," she said in her calmest voice, though her fists were clenched.

Reggie's face turned red. "I will not!" he exclaimed. "I said what I said. She's a no-good junior college dropout, and I wouldn't be surprised if that ragamuffin of hers ends up with a drug addiction and her picture on the centerfold of a men's magazine."

He looked at her as if daring her to make a rebuttal. Instead, Barbara took several deep breaths, released her fists, and went to pick up her baby.

"Get the hell out of here," she said to him through her teeth. "I can't even look at you. Just get out. I don't care where you go, but just leave. Didn't you hear me? I said *get out of here!*"

For the first time, Reggie appeared uncertain as to what to do next. Then he nodded. "Okay," he said, "I'll go. I'll spend the night at my parents' house. But I'm coming back tomorrow."

"You'll come back tomorrow to pack your things," Barbara told him. "Enough until we figure out what to do next. But I won't be here. If you do come back, I expect you to be gone again by three, understand?"

Reggie looked at her with no expression. "Okay," he said calmly. "I understand. I'll go now." He walked backward for a few steps, turned around, grabbed his coat, and was gone.

It was only then that Barbara noticed the baby in her arms was red-faced and screaming. And that her own tears had been falling onto Darlene's face. She rushed to the sofa, pulled up her shirt, and started to nurse her daughter. The baby quickly calmed and grabbed onto her hair.

She realized that Reggie had not said a word about the baby the whole time they were arguing, and when he left, he didn't tell her goodbye or even glance at her at all. All that Barbara could think at that very moment was that she was a terrible mother, because she was feeding her baby sour milk.

Chapter 4

WHAT'S NEXT?

BY SPRING, BOTH BABY GIRLS were walking and getting into all sorts of mischief. Victoria was getting closer to completing her real estate classwork, and after that she would have to take her exam. Barbara helped her study and quizzed her on the material. The girls were close to sleeping through the night now, and both mothers were getting more rest. And Reggie was in and out of the house.

Reggie was motivated to be back with his family, and sometimes, he was able to participate in the activities that made Barbara want to welcome him back. Now that Darlene was a little bit older, she didn't require quite as much intensive care, and Reggie could play and roughhouse with her and make her laugh. He even tried his hand at giving her baths and putting her to bed.

Reggie could maintain this level of parenting for two to three weeks before cracking, and then either he would storm out to his parents' house, or Barbara would strongly encourage him to remove himself from the premises. Their arguments would get loud and heated, and as time passed, Barbara became increasingly resentful, sending barbs back in Reggie's direction. She hated herself for stooping to his level, and any time she heard Darlene's cries during an argument, she would be engulfed with guilt and whisk the baby away, either to the bedroom or to her mother's house. But when Darlene wasn't crying, she was watching. And learning.

There were no more babies. There was one night, when Reggie had finally talked her into going to the Aries Corps Christmas Party, 1969, where they both drank enough to make them amorous, but two weeks later, Barbara started her period, and that ended that.

Victoria became a licensed realtor and began to work for a local agency run by an older couple. Her mother watched the baby while she worked, and Victoria finally felt like a contributing member of society. She had more juicy stories to tell Barbara.

"So I was showing a house to this man and woman, a married couple, and we went down to the basement. They're looking around, and making comments about turning the area into their fun room. So I asked them if they were planning to have kids, because I'm figuring the fun room is like a rec room, right? They say no. Then they say they need to have Joshua and Felice come over and see the place, to see what they think, and I asked them if they're trusted friends, and the guy says, 'No, they're this other couple we know that swings.' So I have no idea, and I must have looked like a childish moron, so I say, 'Like a swing set?' And they start to laugh. And they proceeded to tell me, in graphic detail, what swinging actually is." She leaned in closer to Barbara and covered Kim's ears with her hands. "Barbara, have you ever heard of swinging?"

Taking Victoria's lead, Barbara leaned in and covered Darlene's ears. "Isn't it a kind of dancing?"

Victoria laughed. "Kind of," she said, forgetting about Kim's ears for the moment. "Swinging is when more than one married couple gets together, and they, well, I guess 'make love' isn't really the term for it, but you get my drift. They have intercourse with other people's spouses! And everyone's okay with it! They even have parties, where people socialize, and then go off with each other to the other rooms, you know, to *swing*! So that's what this couple was looking for. A house where they could have these parties! They didn't even seem embarrassed by it!"

"Did they buy the house?" Barbara asked.

"No, they passed on it and decided to stay in Framingham. But now, you know, I have to wonder. Are there a lot of people who do these things? And why did I never know?"

"Mommy," Darlene said, "can we go to the park and go on the swings?"

Kim perked up. "Yeah, the swings! Can we, Mommy?"

Barbara and Victoria laughed, and they got off the floor to prepare to walk their kids to the park. Victoria leaned toward Barbara. "I guess we have to start remembering now," she said quietly. "They're not babies any-more. Little pitchers have big ears!"

Barbara froze. That was the moment she knew: She had to ask Reggie for a divorce. For Darlene's sake.

She brought it to his attention the next time he was home. "Reggie, I don't think this arrangement is working out anymore," she told him while Darlene was off playing in her room. She spoke softly so her voice wouldn't carry. "I'm not happy, and I worry about Darlene seeing us arguing, no, fighting all the time. It's not good for her. And you can't possibly be happy either."

"So what are you saying, Barbara?" Reggie said, his voice starting to elevate.

Barbara shushed him. "I don't want her to hear us. What I'm saying is I think our marriage is not working out. I think we should start talking about getting a divorce!"

"Oh, do you?" Reggie said, standing up out of his chair, with no regard to the volume of his voice. "What, is this something that your friend thinks you should do? Just give up on seven years of marriage so you can go out and party and meet men with her to bring home to your child? To our child?"

Barbara forgot about Darlene and the volume. "What in the hell are you talking about Reggie?" she shouted. "I have never once, one day in my life, even considered being unfaithful to you! Can you say the same? I mean, all those late nights at work? And long lunches at the country club? For all I know, you've got a whole second family out there while I'm struggling to keep things together here for me and Darlene! Where do you get off—"

"Where do *I* get off?" Reggie yelled.

This went on for several minutes. Upstairs, in the back of the house, Darlene stood alone in the middle of her bedroom with the door closed, but it still didn't block out the sound of her parents' angry voices. She closed her eyes and started to hum a song she'd heard on *Sesame Street*. She hummed it again, louder. Then she could hear the song in her head. She started to sway and bounce on her feet. Pretty soon, she had tuned them out completely. All she could hear was the music, and all she could feel was the beat. This was what got Darlene through these times. She would just make them go away like they never happened.

Chapter 5

Two Houses

DARLENE SPENT ONE OR TWO nights a week at her father's new house, in her new room with the walls painted pink and the fancy bed with the pink-striped bedspread. Her father had let her choose what she wanted. And he had bought her a stuffed turtle to sleep with. When they got together, he would take her to the movies, or to playgrounds and amusement parks, or on long walks around magically beautiful ponds and lakes. They found frogs and tadpoles and chased butterflies with a special net. Darlene loved their time together and the fun they had. But she didn't like pickup or drop-off times. Her parents just couldn't keep from saying mean things to each other, and sometimes, they seemed to forget that Darlene could hear them when they yelled with hushed voices. That's when she would start to hum and sway. Sometimes she would start before the yelling began, just to be ready. And she would rock on her feet. Eventually, one of her parents would come and take her hand and lead her away, and no matter where they ended up, they would pretend that everything was just fine and wonderful.

The truly wonderful times were when she played with Kim. Kim liked to run around and get dirty with her, and to play with stuffed animals. She also liked *Sesame Street*, and they would watch and sing together.

Sometimes they would play quietly with their toys while their mothers sat at the kitchen table, talking and drinking tea or coffee. Victoria would tell long and detailed stories about the people she met at work, and her own mother would tell secrets about other people. She would lean in close toward Victoria and tell her what she knew. Sometimes, it was about other mothers, and sometimes, it was about her grandparents, and other times, it was about people that Darlene had never heard of. Sometimes Victoria would laugh so hard at these tidbits of information that she would spit out her tea. Kim didn't even notice, but Darlene couldn't help but be intrigued.

"How do you know all this stuff?" Victoria asked her one day as she dabbed her spit tea off her bare arm.

"It's easy," Barbara told her. "You just use your eyes and ears. Keep them open. In the grocery store, you could be reading a box of instant mashed potatoes, but really, you're listening to Mrs. Farmer in the next aisle complaining to her daughter about how her neighbor walks around in the altogether nude with the curtains wide open. Or you might be having gas pumped at the station with your windows down, but your ears are facing the car in the other lane, where Paula is confiding to her friend Risa that she kissed Tina's boyfriend under the bleachers at the football field! Of course, none of this really matters if you don't know Paula, Risa, and Tina, but sometimes, you hear something about someone that you know. Or know of. So you use your eyes to spot the target, and then you focus your ears on the conversation. You learn to listen to more than one thing at once. And people actually speak louder when they think they're being so discreet!"

"Eyes and ears, eyes and ears," Darlene mumbled. "Use your eyes and ears." She hummed. Then she sang the words. "Eyes and ears," she sang quietly.

Kim looked up. "Do you want to go play house with your doll house?" she asked.

Darlene nodded, and they both stood and ran to her room.

Chapter 6

WORDS HURT

THE SUMMER OF THEIR FIFTH year seemed to fly by. There were outings to the DeMarco Elementary School playground to get the girls used to the area for when they started kindergarten in the fall. The girls would play on the swings and go down the slide and peek in the windows of the classrooms. Sometimes their mothers took them to Friendly's for an ice cream cone after. One day, they ate lunch at Friendly's as a special treat.

Victoria cleared her throat. "Girls," she said, and Darlene and Kim looked up. "Mrs. Feinman and I are going to go on a little mommy trip next week, and we'll be gone for five days. While we're gone, Kim, you'll stay with Grandma."

"And Darlene," Barbara said, "you will stay with your daddy. That will be fun, won't it?"

Darlene looked from her mother to Victoria and back, and saw them meet each other's eyes, and they were not smiling.

"Where are you going?" Kim asked. "Can't we just go with you?"

Victoria smiled at her daughter. "Babe, Mommy and Mrs. Feinman are going to a special place where only grown-ups can go and stay. It's called

Atlantic City, and we are just going to have some mommy time. We have never been away from you girls for that long, I know, but I think you'll have fun while we're gone, and you'll hardly miss us. And you can get together and play with each other while we're gone. We'll make sure of it. And when we get back, it will be time to get ready for you girls to start school! Isn't that exciting?"

Darlene looked at Kim, and Kim nodded. Darlene nodded too. She felt her feet start to rock below her.

Her mother dropped her off at her father's house on Thursday night. When they went inside, her father had pieces of Weaver fried chicken and French fries waiting for her on the table, as well as a glass of milk. As Darlene ate, her father told her all the fun things they would do together.

"We can go swimming at the JCC tomorrow, and then we'll go to McDonald's. On Saturday, you'll go play at the Lesters' with Kim. On Sunday, if you want and the weather is nice, we can go see the polar bears at the Natural Science Museum. Remember when we did that last year? I remember that you liked the gift shop. I got you that shirt with the bears on it. Maybe on Monday, I can take you and Kim to the big playground, or we can go to Carson Lake Beach. Does that sound like fun?"

Darlene nodded as she chewed her fries. It did sound like fun. She couldn't wait to have all that fun.

It was all fun until Saturday night. Her father picked her up at Kim's house and brought her home for dinner. But he had forgotten about dinner until just before he came to get her, so he was in a rush. "I just got back from golf with Mr. Finch," he told her, like this was something important that she should understand. He poured a can of peas into a saucepan and put them on the stove.

"I don't like peas," Darlene told him as her stomach rumbled. She had not eaten anything since snack time, which had been just one cookie.

"Well, peas is what we have," he told her as he took a box of fish sticks out of the freezer.

"I don't want fish," Darlene said.

Reggie turned around and glared at her. "Does your mother let you dictate what you have for dinner? I don't think so. You eat peas and fish, or you don't eat!"

Darlene froze. She felt sick in her stomach. Her father had never spoken to her like that before. That was the voice he used with her mother. When she was with her father, they had fun. They did fun things. This was not fun.

Darlene kept her mouth shut and climbed up on her chair to sit. Her shoulder knocked into something, and she felt cold liquid run down her arm.

"Now look what you did!" her father yelled. "You knocked over my beer and got it all over my newspaper! It's ruined! What the hell is wrong with you? Ugh, you smell like a brewery. Go to your room and get out of those clothes."

"But Daddy, I'm hungry!" Darlene insisted.

Reggie went quiet and stood very still. "Darlene Renee, you will go straight to your room, right now, before I get really angry. And you will stay there until I decide you are ready to leave. Do you understand?"

Darlene searched her father's face for some understanding, but she couldn't find any. She had messed up her father's beer and his newspaper. She had been bad. Now she needed to go to her room. She turned around, ran upstairs, and fell face-first onto her bed, crying. She wanted her mother. She wanted her pale-yellow painted room with its regular bed and tan-colored bed spread. But she was stuck at her father's house for three more days. And she was no longer having fun.

When her mother picked her up on Tuesday afternoon, Darlene felt a sense of relief. Her mother ran up to hug her, and Darlene buried her face in her shirt and smelled her hair. Her father came to the door with her bags.

"That's everything," he said, pleasantly. "I'll miss you, sweetheart." He leaned down to give her a kiss, and Darlene stayed very still and quiet.

Her mother looked at her curiously. "Say goodbye to your daddy," she prompted.

"Bye, Daddy," Darlene said softly, and she reached for her mother's hand. Her father had not yelled at her again for the rest of the time she was there, but she couldn't forget. Her mother and father really didn't like each other, she could tell. And now it seemed her daddy didn't really like *her* much either.

They got into the car, and her mother strapped her in. Then she went around to the driver's side, got in, and started the engine. "Sweetheart, what's wrong?" she asked. "Are you mad at me for going away for so long?" Darlene shook her head. "Then what is it?"

Darlene shrugged. "I don't want to stay at Daddy's house anymore," she said. "If you go away again, I want to stay with Kim or Grandma. Please?"

Barbara had been driving toward home, but now she pulled over to the side of the road, put the car in park, and turned to Darlene. "Doll, did something happen at Daddy's house?" she asked. "Did Daddy do something to upset you?"

Tears fell from Darlene's eyes, and she pushed them away with her fist. "No, nothing happened," she said. "He made me eat fish and peas. I don't like fish and peas."

Somehow, Darlene knew, if she told her mother that she believed her father didn't like her anymore the way he didn't like her mother, and that he yelled at her, it would lead to more yelling and fighting between them. It was better to keep quiet. That's what she would do. She would keep quiet and use her eyes and ears. And she would only use her mouth to tell stories about other people, like her mother did. Her father didn't like her mother, and her mother made herself happy using her eyes and ears and telling things to Kim's mother. That was Darlene's new plan. She would make herself happy by finding and telling secrets.

Her mother sighed. "Doll baby, I'm sorry that every moment with your daddy wasn't fun, but sometimes, you just have to eat fish and peas. But don't worry. I'm not going away again anytime soon. You'll just be going to Daddy's house every other weekend like you did before. It will be okay. I promise."

Chapter 7

First Love

FOR DARLENE, IT WAS LOVE at first sight. She saw the girl with the orange hair, and she knew she must be her friend. But she didn't have any secrets to tell yet, so she waited. She and Kim were in different kindergarten classes, but that was okay. They would still see each other all the time.

When Darlene looked for Kim at recess, Kim was by the swings with a very small boy. Kim was smiling at the boy, and he was smiling at her. And Kim didn't even see Darlene. So Darlene walked around by herself. And she watched and she listened. And she remembered what she heard.

The next day, she planned to go up to the little girl with the beautiful orange hair and tell her the secrets she had heard, but before she could, the orange-haired girl approached her and offered her a cookie. And just like that, they were friends.

At recess, Kim was with her new friend Carl again. She had told Darlene that she loved Carl and was going to marry him. That was okay with Darlene. Now she had Michelle of the flaming orange hair. And she was gonna win her love. She told Michelle everything she had heard the day before on the playground, and Michelle hung on her every word. Thereafter, they spent every day together on the playground. Michelle didn't know much about secrets, but she was good at listening, so Darlene just kept talking.

When she went back to her father's house the next time, there was no more yelling. They went to the park and then to her grandparents' house. And the next day they watched cartoons together after breakfast until her mother picked her up at noon so her father could go play golf. But the whole time she was there, she was careful so she didn't knock anything over or object to anything her father said. She was a good girl, and everything was okay. She just had to be good with her father all the time. Even if it made things not as much fun.

Darlene made everything work. She had her mother in the blue house, and her father in the yellow house. She had her best school friend, and her best home friend. She kept everything in its place and knew how to act when she was with her different parents or friends. Her anxiety decreased, and her life took on a rhythm. The only problem was that she was the only one who knew her structure and requirements. Sometimes, the rest of the world was not so accommodating to her needs, as she learned in second grade.

Darlene had never taken much notice of boys. She didn't have any brothers, and neither did Kim. She got along with the boys in her class, but they were just accessories to her time with her best school friend, Michelle. They were of no consequence.

But it was not like this for everyone. As the year went on, a division developed between the boys and the girls, and it slowly built into a sort of animosity. As this increased, leadership roles started to emerge. On one side was Chris Mahoney, who led a pack of three other boys, Carl, James Newell, and Pete Cooper, who he called his posse. And on the other side was Kim Lester, and now she was in charge of Darlene and Michelle. And two of Darlene's worlds had collided.

Kim had started by following Darlene and Michelle at recess when they tried to play and getting angry when they didn't pay attention to her. Darlene didn't like anger, and she definitely didn't like yelling, so she soon folded and shared her precious time with Michelle with her home best friend, Kim. And Kim had definite ideas on how she wanted her friends to act. The boys were off-limits, and the only interactions they had with boys were to chase them around the playground or show them disdain. Even

Michelle was getting fed up with Chris and the other boys, and she gave in to the pressure of the boy/girl feud.

So Darlene reinvented herself again to make room for her two friends at once. Inevitably, Kim and Michelle both became home *and* school friends, and since Kim had the strongest will among the three, Darlene found herself adapting more and more to Kim's needs. But she ached for her alone time with Michelle, the one person with whom she felt the most in control and the most accepted for who she was.

Chapter 8

THERE FOR YOU

KIM'S MOTHER, VICTORIA, HAD GOTTEN married, and was now called Mrs. Drake. Darlene and her mother, Mrs. Feinman, had gone to the wedding. It was a small gathering of friends and family in the backyard of the Drakes' new home, which was very close to Darlene's home with her mother. Mr. Drake had adopted Kim, and now she was Kim Drake. And Mrs. Drake had adopted Mr. Drake's two small children, who had been abandoned by their mother. So now Kim had a big, noisy family and a new house. Kim seemed slightly less angry at the boys now, but she still refused to associate with them. But she loved her new daddy, even if he was a boy. Her eyes became bright and she smiled when she talked about him. Mr. Drake was sweet, and his voice was soft and reassuring. He was nothing like Darlene's father, who was always so serious, even about their fun. Mr. Drake always just seemed to have fun, and he played with Kim and her friends when they came to their house. Darlene could see why Kim loved him so much.

Darlene also liked going to Michelle's house, where there were always fresh cookies or cakes and twin baby boys with bright red hair. Michelle also had a sister who went to a special school because she was a slow learner.

She was three years older than Michelle and her friends, but she loved to play, and she had a contagious laugh.

Things were progressing well in elementary school for Darlene, and she got used to her new routine. She still made sure she was always a good girl when she went to her father's house, but she could barely even remember why it was so important. She always did what he told her, and ate what he made her, and said *please* and *thank you* to be polite. Every now and then, he would tell her she was a good girl, and she would be pleased. But she never completely let her guard down. It would only take one time, she knew, and everything would change again. She just knew.

Mr. and Mrs. Drake had a baby boy soon after they were married, and now they were expecting another child, which would arrive in the summer. Kim was excited because now, at age ten, she could help more with the baby and take more control at home. Michelle went off to camp, and Darlene found things to do with her mother on weekdays, and her father on weekends, with frequent get-togethers with Kim.

In early July, Darlene was lying down on her bed, listening to music on her radio and reading a book, when she heard several sirens speeding by on her street. Soon after, the phone rang. Her mother was out in the backyard working in the garden, so Darlene just let it ring. Over the next hour, the phone rang two more times, and eventually, Mrs. Feinman came in and caught the ringing on time.

"Oh, no!" Darlene heard her saying. She closed her eyes and focused her ears on her mother's voice. "Oh, Susan, I am so sorry! What can I do to help? Okay, I can do that. We can be there in about twenty minutes. It's okay if Darlene stays there while I go? Maybe she can help. Oh, Susan. I don't even know what to say. We'll get there as soon as we can. Can I bring anything for you? Okay, we'll see you soon."

Susan was Kim's grandmother. Something was wrong at Kim's house. Darlene jumped off her bed. Her mother walked into her room.

"Darlene," she said, "we need to go right now. Mr. Drake's had an accident, and they've taken him to the hospital, and now Victoria is in labor. I need to drop you off at the Drakes' house and then go to the hospital to be with Vee. But first, we need to stop at the store to get something for them for dinner. And oh my goodness, after I drop you off at the Drakes' I'll need to put some gas in the car. Go ahead, put your shoes on."

Mrs. Feinman rushed out of the room before Darlene could say a word.

Darlene stood there for a minute in shock, and then she moved. She put on her shoes and rushed toward the door.

"What happened to Mr. Drake?" she asked her mother, who was gathering her belongings and her purse.

"He fell off a ladder," Mrs. Feinman said. "He hit his head and he's unconscious, that's all I know. And Vee is all alone at the hospital. I need to get to her. Let's go."

They got into the car and strapped in, and Mrs. Feinman turned the key. The engine didn't turn. She tried again. Nothing. "Oh, shit," she said, and then put her hand to her mouth. She pressed the gas down and tried one more time. Same results. "I think we're out of gas. I knew I was close, but the gauge must be off. I'm gonna have to call the auto club to come and bring us a can of gas. Oh, of all the worst days for this to happen!"

"Mom, I need to be with Kim," Darlene said. "I can just walk over there. It's really close."

Mrs. Feinman sighed. "No, doll, I need to make sure you're there safely since I don't know how long I'll be gone. C'mon, I'll walk you over there, and then come back." They got out of the car, and Mrs. Feinman reached for Darlene's hand. Normally, Darlene would complain that she was too old to hold hands with her mother and pull away, but this time, she grabbed on tight.

They arrived at the Drakes' house in less than five minutes and rang the bell. Grandma Susan answered the door.

"Susan," Mrs. Feinman said, "I couldn't stop at the store because the gas tank was empty. I have to call the auto club to bail me out. But Darlene wanted to be with Kim, so I walked her over. It's gonna be a bit before I can get to the hospital."

"You can take my car," Grandma Susan offered.

Mrs. Feinman shook her head. "No, Susan, you might need it if anything comes up. And plus, I can't drive a stick. I keep meaning to learn. No, I'll just get moving now and get over there as soon as I can. Any word yet?"

Grandma Susan sighed. "They're both in surgery last time I heard. I'll keep calling for updates. Maybe you can call me as soon as you get there if you can find anything out."

Mrs. Feinman hugged her. "Of course I will." She turned to Darlene.

"Doll, you be good, okay? And just sit with Kim and do whatever she wants. If she doesn't want to talk, that's okay. Maybe you can listen to some music or something. I'll check in with you later. I'll call your dad, and if you need anything, you can call him. I love you, doll." She kissed Darlene's cheek.

"I love you too, Mom," she said. She turned to the stairs and ran up to Kim's room.

Kim was sitting at the edge of her bed, her hands on her knees, her feet bouncing against the floor. Her facial expression was strained. She looked up when Darlene knocked.

"Darlene," she said, standing up. "What are you doing here? Oh my God, are they dead? Did they send you to tell me?"

"No, no," Darlene assured her, walking toward the bed. "No, my mom is going to the hospital to be with your mom. She brought me here to be with you. Your grandma told my mom they're both in surgery. Kim, what happened?"

Kim sat back down and looked at the floor. "I was helping him. I walked away for just a minute and he fell off the ladder! There was blood. Look." She showed Darlene her shoes. There was blood on the sides. "I stepped in a puddle of blood."

"Kim, let's take your shoes off," Darlene said. She kneeled in front of her and untied her laces. Kim kicked the shoes off. Darlene picked them up gingerly, brought them to the bathroom, and dropped them in the tub. Then she went back to Kim's room. Kim was back to looking at the floor.

"I can't help," she told Darlene. "I can't do anything for my daddy. He wouldn't wake up, even when the ambulance men came. And then my mom . . . . She looked like she was gonna fall over. They had to put her in another ambulance. I don't know why she's in surgery. I just keep waiting for the phone to ring, but it's not ringing. Why won't anyone tell us what's going on? We need to know! Don't they care?" She started to cry.

Darlene sat on the bed and put her arms around Kim. Her sobbing got stronger, and Darlene felt tears in her own eyes. They sat like that for a long time.

Kim finally pulled away. "I don't want my daddy to die, Darlene. I only just got him a few years ago. It's not fair! And what if Mom dies? And the baby? Who will take care of us? I can't take care of them all."

Darlene wasn't sure what to say. She didn't know if Kim's parents were

going to die. But she did know that no one would make a ten-year-old girl
take care of her little brothers and sisters if that happened. She tried to
reassure Kim. "It's gonna be alright," she told her. "No matter what happens, it'll be alright. My mom will make sure you're okay, and so will your
grandma."

They stayed in Kim's room talking for some time, and then Grandma
Susan called them down for dinner. She fed the small children while Darlene ate and Kim picked at her food. After dinner, they sat in front of the
TV for much longer than their mothers would normally allow them. Eventually, the phone rang. It was Mrs. Feinman. She was finally able to get in
to see Mrs. Drake. She had done well in surgery and was in her room with
her baby, a healthy little girl. But there was no news yet on Mr. Drake.

"Her name will be Sophia," Kim told Darlene. "They chose Sophia for
a girl, and Thomas for a boy. Sophia was Daddy's grandmother. So now I
have two brothers and two sisters." Her shoulders relaxed slightly. "And
my mom is okay."

"Mrs. Feinman is going to stay with your mom as long as she can,"
Grandma Susan said, "so Darlene is going to stay over here tonight, unless
you'd rather call your father and go to his house, Darlene. Your mom said
that would be okay, too."

Darlene didn't want to go to her father's house. She didn't feel she could
be who she needed to be with her father with everything going on, and that
didn't feel safe. She was about to say something when Kim spoke.

"Darlene, please don't go," she pleaded. "I don't want to be in my room
alone. Please, stay with me."

Darlene couldn't remember a time when Kim had ever expressed that
she needed her, or even that she needed anyone. Kim usually just stated
what she wanted, and she usually made it happen. Darlene felt her heart
hurting for Kim. She loved her daddy so much. She would hurt so much
if she lost him. Darlene wanted to help Kim so she wouldn't hurt so badly.

"I'll stay here with Kim," she told Kim's grandma. She turned to Kim.
"I'll be here with you, Kim, as long as you need me."

PART TWO

STAVROS: THE CHILD

Chapter 9

FLOWER POWER

STAVROS STARTED COLLEGE BEFORE HE even started kindergarten. His mother was an undergraduate with a philosophy major and an English minor, and his father was a professor of Ancient Greek Literature. They lived in an off-campus apartment for university faculty, which was only slightly larger than housing for married students but smelled of the same industrial cleaner. His mother was a hippie. His father wore a corduroy blazer with patches on the elbows and a wide tie. His father was iron-resistant and constantly looked like a pile of unwashed laundry. His mother was averse to excess clothing.

The year was 1965. Stavros's father, Andreas Karras, was thirty-five years old, his mother, Rebecca Rosenberg Karras, twenty-eight, but she spent so much time with other students that she felt like she was nineteen. She wore halter tops even in the cool weather, and claimed they made it easier for her to nurse her baby. She had no excuse for the bell-bottom pants, wide belt, oversized sunglasses, and platform shoes. The headband across her forehead held back no hair but added a splash of color over her garish face of makeup. It was an exciting time to be at the university, and to be alive. The world was changing. Culture was changing. And little Stavros slept in a blanket-lined dresser drawer in his parents' bedroom and went to classes with his mother.

Rebecca went by Rebel. She was going to college for free because her husband was faculty, but she had found her calling in philosophy. It was edgy and today, even if most of the philosophers were long dead and buried. There were always heated discussions about interpretations of text and theory. Philosophy students liked to gather in circles to discuss their thoughts and arguments over drinks and cigarettes. Stavros would always be there, on his mother's breast or slung onto her body with a makeshift sling. Stavros was the mascot of the philosophy department.

The Karrases had moved to Amherst, Massachusetts, two years earlier from Pittsburgh, Pennsylvania, for Andreas's career. He was on a tenure track. Rebel had left behind her parents, a twenty-three-year-old sister, Sarah, and a seventeen-year-old brother, David. The Rosenberg family was living in a state of fear. The war had begun in Vietnam, and David was in danger of being drafted when he turned eighteen. Some of his classmates had already had their draft numbers drawn. He was trying to get good enough grades to get into college so he could stay at home, but academics were never his strong suit. Rebel was against the war, and she was very vocal about her displeasure. She lived with anxiety in the pit of her stomach due to worry over her baby brother.

Andreas was the youngest of five children born to Greek immigrant parents. His mother had died from heart disease at age fifty-six. His father was sixty-seven, but he looked eighty. He was lost without his wife and denied any ability to take care of himself. Andreas's four sisters took turns caring for him daily and complained to him bitterly on the phone about how ungrateful and demanding the old man could be. Everyone was proud of Andreas, the baby brother called "doctor," teaching at the fancy university. No one dared to call him Andy. Andreas was proud of his Greek heritage, as evidenced by the fact that he made their old stories his life's work. He would raise his young son Stavros to know the stories of his ancestors, and to be proud of his people and his culture.

Stavros took his first steps on the university quad. His first real word was *papa*. He was weaned onto souvlaki and baklava. He marched at his first antiwar rally on his own two feet at eighteen months. By age two, storytime included Jack Kerouac, Plato, Sophocles, and Dr. Seuss. His playmates were underclassmen and women. He never lacked babysitters, but his mother barely ever left his side if she could help it. Stavros would be her only child. She didn't believe in overpopulating the planet.

Stavros was three when his mother completed her degree. There was a large commencement for the whole university, and then the separate colleges had their own ceremonies so graduates could walk across the stage and accept their degree certificates. When Rebel's name was called, she carried Stavros across the stage. Andreas was given the honor of handing his wife her certificate, and when she kissed and hugged him with her proof of graduation in one hand and her son clinging to her neck, there was a huge round of applause, and the other students started chanting, "Stavros! Stavros!"

Rebel considered starting work on her master's degree but then decided to wait. Stavros would be starting school in two years, and she didn't want to miss a thing. She also felt it was important to teach him about the world before the public school system indoctrinated him with their capitalistic beliefs. So she took a break.

Chapter 10

WORSE THAN HELL

IT WAS 1968. REBEL'S BROTHER, David, had not been able to maintain his grades to stay in college, and he had been drafted. He would complete basic training and then ship out to Vietnam to join his unit in combat. The news from Vietnam was not good. It was the year of the Tet Offensive, and there had been mass casualties. Almost weekly, Rebel's mother would call her and report that another boy from Pittsburgh had lost his life in battle. There didn't appear to be an end in sight.

The antiwar movement was picking up steam, and the country was in turmoil. Rebel brought Stavros to marches, but they were becoming more violent, and the opposition was strong, so eventually they stayed home. She still volunteered for the movement, made phone calls, and spoke animatedly to anyone who would listen to her opinion. Rebel was thirty-one years old, and the prevailing theme of the time was "don't trust anyone over thirty." She was fighting against time. She had to make an impact before her influence faded away.

In May of 1970, the National Guard shot into the crowd at a war protest at Kent State and killed four innocent bystanders. And in June, Rebel got the call she had been dreading. David would be coming home from Vietnam but not in the manner that his family had been praying for. He had been shot, and he had succumbed to his wounds. He would be coming home for his final farewell.

Andreas and Rebel took Stavros back to Pittsburgh immediately so they could be with Rebel's family. The atmosphere was somber, and Rebel's mother was inconsolable. Her father was stoic. They were waiting for David's body to arrive in Pittsburgh to much military pageantry, but this was a Jewish family. They needed to bury their son as soon as possible so they could sit shiva. Time was passing, and they received no solace in the process.

Rebel traded her hippie garb for dark dresses and minimal makeup. She moved mechanically through her days and nights, trying to be present for her family and especially her son. But her brother's death had changed her. She was somber, subdued. Stavros would climb onto her lap, she would hold him close, and they would cuddle for long periods of time with no words. Rebel had known the world was a dangerous place, and she had been doing her part to try to make it safer for her son, but now she felt that one person couldn't make that kind of difference.

But she had another chance. She had her son. She would focus on him. He was the hope of the future. She would teach him to be a good person. She would make sure he knew he had a voice. She would teach him to be vocal and make his mark. And she felt she had to start now. The world was unsafe. She didn't feel that there was much time. She prayed that the war would end before her son came of age to be drafted.

The Karrases stayed in Pittsburgh for two weeks, and Andreas took the opportunity to visit his father and siblings. His sisters cooked for him and updated him on their father's ongoing ailments. Andreas took his father and Stavros to church on Sunday, and after, they went for lunch. They stayed for two hours, sipping on coffee and talking, as Stavros heard stories of his ancestral home and great-grandparents in Greece. Stavros sat quietly and listened. Andreas was proud of his son's attention and patience with his father's musings. He knew how important it was for these stories to be passed on to future generations. Andreas treasured his cultural and family traditions, and he was happy to watch this process.

Chapter 11

THERE WASN'T MUCH TIME UNTIL kindergarten would start, and this would be Stavros's first time being away from his mother every day for any length of time. Rebel decided to make the most of the time they had together.

"Stav," she said, "I'm going to teach you some of the things my mother taught me when I was your age. You come from two very strong families, and even though they're quite different, Jewish people and Greek people have a lot in common. One of those things is food and eating. We're going to make challah today, and then tomorrow, we'll make some baklava. Then later, I'll take you to the Greek Heritage Museum. On Saturday, we'll go to the synagogue for a Shabbat service so you can see what's the same and different from the Greek Orthodox Church."

"Can we eat the food that we make?" Stavros asked. "I love challah."

Rebel laughed. "Yes, you can eat some. I'll even let you make your own little challah. It will be just for you."

For the next several weeks, they cooked and baked, and ate, and went to museums and libraries. Rebel took him to the Jewish Nursing Home to meet the elder members of the community. They all doted on Stavros and spoke kind words to him in Yiddish. They told stories from their own childhoods. Some of them could not remember where they currently lived, but they all remembered growing up and hearing stories from their grandparents, their bubbes and zaydes. Stavros listened with wide eyes, and sometimes asked questions. His innocence made the crowd smile.

A week before kindergarten started, Rebel brought Stavros to Sears to buy new clothes. She let him make his own choices based on his own taste. He liked corduroy and vertical stripes, and he favored the color brown. Later, they went to Friendly's for ice cream sundaes.

Rebel held her spoon in the air and ice cream dripped back into the dish. "Stavros," she said, looking at him. "I want to talk to you about something important, because you are part of the family, and I think you have the right to be part of the decisions we make."

Stavros swallowed his mouthful of vanilla ice cream and hot fudge and looked at his mother curiously.

She took a deep breath. "Your father and I have been talking," she started, "and ever since Uncle David died, I've been thinking of what we can do to make the world a better place. I miss him so much, and I want to honor his memory." She put her spoon down and put her hand over her son's. "Stavros, we have decided that we are going to try to have another baby, a little brother or sister for you, and another person we can raise to try to do good in the world. We think that you can make a difference, and imagine what two of you could do!"

Stavros looked at her with a confused expression. "But I'm an only child," he said. "You told me."

Rebel smiled. "You are an only child now," she explained. "But if we have another baby, you won't be an only child anymore. Our family would be one person bigger, and you would be the big brother. You would be much older, but you could still play with your brother or sister and teach them new things. You can have adventures together."

"What if I don't want to be a big brother?" Stavros protested.

Rebel sighed. "I know I said you are part of decisions in our family," she said, "but in this case, it's more like you get to decide things during the whole process, like what we will need to do in our family to make our home welcoming for a new baby, and what the baby will need. Having a new baby is something that moms and dads decide together, and we've already explained how that all works. So that's a grown-up thing. But we will ask for your advice and help along the way. You are a very wise boy. You will help us make good choices."

Stavros thought about it as he took another spoonful of his dessert. He didn't know any babies. He didn't know what they were like. When he saw a baby at Sears earlier that day, it was sleeping in a carriage. It didn't look so bad, and its older sister didn't look too unhappy. And besides, Stavros didn't want his mother to be sad about her brother anymore, and if a baby made her happy, that would be okay.

"Okay," he told his mother. "If it's a boy, you should name it David. When will the baby be getting here?"

A tear ran down Rebel's cheek. She had already decided to name her baby after her brother. "Well," she told Stavros, "there's no baby coming yet, but once we start a baby, it will take nine months for it to come, so I would say hopefully in about a year."

Stavros nodded and took another spoonful of ice cream. "Okay, Mommy," he said. "You can have another baby. I'm okay with that."

Chapter 12

SCHOOL THE CHILDREN

STAVROS'S KINDERGARTEN TEACHER WAS NAMED Miss Abbie. She looked very young and dressed like a teenager. She had big bouncy dirty blond curls held back from her face with a headband, and she wore dresses with swirls and whirls in lime green, orange, and hot pink. She never wore pants. Her boots looked like white plastic. She had an extremely sweet voice, but she could make it travel across a noisy room. She passed out crayons and paper at the beginning of the first day and had the students draw whatever they wanted. Stavros drew a box. Then he added lopsided windows, but no door, and a triangle for a roof. Then he drew a baby in front of the house. Miss Abbie went around the room and asked each child to tell her about what they drew.

"This is the house we moved into when my mom and me graduated from college," Stavros announced. "And my mom is going to get a baby for us next year and the baby will live with us. He'll be called David like my uncle who died in Vietnam."

The little girl sitting next to Stavros raised her head and turned to Stavros. She smiled. "My uncle died in Vietnam too!" she told him. "My daddy says that war is stupid but my grandpa says we should trust the gumber-bent. And the president. My mommy says my grandpa has his head up his—"

"Thanks for sharing, Stavros," Miss Abbie interrupted. "And Deanna," she said to the little girl, "tell me about your picture."

"It's a bowl of alphabet soup," she started to explain, pointing to a circle with scribbled figures inside.

After coloring, Miss Abbie had the class stand, put their hands over their hearts, and face the American flag on the wall. She told them the Pledge of Allegiance. Then she had them repeat the words one by one after her. And lastly, she taught them a new song, "My Country 'Tis of Thee." She informed the class that they would say the pledge and sing the song every morning before class all year.

At recess, the children all ran around exploring the playground and taking turns on the swings. Stavros watched Deanna running around by herself, and he wondered what it would be like if she were his friend. He wondered if she was Greek or Jewish and knew what challah was. Maybe he would try to talk to her tomorrow.

School let out at lunchtime. Stavros was happy to see his mother in front of the school, there to walk him home.

"Are you hungry?" she asked him.

"A little, but not much," Stavros told her.

"Let's walk to the brook," she said, taking his hand.

They walked the two blocks in silence, then came to the little grass clearing that housed the stream of rain runoff that otherwise ran on pipes underground. They gathered small stones and sat by the water. Then they tossed the rocks into the water, watching and listening to the splash.

"Tell me about your day," Rebel said.

"Miss Abbie is pretty," Stavros said. "And she sings nice. We colored. And we had to say stuff to a flag and sing a song about America."

"Oh," Rebel said. "I guess they have you do the Pledge of Allegiance. I forgot to tell you about that. Stav, you don't have to say the words or cover your heart if you don't want to. You're free to say no."

Stavros shrugged. "I don't mind," he said. "Everyone else does it. We had recess and there's a girl and I can't remember her name but her uncle died in Vietnam, too, and she runs really fast."

Rebel gave him a smile. "Did you talk to her at all?"

"Not yet," he said. "Maybe tomorrow. When am I going to learn about philosophy?"

Rebel laughed. "Oh, sorry, Stavros, I'm not laughing at you. I just sometimes forget that you're already versed in all the scholars. I don't think you'll learn about philosophy in kindergarten, but we can still talk about it at home. Now you just focus on letters and numbers and learning to read, so that someday you can read Plato on your own."

"I can read a little," Stavros said.

Rebel looked up from the water to his face. "You can? I've never heard you read anything."

"I do it inside my head," Stavros said.

Rebel bit her lip. "Well, with Andreas as your father, I'm not surprised at all. When we get home, can you read me something out loud while I make you lunch?"

"Okay," he agreed. "But it's not very interesting stuff. You might get bored. It's just stuff about kids and dogs and cats. I don't think I could read you any philosophy yet."

Rebel laughed. "Oh, don't worry, Stav," she said confidently. "I'm sure you will be able to soon. Miss Abbie's gonna have her work cut out for her with you for sure!"

Chapter 13

Circle of Life

BY DECEMBER, STAVROS HAD TWO friends, Deanna and Joseph, and they played on the playground together during recess every day. Sometimes, they went to each other's houses after school for lunch and play, and sometimes, their mothers took them all to the park. These were Stavros's first friends his own age, and although they couldn't read yet and they had never heard of philosophy, they did know how to run and play games. Stavros was having fun.

Later that month, Andreas and Rebel announced to Stavros that a baby had started to grow in Rebel's uterus and should be coming sometime in July. Sometimes, Stavros saw Rebel run to the bathroom and throw up. She told him it was okay; it was part of growing a baby.

In January, Andreas's father closed his eyes one night and stubbornly kept them closed forever. His sister Alexis called with the news, and Andreas decided to take Stavros back to Pittsburgh with him for the very traditional Greek funeral. Rebel, who was still experiencing morning sickness, would stay at home. She could not stomach the idea of copious amounts of Greek food.

They left the next morning. It was an eight-and-a-half-hour drive in clear weather and traffic. There would be a three-day wake and a funeral on the third day. That was when it was believed that the soul left the body. When they arrived in town, they went straight to Andreas's father's house, Andreas's childhood home, to view the body. The body would remain in state for two more days and then be brought to the funeral home.

Andreas approached the body with Stavros in tow. "He's not going to look the same," he warned him.

Stavros looked at his grandfather's face. "He looks like he's sleeping," he said, "except he's so still. And his skin is so white."

Andreas nodded. "Is there anything you want to say to him?" he asked gently. "If his soul is still present, he can hear you. And it's nothing to be afraid of. He's at peace."

Stavros let go of his father's hand and stepped closer to his grandfather. "Papou, I'm sorry you died, but Papa says you're at peace, so that's good. I liked talking to you and hearing your stories. I hope your soul can hear me. Goodbye, Papou. I'll miss you." He stepped back.

"Very good, Stavros," his father said. "Now would it be okay if you went into the kitchen with Auntie Alexis so I can be alone with my papa for a few minutes?"

Stavros nodded and walked off to the kitchen. Aunt Alexis immediately handed him a plate of food.

They spent the majority of the next two days greeting friends and relatives who had come to say goodbye to Papou. Some told stories in Greek, and there was much laughter. Andreas could follow most of what they were saying, and he filled in Stavros the best he could. Others told their stories and memories in English, and Stavros listened intently. He knew it was important to listen so the stories didn't get lost.

On the third day, the body was retrieved by the funeral home, and in the afternoon, the family all headed over there for the service. The priest spoke about Papou in glowing terms and made many references in Greek. He knew Papou well. Others came up and spoke, including Andreas, who spoke about his father's faith and pride in his culture and how he instilled the love of all things Greek in his children and his grandchildren. Then Papou was transported to the cemetery, and all the cars followed behind.

At the grave, Papou was lowered down into a hole in the ground. The priest said some words over a plate of food that Andreas told Stavros was koliva the priest had blessed. Then, he scattered the koliva in the wind. He took the plate that held it and shattered it on the grave. The service ended, and people clad in dark-hued clothing approached the family for hugs and handshakes. "May his memory be eternal," many said, and others said "kalo paradiso," which Andreas translated to mean "wishes for a good heaven" to Papou.

When the funeral was over, Stavros and his father went back to Papou's house to get their belongings. Then they went to Aunt Alexis's house to spend the night. They would leave for home early the next morning. Andreas would come back in forty days for the traditional memorial service. Stavros would not be going. The Rosenbergs, who had attended the service, came by for coffee and to say goodbye to their son-in-law and grandson. They were all still wearing swatches of black on their clothing to show they were still in mourning for the loss of David. Aunt Sarah was getting married in August, so the Karrases would return to Pittsburgh at that time to help them celebrate, along with their brand-new baby.

Chapter 14

EGGPLANTS & ZUCCHINI

IN FEBRUARY, REBEL WENT TO the doctor to check on the progress of her baby. Everything was progressing well with the baby's growth, but Rebel's blood pressure was slightly high. The doctor urged her to rest more and eat less salt and to come back in a week. Rebel thought the doctor was insane.

"Pregnant women should move around and exercise," she told Andreas. "It's good for the baby."

But she did rest more and started reading after dinner every night on her bed. When she went back to the doctor, her blood pressure was the same but not higher.

"We'll keep checking you weekly," the doctor said. "We don't want to take any unnecessary risks. And I'd rather not have you take any medications yet."

Rebel's belly was getting bigger, and she was feeling tired, so she agreed to partial bedrest. Andreas got Stavros up and ready for school every day, and Stavros came to her bed to kiss his mother goodbye when it was time to leave. Andreas served her breakfast before he left for work, and then Rebel took it slow and easy until Stavros came home at noon. They ate a simple lunch and watched television together or played, and when Andreas got home, they all took gentle walks to the park and back. After dinner Rebel and Stavros lay in the big bed together, Rebel reading the classics, and Stavros reading the books Miss Abbie had given him to practice reading at home. Sometimes he read to his mother as she rested, and sometimes, she read to him. It was a soothing routine that they all enjoyed and grew used to, and it went well through the rest of the school year.

As summer began, Rebel's blood pressure increased, and her doctor feared a condition called pre-eclampsia, which could put Rebel in danger. He ordered complete bedrest for Rebel. Andreas took time off from work to care for his wife and son during summer break. He arranged for Stavros to play at Deanna and Joseph's houses a few days per week. Andreas's sister Alexis, who was unmarried, came to Amherst to help.

The first thing that Alexis did when she got there was rearrange the kitchen and take inventory. "I need to go shopping. I don't see one olive in this kitchen. What kind of Greek kitchen has no olives? Stavros, put on your shoes. We're going to the market."

Stavros ran up the stairs to kiss his mother goodbye, and then left with his aunt for the store. She sent him running down aisles to find what she needed.

"Eggplants!" she commanded. "Get me three good-sized eggplants, and some nice zucchini. And we'll need a loaf of good bread from the bakery. And some lamb. I hope they have a good meat counter here or we'll have to find a butcher shop next. What do you like in your salad, Stavros? Let's get some ingredients for baklava. We'll make a nice baklava for your family, okay? And where do they keep the cheese here?"

Stavros led Alexis around to all the right places. He went shopping with his mother every week and knew the aisles like the back of his hand. Soon they had a cart full of food and were headed to the checkout counter.

"You can pick out one sweet at the counter," Alexis told him. "You've been a good helper. I couldn't have done this without you." She leaned over and gave him a big wet kiss on the cheek. When she turned away, he wiped off his cheek.

When they got home and unpacked all the groceries, Alexis turned to Stavros. "Let's start with the baklava. I will show you how to make real Greek baklava."

"My mommy and I made baklava together last summer," Stavros told her.

"Probably from a recipe?" Alexis shook her head. "I will show you how to make it the way my mama, your Yaya, showed me when I was your age. Pull up a chair to stand on so you can reach the counter."

They made the baklava, and then Stavros helped her make dinner. They made a plate for Rebel and brought it to her bed. She loved every bite and the fact that Stavros had participated in the preparation. Every night for the next week, Stavros helped Alexis in the kitchen, fetching ingredients, stirring things together, and presenting the food in an artistic manner on the plate. Stavros was happy. He loved the feeling of creating something out of nothing, and the joy it brought to the faces of his parents. He brought his plate up to eat with Rebel, and they talked softly on the bed while consuming their food.

Rebel started getting headaches. They were bad enough that aspirin didn't help. Andreas called the doctor.

The doctor sighed. "It's time for Rebecca to come to the hospital," he told Andreas. "I'm going to admit her for a monitored bedrest and start her on some blood pressure medication. You can bring her to the hospital right now. Bring whatever she wants to have with her, because she will be in the hospital until the baby comes. And if we can't get her blood pressure under control, that might be sooner than later."

Andreas stretched the phone cord around his fingers. Rebel and Stavros were watching him intently.

"But what about our son?" he asked. "Will they be able to see each other? They can't go that long apart. I don't think that would be good for my wife's health." He saw Rebel grimace.

"I agree with you," the doctor said. "I'll make arrangements for Rebecca to have a private room, and we'll allow visits. This isn't the normal protocol, but this isn't a normal situation either."

Andreas hung up the phone and explained what the doctor said. "We need to pack your bag," he told Rebel. "Stavros, you will stay with Aunt Alexis while we get your mother situated, and then I'll bring you to visit her tomorrow."

"But I don't want Mommy to go," Stavros protested. "Mommy, don't go away. How can we make you dinner if you're in the hospital?"

Rebel motioned for him to get up on the bed with her while Andreas got her travel bag. "Stav," she said, cuddling up close to him, "I know it will be hard to be apart. It will be hard for me too! But we have to do what the doctor says. I need to stay healthy, so I can have a healthy baby. That's all that I want—for my children to be safe and healthy. And you'll come see me. It'll go by quickly, you'll see, and then when we come home, we'll come with your brother or sister. And when the baby is old enough, you'll be able to make him some yummy baklava!"

"Can we read together at the hospital like we do here?" Stavros asked.

"Of course we can," Rebel promised. "Andreas, make sure to pack me some books, okay? Lots of books. I'll have time to read them. And pack some extras for Stavros."

Soon, his parents were ready to go, and Andreas helped Rebel get dressed and go downstairs. Stavros followed them down.

"Make sure and mind Aunt Alexis," Rebel instructed. "But don't let her push you around. You still have free will, remember that." She embraced her son. "I love you more than all the love in the universe," she said softly. "And I'll see you tomorrow." She released him.

"I love you, Mommy," Stavros croaked, trying not to cry. As soon as they were out the door, the tears came.

Stavros visited his mother for two hours every day. She looked so small in the big white hospital bed. She was allowed to wear her own clothing, but she was constantly hooked up to monitors to check her blood pressure and the baby's heart rate. She had needles in her arm to give her medicine, and she always looked tired. When it wasn't too hot outside, Stavros and his father were allowed to push Rebel out to the courtyard in a wheelchair to get some fresh air. She would close her eyes and inhale deeply. Stavros would run around the courtyard and bring her back objects to hold, such as warm rocks or rose petals that had fallen from the bushes.

"Things from the earth ground me," she said. "They make me feel like I'm part of everything. It's like that when I plant flowers and dig in the dirt. I feel a part of the dirt. We all come from the earth, and someday we will all return to the earth. Stavros, next time you come, please bring me some things from our yard at home that I can hold."

Stavros surveyed the yard that night and found a small, pretty white rock, a moss-covered twig, and a green maple leaf. He brought them to his mother the next day, and she treasured the objects like they were gemstones.

"You did well," she told him. Then she needed to take a nap.

It was July now, and the baby was due in two weeks. Rebel was still struggling with headaches, and the doctor was struggling to control her blood pressure. They decided the baby would come early, and the doctor would take the baby out in an operation called a cesarean section. Rebel wasn't scared.

"The doctor knows what he's doing," she told Stavros the day before the surgery. "He's done this many times before. He says when the baby's out, I should start to feel better. It might take me some time to get back to normal, and I may need to take medicine for a while, but that's okay. We do what we have to do. And tomorrow, we'll meet our baby!"

"Baby David," Stavros stated.

Rebel laughed. "If it's a boy," she said. "We have no idea what we will name her if she is a girl. But we'll figure it out. Or we'll just wait until she's old enough to choose a name for herself." She laughed again. "No, I'm just teasing. We'll give her a good, strong name. Now Stavros, climb up here with me."

Stavros got on the bed and lay down next to his mother. She put her arm around him. "I'll see you after my surgery tomorrow, and you'll see the baby. Papa will need to be with me tomorrow, so you'll stay with Aunt Alexis until it's time for you to come. Remember, you're a strong boy. I suspect you're stronger than all of us, so make sure you're kind to your father tonight. He's worried. He's a worrier. It's in his nature."

"I'll be kind to Papa," Stavros promised. "I'll read to him at bedtime."

Rebel smiled, then hugged and kissed Stavros. "I think he would like that. I need to rest now, Stav. I love you. I'll see you tomorrow, okay?"

"Okay, Mommy," Stavros replied. "I love you more than all the love in the universe. Bye."

He walked out of the room. Andreas was pacing out in the hallway. "I'll go in and say good night to your mother, and then we'll head home," he said.

Chapter 15

IMPORTANT THINGS

THE NEXT DAY, REBEL WAS PREPPED for surgery, and she was brought in early in the morning. When the surgery was complete, Andreas called Alexis and informed her it was time to bring Stavros to see his mother, and his new baby sister.

"What's her name?" Stavros asked Alexis.

"They still haven't chosen," his aunt reported. "They still have some time. Let's go see them."

Rebel was in her room, and she was groggy. The baby was in the nursery. Andreas went to see if he could get her.

"Stavros," Rebel said wearily. "Your sister looks just like you did when you were born. She's going to be your closest friend for the rest of your life, and you have to take good care of her, okay? She came into the world in a rough way, but she has a strong voice, I can tell. You'll need to teach her everything I taught you. All the lessons, the philosophy, how to be a good person and make a difference. You'll have to tell her the stories I told you about Uncle David. You'll carry on the oral family traditions."

"Mommy, you can tell her the stories, too," Stavros said. "I like it when you tell the stories. And I might forget something."

Rebel shook her head. "No," she told him, "you won't forget anything. You've heard the stories hundreds of times. You'll know what to say. It's your turn now."

"Okay," Stavros said skeptically. He knew there was no use in arguing with his mother. "When are you going to come home?" he asked her.

Rebel looked up at the ceiling. "I don't know yet," she said. "The doctor is still trying to get my blood pressure back to normal. Stavros, I want to come home more than anything, I promise. My love, I want to be with you, and your sister, and your father. Please, always remember how much I love you all and how important you are to me. You are my everything."

Stavros had a funny feeling in his stomach. The door opened and his father came in, carrying a small bundle. "Come meet your sister," he said quietly.

Stavros took some tentative steps toward his father. He looked in his arms. The tiny baby was sleeping. He could see the blanket rise and fall with each of her rapid breaths. Her tiny pink fingers poked out of a gap in her wrapping, and her fingernails were merely dots on her fingertips.

"She looks like a doll," Stavros said softly.

"I'm going to help your mother hold her now," Andreas said. "She can't hold her on her own yet because she's not strong enough."

Rebel held out her arms, and Andreas held the baby and rested her lightly in his wife's embrace. Rebel smiled. "She's so perfect," she whispered. "Hello, baby girl, you made it."

The door opened again, and this time a nurse came in. "I need to put some medicine in your IV," she told Rebel. "Your husband can hold the baby. Can your little boy wait outside for a bit?"

Rebel looked at her son. "Stavros, why don't you go find Aunt Alexis in the waiting room, okay? This shouldn't take long." She looked into his eyes with tears in her own. "You will do such marvelous things, my son," she said firmly. "I'm so sure of this."

When Stavros got to the hallway, he felt a tear run down his cheek, but he didn't know why. He found his aunt, and they sat in the waiting room, waiting. And waiting. Stavros checked the clock. It had been a half hour. It shouldn't have taken this long. But he continued to wait.

Fifteen minutes later, his father came out. He walked slowly toward his son and sister. "Stavros," he said in a tired and strained voice. "Sit down." They sat next to each other on the plastic chairs. Aunt Alexis looked on expectantly.

"Stavros, while the nurse was with your mother, she complained of a bad pain in her head, and the nurse went for the doctor. Then, your mother told me she loved me, but she needed to close her eyes and rest. Stavros, when the doctor came back in, your mother had stopped breathing. They did everything they could to get her to start again, but, you see, her heart had just stopped. The doctor thinks she had a massive stroke from the stress of surgery and the high blood pressure. Stavros, they couldn't save her. She-she died, my son. I am so, so sorry."

Stavros stared at his father. "No, that must be wrong. I just saw her. She was fine. She was tired. Maybe she's just sleeping. Sometimes, people look dead when they're sleeping!"

Andreas shook his head. Tears fell down his cheeks. "No, I am so sorry, Stavros, but that's not what happened. She's not sleeping. She's gone."

Stavros felt his chest heaving. His face was wet, but he couldn't feel himself crying. "I want to see her!" he insisted.

"I don't know . . ." his father started.

"Is that a good idea?" Alexis asked, tears running down her face.

Andreas put his hand on Stavros's arm. "Stavros, there are rules."

Stavros shook his head. "Her soul is still in her body. For three days. I'm going to see her at the wake—"

"There won't be a wake," his father explained. "It will be like it was with David. A quick funeral, and then sitting shiva. Your mother was raised Jewish, and you know their beliefs are different."

"They can't bury her if her soul is still in her body!" Stavros insisted. "She'd be too scared!"

He broke away from his father's grasp and ran back to the room where he had last seen his mother. He pushed in the door.

She was still there on the bed. The monitors and needles were still there. The baby was gone. There was no one around. He rushed to her side and tapped her arm.

"Mommy," he said softly. "You have to wake up and say something. They think you're dead. But you're just sleeping." He remembered seeing his Papou in his bed at the wake. "You're not dead," he said. "You look pink, and you feel warm. You have to wake up. They'll bury you if you don't say something."

He could feel that his father had entered the room, but he didn't look back. He took his mother's hand. Her eyes were still closed. Tears continued to roll down his face.

"Mommy, you're the only one who can feed the baby. Who's gonna feed the baby? She's gonna be hungry! Mommy." He squeezed her hand. He started to sob. "Wake up!" he yelled. "Wake up!"

His father rushed to his side and got down on his knees. He pulled Stavros close to him and held on tight. Stavros resisted, but his father did not relent. He fell limp in his father's arms.

"But I have to wake her up," he said with resignation.

His father just held on to him, and he started to sob again. Then Andreas sobbed with him.

They stayed this way for a long time, until a clergyman came in and led them from the room into a little office. Alexis joined them there, clutching her damp handkerchief.

"Do you need to call anyone?" the minister asked.

Andreas nodded. "I'll need to call her parents, in Pittsburgh. Alexis, you can call our family, but I need to talk to the Rosenbergs. Oh God, it's less than a year since they lost David. I can't bear this. How will they bear it?" He started to sob again, and Stavros joined him.

Alexis was quiet for a moment. Then she spoke up. "We need to arrange for someone to be with them when you call. Someone who can support them. Who would that be?"

Andreas composed himself and then nodded. "Their best friends. The Cohens. I know the number is in Rebel's address book, and it was here with her. I will call the Cohens. They can help. Thank you, Alexis."

The baby was named Drea Adira Karras. *Drea* meant "courageous" in Greek and started with D for David. *Adira* meant "strength" in Hebrew. Andreas and Stavros agreed that Rebel would approve of this name, and Andreas felt it reflected the strength and courage of his daughter's mother.

Rebel was buried in a nondenominational cemetery and mourned in the Jewish tradition. Due to the family needing to travel, the funeral was three days after her death, and Stavros, even knowing it wasn't part of his mother's belief system, felt relief knowing that her soul was safely out of her body before it was buried. There were dozens of mourners by her graveside, including the many friends she had made in college and in her antiwar efforts. Rebel's parents and sister were devastated, as Andreas had predicted, but they agreed that Sarah's wedding should go on as planned in August. They knew that Rebel had lived by the credo "life is for the living" and would want her sister to start her married life and have as much happiness as she could.

They sat shiva at the Karrases' house for three days. During that time, friends and family came and went and told their favorite stories and memories about Rebel. A rabbi came to the house once a day to conduct a short service, and Stavros listened carefully to his words, both in English and in Hebrew. This reminded him of the Greek spoken at his Papou's wake, and aside from the differences in culture, he found a lot of similarity between his father's traditions and those of his mother's family.

There was always food coming into the house, and it was very different, too. There was challah, of course, but there was also kugel and casseroles, and gefilte and other white fish and lox. Someone brought a big batch of borscht, which was cold beet soup, and someone gave a bowl to Stavros with a dollop of sour cream on top. He mixed it all together, and the soup turned a brilliant shade of pink. He tasted it, and it was different than anything he had ever eaten, but it was okay. Aunt Alexis spent most of every day cooking and cleaning up after cooking. Andreas let Stavros help her sometimes, but at other times, he wanted his son with him on the couch.

The baby was passed around the room but could mostly be found in Mrs. Rosenberg's arms. Mrs. Rosenberg sat in Rebel's favorite armchair, stared at Drea, and gave her bottles when it was time to eat. Mr. Rosenberg sat in a metal folding chair by her side. He held plates of food on his lap left untouched for hours. He would speak to visitors when spoken to and watch over his wife while she sat. When Andreas took the baby from his mother-in-law, Mrs. Rosenberg called Stavros over to her and pulled him onto her lap. He stayed with her as long as she needed, absorbing her tears in his shirt and sometimes crying along with her.

"My Stavros," she whispered to him. "My beautiful Stavros. Will you be okay?"

Stavros nodded his head. "Grandma," he said, "can I call you Bubbe?"

For the first time in days, he saw his grandmother smile. "I would love for you to call me Bubbe," she told him. "That's what I called my grandmother. She only spoke Yiddish. I knew some Yiddish, but not enough. We communicated through our culture. She taught me to cook, and light the candles on Shabbat. I taught these things to your mother. Maybe those are things I can teach you and Drea someday." Tears rolled down her face again.

Chapter 16

PITTSBURGH BOUND

AFTER SHIVA ENDED, NEW PLANS were made. Alexis would stay with Andreas and help care for baby Drea. Stavros would go back to Pittsburgh to stay with the Rosenbergs. Andreas and Drea would fly out to Pittsburgh for the wedding, and then the Karras family would return to Amherst to prepare for the new school year for Andreas and Stavros. Then Alexis would return home, and Andreas's other sister Iris would be coming to stay and take care of Drea.

It was Stavros's first time on an airplane. He sat in the center seat between Bubbe and Aunt Sarah, who both remained quiet throughout the short flight. His grandfather sat in the row behind them. Stavros sat in his seat, swinging his legs back and forth, careful not to kick the seat in front of him. Then he read his book for a few minutes until the plane started its descent and got bumpy. When it was time to get off the plane, he put his knapsack on his back, and his bubbe took his hand as they walked through the airport. They got their luggage from baggage claim and headed outside to get a taxicab home.

The first thing Stavros noticed when they walked into his grandparents' house was that it was dark, and it didn't smell like food. Bubbe threw her bags down, flipped on the lights, and went immediately to the kitchen. She removed a package of chicken parts from the freezer and put it on the counter.

"We'll have chicken and potatoes for dinner tonight," she told Stavros. "Do you know how to peel potatoes?" He nodded. "It will take a while for the chicken to defrost. Can I make you something to tide you over until then? A can of soup?"

"Okay," Stavros said.

"Go into the den and have your grandfather turn on the television for you. And then just sit and rest for a while."

Stavros went into the den and asked for the TV. Mr. Rosenberg stepped up to the TV, turned it on, and turned the channel dial. He found a channel playing Looney Tunes cartoons and left it there. Then he sat next to Stavros on the couch. He looked at his grandson.

"It's good that you're here, Stavros," he said. "Your grandma needs to have you here so she feels her life has a purpose. I do, too. We're both glad you're here."

Stavros smiled shyly at his grandfather. "Grandma said I could call her Bubbe. Can I call you Zayde?"

His grandfather looked at him for several seconds. "Stavros," he said. "It would be an honor if you called me Zayde. I never expected that you would. But it's a special name. You're my first grandchild, and my only one until Drea was born. We'll have Drea call us Bubbe and Zayde, too, okay?"

Stavros nodded. "Okay," he said. He watched the TV for a few minutes, then turned back to his grandfather. "Zayde," he said, "do you like being Jewish?"

Zayde looked surprised. "Do I like being Jewish?" he repeated back. "Well, no one has ever asked me that before. I would say, yes, I do. I think it's amazing to be able to know where we come from, and that generations back, our ancestors had the same beliefs that we have now. Our traditions are so special, and our food is delicious. There are some difficult parts, just like anything else. We'll talk more about those when you get older. But overall, yes, I like being Jewish and I'm proud of my heritage. Why do you ask?"

Stavros considered what to say. "My mommy was Jewish, and my papa is Greek Orthodox. They say really different things about everything. Both like to eat and talk. When my Papou died, his soul stayed with his body for three days, but when my mommy died, her soul left right away. What do you think happens when someone dies?"

Zayde's eyes became misty, but he nodded his head. "That's a big question for such a little guy," he said. "I can see that it could be confusing. There are a lot of people who think a lot of different things about what happens when you die. They come up with beliefs that bring them comfort when they lose someone special to them. If they don't have beliefs, then they just have to accept that the person is gone, and that just hurts too much. Many religions came to be because people needed to believe in something so they didn't feel so alone in the world. But you asked what I think. Well, I am not totally sure. Sometimes I am positive that there is a heaven, a place where people go where they don't feel any pain, and they have peace. Other times, I see no meaning in death at all. For instance, why would God make me lose two children in one year? It feels so meaningless. Then, we sat shiva, and I felt the support of my family and friends, and I knew I wasn't alone in my pain. I knew that I could go on, move on with my life, never forgetting your mother or Uncle David, but knowing that their lives had meaning. You and Drea are proof of your mother's meaning on Earth. Your mother was so special. She had a sense of the world, of what was just and fair, and she fought for what she believed in, every minute of her life. She taught you that belief, and you will teach Drea. And the two of you will teach your children. So in that sense, your mother will never die, and that brings me comfort. Does any of this make sense?"

Stavros bit his upper lip and thought. "I guess so," he said. "But what am I? Am I Jewish, or Greek Orthodox? And if I am one, does that mean I can't believe things about the other? Can my mommy's soul be in her body for three days but also go to heaven right away at the same time?"

Zayde shrugged. "You ask the questions of a forty-five-year-old philosopher," he said. "I don't know the answer to your question, but I can tell you this: whatever brings you comfort is the right answer. There is no right or wrong, even if anyone tells you there is. By Jewish law, you are a Jew because your mother was a Jew and it passes through the mother, but your father's religion may disagree. As you grow older, you keep asking these questions, okay? And you decide the answers for yourself. Until then, just remember that your mommy loved you more than anything, and wherever her soul is, it will remain happy as long as you are safe and secure. And she will always, always live in your memory. And you and your papa will provide the memories for your sister."

Stavros nodded. "Okay, Zayde," he said. And he went back to watching cartoons until Bubbe came in to tell him his soup was ready.

Bubbe introduced Stavros to children in the neighborhood that were close to his age. He went to their yards to play, and sometimes they went to other places, like children's museums and the zoo. Sometimes, Stavros would be having fun, and then he would see a child hugging his mother, and he would remember his loss. At times like those, he would run to his Bubbe and sit by her side holding her hand until the urgency of his grief fell away.

Zayde went to synagogue each day to say Kaddish for his children, and on Friday night, Bubbe brought Stavros to the family service. There were other children there, and there was a lot of music and singing. After, they had a gathering called an Oneg Shabbat, where there was challah, cakes, cookies, and juice, and people could socialize. Stavros met his grandparents' friends, and they all hugged him and said they were sorry for his loss. "May her memory be a blessing," they would say, and then they would kiss him on the cheek.

The time was approaching for Aunt Sarah to marry her fiancé, Arthur. There were many details to focus on to keep the Rosenbergs busy and their minds occupied. On Thursday, Andreas arrived at the airport with Drea, and Zayde brought them back to the house. Even though he had talked to his father every night he had been away, Stavros cried when he saw his father and ran into his arms. He held on to him for dear life. He half expected his mother to walk in the door behind him. But of course she didn't. Eventually he went to look at his baby sister.

"She's so much bigger," he said.

"Do you want to hold her?" Andreas asked him. Stavros nodded. He walked over to the couch and sat back against the cushion. His father laid the baby onto his arms and then propped her up with a throw pillow. Then he sat down beside them.

Stavros looked at his sister. She was awake, and she was looking at him. Her arms were flailing, and her lips twitched at the edges. It almost looked like a smile. Stavros smiled at Drea. Her mouth opened. A small noise came out.

"Hello, Drea," Stavros said softly. "I'm your big brother, Stavros. Hello. I'm gonna tell you stories and play with you. I'll teach you to make challah and baklava when you get some teeth. But I don't want to change your diapers. Hello," he said, and he smiled. "Hello." Drea's mouth moved some more. Stavros sat quietly staring at his sister's face, with his father sitting silently beside him.

The wedding was on Sunday. The occasion was happy, but there were many tears. The bride was beautiful, and the groom was attentive and sweet. At the reception, speeches were made, and Rebel was eulogized. There was some dancing, but it was kept soft and slow. There was no celebratory circle dancing, or lifting of the bride, groom, and their parents on chairs, celebrating the last child being married. But there were words of hope for the future. The bride and groom were given blessings from their family and community.

After the wedding, it was time for the Karras family to go home. They packed Stavros's bags, and Bubbe and Zayde drove them to the airport.

"My sweet boy," Bubbe said as she knelt in front of him at the airport. "I will miss you. But I know you'll be there, and that's enough for me. We'll call, and you'll come and stay with us for Chanukah and during the summer, okay? And I'll teach you to make a nice kugel. You'll like that. Take care of your sister, please."

"Stavros," Zayde said, "I've enjoyed our talks. You are a bright boy. You'll do well in school this year. We'll have a good time at Chanukah. We'll call you next week to check that you've settled in, nu?"

After tears were shed, and cheeks were kissed, the Karras family of three got on their plane and headed home.

Chapter 17

STAY CURIOUS

"WHAT DO YOU THINK HAPPENS to a person after they die?" Stavros asked Deanna and Joseph on the playground. They had finished running around and were sitting on the ground, picking petals off dandelions. Now both of his friends looked at him like they thought he had asked why they each had two heads. Finally Deanna spoke up.

"My Nana says that when people die, they go up to heaven to be with Jesus," she said.

"But not everyone knows about Jesus," Stavros told her. "My mom was Jewish, and they don't believe in him."

Deanna nodded. "My nana says that if you die without Jesus in your heart, that you'll go to hell for eternity."

Stavros looked at her carefully. "My mommy was a good person," he told her. "She would never go to hell, even for a little while. Do you think she would?"

Deanna shrugged. "That's what my nana says, but my mommy says that my nana is batshit crazy so I don't know."

"What's batshit crazy?" Joseph asked. Deanna shrugged again. "When my grandpa died," Joseph went on, "my mom said he lives on in our hearts, but I don't think he could live in all of our hearts, and he was too big for that. I mean, he was really fat."

"Sometimes grown-ups say weird things," Deanna said. "When mommy's aunt died, they buried her in the ground. So she went in the ground. I guess that's where people go when they die."

Stavros considered what his friends had said. He thought there was more to it. He knew about souls, but he didn't know how to explain it to them. Souls were everything you loved about someone that was inside them, and not their body. They didn't need their body when they died. So their body went into the ground. But where did their soul go? Zayde said to keep asking questions, so that's what he would do.

Aunt Iris didn't take Stavros to the grocery store, and while she was a wonderful cook, she didn't have the patience to teach him to make the food. She had raised four children already, and now, she just wanted to make the food and feed the family. Stavros sometimes stood and watched what she was doing, and she gave him looks of exasperation. Then she'd tell him to go read a book. He never had a good chance to ask her what happened after you died.

But he did ask his teacher. "Mrs. Carver?" he asked her one day before leaving to walk home.

She looked up and smiled at him. "Yes, Stavros?"

"What do you think happens to someone's soul after they die?"

The smile fell away from the teacher's face. She had been told about Rebel's recent death. "Well, Stavros," she started, "there are a lot of different thoughts about this. Maybe it would be best to ask your father."

Stavros shook his head. "I know what my papa thinks," he said. "I want to know what other people think. Do you believe in heaven?"

Mrs. Carver cleared her throat. "Um, Stavros," she said, "I do have my own thoughts about this, but it's not something I can talk about with my students. Maybe a minister at your church? Or a family friend?"

Stavros was discouraged. Why couldn't she just tell him? It wasn't a hard question. Everyone died someday. They had to go somewhere. "Never mind," he said, and he trudged toward the door.

"I'm so sorry, Stavros," she called after him, but he kept going. Mrs. Carver went to the office and spoke to the principal.

The next night, Andreas called Stavros to the kitchen table when he got home from the university for a talk. "Stavros, you're not in trouble, I assure you. But your school called. It seems you've been asking people about what they think happens when you die. Is this true?"

Stavros nodded. "Just Deanna and Joseph and Mrs. Carver. But I didn't get any good answers. My friends really didn't get it, and Mrs. Carver wouldn't tell me."

Andreas nodded. "Okay, well, Stavros, why are you asking these questions to people?"

"Zayde told me to never stop asking questions," Stavros said matter-of-factly. "And it's something I want to know."

"It's okay to ask questions," Andreas told him, "but some questions are appropriate to ask at school and some aren't. For instance, it's okay to ask your friends about what they did over the summer, or about their pets and brothers and sisters, but what you've been asking is what is considered not appropriate for school. They are the questions you speak to me about, or other family and adult friends, do you understand?"

Stavros wrinkled his forehead. "Kind of," he said, "but if someone asked me what I did this summer, I would have to tell them that my mommy died. Why is that different?"

Andreas sighed. "Oh, Stavros," he said. "It's a blessing you have such a mind, but it's also a curse sometimes. You could also tell them that your aunt got married and you have a new baby sister. In school, we don't really ask the kinds of questions that make people feel their privacy is invaded. You may not understand now, but you will as you learn and grow more. You'll just have to trust me."

Stavros didn't really entirely understand, but still he nodded. "Okay, Papa," he agreed.

His father perked up. "I have an idea," he said. "Let's take a trip to the public library and find some books for you to read about your questions. And then, if you want to talk about what you've read, you can talk to me about it. Does that sound okay? Do you think you would be ready to read books at that level?"

"I think so," Stavros said.

So the next afternoon, they went to the public library and got Stavros his first library card. And thus opened a door in his world to all the answers, and all the new questions, that he would ever need to know.

DARLENE: THE MIDDLE YEARS

Aspen held her pen between her first and second fingers, and her hand hovered over her writing pad, but she didn't write anything down.

"Tell me more about your father during your preteen years," she said. "Did it stay the same as you got older, or did things change at all?"

Darlene looked at the wall behind Aspen's chair. "Same and different," she replied. "Or it could have been me changing. I don't know. But the summer of Mr. Drake's accident, I spent most of my time with Kim. Michelle was at camp, so it wasn't too hard. And then at the end of the summer, my dad and I went to Disney World for five days."

"How was that?" Aspen asked.

Darlene exhaled hard. "It was fun. At first. He had a tolerance level of about forty-eight hours, and I knew that, so after the second day, I tried to be really, really good. I remember going on a ride that he wanted me to go on, after eating a hot dog. I didn't want to go on it, but he seemed to really want me to, so I did. I ended up feeling sick the whole time, and when the ride finally ended, I needed to throw up. I told him I needed to go to the bathroom, and then ran in there and puked my guts out. My stomach was *throbbing after. But I just washed my face, put on a smile, and went back out there like everything was fine. And he bought it."*

Aspen's forehead wrinkled. "You were ten?" she asked. Darlene nodded. "Wow, Darlene, you really took on a lot of responsibility for your father's emotions back then. When you did things like this, so as not to upset him, did it keep him from actually getting upset?"

Darlene shook her head. "No," she admitted. "Not always. He would get upset about things I never would have expected. Nothing I could have prepared for. Like when my toothbrush fell into the sink at the hotel on the night of day three. I didn't put it there, but you would have thought I had just deliberately stepped on his kitten or something. How could I? Why couldn't I just follow a simple rule? Did he have to watch everything I did to make sure I didn't screw it up? And then at the airport, going home. We almost missed our connection. We were running to the gate. I was lugging my five-day suitcase and a backpack, and I couldn't keep up with him. He told me if we missed our flight, it would be my fault, and he would never take me on a trip again because I was more trouble than I was worth. We made our flight, and for two hours I sat next to him quietly, afraid to move. I was so worried that I had angered him so much. But when we landed, he turned to me and smiled like nothing had happened. When I got home, my mother asked me if I had fun on my trip. I said yes and went to my room. She believed me. I don't think I was that convincing. Could she really have believed me?"

"How were things after the trip?" Aspen asked.

"Back to normal," Darlene said with a sigh. "Every other weekend, just like before. But I was so busy being with Kim that I didn't even think of my father. It was like that all through sixth grade, too. Michelle, Kim, and I would be together at school, but Kim still needed me. I was hoping that, over time, her father would keep getting better, and things would be normal for us again, but things were never really normal again."

"And what about Michelle?"

Darlene was quiet for a moment. "I did something I'm ashamed of," she said. "I was mean to Michelle, really rude the first day of school, and I could see she was really confused and hurt."

"Why were you mean to her?"

Darlene shrugged. "Because Kim and I had been together all summer, and Michelle went to camp. I guess Kim and I had gotten into this sort of routine that didn't include Michelle. You have to remember, I loved Michelle. I still love Michelle. But I just didn't have the energy for both of them. I just couldn't be my Kim person and my Michelle person at the same time, and I had been yanked into Kim's vortex by her irresistible gravity. I was stuck. It wasn't exactly a bad place to be, but it wasn't exactly where I wanted to be, either. But I never felt I could talk to Kim about it."

"You were worried she'd become angry, like your father."

Darlene nodded. "So I was mean to Michelle, and I hated myself. The next day, I walked home from school with her, and we talked. I apologized. But then, I did something that pushed her further away. I told her that Kim needed me more, because of her father and all, and since we weren't in classes together, and Kim and I were, it might be good for her to try to meet new people. She had made a new friend already, Sally, and I encouraged her to be friends with Sally. Sally was nice. We all had lunch together. But then they got really close, and I hated Sally. But I didn't really hate her. I was grateful for her, because now Michelle wouldn't be alone and sad. Now Sally's actually one of my best friends. But I was so jealous. All through junior high, we all ate lunch together, me, Kim, Michelle, and Sally. But outside of school, it was me and Kim, and Michelle and Sally. But when high school started, Sally left and went to private school."

"Let's go back to junior high for a moment," Aspen said. "A lot of girls find themselves starting to notice boys a lot more at that age. What was that like for you?"

Darlene considered this. "I don't know," she said. "The only boys I really knew were James, Chris, Carl, and Pete, the posse boys from DeMarco. Kim liked to look at boys, and Michelle and Sally had lots of crushes, especially Sally. She loved the posse boys. But I don't really remember having any specific crushes, or even thinking much about it. My mind was always on so many other things."

Aspen nodded. "It must have been so hard to keep things straight. You had so many different roles you had to remember. Did you ever get your roles mixed up?"

"Not really," Darlene said. "I feel like my life back then was like a game of Jenga. If I pulled out the wrong piece, the whole thing would just collapse to the ground. There was the time that my father decided my whole future for me, and I almost waivered . . ."

"How did he do that?"

"He suddenly decided that I was going to be a scientist when I grew up. He started bringing me on lab tours and buying me books about women in science. He said that science was the up-and-coming field for women. He bought me chemistry sets and brought me to movies that had scientific themes. It wasn't as if I ever even expressed an interest in science. I mean, these things were interesting, but I didn't see them in my future as my career. And one day, I was talking to Kim about what we wanted to do, you know, when we grew up. Kim wanted to be an actress at that time. She would have been great at it, too. She could tell stories like no one you've ever met. She could make you laugh, and cry, and wish you had been there when it happened. Being an actress seemed kind of cool. The next time I was at my father's house, he had a friend there, and the friend asked me what I wanted to be someday, and I said an actress. My father corrected me. He said no, no, you'll never get anywhere in life being an actress. She really wants to be a scientist. He gave me this look, like I had just humiliated him in front of the queen. So when the friend asked me what kind of scientist I was going to be, I said a biologist. Just said it, for no logical reason. And suddenly, it was like I had written it in stone. My father told anyone that would listen that his daughter was going to be a biologist. It made him so proud. It wasn't long before I thought I was going to be a biologist too. I believed it with all of my heart and soul. I thought that was what I wanted. Because if not that, then what?"

"You didn't become a biologist, though."

Darlene shook her head. "Not for lack of trying. Everyone knew I was going to be a biologist. Everyone, even my friends, thought it would happen. I had convinced them all. Except for one person."

Aspen tilted her head. "Who was that?"

Darlene smiled. "My new friend in high school. Traci. She saw right through me. She was really intuitive. She knew everything. But I didn't believe her when she told me I would be unhappy all alone in a cold science lab. No, she just made me want to work even harder toward my goal. But she was ultimately right. About that. About everything, it turned out."

Aspen nodded. "Darlene, I'd like to talk more about your time in high school," she said, pointing at the clock, "but we're out of time. Same time, next week?"

Darlene nodded. "Yeah, that would be great. Yeah, high school was something, that's for sure."

Chapter 18

High School Days

DARLENE WAS WORRIED ABOUT MICHELLE. She had definitely been quiet since the school year started and was missing her constant companion, Sally. Darlene secretly cursed Sally for going to private school and messing everything up. There had been such a fine balance of things, and now it was all askew. She couldn't stand seeing Michelle so sad and lonely looking. Michelle had this thing she did where she scrunched up her little freckled nose when she smiled. It always made Darlene smile too. Now there was much less of the scrunched-up nose, and Darlene wanted it back. So for the first time, she defied Kim.

Kim had a doctor's appointment after school on Monday. "Come over tomorrow, though," she told Darlene as they walked home together after last period. "We can hang out and watch soap operas with my dad."

Darlene took a deep breath. "I can't tomorrow," she said. "I asked Michelle to join the decorating committee for homecoming with me. It's tomorrow after school."

Kim met her eyes. "Really?" she said. "That's not something that I thought you would enjoy."

Darlene shrugged. "I like decorating things," she said. "And I like to hang out with Michelle. I'd also like to meet some other girls from other schools. It's a good time to do that. And it will be good for Michelle. She misses Sally. She needs some new friends."

Kim gave her a baffled look. "Okay," she said, shrugging. "I guess we can just hang out on Wednesday instead." She kept walking.

Darlene stopped for a brief moment and looked after her. She pretended to pick a rock out of her shoe. She had just said no to Kim. And against all her firmly held beliefs, Kim had not gotten mad, or yelled, or stormed away saying she wouldn't be her friend anymore. This seemed odd. But when she thought about it more, she realized that she didn't have any reason to believe that Kim would blow up at her if she wasn't one hundred percent agreeable with her all the time. Darlene had just assumed that would happen. Kim had never had a chance to hear her say no before. She might not have been thrilled, but she had, literally, just shrugged it off.

Darlene caught up with Kim, and they continued toward home.

Darlene and Michelle did make a new friend while decorating the gym on Tuesday. Her name was Traci, and she had a special gift. It was almost as though she could read minds. But she denied that she had any special powers of magic. She was just intuitive, and she could read people's body language. Almost immediately, she told Darlene she didn't see her as a biologist, that she saw her working in a field where she would be surrounded by people, and she would be happy. Darlene became defensive. She was going to be a biologist, and no fake psychic mind reader was going to tell her differently. So what if, so far, everything Traci said had turned out to be right? It didn't mean anything. Darlene decided to double her efforts to do well in biology class, just to prove that Traci was wrong. But deep down inside, she knew Traci was not wrong.

As the weeks went by, she became closer to Traci, as did Michelle and Kim. Traci told them things, things they wished for themselves, and encouraged them if she thought they were going in the right direction. She also saw things that she didn't think would work out, like relationships, and she hoped that maybe she was wrong. But Darlene doubted that.

One Saturday, Darlene and Traci went to the Main Street Mall to shop and walk around. They went from store to store, riffling through racks, looking for something that would be *just right*. Then they took a break to eat.

"Traci," Darlene said after swallowing a bite of her chicken salad sandwich. "You've had a lot of, I guess, intuitions about everyone about a lot of things since we met, but the only thing you've ever said about me is that I won't be a biologist, even though I know I will. What about my love life? Can't you sense anything about that?"

Traci looked at Darlene silently for several seconds. "No, I really can't, Darlene," she said apologetically. "I want to, but when I look at you, it's like looking at a thick brick wall. It's like you're a fort, and the wall is your defense. There isn't even a door on the wall. It's just solid."

Darlene was confused. "Then how did you know anything about what I would do when I grow up?"

Traci nodded. "That was easy. That one is hard to stow behind the wall. That one is big, but really fragile. It comes from a place of great desire, but also a lot of sadness and fear. But it's so much more complicated than that. It's like there's more than one person in there." She reached out and touched Darlene's forehead. "Tons of them, but they're all locked in their own separate rooms behind the brick wall, like if they ever came together, they would all be doomed. I don't really understand it, Darlene. It's just what I feel. Does that make any sense to you?"

Darlene quickly shook her head. "No, not at all, Traci. I can't even imagine what that all means." But that was a total lie. She knew exactly who all the people were in her head. Every one of them was Darlene. A different Darlene for every occasion and every person, depending on who she needed to be. But she had no idea which one of them was the real Darlene, or even if there was one.

Chapter 19

TEENAGE WASTELAND

KIM WAS GETTING MOODY, AND Darlene didn't know why. She wondered if she had done something to upset her, but then she noticed that it wasn't just around her. She was like that with everyone. And she was acting weird. At the beginning of the year, Kim had made sure to sit next to Carl Bishop in every class they had together, but it seemed that she had done that just to be able to torture him more. She called him a moron, and other derogatory names, but then would get irritated when he didn't pay attention to her.

"Why do you put up with the way she treats you?" Darlene asked Carl one day in Spanish class.

"The way who treats me?" Carl replied.

"Kim! She's so mean to you, and you just sit there and take it! Why don't you ever just tell her to stop?"

Carl shrugged. "I don't know. She's my friend. She's always been my friend. I figure if she's talking to me, then that's good. I guess I just let all that other stuff go. I mean, she sits next to me. We're friends."

Darlene didn't understand boys, but Carl also didn't seem like most boys. He played so dumb, but he was doing so well in school. Maybe he had lots of Carls in locked rooms inside his head, just like her.

There was one boy who seemed kind of different, though. He was in her history class, and she watched him a lot. His name was Charlie Palmer. He laughed a lot with his friends. He was very thin but had a handsome face. His hair was light brown and unruly. His eyes were a shade of brown that reminded Darlene of a cow's eyes, and he had a mole in front of his right ear. He wore striped polo shirts that always looked loose and tan corduroy pants over well-worn sneakers.

Darlene was not sure how or why she knew all this about Charlie. Even at gunpoint, she would not be able to describe the color of any of the posse boys' eyes. Maybe one of them had blue eyes? Or maybe two. But Charlie had eyes that could make all the thoughts in Darlene's head clear out. She could focus on Charlie, and nothing else mattered.

This must be what a crush feels like, she thought. *No wonder my friends freak out so much about crushes. I wonder if he knows my name.*

Charlie walked by Darlene every day to get to his seat in the back row of the classroom. Sometimes, he caught her eye and he smiled, then kept walking. Darlene would sink down slightly in her seat and stare at her feet. When Charlie smiled at her, there was no chance she would be learning any history that day.

But Darlene didn't know what to do with her crush. So for now, she just stuffed it down and focused on her eyes and ears again. She started paying attention and telling her friends what she saw and heard. They loved to listen, and to join in. Sometimes, all eyes would be on her, and they were filled with anticipation. So she looked and listened even more. Sometimes, she would listen where she shouldn't, like in the girls' room. It was as if the other girls thought the bathroom was a chamber of secrecy. Sometimes, she got some juicy tidbits; sometimes, she heard things she didn't care to hear, like Rhonda Jenkins talking about her crush on Chris Mahoney. Bad Boy Posse leader, Chris Mahoney. She couldn't keep this information to herself.

"Rhonda Jenkins likes Chris Mahoney," she said, and thus started the conversation among her friends. She sat back and watched. And listened.

"What was it that made Christmas sophomore year so significant?" Aspen asked.

"Kim lost her virginity at a party, and it was my fault."

"Were you there while it was happening?"

Darlene squirmed in her armchair. "Not exactly," she said. "But if I was there, I think maybe it wouldn't have happened. I left her at a party. She didn't want to leave, but Michelle got sick, and we had to go. We were going to have our friend James watch out for her, but he had hooked up with this girl, and I just felt weird interrupting him and I figured Kim would be okay. It was only for one hour. What could happen in an hour, right? But I should have known better."

"Were you responsible for Kim's actions?" Aspen asked. "Had there been some sort of agreement that you would be watching out for her?"

Darlene looked down. "No," she said. "But I should have known Kim would do something impulsive. It was just a matter of time. She was a ticking time bomb back then. So much repressed anger and grief about her father. She called me the next day in hysterics. She was crying and hyperventilating, *and I had to get her to calm down before she could tell me what was wrong. And when she told me, I kind of froze. I listened and she went on and on about this guy coming out of the bathroom, and they were both wasted, and it just happened, and she didn't mean for it to happen, and it wasn't what was supposed to happen, and now she couldn't take it back and everything was ruined. She swore the guy didn't hurt her, or force her to do anything, that she was just as much to blame, but then she downright refused to tell me who it was. She never told me. Even to this day I don't know."*

"What did you do after she told you?" Aspen asked.

"I comforted her, told her it would be okay. I asked her if she wanted me to come over, and she said she had to go to her grandmother's house, so no. And then we got off the phone, and I immediately called Michelle."

"Was this one of those eyes and ears situations?"

Darlene shook her head. "No, I would never want to betray Kim's trust. But I knew I could trust Michelle. And I knew this was not a secret I could hold on to alone. And it helped. Talking to Michelle helped me realize that it was possible that maybe Kim had a thing for Carl. It just made sense. The way she treated him. She wanted to be with him, and she didn't know how. And now, she had been with someone else, and it hurt, and she could never make it go away."

"How did Michelle respond to all of this information?"

Darlene sighed. "She told me she wished I hadn't told her. Because now it was her secret, too, and she couldn't let on to Kim that she knew. I felt lighter right away because I had told her, and she shared my burden. But then later, I felt guilty. Guilty for leaving Kim. Guilty for telling Michelle. Guilty for not being able to keep this to myself."

"It's been about ten years," Aspen said. "Have you and Kim or Michelle ever talked about this again? About how this all made you feel?"

Darlene shook her head. "No," she said. "We never talked about it in high school. Then Kim moved to California the summer after graduation. Then Michelle and I went to college. And then Michelle stayed in Amherst. It just never came up."

"What do you think Kim and Michelle would say today if you were talking about this event, in retrospect?"

Darlene thought for a moment. "They'd probably say they've moved on. And everything worked out fine. And it did for them. They're both married now, to cousins who are best friends. They probably don't look back on these sorts of things."

"You don't think that Kim thinks about her first time?" Aspen wondered.

"I don't know if Kim thinks about her first time," Darlene said. "But I think that I think about Kim's first time more than I think about my own first time. Maybe that's because there were so many years in between. And because hers mattered so much more."

"So you put a lot of weight on Kim's experience over your own then?"

Darlene considered the best answer and went with the honest one. "Maybe," she said, "or it just might mean that my own experience just wasn't all that worth remembering."

Chapter 20

THE JUNIORS

THERE WERE THREE THINGS THAT stood out the most about the start of junior year. First was that Chris and Rhonda were now in an established relationship. Next was that Sally returned to public school and was now at McKinney High. And last, Sally and James from the Bad Boy Posse fell in love. Darlene watched this all occur from a distance, and she heard it from Michelle.

"Sally is totally head over heels," Michelle said. "And James is so sweet with her. Did you know, he lets her call him Jamie? He hasn't let anyone call him that since junior high. And they kissed on the top of the big bridge at Twin Bridges Park." Michelle sighed. "I hope someone kisses me up there someday."

Darlene thought about being on the top of the bridge with Charlie Palmer. She wondered if they'd kiss. The idea was intriguing. Charlie was in her English class, and this year she was seated behind him. She could stare at the back of his head for fifty-five minutes each day. She could see him scratch his neck. She could see him whisper to his friends when the teacher's back was turned. And she could make eye contact with him if she came into the room after him. So she did. Every day. She'd give him a little smile. He'd smile back. And as she sat down, she would smile even bigger to herself.

"Who do you want to kiss on top of the bridge?" Darlene asked Michelle.

Michelle sighed. "I don't know. I can't picture him yet, but I think he's tall. Well, everyone's tall to me." Michelle was just about five feet tall.

"Maybe Freddy Pierce will break up with Marla," Darlene said, "and he'll realize it was you he wanted the whole time!"

Michelle laughed. "Freddy *is* tall," Michelle agreed. "But I don't think I would want to go out with him. It was uncool how he ditched his brother last year when their parents went away over Christmas. No, I want a guy who looks out for me. And if he doesn't even look out for his own brother, how could I trust him with me?"

Darlene knew how important it was to look out for and take care of people you loved. And to try to do everything you could to make them happy. "Yeah," she said. "I get that. Same with me."

As December approached, the smiles with Charlie increased. A couple of times, Darlene could feel him following her with his eyes as she walked back to her seat. And one day, when she sat down, he turned around in his seat, facing toward her, and he smiled again.

The next day, when Darlene approached Charlie's desk, he looked up and said, "Hey, Darlene."

Darlene stopped short. "Oh, hi Charlie."

"How's it going?" he asked while grinning.

"Good," Darlene said. "Are you ready for the quiz?"

"I hope so."

The bell rang. "I'd better sit down."

"Okay."

Darlene tried not to squeal as she walked back to her desk. She had never seen Charlie talk to any other girl like that. He seemed to like her! Her heart started thumping and she sat down. Charlie turned back to look at her, and he smiled again.

After the quiz, Darlene doodled on her notebook throughout class and tried not to write Charlie's name. She wrote his initials, then scribbled them out. She drew hearts and flowers around the cross outs. When the class ended, she stood up to leave. Charlie stayed in his seat until she approached.

"Darlene," he said, getting to his feet and facing her. "My friends and I are going down to Carson Lake to skate on Sunday. They're gonna plow it off on Friday. Maybe you want to meet up with us there? You can bring your friends, too. It's free."

Darlene didn't speak for a moment while she sorted words in her brain. "Okay," she said. "Yeah, I'll see if my friends want to go. Sounds like fun."

Charlie smiled. "Great. We'll be there at two. Are you a good skater?"

Darlene nodded. "Kim and I took lessons when we were younger. I can even do a few tricks."

"You'll have to show me," Charlie said.

"I will." There was an awkward pause. "I have to go meet my friends for lunch. I'll see you later."

"Later."

Darlene walked out of the room, and when she got to the hall, she picked up her speed so she could get to her friends. She needed to beg them to come skating with her. She definitely couldn't do this on her own.

Much to her joy, Michelle and Kim agreed to go with her to the lake, although Traci couldn't make it. Darlene walked around the lake with them both after school, and all the attention was on her.

"I can't believe Charlie asked me to do something with him!" she exclaimed. "I wonder why now? We've kinda been flirting since last year. Oh my God, I need to figure out what to wear! I need to make sure my skates still fit! Maybe I should get new skates!"

Michelle laughed. "Darlene, it's gonna be like zero degrees on Sunday! You should wear lots of layers and a hat and a scarf! If Charlie likes you, he's not gonna want you to freeze to death!"

"I don't think I'll even feel the cold, I'll be so nervous!" Darlene sighed. "Do you think he'll want to hold my hand? I'll let him if he wants to."

She felt giddy. She was feeling a new Darlene emerging inside her, and she really liked this one. This one made her energetic and excited. Maybe this one would stick around. She really hoped so.

"Do you want me to come over and help with your makeup?" Kim offered. "I can bring some of my stuff, too."

Darlene nodded. "That would be so cool! Michelle, can you come, too? You can help me with what to wear so I can look sexy and not catch pneumonia. And then we can walk to the lake together."

"That would be fun," Michelle said. "I don't have any other plans on Sunday. Sally's working that day, and my parents and brothers are taking my sister to the movies."

It was all set. When Darlene got home, she told her mother her plans.

"You're supposed to go to your dad's this weekend," Mrs. Feinman reminded her.

Darlene's heart sank. She had forgotten. "But Mom, this will be my first date," she protested. "I can't cancel! Can you call Dad and let him know I'll come next weekend instead? Please?"

"Why don't you call him yourself?" her mother asked. "You're sixteen. You can do these things now."

Darlene's face went cold. She thought quickly for an excuse. "Mom, can you just do it for me? I need to go do my homework. I have a test to study for. Just this once, okay?"

Mrs. Feinman smiled at her daughter. "Go upstairs and study. I'll call your dad. Just this once. Now get to it."

Darlene hugged her mother. "I love you, Mommy." She grabbed her book bag and ran toward the stairs. When she got to the top, she stopped and caught her breath. She tried not to panic retroactively.

The thought of calling her father to cancel their time together terrified her. If she had been forced to call him, she wouldn't do it. She would have just had to let Charlie know that something else had come up. She would have simply canceled her date. Now she wouldn't have to. That was too close. But everything had worked out okay.

On Sunday, the girls met up to get ready for skating. Then they walked over to the lake they all knew so well. It didn't take long for Darlene to find Charlie. She made eye contact and waved as she laced up her skates. Soon, the girls went out to the ice and got the feel of the terrain. Darlene skated skillfully over to Charlie. Michelle and Kim followed awkwardly. Soon, the whole group was skating around in circles, and Darlene showed Charlie how she could twirl.

"Impressive," he said. "I mean, not anywhere near ready for competition or anything, but it's a start."

"Thanks?" Darlene said. She had thought her twirl was spot on. They skated in silence for a few minutes.

"Aren't you cold?" Charlie asked.

"A little," Darlene admitted, crossing her arms in front of her and trying not to shiver. She had opted for less winter attire than was required because she wanted to look good for Charlie.

"You should have worn a hat and scarf," Charlie said. "Maybe I can help warm you up a bit."

He reached out for her hand. Darlene reached her hand back toward him, and he grabbed it. They skated together like this for some time. Then Darlene noticed that her friends had backed off to give them more space.

"Do you want to go to a movie or something next weekend?" Charlie asked.

Darlene felt butterflies take flight in her stomach. A date! A real date! And her father was going to be away that weekend, so she didn't have to go over there, after all.

She shrugged. "Yeah, I could do that. I think *Starman* opens next weekend. Maybe we can see that."

Charlie shook his head and made a face. "I don't like all that sci-fi crap. It's kind of stupid. Like *Star Wars?* I hated that shit. Maybe we can find a comedy or action film instead. I can call you to let you know what's playing and what time. Saturday night?"

Darlene nodded. She had wanted to see *Starman*, but she didn't want to see a movie that Charlie wouldn't like. She wanted him to have a good time on their date. She liked comedies, but she didn't really like action movies. The intensity made her anxious. *Terminator* had given her nightmares for a week. She hoped they would see a comedy. She would trust Charlie to pick a good film.

Darlene told Charlie how to find her number in the phone book. They skated around for another half hour, and then Darlene's feet started to hurt.

"I think I'm ready to stop," she said. She hoped maybe Charlie would suggest that they all go for a hot cocoa or some ice cream or something. It would be a nice way to end the afternoon.

"I'm gonna keep skating for a while," Charlie said. "You need to work on your stamina if you're gonna skate with me again. I have at least another half hour in me. I guess I'll see you in school tomorrow."

He squeezed her hand, then let go and skated away. Darlene watched him go. It felt kind of abrupt. She waved to her friends to let them know she was done. They were talking to two boys. She hoped she wasn't interrupting something.

"Did you have fun with Charlie?" Kim asked as they were putting their shoes back on.

"Yeah," Darlene said. "He held my hand! And he asked me to go to see a movie next weekend. He's gonna call me!" She shrieked.

Kim laughed. "That's wicked awesome! You two looked cute skating together. And guess what? Michelle met a boy, too! He obviously likes her."

Michelle gave a shy look. "So you really think he liked me, huh?"

Kim laughed again. "Michelle, if I don't hear from you tomorrow that he called you tonight, I will give you ten dollars. That's how sure I am."

"What's his name?" Darlene asked.

"Joey Cafaro," Michelle answered. "He goes to Murphy. And he has the best eyes!" Now she gave a shriek.

Darlene smiled at her friend. She was so happy for her. Darlene and Michelle had both never kissed a boy or been on a date before. It was something they had been able to connect about. Maybe they would all end up going to prom together in the spring. Now if only Kim could find someone. She looked at Kim. Kim smiled at her.

Darlene suddenly flashed back to Kim crying hysterically on the phone last year after the Christmas party. She tried to push the thought out of her head. Kim was okay. She had to believe that. Kim was not damaged goods.

"Hey, you guys," Darlene said, smiling brightly. "Hurry up, okay? I'm freezing. I'm obviously underdressed for the weather. Let's go home. We can have my mom make us some hot chocolate with marshmallows."

"Tell me about substance use," Aspen said. "High school is a time of experimentation. Did you and your friends try drinking, or smoking pot?"

Darlene nodded. "It was never too much of a problem for me, but I worried about Kim. She seemed to check out when she drank or smoked pot. And she also smoked cigarettes, at least until she got caught at school and got detention. But I tried stuff, too. The first time we all experimented was at the Christmas party. We all had a drink, and Kim had at least two. Then a joint got passed around. We all took a hit. I think it was the first time for all of us. I thought it felt pretty good. Michelle had something like an asthma attack, and that's why we had to leave. But Kim just kept on drinking and smoking.

"Our friend Sally and her boyfriend James didn't drink or smoke, at all. They didn't really like to be around us when we were doing it. The last time I remember them being there was on Halloween junior year. There was a party, and Kim was there. Chris and Carl were there, too. Carl had a date with him, someone we knew from elementary school. Kim was looking sideways at her all night, but at the time, I didn't know why. So that night, I *was determined to drink. Neither Kim nor I were able to find any alcohol in our moms' houses. They would drink sometimes, but it was always at a restaurant or bar, and they'd get cocktails, but they didn't drink at home. So nothing there. So I did something sneaky."*

"What did you do?" Aspen asked.

"I broke into my father's house when he wasn't home and I stole a bottle of rum from his liquor cabinet," Darlene admitted.

Aspen looked at her curiously. "Weren't you afraid he would be mad when he realized it was gone?"

Darlene shook her head. "No, I knew he would never notice. My dad didn't drink. He always had bottles of something in there, either a gift he had gotten, or something he bought for his guests. I mean, of course he drank. He drank beer. But he didn't think of beer as drinking. That's weird, isn't it? Beer is totally drinking. That seriously never even occurred to me until this very moment. My dad drank beer all the time." She paused.

"So your memory of your dad had you picturing him as someone who didn't drink alcohol," Aspen summarized. "And now you're figuring out that this wasn't exactly true. Do you think the beer might have affected his moods?"

Darlene thought about it. "I don't know. I mean, I always noticed that my dad could last about two days with me before he started getting upset by my behavior. That's why the weekends were usually okay. I would even start to change my behavior on day three, like at Disney World, so I wouldn't make him upset. Now that I'm thinking of it, it's possible it could have been a couple of things. Either he was jonesing for a beer and going through withdrawal of some sort, or he had gone two days without drinking because he was around me, and finally went and got a beer. Could my dad have been an alcoholic, do you think?"

Aspen gave her an empathetic look. "I don't know, Darlene. I would have to have a lot more information about him and do an assessment before I would be able to make a determination like that. Do you think he might have had a drinking problem?"

Darlene sighed. "I do now. And it really makes me wonder about all the things that happened back then."

Chapter 21

EXPECTATIONS VERSUS REALITIES

DARLENE HAD BEEN DATING CHARLIE for three months. It had been going okay. He seemed to like her, and he kept calling to ask her out again. They kissed on their first real date. They went to an action movie, and after, Darlene's shoulders felt tense. But she wanted Charlie to think she had a good time. So she acted like she had a good time. And when he brought her home after the movie, he kissed her in the car. It was her first kiss. She wanted to savor it. But then he put his tongue in her mouth, and she didn't know what to do, so she kept pulling back. She didn't know if she was supposed to do something with her tongue. No one had ever told her. It didn't feel like she thought it would. Then, eventually, Charlie walked her to the door. They said goodnight, and he gave her a small kiss. That one felt right. She wondered how she could make all the kisses like that.

She dared to ask Kim the next day. "What do you do when a guy puts his tongue in your mouth?"

Kim made a face. "Gross," she said. "I've only kissed a couple of guys, and there was never a tongue involved. Well, they might put it out a little but not in my mouth. Charlie did that?"

Darlene nodded. "I didn't know what to do. I wanted to do it right, but I didn't know how. I want to be able to do it right next time we kiss."

Kim looked at her like she was crazy. "Did you like it?"

Darlene waivered. "It was okay," she lied. "I could get used to it. But I don't want to gross him out." She let the subject drop and talked about the movie they saw.

Prom was coming up now, and everyone had their dates. Michelle was going with Joey Cafaro, Sally was going with James, Rhonda was going with Chris, Traci was going with her crush from Murphy High, Doug, Darlene was going with Charlie, and in the biggest surprise twist, Kim was going with Carl. When Darlene found out about this, she was baffled.

"How did that happen?" she asked when Kim told her on the way home from school.

Kim shrugged. "Last year, Carl and I made a prom pact. We decided that if neither of us had a date for junior prom, we would go together as friends. So that's what we're doing." She smiled. "Remember I talked about having a backup plan last year if no one asked me?"

"But didn't Sam Johnson ask you to the prom?"

"Sort of," Kim responded. "He asked me if I was going with anyone, and I said I was. I just didn't specify."

"Oh," Darlene said. So Kim *did* like Carl! Now Darlene was fairly sure. And the timing made sense. Kim's moodiness seemed to evaporate overnight the previous spring when they had been talking about prom and she mentioned forming a backup plan. That must have been when she talked to Carl and knew that she would be able to manipulate him into going to prom with her. Kim was a genius! Darlene was proud of her work.

"It should be a lot of fun," Darlene said. "I'm looking forward to the dancing. And the after-party!"

Kim gave a giddy smile. "Me, too."

The prom itself was fun. So was the dinner before. The after-party started out well. The group drank wine coolers, beer, and champagne, and before anyone knew it, they were all tipsy and amorous. James and Sally left to have a private night together at his house, then Kim shimmied up close to

Carl. Carl seemed to be noticing and touching her more. Then Kim got up and pulled Darlene into the bathroom and begged her to get the keys to Charlie's car, because she wanted to go out there with Carl to be alone.

Darlene thought the whole thing was hysterical. It might have been the champagne talking, but she agreed and went out to the room and found the keys in Charlie's discarded tux jacket pocket. She showed Kim, who then asked Carl to go for a walk with her. Darlene slipped the keys into Kim's purse as discreetly as she could, and Kim and Carl left.

Michelle brought Joey into the corner so they could make out. Chris and Rhonda were kissing and getting handsy on the armchair, and Traci and Doug were sitting between the beds, looking into each other's eyes. Then Doug reached forward and kissed Traci. Suddenly, Charlie took Darlene's arm and led her into the bathroom. Darlene got excited. They were going to make out.

But when they got in the bathroom, Charlie locked the door, took an open bottle of champagne from the tub, and chugged some down. He looked at Darlene angrily.

"Why the hell did you do that?"

Darlene was confused. And a bit tipsy. "Do what?"

"Why did you give Kim my keys?" Charlie demanded. "Yeah, I saw you trying to be so sneaky. What were you thinking? They're just gonna go down there and do it in my car. They're gonna mess it all up! And if you were so into people doing it in my car, why didn't you suggest going down there with me?"

Charlie grabbed her arms roughly and pulled her toward him to kiss him. He put her tongue deep in her mouth. She pulled away.

"Charlie, you're hurting my arms," she told him. He let go of her. "I'm sorry. I didn't mean to make you mad. I just wanted to help my friend."

This was confusing. She didn't know how to keep both Charlie and Kim happy at the same time.

"Well, you did make me mad. And I think you need to make up for it. Let's just do it in here, then." He reached for his belt.

Darlene hated to be disagreeable to Charlie, but she knew this wasn't right. "No. I've never done it before. I can't do it in the bathroom. And I don't want to."

Tears ran down her face. He was going to get so mad at her. She was losing control.

Charlie softened his voice a little. "Okay, fine. But you still owe me. I had to put out a ton of money for prom, and that dinner I bought you wasn't cheap, you know. And now I'll have to clean out the back of my car. You can at least give me a blow job to make up for it." He pulled down his zipper.

Darlene was stupefied. She didn't feel she owed Charlie anything. It was his prom, too. All the boys had paid for the girls, except Carl, because Kim didn't let him since they had gone as friends. This was wrong. Charlie was bullying her into doing something she didn't want to do. But Charlie was so mad, and she had made him that way. She had to fix this. She had to do what he asked, even if the thought made her feel sick. It wouldn't actually kill her. She didn't even really know what a blow job entailed, but she knew it wasn't something she wanted to do.

"Okay," she said shakily, tears still falling swiftly. "I'll do it. But I don't know what to do. You'll have to tell me."

She braced herself for what was coming next.

When it was over, Charlie zipped up his pants and fastened his belt. Then he left the bathroom without saying anything, closing the door behind him. Darlene quickly went to the toilet and threw up, for a long time. Then she cried. Then she washed her face.

She had left her overnight bag in the bathroom earlier, and now she opened it up. She put on some fresh makeup, fixed her hair, and straightened her dress. Then she stepped out of the bathroom.

And she stuffed what had just happened all away in the back of her head, behind the wall. No one would know, not even Kim. This was to be her dirty little secret. She would keep it forever.

And after the next morning, she never, ever wanted to see Charlie again.

Everyone was back to talking and hanging out when she came out, and no one said a thing about how she looked. Darlene smiled, sitting down on the bed next to Charlie. She folded her hands on her lap and focused on the conversation.

When Kim and Carl came back, it was obvious something had happened while they were gone, because Kim's makeup was gone and she looked like she'd been crying. Darlene switched gears. Now it was about Kim. She gave her a look. Kim returned it, smiling to let her know she was okay. Darlene didn't believe her, but Kim didn't want to talk about it and went to get ready for bed, which prompted everyone to prepare to sleep.

Charlie had gotten dibs on one of the double beds, so now Darlene was expected to sleep next to him all night. Her nausea flared. She swallowed it back down. After she brushed her teeth and put on her sweats, she crawled into the bed and turned her back to Charlie. He yelled out good night, and Darlene said it back. Within five minutes, Charlie was asleep, but Darlene lay awake for hours. She just couldn't shut off her brain.

The next morning, they all went to IHOP. Darlene was exhausted. She didn't speak too much, which her friends thought was strange.

"Are you okay, Darlene?" Kim asked. "You're so subdued. Are you feeling sick?"

Darlene shook her head and smiled. "No, I'm fine. I think I may be a bit hungover or something. But I'll be okay after I get a good night's sleep tonight."

That answer appeared to satisfy Kim. She turned back to the group, and they all continued their conversation.

Charlie drove her home after breakfast. He blasted the music on the radio. When they got to her house, he leaned over to kiss her before she got out. She let him for a few seconds, and then pulled away.

"Goodbye, Charlie." She climbed out of the car with her bag.

"See ya tomorrow," Charlie called out. "Maybe we can get some pizza next weekend."

Darlene didn't say a word. She just kept on walking. When she went inside, her mother asked her how prom went, and she said it was good, and her mother believed her.

Over the next few weeks, she told Charlie she was busy every time he called. At school, if she saw him in the distance, she would turn and walk the other way. She started to tell her friends that she was thinking of breaking up with him, although in her mind, they were already done. Her friends felt bad for her and wanted to help, but she told them she just didn't feel it anymore for Charlie. Charlie continued to attend group events with her until the end of the year. She knew that was when she could do it. The end of the year. Then she wouldn't need to see him again for more than two months.

He came to pick her up at her house. She got in the car, and she told him to wait.

"Charlie, we need to break up," Darlene announced.

Charlie looked at her and laughed. "Yeah, right. Very funny."

Darlene shook her head. "Charlie, I'm not joking. We need to break up. I don't want to go out with you anymore."

A voice inside her head started yelling at her, *Darlene, what are you doing? Stop, please stop!*

"What the hell, Darlene?" Charlie said angrily. "You're seriously breaking up with me? Why?"

Darlene hesitated. "I don't know, I just don't feel like it's working for us anymore. We just don't have that much in common."

We just want to make you happy, Charlie, the voice insisted.

Charlie sneered at her. "We don't, huh? Well, I don't know why I'd want to have anything in common with you anyway. You're kind of boring, and your friends are so weird. And you're really not all that good-looking. I'm surprised that I didn't break up with you already. Fine. We're broken up. Are you happy now?"

Darlene felt her anxiety rise. "No, I'm not happy. I didn't want to have to break up. I wanted things to go well with us, but they're not. It just makes sense for us to move on."

Don't move on, say you're sorry, Darlene! Make this better!

"Then move on already," Charlie yelled. "Get out of here!"

He started to lunge toward her as if he was going to shove her into the door. She flinched.

"Stop it Charlie, I'm going!"

She opened the door of the car and practically fell out. She slammed the door and ran down the driveway, up the walk, and into her house. She closed the door, locked it, and tried to catch her breath.

She could hear Charlie's car still running outside her house. She went to the window to look. Charlie was sitting there, staring at the front door. Darlene pulled down the shade and then ran up to her room. Charlie was still there. She pulled that shade down, too, and sat on her bed, still breathing hard. She was terrified. She had never seen anyone so angry. She had never made anyone that angry, not even her father. She was scared he was going to hurt her. Her mother wasn't home. Charlie could see that her car was not there. He knew she was alone. She started to cry. She wondered if she should call the police. But finally, Charlie put the car in gear and drove away.

Darlene sat on her bed and rocked and swayed. She hadn't done that in years. Eventually her heart rate decreased, and her breathing regulated. She listened for the voice inside her head that belonged to the Darlene who always told her how to act around Charlie. It was silent now. She let herself fall onto her bed and sob.

Charlie called the house the next day. Mrs. Feinman answered. "Darlene, Charlie's on the phone," she yelled out.

"I can't come to the phone," Darlene called back.

"Okay, I'll let him know."

He called again later that night. "Darlene, it's Charlie again," her mother said.

"I'm in the bathroom," Darlene told her. She went into the bathroom and closed the door in case her mother checked.

Her mother came up a few minutes later. She sat next to her on her bed. "Darlene, is there something going on with you and Charlie? He sounds upset, and it sounds like you don't want to talk to him."

Darlene sighed. "I don't, Mom. I broke up with him yesterday. He wasn't happy about it. He got angry. He's probably calling to try to get me back."

Mrs. Feinman looked at Darlene carefully. "I'm so sorry, Darlene. I didn't know. Oh, first love is so hard. Are you okay?"

First love, huh. Darlene gave her mother a reassuring smile. "I'm gonna be fine, Mom. I just wish he would stop calling. I don't want to talk to him."

Mrs. Feinman nodded. "The next time he calls, I'll ask him to stop calling, okay?"

Darlene nodded.

"And I'm going to make you whatever you want for dinner tonight. What should I make?"

Darlene didn't really want to eat, and she didn't really have a favorite, but she knew her mother's favorite. "How about orange chicken and rice?"

Mrs. Feinman smiled. "Yes! I think I have everything I need for that tonight. I'll go get started. And don't you worry about the phone. I'll answer it tonight. I'll only get you if it's one of the girls." She got up, smoothed out her shirt, and started toward the stairs. "And let me know if you want to talk about this thing with Charlie, okay? I can really be a good listener."

"Thanks, Mom," Darlene called out. She sighed. At least she always knew exactly what to do to make her mother happy.

"Darlene, I'd like to talk more about the people, the voices in your head. Can you tell me about them?" Aspen assumed a listening position.

Darlene laughed. "I'm not psychotic," she said. "I know they're not real people. They're not really voices, they're more like loud thoughts. And they're not multiple personalities. I never black out or lose time, and I am always in control of all my actions. I never even called them the people in my head until Traci said that phrase, and it seemed to fit. So, I guess when I was born, there was just one of me. Maybe for several years. But as my parents started fighting more, things got more stressful. I might have even been a toddler when it all started, but I can't really remember. I would have a certain level of anxiety all the time. I could bear that. But if my anxiety went up, it would become intolerable, and I would have to find ways to bring it down. So what I did was adjust. I would figure out how to make the anxiety go away with my own actions. So with my father, I would be good, so he wouldn't get mad at me anymore. With my mother, I would act like everything was always okay, and she would believe me, no matter what. With Kim, I would be a support, a constant friend and companion, and she would always be my *friend. With Michelle, I would have to be as genuine as I could. She could tell if I wasn't. So those were my first four people. They were like a little family in my head. When I was with one person, I was one way, and with another person, another way. Some of them were similar enough so I didn't screw up, but some were really different."*

"Give me some examples of that," Aspen said.

Darlene thought. "When I was with Kim and Michelle together in elementary school, I was tough. We were tough around the posse boys. It was a group persona that lasted until junior high. I kind of liked being tough. So it was okay sometimes if I was tough around Kim or Michelle alone. But never with my mom or dad. I always had to be a good girl with my father; that was all I could be with him. It wasn't safe to be anyone else. But I could also be a good girl with Kim. I was afraid to make her angry. I didn't want her to reject me. I had to make adjustments after I found out that Kim wasn't going to abandon me if I wasn't perfect with her, so I did. I didn't have to be a good girl with Michelle. She wouldn't have bought it. She would have known immediately that something was off. And it wasn't safe for anyone to know that I was doing this. I knew this instinctively.

"Developing new people was like making a plaster mold. You put the plaster in the mold with all the right ingredients, and when it's in the right form, it starts to set. I would feel if the person in my head would make me feel less anxious in a certain situation, and then I would let it solidify. But as life went on, there were more and more people. There were classmates, and teachers, and skating teachers, and people at my father's temple. And then there was Sally and Traci. And then Charlie. My Charlie person was super compliant. She didn't want to be abandoned, so she always did whatever Charlie wanted. But eventually even she had her limits. And after we broke up, she disappeared. Or so I thought. So, pretty soon, my head was so full of people that it got kind of noisy, and it got harder to figure out which one I needed at which time. After Charlie, I had a hard time with that. It took a while for that to settle down, and the good thing was that my friends just thought I was sad about the breakup."

"But what was really happening?" Aspen wondered.

"I was repairing my house, I guess," Darlene said. "I was weeding out the garden. My friends offered for me to go out with them to do things. I always had a reason I couldn't. I had to help my mother with something. I was going

to my dad's house. I didn't feel well. Or I didn't want to be a third wheel with them and their boyfriends. But what I was really doing was sitting on my bed, thinking. And sorting. And discarding. And pretty soon, I had weeded out all the unwelcome people. I narrowed my world down to a very small town. It was my mother, my father, Kim, Michelle, Sally, Traci, Chris, Carl, James, and our friend Pete who went to Murphy. And everyone's boyfriends or girlfriends at the time. Then there was a generic Darlene that I used with everyone else. These were the knowns. I didn't want any more unknowns. I knew that there would have to be new people when I went to college and into my adult life, but at that time, I was fine with my little tribe. And I didn't have room for another boyfriend, that's for sure. But everyone seemed to think I needed one, and wondered why I didn't do anything about it. So they focused on just being with me, consoling me, making me feel better. I just let them think and do whatever made them happy."

Aspen nodded. "It was always about making sure everyone was happy all the time, wasn't it?"

"Yeah," Darlene agreed. "It was. I thought that I could make everyone happy when I was being their person. Sometimes it worked, but sometimes it didn't. But the biggest problem was that I didn't have any person up there in my head looking out for me. I was never happy. And it was going to get even worse after high school."

Chapter 22

The Future is Now

WHEN SENIOR YEAR BEGAN, DARLENE started the day feeling prepared and calm, but that feeling didn't last long. First, she had history class with Charlie. He kept shooting daggers at her from his eyes, and she felt violated. She felt that everyone else in the class knew what he was doing. She ran out of the room as soon as the bell rang. She looked for her friends but couldn't find them. Even in the classes they shared that morning, they didn't show up. She didn't see Chris, but she did see Rhonda in English. And then Traci wasn't in math. At lunch, all was revealed.

Traci arrived in the cafeteria and tearfully announced to the group that she was leaving immediately for Michigan. Her father had relocated for work. Darlene felt a stabbing in her head as her Traci persona wept inside. Then, when Traci left, Chris arrived to say Rhonda had broken up with him. She had blindsided him. He was broken. Now Darlene stayed silent, but she felt herself get out of her chair and retrieve Chris a glass of water. She didn't know what else to do. Getting a glass of water was at least *something*. It reduced her anxiety for a minute. She remained calm on the outside, but inside, she was having a multi-person panic attack.

Luckily, Sally took charge. She had everyone announce their afternoon schedule and assigned them each a time to watch over Chris, to make sure he got to class and was okay. Now there was a plan. Darlene could follow instructions. She didn't have to think. She could just do.

When she got home that afternoon, she sat on her bed. She had to reassess. She had to discover how to exist in her friend group without Traci. She already felt the ache of her absence. And she had to figure out how to be Chris's friend again. None of her friends had ever been broken up with before. She didn't know what he needed. She would have to watch her friends over the next few days and take their lead. Then she could develop a new Chris persona. A little while later, Kim, Carl, and Chris stopped by and they all went out to the clearing to talk and smoke a joint.

The days passed. Then the weeks. The seven friends stuck close by each other, both in and out of school. They worked on college applications and took their SATs. Darlene was happy with her score of 1190. It would be enough to get her into the schools of her choice. Her mother congratulated her. Her father sighed over the phone. Darlene apologized for not doing better. Her father told her they would make the most of what they had. She didn't respond.

Darlene applied to Boston University, UMass, Ithaca College, University of Rhode Island, and Eastboro State as her backup. She knew that Michelle had applied to UMass and wanted to go to nursing school there. Darlene secretly had already decided to go to UMass to study biology if she got in, and she was sure she would. She wouldn't be in most classes with Michelle, and they wouldn't be living together, but they would be able to see each other as often as they wanted. The thought brought her close to happiness. She could almost feel it.

Her mother took her to college interviews. They listened to music in the car on the long drives and chatted about the latest celebrity gossip. Darlene knew her mother was feeling sad about the idea of Darlene leaving the next year to go to college; she had heard her telling Mrs. Drake on the phone when she thought she couldn't hear her. Darlene could always hear her. So Darlene was trying to spend more time with her, to make sure her mother had plenty of happy memories to keep with her after Darlene left.

When they arrived at interviews, her mother would walk her inside and wait with her until she was called in. Right before she went in, Mrs. Feinman would look her in the eye and say, "Just be yourself. Good luck."

Just be myself, Darlene thought. *Yeah, okay. But which one?*

She was accepted to all the colleges she applied to. She was excited to fill out her commitment form for UMass. Her mother urged her to bring the paperwork over to her father's house that weekend so he could write any checks she might need. She put all her acceptance information into an envelope, and then she placed the envelope in her overnight bag. After dinner that night, she took out the envelope and sat down on the couch next to her father after the news ended.

"Dad," she said, "I'm ready to fill out my commitment letter for college. I brought everything over so we can do it together. Mom thought we might need to send in some checks."

Mr. Feinman smiled. "I'm proud of you, Darlene," he said. "Ithaca's going to get a great biology student."

Darlene grew cold. "Dad, I'm planning on going to UMass. I thought you knew that."

Mr. Feinman gave her a confused look. "UMass?" he asked. "Why would you want to go there when you were accepted to Ithaca? UMass is a fallback school. It's like an extended high school! No, you'll go to Ithaca. That's where you'll learn the most, become the best you can be. Your chances for a better career come through Ithaca."

"But Dad, I've really had my heart set on going to UMass. Michelle is going there, and—"

"Darlene, you don't choose a college based on where your friend is going," Mr. Feinman said sternly. "You go to a college based on what's best for you academically! You need to make the correct choice."

Choice? Darlene thought. *It seems that maybe I don't have one, really.*

Darlene let a minute pass while she stared at the paperwork. Her next words almost choked her. "Okay, Dad. I'll go to Ithaca."

Her throat felt like it was closing.

Mr. Feinman smiled and patted her on the shoulder.

"That's my good girl," he said, rising. "Let me go grab another beer, and then we'll fill out the paperwork, and I'll write as many checks as you need. And I got us some ice cream for dessert. We need to celebrate your success!"

Darlene glanced at the UMass paperwork in front of her. Her vision grew blurry, and she blinked. Then she reached back in the envelope and pulled out the forms from Ithaca. She took out a pen.

She felt like her life was not her own. Her choices were taken away. She wasn't going to be with Michelle. Again.

But her father had said she was a good girl, so that was something. Wasn't it? So why didn't it feel like something? It felt like nothing.

She was able to get ready for bed, read a chapter of a book for English class, and crawl under the sheets with the lights off before allowing the tears to finally burst free.

Chapter 23

Prom Drama

DARLENE KNEW SHE WOULDN'T BE asked to the prom, and she had come to peace with that fact. There was no one she wanted to go with. She was okay with staying home that night and watching movies with her mother. Her mother would feel bad for her and cook her a nice meal. She might also make her a nice dessert. It would be low stress, low fuss, and no muss.

But there was one thing she could not tolerate: her friends being hurt. Michelle's boyfriend, Joey, went off and joined the Marines before prom and left her without a prom date. He didn't even break up with her so she could find another date. Now Michelle wouldn't be able to go to the prom, and Darlene was not okay with that.

Chris didn't have a date either. Darlene sensed a familiar energy coming from Chris. She didn't think he really cared if he went to the prom or not. He was still smarting over the loss of Rhonda. But when Carl suggested they all go as a group, so no one would have to miss prom, Darlene jumped on the opportunity. She didn't want Michelle to be sad and lonely. They were seniors. This was their last prom. She enthusiastically endorsed the idea. Michelle got on board, and it didn't take long for the six friends to talk Chris into it. So the plans were made. They would be a prom date of seven. Darlene even started to get excited.

They did girl things to prepare for prom. They bought dresses and shoes. They had their makeup done at Filene's and helped each other decide what products to bring home. They had lunch together at the mall and talked about how they would do their hair and the fun they would have. A limo was rented, an after-party was secured at Chris's house, and dinner reservations were made. Darlene regretted that she would miss movie night with her mom, but she looked forward to spending some pressure-free quality time with her friends. Their last hurrah before graduation.

After dinner, they went to the dance. They had a plan in place. No one would be left without a dance partner while everyone else was dancing. Sometimes that meant dancing with someone else's girlfriend or boyfriend or dancing in groups of three. Everyone was laughing and having a fun time.

Darlene noticed Rhonda on the other side of the dance floor, dancing close with her date, Kyle Newkirk. Darlene glanced at Chris. He hadn't noticed Rhonda yet. Rhonda and Kyle were moving around the floor slowly, kissing from time to time. Rhonda seemed to suddenly notice Chris with his friends and the fact that he was having fun. Darlene didn't know if she did it on purpose, but Rhonda appeared to be slowly making her way across the floor toward her group. Finally, Chris looked up and saw her, just as she kissed her boyfriend.

Darlene saw Chris's face drop, all of the fun draining out of him over the span of a single second. Darlene had to do something, and fast. Her first impulse was to approach Rhonda and tell her off, but that wouldn't get the results she needed. Then she remembered that when they had all planned to go to prom together, Darlene had jokingly promised to give Chris a huge French kiss if Rhonda caused him any grief. Well, there was no time like the present.

She walked over to Chris and stood in front of him. He didn't notice her at first because his head was turned toward Rhonda, so she tapped him on the shoulder. He turned to her, and she grabbed him around the neck and pulled his face closer. She kissed him hard, and long enough so that she knew Rhonda would have seen. He kissed her back, most likely out of surprise. Just before she pulled away, she nibbled lightly on his lower lip. Chris jumped back, shock evident on his face.

"Better now?" Darlene asked. Chris nodded and stared at her, his grief instantly forgotten. "Told you I'd do it."

By the time she looked around again, Rhonda was nowhere in sight. Darlene and her friends went back to dancing. With a rush of adrenaline, Darlene started to let loose. She could dance all night.

The kiss was the talk of the after-party. "I can't believe you did that," Sally said. "It was perfect! The look on Rhonda's face! I wish you could have seen it! It was classic. Darlene, you are the real prom queen!"

The others agreed, and Darlene grinned shyly. "Well, we look out for our friends, don't we? That's kind of what we do."

Pete arrived with his girlfriend, Carolyn, and the party got started. Everyone had a drink in their hand, and Michelle was quickly getting a buzz. Kim and Carl disappeared for about half an hour, and everyone knew what they were doing. Everyone else sat around, sipping on their drinks and eating the food Mrs. Mahoney had made for them. There was laughter, and at one point, Darlene noticed some tears from Michelle. But Sally was taking care of her, so Darlene knew she would be okay.

After a while, everyone decided to go to sleep. Darlene had unrolled her sleeping bag on the floor to the right of Michelle, and now Chris had his to the right of her. As they slipped inside, Chris turned to Darlene.

"Darlene," he said. "What you did at the prom, I don't even know what to say. It was awesome. I couldn't have asked for anything better to help me get through that. I owe you one." He paused. "And for what it's worth," he went on, "that was a pretty good kiss. Any guy would be lucky to be able to kiss you." He leaned closer and gave her a soft kiss on the cheek. "Good night, Darlene."

"Good night, Chris," Darlene said. She turned on her side away from Chris and smiled. She had done something good. She had helped Chris. And he said she was a good kisser! And she didn't even use her tongue. She had kissed him the way she would want to be kissed, and that was okay. And she had danced all night! It was a good night. She couldn't deny it. Her friends were the best. She really loved them all. And, in a small and distant part of her brain, Darlene wondered what it would be like to kiss Chris again someday.

Chapter 24

Endings and Beginnings

DARLENE'S PARENTS ATTENDED GRADUATION AND sat together, along with Kim's family. Darlene couldn't help but notice that her parents didn't fight anymore when they got together. They had learned to be civil, and they had even progressed to bits of small talk. Darlene guessed they just didn't have any reason to fight anymore. Now they were just two people who once loved each other, many years ago, and shared a child. Darlene felt a mild jealousy. She wished her relationship with her father could be so free and easy.

After the ceremony, the Feinmans and the Drakes went out for dinner. With ten diners, it was a noisy but joyful meal. Kim was smiling, and Darlene's father was smiling. So Darlene smiled, too. It was a happy occasion. She let herself relax and enjoy it.

Darlene was worried about Kim, because she still didn't know what she wanted to do in the fall. She was waiting to see what Carl wanted to do, and Carl was making no plans for his immediate future. Darlene feared that Kim would just decide to stay home and take care of her father. But that was no life for Kim. She was spirited, and bright, and she needed an outlet. If she stayed at home, her colors would start to fade.

But the solution to this problem was not at all what Darlene was expecting. Kim had announced that Carl was moving to California to be an electrician's apprentice to his cousin, Laine. Kim decided that she would go with him. Which meant that Kim would be gone. Darlene would be gone, too, but Darlene would be able to come back to Eastboro whenever she wanted, and for sure for holidays and the summer. But Kim would be staying in California. It would be her new home. Carl would be her new family.

This was a loss that Darlene didn't know if she could bear. In her whole life, she had never gone more than one week without seeing Kim, and most often, she saw her every day. How could she just be gone?

She did what she usually did in these situations. She brought out neutral Darlene. Neutral Darlene was the one who could just go with the flow. She did what she had to. She listened to her friends when they talked about their grand plans. Michelle was going to become a nurse. Sally was going to be a writer. James would be at culinary school, and he was excited about learning to be a chef. Chris would study to become a teacher. Chris, a teacher! Kim and Carl would be starting their new lives in Seska, California. And Darlene. She would be going to a school she didn't want to go to, to prepare for a career that she had no interest in.

The summer flew by. She spent as much time as she could with Kim. She took tons of pictures that she could put up on her dorm room wall. She helped Kim plan what she just had to bring with her to her new home, and what could be left behind. They made plans for how they would stay in touch, by phone, and by letter, and maybe someday, Darlene could come visit in California.

There was a goodbye party at Carl's Gram's house. The friends were all there, and they were all feeling the loss. They talked about old times, and about times to come. They talked about the adventure that Kim and Carl would be embarking on. Then Chris lit up a joint, and they all, with the exception of James and Sally, got higher than kites. Some got mellow, some got jittery, and Darlene just got numb. She had hitched a ride to the party with Chris, but neither of them were safe to drive. Chris's Gram drove them home. And Darlene, for once in her young life, fell onto her bed and went right into a deep and dreamless sleep.

She would be the last of the friends to see Kim and Carl before they left later that week. They decided to go out to lunch. None of them had ever tried sushi before, so they decided to try a sushi restaurant that had just opened near their neighborhood. They had no idea what to expect. The menu was made up of foods they had never heard of, so they guessed what to order. When the food came, it was pretty, and colorful, and came with a variety of bright sauces. They each took a bite of their sushi, and then they all made eye contact. It was awful. They all hated it. Darlene tried to take one of the rolls apart and just eat the parts that looked palatable. She tried dipping some of it in a green sauce. Her mouth caught fire. There wasn't even any bread on the table. The three friends stopped eating and just talked while drinking water. Finally, they paid their check and walked out.

As soon as they got to the sidewalk, they said what needed to be said. "Oh my God," Kim said with a disgusted face. "That was so gross! I can't believe I even put that stuff in my mouth! I've had Japanese food before, but never anything as disgusting as that!"

Darlene nodded. "I don't even know what I ate. What was that black stuff?"

"I think it was seaweed," Carl said, grimacing. "It tasted like they just pulled it out of the fucking ocean!"

They looked at each other quietly for a moment, and then they started laughing.

"Is this what being an adult is going to be like?" Kim asked. "We have to try new things and pretend they don't make us sick? I'm gonna be awful at that. I can't keep my opinions to myself. I'm gonna get myself banned from all the hip adult places."

"Or you could be an excellent food critic," Darlene suggested. "They never like anything!"

Carl laughed. "But I don't think you can pan a whole genre of food! Maybe just systematically write bad reviews about every sushi restaurant until they start serving hamburgers or something for people like us!"

"American restaurants have gross food, too," Kim admitted. "My dad actually likes the liver and onions at Friendly's. Gag me."

They got into Darlene's mother's car, and she drove them back to Carl's Gram's house. Darlene could see Carl and Kim's cars parked in the driveway, loaded with all of their belongings—very concrete evidence they would be leaving soon. Darlene swallowed back tears.

Then Kim started to cry. Darlene couldn't keep her tears inside any longer. They got out of the car and embraced each other tightly. They cried and rocked back and forth.

"I don't know what I'm gonna do without you," Kim whispered. "You're my best friend. You've always been my best friend, since we were babies. I will never have another friend like you."

Darlene pulled away but kept her hands around Kim's neck. "I know," she said through her tears. "You're like a sister to me. But you have to promise me, Kim. You have to make new friends. I don't want you to be lonely. I want you to be happy. That's all I want for you. I want you to have Carl and friends, and some great career that makes you happy. Promise me."

Kim nodded. "I promise. But my friends will just be second to you. You have to promise me, too, Darlene. I want you to be happy, too. I don't hold the market on happiness. I want you to be happy at Ithaca. I know you wanted to be with Michelle, and I know you don't want to talk about what happened, so I won't ask again, but just make the most of what you have, okay? Make friends. Take classes you love. Maybe meet someone special. It's been a long time. You deserve someone special. And don't forget about me."

Darlene shook her head. "I will never forget about you, Kim. I love you."

Kim hugged her again. "I love you, too. I'll call you when I get settled in to tell you my address and phone number. Take care of Michelle, okay? Make sure she's okay. And if you ever think of it, check in on my mom and dad."

Darlene moved on to Carl and hugged him. "Carl, I hope you love what you're doing in California. And take care of Kim. She's more important than anything. And thanks for being my friend all these years. I'll miss you."

Carl smiled. "Darlene, I promise I'll take care of Kim. She's the most important thing to me. Everything else is just frosting, okay? I'll miss you, too. But we'll see each other again, I know it."

Finally, Kim and Carl had to go inside. Darlene got behind the wheel and watched as they walked to the door, then turned around and waved. She pulled away and drove toward her house, tears still running down her cheeks.

When she got home, she finished crying, washed her face, and went to find some food she could stomach. She was starving.

There were more goodbyes to endure before Labor Day, but they were not quite as hard. Everyone was leaving for their first year of college. They would all come home for Thanksgiving and Christmas. They would see each other. They would talk on the phone. Darlene said goodbye to Chris and Pete before they left to drive Kim's car to California. Then she said goodbye to Sally and James.

The last goodbye was the hardest. She had to say goodbye to Michelle, her second-oldest friend, and the first one to choose her. They met at Friendly's for dessert and coffee the night before they would both leave for college.

"Thank you for the chocolate chip cookie in kindergarten, Michelle," Darlene said.

Michelle laughed. "Thanks for taking it. And thanks for all of the days and years on the playground with me."

Darlene smiled. "I couldn't imagine any other life than the one we had when we were at DeMarco. I think those were the years that made us who we are."

Michelle nodded. "I think so, too."

Darlene took a breath and exhaled. "Michelle," she said. "I'm sorry I haven't been closer to you since then. I always wanted to be, but it was so hard. . . ."

Michelle put her hand over Darlene's hand. "Darlene," she said softly. "I know Kim, too. I know her well. I know she's a force to be reckoned with. I don't know how you lasted as long as you did, being with both of us all those years. I always understood why you did what you did. I might have been sad, but I never resented you. You will always be one of my very best friends, Darlene, and if you ever need me, I'll be there for you."

Darlene's tears were running down her cheeks. She dabbed them with a napkin. "Michelle," she said. Then she paused. "I wanted to go to UMass, but it didn't work out for me. I would have loved to be able to see you whenever we wanted. We'll see each other at Thanksgiving. But I still want you to know, I love you. I have loved you since the first day of kindergarten, and I will always love you, even if we don't see each other. Just remember that."

Now Michelle was crying. She squeezed Darlene's hand. "I love you too, Darlene. Why do you think you were the one who got my cookie in kindergarten? Cookies are a sign of love." She reached into her purse and extracted a small plastic baggie. She handed it to Darlene. It was filled with chocolate chip cookies. "My mom and I made these today so I could bring them to my dorm to bribe people to be my friend. So you can either eat these or bring them to Ithaca to bribe some new friends for yourself. But remember, they're a token of my love. Think of me every time you eat a chocolate chip cookie."

They parted later in front of Darlene's house. It was dark outside. Soon it would be time to go to sleep, and tomorrow, she'd wake up to a new, exciting, and frightening experience.

Darlene walked into her house and saw her mother reading her new *People* magazine on the couch. She looked up at Darlene and smiled. "How did it go?"

Darlene was about to say everything was okay, like she always did, but she couldn't make words. And there was a lump in her throat. She started to sob. Her mother's arms were suddenly around her, holding her tight.

"I know, doll," she said. "I know how hard it is to say goodbye. I remember. It's gonna be okay. You'll see your friends again soon. And you'll make new friends. And you always know that your mom loves you so much. I'll miss you so much."

She squeezed Darlene tight and started to sob with her. They stayed that way for a few minutes but finally said goodnight. Darlene headed upstairs to get ready for bed for the last time before becoming a full-time Ithaca College biology student.

Part Four

Stavros: The Great Teenage Love Experiment

Chapter 25

GROWING UP

AS THE YEARS PASSED, STAVROS started to come into his appearance. His hair was deep brown and loosely curled. When it was short, it appeared straight until it started to grow out, then it would take on a life of its own. It would point in every direction. He would have to decide to keep it long or maintain getting a haircut every three weeks to keep everything in place. In high school, he opted for long with occasional trims. He had thick, dark eyebrows and long, lustrous eyelashes above his milk chocolate–colored eyes. His skin was olive, but a lighter shade than his father's. His skin was smooth, and his lips were full. By the age of fourteen, he was close to having to shave.

His eight-year-old sister, Drea, by contrast, had lighter brown, straight hair, fair skin, and blue eyes. The eyes were the mystery. Everyone knew blue eyes were recessive. No one remembered any of the Greek side of the family ever having blue eyes, but they suspected maybe, at one time, there had been a traveler from another country who might have left behind the blue-eyed gene. Andreas laughed it off when anyone suggested the child had been fathered by the milkman.

"There was no milkman," he would say, "and no mailman either. We had a post office box. Yes, I am pretty certain the girl is my flesh and blood. Just look at the shape of her face. But who could blame her for wanting to look just like her mother."

Drea did look like her mother. She was a stunning little girl, and she was sweet, curious, and inquisitive. She would sit, and watch, and take in the details. She was the perfect audience for Stavros's stories, and after eight years of the stories going in her ears, she now could tell them back to Stavros. He would lay on her bed with her at bedtime and encourage her to speak. He would correct her if she got any details wrong or mispronounce any of the Greek words.

Their favorite time together was in the kitchen. Stavros could make baklava and challah from memory now, and he taught Drea each step. He was patient with her as she tried to recall how many eggs were needed, or how much salt to add. Sometimes, Andreas would watch his children from the kitchen doorway, just out of their line of sight, and listen to their voices as they cooked, the soft questions and the gentle answers. Sometimes, tears would come to his eyes, and he would have to take out his handkerchief. Then he would go back to his chair and read or do his work. He was proud of Stavros and Drea. So much like their mother, and so eager to learn and teach.

Stavros learned to make meals from his Jewish bubbe and his Greek aunties when he visited them in Pittsburgh. He knew what to make for every holiday and every event. He knew every dessert. He knew how to make a honey cake that was unleavened for Passover, and vasilopita cake for the New Year. He could make fluffy matzo balls for soup and flaky, savory spanakopita. Drea was always standing on a chair beside him, watching, talking, and asking questions.

Every day when they got home from school, Stavros would say to Drea, "So tell me about your day," and she would. And as she got older, she asked him about his day. Then they would both sit at the dining room table and do their homework. The rest of the day was theirs. Sometimes, they watched TV. Sometimes, they walked to the park. Sometimes, their father took them to a family friend's house to visit and eat dinner. And sometimes, they spent time with their own friends.

Stavros was still friends with Deanna, but Joseph had moved to

California. In junior high, Stavros met Mario and Alec, and Deanna met Lindi, and now they all ate lunch together. Alec's father also worked at the university and lived close to the Karras family, so he was able to come over after school to watch TV or hang out. Mario lived further away, but he had a bus pass, and sometimes Stavros and Alec would scrounge up change from around their houses and take the bus with Mario into town. Then they would walk around past the stores and restaurants, among the students from UMass, Amherst, and Hampshire College.

This year, they were all going to be freshmen, and now the girls were allowed to go out after school as long as they stayed together and got home before sunset. Their favorite place to go was the elementary school playground. They would wait until most of the younger kids were gone and then swing on the swings, twirl on the merry-go-round, and act goofy on the seesaw. It was innocent fun, and if any parents complained about them being too loud and rowdy, they would walk away and sit in a circle on the grass.

It was the day before school started. It would be their last year at junior high. "I hear Jessica Fields is having a back-to-school party," Deanna announced.

"Boys and girls?" Alec asked nervously. He was still pretty shy around girls he didn't know well and tried to avoid any unnecessary contact.

Deanna nodded. "It's gonna be in her basement. She's gonna play albums and have food and punch. Maybe even some dancing if anyone's into it."

"I hope she's not gonna play any disco," Mario said. "Disco sucks."

Lindi leaned in toward the center of the circle. "I heard she's gonna have kissing games at the party," she confided.

Stavros made a face. It wasn't that he was against kissing; he just thought people should have a choice about who they were going to kiss. Not that he had ever kissed anyone.

"We might not even get invited to the party," he said. "I mean, we're not even friends with her. So then we wouldn't even have to worry about disco or kissing games."

"No, I'm pretty sure we will be," Deanna said confidently. "I have it on good authority that Jessica's friend Sandy has a little crush on our friend Mario here."

Mario had been digging in the dirt with a small stick. Now his head jerked up. "Say what? That's crazy. I've never even talked to Sandy!"

Lindi laughed. "You don't have to talk to someone for them to have a crush on you. That's why it's a crush. You watch from far away and just hope the person notices you."

Deanna nodded. "And she's definitely noticing you, Mario. She's hoping you'll be at the party, and if you go, you'll have to bring your friends, so we're all in. Plus, Jessica's family goes to the same church as my grandparents. Her parents will make her invite me."

Stavros considered this situation. Kissing games. What would that even entail? Spin the Bottle? Seven Minutes in the Closet? Seven minutes in a closet sounded like a long time! But he wondered what it would be like to spend seven minutes alone in a closet with Lindi. He forced himself not to look at her. As it was, he hardly ever spoke to her directly. It was just like she had said: you didn't have to talk to someone to have a crush on them.

He pretended to look around the playground but let his eyes pass over Lindi. There was a breeze blowing, and it was catching the strands of her straight dirty-blond hair and blowing it about. She repeatedly had to push her hair behind her ears so it wouldn't blow in her eyes. Her blue eyes. She had pale skin and pink lips. She still had very small breasts, but Stavros didn't mind. Breasts scared him. And Lindi hadn't hit her growth spurt yet, he had heard her say to Deanna. So maybe by the time she finally grew breasts, he wouldn't be so afraid of them.

"Aren't you coming?" Deanna asked.

Stavros realized that while he was in his revery, his friends had started to get up. He had no idea what they were going to do next. "Yeah," he said. "I was just thinking about what to make for dinner tonight."

"You're still making dinner for your family every night?" Deanna asked as they started to walk toward the street with their group. "I thought your dad was going to get someone to come and do that for you guys."

Stavros shrugged. "He's talked about it, but I like doing it, so he hasn't really had to. And Drea likes to help."

"I hope Drea makes some friends this year," Deanna said. "I can't believe her only friend moved away. That really sucks. And third grade is hard, I remember. Girls can be real bitches at that age."

Stavros was worried, too. It had taken quite some time for Drea to find someone she felt comfortable enough with to ask her to come over to play, but now Sasha was gone and Drea had to start over. Drea was quiet, and sometimes passive. She didn't normally make the first move. She would even get shy around her own aunties when they went to Pittsburgh, and it would often take two to three days before she would warm up. He wished there was something he could do to help, but he knew she would have to find her own way. If only their mother was still alive . . .

Apparently, they were all walking home now. It was almost time for dinner. Deanna was the first to turn off on her street, and then Alec. Lindi was next, and then Mario came to the bus stop. Stavros walked the final three blocks to his house alone.

Drea was sitting on the couch next to their father. She was holding up a book about Plato, but on top of it was an early reader chapter book. Drea was not too into reading Plato yet, but she wanted to fit in. Stavros laughed. Drea smiled.

"What do you want for dinner?" Stavros asked them both. "It needs to be something that won't take a long time. It's getting late."

"Do we have Velveeta?" Drea asked. "I want macaroni and cheese."

Stavros nodded. "I can make that. Wanna help?"

Drea dropped her books on the couch and followed him to the kitchen.

That night, after they said goodnight to their father, Stavros read to Drea in her room. He had been able to find some books at the library that had philosophical lessons in them but were written in a language she could understand. He had also found her tales of ancient Greece in children's books, and some she could read on her own. After reading, he told her a Rebel story. Those were her favorites. Drea had a framed picture of Rebel on her nightstand. She loved to hear about their beautiful mother and all of her adventures.

"Were you scared when Rebel took you to the war marches?" she asked.

Stavros shook his head. "I didn't feel scared because I knew that she wouldn't let anyone hurt me. Everyone was carrying signs with the peace symbols on them and other signs I couldn't read yet. But people were singing, and there were some marching with guitars, and sometimes they would chant. Mom stopped bringing me to marches when she felt they were getting too dangerous. It wasn't the antiwar people who made it dangerous. It was the people who came to tell them to go home, to mind their own business and get a job. Sometimes they would throw things at them. I guess it would have been really scary. Mom made a good choice. But if they had peace marches now, I think I would go."

Drea nodded. "I would, too. I would be just like Rebel!"

Stavros smiled at her. "Rebel was your mom," he told her. "So half of you *is* Rebel. She was very strong and brave. And you can be too." He paused. "Drea, I want you to be brave and strong in school tomorrow, okay? I know you're scared because Sasha won't be there anymore, but because you had Sasha, you know that you're good at being a friend. You will be able to make another friend. Maybe not tomorrow, but soon. You really are someone worth being friends with."

He gathered his thoughts.

"Remember when we went car shopping with Papa a few months ago?" Drea nodded. "Remember that guy who tried to sell him the first car? He was really pushy, right? Papa already knew what car he wanted to buy, but this guy had a lot of the other type of car, and he wanted to sell those, so he did everything he could to try to convince Papa. He couldn't, because Papa didn't want the car."

"I don't want to be like that car guy," Drea said, making a face. "He was creepy."

Stavros laughed. "No, you don't have to be as bad as him, but you can still learn from him. You have something valuable that you want to sell, and other people don't know you have it. You need to let them see that valuable stuff, so they want to come buy it. You don't want to overdo it or you'll scare them away. But if you don't show them anything, they won't even know you're selling anything. So you have to remember, Drea, that you're smart, and you're funny, interesting, and friendly. But if you sit quietly and don't say anything, no one will know."

"How do I do that?" Drea asked.

Stavros could tell she really wanted to know.

"You could raise your hand if the teacher asks a question and you know the answer. If you hear someone talking about something you know something about, you can come up and ask them a good question about it, as long as you don't look like a know-it-all. Or you can show them something that you have that will get their attention."

"Like what?" Drea asked.

Stavros had an idea. "I'll be right back," he said, and he ran out of the room. When he came back, he was holding a multicolored piece of fabric.

"What's that?" Drea asked.

Stavros sat down on the bed and showed her. "This was Rebel's," he told her, holding it up in both hands. "It's a headband. She used to wear them all the time to keep her hair back. Can I put it on you?" Drea nodded. Stavros slipped it over her head, and then pulled it up over her forehead. "That looks so good. Go check it out."

Drea jumped down off the bed and went to the mirror. She looked at herself for several seconds and then touched the headband. "She wore this?"

Stavros nodded. "All the time. And it was beautiful on her, too, just like on you. There are a few others in a box in Papa's room. Maybe you can have that be your thing. You can be the girl who wears cool headbands that belonged to her beatnik mother! I bet the other girls will be interested."

Drea nodded, still looking in the mirror. "I want to wear it," she said. "Can you help me pick what to wear it with?"

The next morning, Andreas had to come into Stavros's room twice to wake him up for school. "Come on, Stavros," he said. "I made breakfast. You don't want to be late on your first day."

Stavros stumbled out of bed and into his clothes. He combed his hair, brushed his teeth, and headed downstairs.

And there she was, sitting at the table, eating eggs, smiling brightly, and looking just like their mother. Stavros looked at his father. Andreas nodded to let him know he understood.

"You'll do great today," he told Drea as he sat down at the table. "And if you ever get worried or scared, just touch your headband, okay? And remember, you're half rebel, half Greek warrior. You'll make it through. And tonight, we'll make baklava."

"Okay," Drea said. "I'm a rebel and a warrior." She growled like a rabid dog, and they all laughed.

Andreas walked Drea out to her bus while Stavros got his school supplies together. When Andreas came back, he put his hand on his son's shoulder.

"Stavros, you never cease to amaze me," he said affectionately. "Drea is so excited to go to school. She has never been excited before. You did that.

You believe in her so much. And you know what that means." He paused. "Drea may look just like your mother, but Stavros, you have her spirit. She lives on in you."

Stavros wanted to be a normal teen. He wanted to defy his father and tell him off. But he was fourteen now, and so far, he'd had no reason to push back against his father's authority.

It was so annoying.

Maybe in high school.

"Thanks, Papa," he said quietly. He allowed his father a brief hug, said goodbye, and headed for school.

Chapter 26

Kissing Games

THE FIRST WEEK OF SCHOOL was uneventful but for one thing. Stavros and his friends received invitations to Jessica Fields's back-to-school party on Saturday night. They all agreed to go. Alec was on board, but he acted like he had volunteered to spend a night alone in a confirmed haunted house. Mario contemplated if he wanted to spend seven minutes in the closet with Sandy Parsons. And Stavros tried to remember to ask his father to pick up some mouthwash for him when he went to the store. The girls didn't let on about what they were thinking. Stavros hoped that Lindi was hoping that his bottle spin would land on her, but he doubted it. He had no idea who Deanna wanted to kiss. He didn't think of Deanna in that way. He couldn't picture her kissing anyone. He didn't even think of her as a girl most of the time, just as his longtime friend. But he knew that she really was a girl, after all, and she probably did notice boys. She was probably considering who she wanted to kiss. But Stavros didn't ask her.

"Is it like a birthday party?" Drea asked him when he told her he was going to a party. "Do you have to bring a present?"

"No, it's not like that," Stavros explained. "And there probably won't be any cake and ice cream. Maybe pizza rolls or things you can pick up in your hand."

Drea looked puzzled. "No presents, and no cake? So what do you do the whole time?"

Stavros shrugged. "I'm not sure," he admitted. "I guess we just listen to music and maybe dance. And maybe play some games."

Drea perked up. "Oh, like Pin the Tail on the Donkey?"

Stavros laughed. "I think more like big-kid games."

Drea nodded. "Oh," she said knowingly. "Like Monopoly."

Stavros smiled, but he said nothing.

Andreas looked up from his newspaper. "So this Monopoly requires mouthwash, does it?" He gave Stavros a grin.

"Well, Papa," Stavros said, "it's close quarters. I wouldn't want to offend anyone."

"No, I understand," Andreas said, turning the page of his newspaper. "We certainly wouldn't want you to offend anyone."

The next day, Stavros approached Deanna at her locker. "Dee," he said quietly, "how am I supposed to dress for this party? I don't have to wear a tie or anything, do I?"

Deanna laughed. "How am I supposed to know? I've never been to a party like this either. I guess if there's kissing, you'd dress like you would if you were going on a date."

Stavros had never been on a date. He squirmed a little. "Do we know for sure there will be kissing there?"

Deanna nodded. "Oh, yeah," she said confidently. "I confirmed it. Definitely kissing."

Stavros groaned. "It's too late to back out now, isn't it?"

Deanna grabbed his arm. "You better not back out," she demanded. "Someone's gonna have to handle Alec. And if Mario and Sandy do hook up, it would just be me and Lindi, and someone's likely to want to kiss her. She's really pretty. You've gotta be there for me, Stav, okay?" She pleaded with him through her eyes.

Stavros rolled his eyes. "Fine," he said. "I won't back out."

Deanna smiled. "Good. Do you want me to come over and pick out your clothes for you on Saturday?"

Stavros couldn't tell if she was teasing. "No, I can figure it out. But maybe we should all meet up at my house and go together, though. There's definitely safety in numbers."

Drea was not there when Stavros got home that day.

"She wanted to go over to a friend's house," Andreas told him. "Susan or something. Yes, Susan. I got her mother's phone number. They'll bring her back before dinner."

"Oh, okay," Stavros said. Drea had not told him that she had made a new friend. Maybe he should have been asking. "I guess I'll make dinner myself then. What should we have?"

"The night off, Stavros," his father told him. "Tonight, we order pizza. And I'll pick it up. I'll make you dinner for a change!"

Stavros brightened up. "Athena's?" he asked, and his father nodded. "How about a pizza with feta and black olives? And a Greek salad?"

"Sounds perfect," Andreas said.

When Drea returned, Stavros asked her about Susan. "She liked my Rebel headband," Drea said. "She said it made me look like someone on one of the dance shows on TV. So I told her my mom was a hippie, and she thought that was cool. We played on the playground yesterday and today, and when her mom came to get her, she asked if I could come over and play. And her mom said yes. We went to her house and played outside on her swing set, and then we helped her mom make cookies. I told her she can come to my house, and we could make baklava. She had never heard of baklava, but her mom had. Her mom asked me if I baked with my mom, and I told her my mom died on my being-born day, and then she looked sad."

Stavros nodded. "People get sad when they hear about our mom. They can't imagine what it would be like to not have a mom, and it makes them think about their own moms."

Drea nodded. "I told her I'm not sad because I didn't know her, but I know her stories. Then we ate cookies and milk, and me and Susan played with her Barbies in her room. She has Barbies that were her mom's when she was little. I'm hungry. Will Papa be home soon with the pizza?"

Stavros nodded. He felt some relief. His sister was learning to make friends. She would be okay now. He could stop worrying, at least about that.

Saturday finally arrived. The party started at eight, but Stavros's friends would come over at seven thirty. Jessica Fields lived nearby, so they had decided to walk there. Their parents would pick them up after the party.

Stavros spent much of the day reading and feeling nervous. His father brought Drea over to the university for lunch and to stop briefly in his office to pick up some books he needed. Stavros tried to waste time watching TV, but he had no patience for cartoons, news, or late season baseball that day. He went outside and walked around the block a few times. When he got back inside, only fifteen minutes had passed. He cursed in Greek, like his father.

He made himself some lunch and thought about what to do. His mind wandered to what Lindi would be wearing at the party. He wondered what it would be like to kiss her. Would she be wearing lipstick? Would the lipstick come off on *him*? He had no idea. What if he had to kiss someone else? He didn't even know who would be there. He hoped if he spun the bottle and it landed on a guy, he would be allowed to spin again. That had to be a rule. And what would he do with seven minutes in a closet? If he was with someone he wasn't interested in kissing, he could suggest they play Twenty Questions. That should use up the seven minutes.

Stavros was relieved when he heard his father's car pull into the driveway. It was always better to have distractions. He had learned that at an early age.

When Andreas and Drea came in, he pretended he didn't even notice. "Oh, hey, I didn't hear you guys pull up," he said casually.

Drea came over and pulled on his arm. "Play with me."

"Do you want me to take you to the library and the playground?" he asked her.

Drea jumped up and down. "Yes!" She ran up to her room to put on her play clothes.

Andreas came over and put his hand on Stavros's shoulder. "Doing okay, Stav?" He sat down at the table next to him.

Stavros nodded. "Yeah, Pop, doing fine."

Andreas sighed. "I thought maybe we should just check in, since you'll be going to your first event where there will be, well, girls and boys, and we haven't talked about anything like that since you were about three and your mother insisted that we tell you the facts of life."

"There's more to tell?" Stavros asked.

Andreas laughed. "Oh, my son, there's so much more to tell," he told him. "But we don't have to get into it now. Maybe before your wedding. But I just want to make sure that you know that you don't need to treat girls any differently if you like them or don't like them in a romantic way. No matter what, you always have to remember to be kind."

"I know, Papa," Stavros said. "You've always taught me to be kind. And so did Mom. I think I know how to do it."

Andreas nodded. "Yes, Stavros, I know you know how to be kind. I see you with your sister every day. But this is still something new to you. When someone is your age, they have new feelings they didn't have before. And sometimes, they act differently. But there is no need. If you are with a girl, and she is happy, you be kind. If she is upset about something you did, you be kind. If she is not interested in you, you still be kind."

Stavros looked at his father. "So if she's angry at me, still be kind? Isn't that kind of hard to do?"

"Yes, it is hard," Andreas agreed. "But no one said it was going to be easy. The best way to be kind? Ask open-ended questions. Listen to the answers. Don't try to lead her in a certain direction that just serves your purposes. Really find out how she's feeling and why. And then help her come up with a solution that works."

"Is that what you did with Mom?" Stavros asked.

Andreas smiled. "Who do you think taught all this to me? I wasn't always the sweet, sensitive man you see before you now. Your mother saw potential. So she talked to me and was patient with me. And I learned by watching her. You learned much from her. I just want to make sure you don't forget."

Stavros drummed his fingers on the table. "I won't forget, Papa, I promise. But I don't think there's much to worry about right now. I mean, I don't think there's anyone who's interested in me, and I'm not sure I'm interested in anyone. . . ."

"That might change given the right circumstances," Andreas said. "It's amazing how these things work. But I studied literature, not biology. I'm not an expert. All I can tell you is to be kind."

Drea ran back into the kitchen carrying her library card. "I'm ready to go."

When Stavros and Drea came back, they made dinner, and after dinner, it was time for Stavros to get ready. He took a shower and put some of his father's hair product in his hair to help keep his curls from being too out of control. Then he got dressed. He had already ironed his shirt and his jeans, and everything looked crisp and new. He put on his newest sneakers. He spritzed a bottle of body spray as softly as he could into the air and then stepped through it. He didn't want the smell to be too overwhelming, especially in a small, confined space like a closet. He was ready to go.

Alec and Mario arrived at 7:30, but there was no sign of Deanna and Lindi. The boys sat in the living room and tried to make conversation. They were all nervous. Now they were worried they were also going to be late. Finally, at 7:50, Stavros could see the girls walking up the sidewalk, so they went out to meet them in the yard.

"You guys are late," Mario said. "Now we're all going to walk in late."

The girls laughed. "No one goes to parties right when they start," Deanna said with a smirk. "It's called being fashionably late. We don't want to be the first ones there."

"God forbid," Alec said under his breath.

"What?" Deanna said, and she shot him a look.

"Nothing," Alec said, looking down at the ground with his hands in his pants pockets.

They started their walk toward Jessica's house. When they arrived, Deanna rang the bell, and Jessica's mother answered. "Everyone's downstairs," she told them, and she pointed to the basement door. "Have fun."

They walked slowly down the stairs. The music was playing loud, but not too loud, and no one was dancing yet. They spotted about a dozen other kids from their grade holding cups containing punch or clutching carrot sticks or pretzels. They were talking in groups of two or three.

Jessica approached the group. "Oh, good, you guys made it! Come on down, get some punch! I'm gonna try to get everyone to dance when more people are here. Oh, look, there's Sandy."

Sandy and another girl were on the steps behind them. Sandy looked at the group. "Hi Mario," she said.

Mario looked up awkwardly. "Oh, hi, Sandy," he said and then looked at the floor.

They got food and drinks and started to talk to other kids in the room. More guests arrived, and Jessica and Sandy started dancing with some of their other friends. A few more kids danced along. Someone turned off the overhead lights, and the room glowed with lava lamps and fairy lights. The aura became pinkish and appeared to be crawling with motion. Stavros and his friends danced, too, and Stavros tried to remember if he had put on deodorant. He had.

The night was passing quickly, and Stavros was worried both that there wouldn't end up being kissing games and that there would. At that moment, Jessica approached the stereo and turned the volume down but not off.

"Hey, everyone!" she said. "Let's sit in a circle on the floor."

Everyone found a spot and sat. Then Jessica smiled and produced an empty glass wine bottle from behind her back and was met with groans and laughter. She put the bottle in the middle of the circle.

"Does anyone not know how to play this?" she asked. No one said anything. "Okay, so here's what we're gonna do. I'm gonna spin the bottle, and whoever it lands on goes first. Then the person they get goes second. So everyone gets two kisses. And if the bottle lands on someone twice, the spinner spins again. The last person to go has to kiss the first person so they don't get cheated. And no girls kissing girls or boys kissing boys. Okay? I'm gonna spin."

She gave the bottle a good twirl, and it went around about six times.

It landed on a girl named Kerry. She looked terrified. She reached over and spun the bottle. They all watched as it came to a stop in front of a boy named Cliff. Terry stood up tentatively and walked across to Cliff and bent over. She gave him a chaste kiss on the lips, giggled, and then ran back to her spot and sat. Cliff spun the bottle, and it landed on Alec. Everyone laughed. Cliff tried again. It landed on Denise. After their kiss, Denise spun, and it landed on Stavros. She gave a weak smile while Stavros's heart started to pound. Denise bent over and kissed him. His first kiss. It was okay. Her lips were soft, and she smelled like baby powder.

Now it was Stavros's turn to spin. He looked around the circle and found his friends. Then he sighed, bent over, and spun the bottle. He watched as it seemed to spin in slow motion. He could see all eyes watching to see where it would go. It started to slow down more, and more, getting closer and closer to Lindi until . . .

It landed on Deanna.

They looked at each other in horror.

Everyone who knew them and knew their history as friends either gasped or laughed. Stavros took a deep breath and started his walk across the circle. He could do this. Everyone else was doing this. It was just a small kiss. Now it wasn't even his first kiss. He looked down at Deanna and smiled. She gave him a nervous smile back. Then he leaned over and moved his face near hers. His lips touched hers and applied pressure. Then it was over, just like that. Stavros exhaled and went back to his seat.

Now it was Deanna's turn to spin. She still looked uneasy. She got Kevin and suddenly looked relieved.

Stavros stopped paying attention to the game until he heard someone say Lindi's name out loud. He looked up to see Alec walking across the circle. Lindi gave him a kind smile. Alec looked like he wanted to bolt. But he didn't. He kissed Lindi and went back to his seat. Then Lindi got Chuck. Stavros longed to be Chuck at that moment.

After everyone had been given a turn, they all took a break to get punch. Stavros looked around the room. He found it amusing that everyone in the room had now been kissed, including him. But he had kissed Deanna. That was weird. But it was okay, and she seemed okay.

Next, Jessica pulled out two hats. "The boys take a number from the black one, and the girls pick a number from the blue one. Then find the person who has your same number, and prepare to spend seven minutes in heaven with them! Or in our storage closets, which are the next best thing!"

Some people whooped, and then everyone came up to get a number. Stavros pulled out a small sliver of paper and looked at it. The number 7. Maybe it was good luck. Number 7, Seven Minutes in Heaven. He looked around at the girls. People were finding their partners. Deanna was standing with Ray Spencer. Mario was talking to Terry. He made eye contact with Lindi. She walked over. "Number 7?" she said.

Stavros felt a lump in his stomach. Lindi was number 7? No way. "Yeah," he said. He smiled at her. She smiled back.

"Ok, we have ten couples," Jessica announced, "two closets, and one hour. So no trying to get extra minutes!" Everyone laughed. "Number 1! Number 2!"

Mario and Terry came forward, and two kids that Stavros didn't know. Jessica led them to the storage areas.

"I'll set the timer for seven minutes," she said, "and I'll knock when your time is up." The couples went in, and the timer went on. Then Jessica turned up the music. "No listening!"

Stavros turned to Lindi. "I know this is weird," he said to her. "But we can just talk, or play Twenty Questions, or whatever you want. We don't have to kiss or anything."

Lindi smiled kindly. "I dunno, let's just see. But thanks for offering some choices."

"You're welcome." He didn't know what else to say.

"Do you like your teachers this year?" Lindi asked him.

Stavros was grateful that she had found something for them to talk about. "Yeah, so far. Most of the teachers don't like it when I correct them when they misquote someone, so I'm gonna try not to do that too much this year. I can't help it that my mom and pop read me the classics when I was a baby!"

Lindi laughed. "Yeah, you do know a lot about some pretty weird things. But most of the time, things you say in class are more interesting than what the teachers say. That's why I like being friends with you." She looked at her feet.

"Yeah, I like being friends with you, too," he said shyly.

They talked about school some more until the first timer went off. Mario and Terry walked out, and they were both smiling. Stavros looked at Sandy, and she looked upset.

"Number 3 and number 4!"

Alec stood along with Sandy, and they walked to one of the storage rooms. Mario watched them walk in.

"Do you think Mario kissed Terry?" Lindi asked.

Stavros shrugged. "Either that or they were telling each other really funny jokes," he said.

Lindi laughed. "Terry can be pretty funny," she said. "I bet it was the jokes."

"I'm sure Mario will tell us later," Stavros guessed.

"How about when we come out," Lindi suggested, "we don't tell anyone what we did in there? We can keep them guessing for a long time!"

Stavros laughed. "That's brilliant."

The second timer went off. Stavros was starting to get nervous. Just one more group before them. Alec came out of the storage closet looking like he wanted to vomit. Sandy was smiling. Now Mario looked concerned.

"This is really getting interesting," Lindi said. Stavros nodded. He sipped on his punch. He wished he had his mouthwash.

The minutes ticked by, and the third timer went off. Stavros felt a wave of panic, then another one of anticipation.

"Number 7 and number 8! Oh, I'm number 8. C'mon, Simon." Jessica handed the timer to Sandy. "Don't forget to knock when the timer goes off."

Stavros and Lindi approached the closet, and Lindi opened the door. They stepped inside. It was dark and faintly smelled of mothballs. Stavros brushed up against something woolen. They got to the back of the large storage area and sat on the floor facing each other. He could tell they were looking at each other as his eyes adjusted to the darkness.

"Hi," Lindi said.

"Hi," Stavros said back. *Boom-boom* went his heart. He was sure she could hear it.

"What do you want to do?" she asked.

"I'm not sure. What do you want to do?" Stavros thought they could fill the whole seven minutes back and forth like this.

But then Lindi was quiet, and suddenly, she leaned toward him and kissed him. He kissed her back. They sat several inches apart, kissing shyly, for about a minute. Then they shuffled closer to each other, and their lips made better contact. Then Stavros shifted even closer and put his arms around her waist. Then she put her arms around his neck. And their kissing got harder. And then more urgent.

"Is this okay?" Stavros said when he came up for air.

"Yes," Lindi whispered. "It's okay. It's good. Let's do it some more."

They continued to kiss and move their hands on each other's backs until Lindi pulled one arm back in front of her and grabbed Stavros's hand. She directed it to the front of her shirt. Stavros was stunned, but not too stunned to use his hand as directed. He was right. Her breasts were small. But they were wonderful. They weren't scary at all. He didn't even know why he had been scared. They continued to kiss. The time went on. It felt like the seven minutes had passed, and they didn't want their time in heaven to end. But then Lindi pulled away.

"It's been way over seven minutes," she said. "Did we miss the knock?"

They got up and walked carefully to the door. Stavros opened it and looked out. Sandy looked up.

"Oh my God!" she said. "I put seven minutes on the egg timer, but

I forgot that you have to push start on these things!" She looked at her watch. "You guys have been in there for twelve minutes!" She quickly went to the other door and knocked.

The door opened, and Jessica and Simon came out. Jessica looked at Sandy. "That seemed like a long seven minutes," she said. "There are only so many times you can play Twenty Questions!" Simon laughed. Stavros suspected that Jessica and Simon were not playing Twenty Questions. He also suspected that Sandy had maybe forgotten to push the start button on purpose. He would have to thank her later.

Deanna was in the last group with Ray. Stavros watched her walk in and wondered what Deanna would do in there. But then his attention went back to Lindi.

"So we don't say anything," he said. Lindi nodded. "But maybe, we could do this again sometime?" Lindi smiled and nodded again. She looked sincere. Stavros could not believe this was actually happening.

Half an hour later, it was time to go. Parents were starting to arrive to retrieve their children. Everyone went upstairs to thank Mrs. Fields. Stavros stood with his friends, right next to Lindi. When her mother arrived, she reached out and squeezed Stavros's hand discreetly. Then she left. Then Alec's father was there to drive him and Stavros home. They walked outside.

"Did you kiss her?" Alec asked him.

Stavros shrugged. "We agreed before we went in that we wouldn't kiss and tell. Or we wouldn't not kiss and tell. How about you and Sandy?"

Alec chuckled. "Sandy wasn't very handsy," he said. "She kissed me before we walked out, just to be nice, I think. Or maybe to try to make Mario jealous, I don't know. But, yeah, she talked about Mario the whole time and asked me if he liked her."

"What did you tell her?" Stavros asked.

"I told her I didn't know, because I don't."

They got into the car, and the conversation ended.

Stavros unlocked the front door and went inside. His father was sitting in his easy chair in the living room with all the lights out except for his reading lamp. He inserted the bookmark in his book and took off his reading glasses. "How did it go?" he asked.

Stavros smiled at his father. "It was fun. I took your advice. I was kind. And it worked out well for me. Good night, Papa."

Andreas smiled at his son. "Good night, Stavros. See you in the morning, son."

Stavros went upstairs and got ready for bed. He was going to choose what to read before going to sleep, but then his mind went back to Lindi, and he made a different decision. He turned out the light and crawled under the covers. He let his mind wander back to Lindi, her breasts, and their seven minutes in heaven.

They didn't have a chance to be alone to talk about what had happened at the party until Tuesday. They were outside in the school yard after lunch, and everyone else had somehow scattered.

"Hi," Stavros said, suddenly shy again.

"Hi," Lindi said.

"Look, Lindi," Stavros started, "about the party. I know I asked you if you would do that again, but I understand if you don't want to. I mean, it was a moment in time. Maybe we were caught up in it. I mean, I wouldn't mind if we did it again, but if you don't, I won't hold it against you." Stavros could have kept giving her excuses to back out continually, but he stopped there. She had the general idea.

Lindi looked him in the eyes. "Stavros, I have a confession to make." She paused and took a breath. "When you were drawing your number, I looked over your shoulder. I got number 8. I traded for the 7."

Stavros felt tingling throughout his body. "You did?" he said. She nodded. He couldn't believe it. "So you traded with Jessica?"

Lindi nodded again. "Jessica was watching when people took their numbers. She knew Simon was number eight, and she wanted Simon. I think they both like each other. So she was happy to trade."

Stavros considered this. "So it's not that you traded to get rid of Simon. It's that you traded to specifically get me." He needed to be sure.

Lindi nodded. "Yes, dunderhead," she said, rolling her eyes. "I. Wanted. To kiss. You."

Stavros nodded. "Okay," he said. "Okay. So now we kissed. A lot. And you still want to kiss again?"

Lindi laughed. "Oh my God, Stavros. Yes! I like you! I was just worried that you didn't like me!"

Now Stavros laughed. "Are you kidding me, Lindi?" he asked. "I've liked you since seventh grade!"

Lindi looked stunned. "You have? I had no idea. I've liked you since the first day of eighth grade. You have me beat."

They both stood quietly for a moment. Then they walked over to the brick wall and sat down.

"So you'll go out with me?" Stavros dared to ask.

Lindi nodded. "I'd like that."

Stavros nodded. "Okay. Well, we can go to a movie or something. Maybe we can go on Saturday. We can take the bus so we don't have to have someone drive us. Does that sound okay?"

"Yeah," Lindi said with a satisfied smile. "That sounds good."

The bell rang and they stood. Suddenly, Lindi leaned toward him and kissed his cheek. "I'm happy we're going to go out, Stavros," she said quietly.

They walked back into the school without speaking. But they were both smiling happily.

Deanna came home with Stavros after school to work on their history project. She was quiet, which was not like her. Stavros stayed quiet, too, to give her some space. They set up their notes and books on the dining room table. Then Deanna just sat there. Finally, Stavros had to say something.

"You've been really quiet," he said. "Are you okay?"

Deanna looked at him with a sneer and crossed her arms across her chest. "You're gonna ruin everything!" she said angrily.

Stavros was taken aback. He'd been having a good day until then. He had no idea what he was ruining. "What did I do?"

"I saw you out in the school yard at lunch," Deanna said accusingly. "I saw you talking to Lindi. And she kissed your cheek. You kissed her in the closet, didn't you?"

Stavros didn't want to answer her, but he felt he had no choice. He shrugged. "Well, it was Seven Minutes in Heaven. That's what we were expected to do, right?"

Deanna shook her head. "You could have done literally anything else!

You could have told her a story about ancient Greeks! You're good at that! Or asked her to talk about something. But no, you had to kiss her! Now you've ruined everything!"

Stavros was baffled. "Well, first of all, she kissed me," he corrected. "And second of all, why does this even affect you at all?"

Deanna stared at him. "You just don't get it, do you? Ugh!"

"I guess not!" he snapped back. "How can I get it if you don't explain it to me!"

Deanna just sat there in a huff. Then she started to leaf through her notes. She was angry. Stavros was feeling angry, too, because it was all so confusing. He was about to let her know how angry he was by saying something about how frustrating she was being when he suddenly remembered his talk with Andreas the night of the party. *Be kind, son*, he could almost hear his father whisper in his ear. He took a deep breath.

"Deanna," he said softly. "I'm sorry. I didn't mean to do anything to upset you. I want to know what I did to make you so upset. But I don't understand. Can you just tell me more about what you're upset about? Then maybe we can fix it."

Deanna looked at him, anger still in her eyes. Then it started to fade. She sighed. "Stavros," she said calmly, "I spent all of elementary school with you and Joseph. I got along with everyone okay, but I really didn't have any friends who were girls. But in seventh grade, I met Lindi, and we became friends. I didn't even want to share her with you. I wanted her all to myself, but I knew that was selfish. So we all became friends, and it's worked out really well." She paused.

"It has," Stavros agreed. "I like our friends a lot."

Deanna nodded slowly. "But that's just the thing," she said. "She was my friend first. It was special for me. I shared her. And now, if the two of you get together, everything will change. You'll want to do things alone together. You'll go on dates together. And then, someday, you might break up. And then we won't all be able to be friends anymore. We'll all have to take sides. I don't want to have to take sides! I don't know what I would do." She stopped talking. She had tears in her eyes.

Stavros sat with this information for a while. Finally, he spoke. "Deanna," he said. "You're my oldest friend. I don't want you to feel like that. I want to do what I can to make you feel okay. But I have to be honest."

He paused. "Lindi and I like each other. We didn't know it, but we've both liked each other for a long time. And now we know. And I did ask her out. And we're going out this weekend. I don't want you to be uncomfortable, Dee, but also, I really like her. And I'm not going to cancel our date. We're just gonna have to figure out a way for you to be okay with this."

Tears rolled down Deanna's cheek. She nodded. "I can tell she likes you," she said. "I knew she had a secret crush, but she never said who it was. But now that I know it's you, it just feels so mixed up to me. Why didn't you tell me you liked her?"

Stavros shrugged. "I wouldn't have known what to say to you. And you might have told her. I wasn't ready for her to know. I didn't think she liked me back. It was better to not know than it would have been to have her laugh at me."

"I never would have let her laugh at you, Stavros," Deanna said. "You should know that. You're my best friend. I would stick up for you."

Stavros felt a warm feeling run through him. "Thanks."

Deanna sighed. "I'm not going to ask you to not go out with her. You wouldn't listen anyway, and she would get mad, and you both would get sad. But it just would have been better maybe if you had liked someone else, like Terry, or Jessica. Then it wouldn't be a big deal."

Stavros smiled at her. "It's not gonna be a big deal," he promised. "I won't let it be. We talked about it now, and I know what you're thinking. So now I can do something about it."

Deanna sniffed. "Like what?"

"Like talk to you, and let you know what's going on. Like not leaving you out of things. Like just acting like friends, I guess. I wish I could promise you we would never break up, but Dee, we're fourteen years old. I just don't know what's gonna happen."

Deanna nodded. She pushed her hair up off her forehead. "Okay," she said. "I'm okay. We can work on the project now."

Stavros nodded. Then he laughed. "So we're never gonna talk about the fact that I kissed you at the party, are we?"

Deanna shook her head. "No. We will never mention that again as long as we live."

Chapter 27

THE DATE

THEY SAT NEXT TO EACH other on the bus. It was early. They were going to catch the matinee and then get something to eat. Lindi's mother didn't want her on the bus after dark. It was less embarrassing to be on the bus early than to be in your mother's car and get home later.

They sat in silence for a while, both not sure what to do. Then Lindi reached over and took Stavros's hand. He looked at her. She looked back. They smiled. They both looked away. He squeezed her hand. She squeezed back. It was perfect.

They bought tickets to see *Meatballs* and then stood in line for popcorn. Andreas had given Stavros twenty dollars for the occasion of his first date, but he needed to save some for food after the movie. They went into the theater and Stavros let Lindi pick their seats. The theater was not very crowded that Saturday afternoon. Lindi slid into a middle row and worked her way down to a middle seat with Stavros trailing behind. They sat and made themselves comfortable. Then Stavros reached for Lindi's hand. The previews started. Stavros looked around the theater and then at Lindi. There was no one near them. He leaned over and kissed her. It was a short kiss, but it set the tone. When the movie started, he put his arm around her shoulder, and she settled in against him.

The movie was goofy but funny. They both laughed. Stavros couldn't help but be aware that one of the characters was dealing with the death of his mother. It didn't matter. It didn't make him think any more about his mom. He thought about her every day anyway.

When the movie ended, they walked across the street to Friendly's. They both ordered hamburgers and fries and discussed the movie. They ate their food, and Lindi reached over to Stavros's plate to borrow some of his ketchup. When they finished, they ordered ice cream.

Lindi sighed. "Deanna asked me why I like you."

"What did you tell her?" Stavros asked. He was curious about this, too.

Lindi smiled. "I told her the first thing I liked about you was your hair. You started to grow it out last year, and I love your curls." She reached out and poked one of his curls with her finger. "And I like your eyes. They're a beautiful shade of brown, and they light up when you smile. Just like that!" She thought for a moment. "I remember when I first saw you with your sister. I used to feel sorry for her when I first met you, since she never knew your mom. But when I saw the two of you together, I stopped feeling bad, because she has you, and she adores you. And you're so great with her. After I saw that, that's when I really started to like you."

Stavros sat quietly with this knowledge. Then he asked her, "Do you want to know why I like you?" Lindi nodded. "First of all, I was twelve when I first saw you in the hallway at school, and you were the most beautiful girl I had ever seen. I was doomed the minute I laid eyes on you! And then when I met you, you were so nice. You made Deanna have fun, and do girly things. She needed that. And you're so gentle. And kind. Like my mom." He paused. "And over the two years, you've gotten prettier and prettier. And you've stayed sweet. It's like you're pretty inside and out. God, that sounds so corny!"

Lindi laughed. "It's not corny at all. I don't know any girl who wouldn't want to hear a boy say things like that to her. You really have a way with words, Stavros. I love to listen to you talk." She reached back across the table for his hand.

The ice cream arrived. They both took a taste, and they both made approving noises and then laughed. When they were done, they went back out to the bus stop. They still had a bit of time until sundown. They took the bus as far as the school yard and got off. They walked hand in hand to the playground and over to a bench by the merry-go-round. The playground was deserted. They sat down and turned to each other to kiss. After some time, they decided to walk around the park, talking, remembering things from the last two years that they had thought but never told each other.

"How you looked so pretty at the choir recital," he said.

"How I love to listen to you read out loud in English class," she said.

"How when you giggle, it sounds like music," he said.

"How your friends listen to your opinion and respect you so much," she said.

"How brave you are."

"How handsome you are."

"How you kissed me in the closet."

"How you're gonna kiss me right now . . ."

They finally headed toward home. Stavros walked Lindi to her door. "I had a great time," he said, touching her hair.

"So did I," she replied, pushing her head into his hand.

"We'll go out again next week?" he asked hopefully.

"Yes," she said.

After one more kiss, they said goodnight, and Lindi went inside. It was still early, so Stavros took the long route home. He wanted quiet time to think. He thought about Lindi. How he liked her. How he liked her *so much*. How he couldn't even imagine that she liked him as much as he liked her, *but she did*! He thought about what things would be like at school. If they would hold hands walking to class. If they would kiss in the hallway. If they would kiss in front of their friends. Then he wondered what it would be like to do more than just kiss. But he liked her. He didn't want things to move too fast. They had so much time in front of them. He wanted things to look forward to. She was so sweet and gentle. He didn't want her to change. So kissing. And holding hands. And maybe a bit of over-the-shirt action . . .

He wondered what his father was planning on talking to him about before his wedding.

He cleared his head. He was in front of his house. It was almost Drea's bedtime. It was Drea's time, and he would give it to her. He focused his attention and went inside.

Chapter 28

It's In Her Kiss

STAVROS AND LINDI STARTED TO see each other every weekend. Sometimes they just went to the school yard, and sometimes they went to a movie or to eat. Andreas let Stavros do extra chores around the house for money for his dates, and the house and yard looked better than they ever had. Both Stavros and Lindi made time for their other friends, because Stavros had truly understood where Deanna was coming from with her concerns. They all still hung out as a group, and Stavros restrained himself from touching Lindi during those times unless no one else was looking.

They kissed in the hallway, and they always walked hand in hand together. It was as if their hands and lips were magnetic. As time went by, Stavros found, much to his disbelief, that he actually liked Lindi more and more. It seemed like there was no limit to how much he felt for her. And she felt it, too, he just knew.

In the meantime, Drea was making friends and spending more time at their houses. Stavros missed their time together, but he knew it was important for Drea to have friends her age. They still had bedtime, and now she told him new stories about her adventures with her friends. Stavros would lay back and listen, smiling and reveling in the knowledge that Drea now had her own stories.

Lindi visited the Karrases' house and hung out with Stavros and Drea. They were instant friends. Drea knew that Lindi made her brother happy, and she enjoyed having another girl around. Sometimes, they would all cook and bake together. Stavros let Drea direct Lindi on what she needed to do next. He would stand back and watch. And Andreas liked Lindi. He felt she was a good match for Stavros. She kept him levelheaded and made him smile. She was smart and clever, and she understood his jokes. He couldn't ask for anything more for his son.

The school year passed by, and finally, junior high was completed. Stavros and his friends would be going to high school in the fall. Everyone was either fifteen or would be soon. Stavros didn't see Lindi every day anymore, but they got together as often as they could. They found private places to go to kiss, and now they were exploring each other more. And one magical evening after Lindi got home from four weeks of overnight camp, she let Stavros put his hand under her shirt and over her bra. Her bra was thin, and he could feel everything beneath. It was amazing. Then he had her reach under his own shirt, and she seemed to find that just as enticing as he did, even if he didn't have breasts. He wondered what would happen if they could be in a room together, with the door closed. He imagined them both taking off their shirts, and her taking off her bra. Then they could feel their skin touch. The thought slayed him. But it felt like the next step. If only they had somewhere they could do that.

They all enjoyed sophomore year, and they even made some new friends, but no one really broke into the original group of five. Mario dated Sandy for a while, but they didn't click as well as both had hoped, so they parted as friends. They attended more house parties, but they no longer needed kissing games to get them all going. Now they had beer and mixed drinks. Stavros experimented with having a few drinks, but mostly he liked to be clear and alert when he was with Lindi. At one party, she got very tipsy after one drink, and he had to make sure she got home safe and was clear enough to not get grounded by her parents. Grounding would be hard on both of them.

By the next summer, they had been together for two full school years, and it felt like they would be together forever. They were both content, even with occasional tiffs and disagreements. Stavros practiced kindness all that he could, and it came naturally to Lindi. They talked things over. Sometimes things got heated, but then someone would take a deep breath, and they would start again.

Lindi was going to be a counselor-in-training at her summer camp. She would be gone for eight weeks. Stavros was beside himself, missing her in advance of her leaving. He was going to go with her parents and brother to Family Visiting Day, and they would write letters, but he was positive he would die without her touch. He had his learner's permit, but not his license yet, so he couldn't just drive up to see her for a night.

Their goodbye was hard. "I've never been away from you this long," Lindi said between kisses. "I'm gonna go crazy."

Stavros grinned at her. "You'll be so busy with all the camp stuff that you'll forget to miss me at all."

Lindi pulled away and shook her head. "No. I'll miss you every minute, Stavros." She paused. "I love you."

Stavros's vision went foggy. He restrained himself from saying, *you do?* It was the first time those words had been spoken between them. And she'd said them first.

He looked into her eyes. "I love you, too, Lindi."

They kissed and touched as much as they dared on Stavros's couch with his father and sister upstairs. Stavros pushed her gently back on the couch and felt his weight on top of her. They held each other tight and relished the taste of each other's lips until they both had to stop. They sat up and looked at each other.

"Lindi," Stavros said as he caught his breath. "When you get back . . ."

"I know, Stavros," she said. "When I get back. I know."

It was time for Lindi to go home, and Stavros walked her there. When they got to the door, Lindi wiped a tear from her cheek.

"I don't remember my life without you anymore," she told him. "I know I'll have a good time at camp, but I'll miss you so much."

They hugged each other tight. "I'll miss you, too," Stavros said. "I really do love you."

Lindi smiled. "I love you, too. Goodbye, Stavros. I'll see you on Visiting Day."

One more kiss, and she went inside. Stavros went back home and went up to his room. He was already feeling empty inside after being away from Lindi for fifteen minutes. This summer was going to be hard.

Stavros got a job at the grocery store, stocking shelves in the afternoons. It was mindless work, and his mind wandered off all the time. He thought about Lindi at the lake with the campers in her bathing suit and singing songs with them in the dining hall. He thought about her eyes, her skin, her body . . . Now he had to stock canned peas. *Focus on the canned peas.*

Deanna had gone to Virginia with her parents to visit relatives for two weeks. Stavros, Mario, and Alec spent time together playing video games, walking aimlessly around the mall, and hanging at the playground. Alec liked a girl now, and she was even shier than he was. It gave him confidence. But she was away, too. Mario was still checking out his options.

Letters came from Lindi every other day, giving detailed accounts of her activities and her thoughts. She signed them all with her love and drawings of hearts. Stavros wrote right back and wished he had more exciting things to tell her than just stories of stocking ice cream and discovering an interesting new flavor.

Deanna got back, and she called everyone to action. They were going hiking. They were going to the movies. No more sitting around on their butts! This was summer! She made them all get up and be ready by noon, even on the weekends. But the distractions were good. They helped Stavros get through the days and nights until it was time for Visiting Day at Lindi's camp.

Stavros rode in the back seat of the Plymouth station wagon with Lindi's brother Brian. Brian read *MAD* magazines all the way to New Hampshire and didn't talk to Stavros at all. Lindi's parents, Dr. and Mrs. Leahy, tried to engage Stavros in conversation by asking him the questions that adults always asked: How is work going? What kind of work does your father do? What do you want to do when you grow up? Have you given any thought to where you want to go to college?

Stavros didn't know the answers to the last two questions. Sometimes, he would just say he wanted to study philosophy, but then he would be asked what kind of a career would come from a degree in philosophy. He would say professor of philosophy, but he was pretty confident that was not what he wanted to be. He wouldn't be able to do what his father did,

standing in front of a group of students, day after day, pouring out information and always wondering how many of them were actually paying
attention. Were they taking notes, or just doodling in their notebooks? His
father had seen students doing crossword puzzles during his lectures. No,
Stavros didn't want to be a teacher. But he didn't really want to be anything
else either. So he just gave the Leahys the philosophy answer and imagined
they were wondering how he was going to support their daughter financially someday with a professor's salary.

Mercifully, they crossed the border to New Hampshire and soon arrived
at Lindi's camp. They parked and made their way across the parking lot.
As they approached the main building, Stavros could see Lindi standing
among a group of other girls her age, searching through the arrivals and
bouncing on her feet. She saw them, jumped to attention, and then ran up
to the group. She hugged and kissed her parents quickly, then broke free
and rushed to Stavros, throwing her arms around him and holding him
tight.

"I missed you so much," she said softly into his ear. "I was counting the
hours until you'd get here!"

Stavros closed his eyes and kept his arms clasped firmly around her. "I
missed you, too."

"Okay, that's enough of that for now," Dr. Leahy finally said. "Lindi,
why don't you show us your cabin. But I'm sure we could all stand to find
a restroom first."

While her parents and brother were using the facilities, Stavros took
the opportunity to kiss Lindi. Several times. And tell her some news.

"My father and sister are going to Pittsburgh on Labor Day weekend,"
he told her. "It's been a bit over ten years since my papou died, and they're
going to have a service at his church. And they'll also visit my grandparents while they're there. I told my father I wanted to stay home because
you were coming back. He understood. He's letting me stay." He kissed her
again. "So I'll be home, by myself, for three long days."

Lindi smiled. "Oh my God, Stavros. I can't believe this is happening!
We get to be alone, just the two of us, at your house!"

Her mother came out of the bathroom. Lindi let go of Stavros, and they
waited for the rest of her family.

Lindi gave them a tour of the camp, and then they went to a special lunch for the families. After lunch, they all changed into their swimming gear and went to the lake. Lindi took them out on a rowboat to see the scenery. When they got back, they took a dip in the lake. It was a balmy day, and the water was refreshing. Lindi looked beautiful and fit in her bathing suit, just as Stavros had imagined.

After they changed back into their clothes, they went to the main building to relax until it was time to head back home. Stavros gave Lindi some gifts he thought she would enjoy: two large Hershey bars and *A Wrinkle in Time*, a book she had been wanting to read. She hugged him and said thank you.

When it was time to go, Lindi said goodbye to her family, and they went to the car. "Stavros," Lindi said, putting her arms around his neck. "Our time alone. I can't wait. It's our time, I know it. I'm nervous, but excited."

Stavros got the chills as he held her waist. "I'm both of those things too, Lindi. I'll have everything all set at my house. You won't need to worry about anything, okay? I'll take care of everything."

Lindi nodded. "I understand," she said. "I trust you, Stavros. One hundred percent. With my life." She kissed him and then held him to her. "I love you, Stavros."

"I love you, too."

The last four weeks of summer crept by. Stavros went to the community pool with his friends and continued to work and save his money for when Lindi was back. He started to clean his room, including regular vacuuming and dusting. He washed his mirror with Windex. He hung up his clothes after he washed them. This new behavior was not lost on his father. There were three days now until Lindi was home and four until his father and sister left for Pittsburgh.

When Stavros got home from work the next night, his father called him to the living room. "Before you go upstairs," he said, "I wanted to let you know, I left something for you in your dresser. Just in case. I want you to know, I'm not condemning or condoning anything. I'm just being realistic."

"Okay, Pop," Stavros said, having no idea what his father was getting at. "Good night. See you tomorrow."

"Good night, Stav," his father called after him.

Stavros took the steps two at a time. He peeked into Drea's room to make sure she was sleeping. She was on her back, clutching her stuffed zebra, and breathing softly. He gently closed her door and headed for his room.

When he got there, he opened his top dresser door. Right there, next to his underwear and socks, was a box of twelve condoms. Stavros was both horrified and relieved. Mostly relieved. Now he wouldn't have to go buy them himself. He had been worried about that experience. But he was still horrified that his father had guessed. Stavros figured it was probably pretty obvious. He and Lindi had been a couple for two years. They were both sixteen. He was going to be home alone. He was cleaning his room. His father wasn't a stupid man. Stavros considered yelling a thank-you down the stairs, but he held back. He didn't think anything really needed to be said.

Two days! One day! Today! Lindi was coming home!

Stavros was up early to shower and get dressed. He considered getting her flowers as a welcome home gift, but that didn't feel quite right. He took the bus to the toy store in town and found her a soft, plush brown bear with curly fur, just like his hair. He had the clerk tie a gift ribbon around its neck. When he got home, he had Drea help him bake brownies for Lindi that would still be warm when she ate them. Then he waited. And waited.

Finally, at 4:15, the phone rang. It was Lindi. She was home.

"Come over," she said urgently.

Stavros grabbed the bear and a container of warm brownies and dashed toward the door, calling goodbye to his family. He was at Lindi's door in five minutes, and she was in his arms thirty seconds later. It was like *he* was the one who had been away.

He let her go, picked up her gifts, and put them behind his back. "Pick a hand," he told her.

She picked his right hand. He pulled out the bear. She shrieked and gave it a hug. "It's a Stavros doll!" she exclaimed.

"Pick again," he said.

She picked his right hand again. He knew she would. He brought out the brownies. "Made with love by Stavros and Drea."

She put her gifts on the table and hugged him. "I knew there was a reason I wanted to come home," she said affectionately. "Let's go back to your house so I can thank Drea." She grabbed a brownie for the road, told her parents she was going out, and they left.

They held hands on their walk. They were quiet, but Stavros knew they were both thinking about the upcoming weekend. It was all he could think about.

"So my father and Drea are leaving at noon tomorrow."

"Noon, huh?" Lindi asked. "I need to go see Deanna tomorrow. Maybe we should get together later. My mom says now that I'm sixteen, I can stay out until twelve thirty, so that's good."

"Yeah," Stavros agreed. "It is good. Maybe I can do something with the guys tomorrow afternoon, and we can meet up later?"

"Okay," Lindi agreed. She stopped and turned to face him. "Stavros, I almost can't stand it. The wait. The anticipation. The nerves! How are you handling it?"

Stavros shrugged. "I'll be much better when we're together tomorrow. And alone. Until then, I don't know. I'm just so happy you're back."

Lindi smiled and nodded. Then she grabbed his hand again, and they proceeded onward.

Drea ran right to Lindi when she came in the door and gave her a huge hug. "I missed you, Lindi. And look." She stood in front of her. "I lost two more teeth!" She opened her mouth wide for Lindi to see.

"Wow, Drea," Lindi said. "Impressive. And that's a lot of gum you've got there in your mouth."

Drea nodded. "I can blow huge bubbles with this much," she said. "And I start fifth grade next week. But first I'm gonna fly to Pittsburgh with Papa. But Stavros would rather be with you than come with us. He's a stinker!"

Lindi laughed. "Drea!" Stavros said, throwing her a look.

"What, you don't think she already knows that?" Drea asked with a smirk.

Lindi winked at her. "I already knew," she said. She and Drea shared a conspiratorial smile.

"Dray, eat a brownie," Stavros said, sticking one in her face. "I think that's the only way to get you to stop talking." He turned to Lindi. "Remember when she used to be shy? I really miss those days."

They decided to watch a TV movie, and Stavros sat between his two favorite girls with his arms around their shoulders. It was the best he'd felt in months.

Chapter 29

Olympia's

ANDREAS CAME HOME FROM HIS office and decided to take them all out to dinner to celebrate the end of summer vacation. "Can we go to Olympia's?" Drea asked.

Andreas agreed to the family's favorite Greek restaurant. Lindi called her parents to let them know, and they all piled into Andreas's Volvo.

When they were seated at their usual table, Andreas turned to Lindi. "We haven't brought you here before. Have you ever been to a Greek restaurant?" Lindi shook her head. "Would you trust me to order for us all?" Lindi nodded. Andreas nodded back.

"Smart move," Stavros told Lindi. "You never know what you'll get if you don't know what you're doing."

When the waiter approached, they ordered drinks, and Andreas ordered appetizers for the table: tzatziki, kolokithokeftedes, olives and flatbread, and Greek salads.

"That sounds like a lot of food," Lindi said to Stavros.

Stavros laughed. "He's just getting started. Wait until we get to the entrees."

When the appetizers arrived, Lindi looked baffled. Stavros told her what to do. "You eat the kolokithokeftedes with the tzatziki, and you don't have to try to pronounce anything. You can just dip it in. And you know what to do with bread and olives. The bread is really good dipped in oil."

Lindi tried it and made noises indicating she liked it. "What's in the kolo-stuff?"

"It's a zucchini fritter," Stavros explained. "I've made them before. We make a similar thing for Chanuka, too, called a latke, but it's made with potatoes instead of zucchini, and we eat it with sour cream and applesauce."

"If I had to eat this stuff every day," Lindi said, reaching for another fritter, "I would weigh eight hundred pounds."

Andreas was ordering the main course. "Moussaka," he said. "Lamb skewers. Beef skewers. Lindi? Do you like eggplant? Good. Some nice Papoutsakia then. Retsina for me, and whatever they're drinking, bring them refills. Stavros, did you bring your permit? I'll let you drive us home. Ouzo after dinner. Tomorrow, we fly. Tonight, we celebrate."

When the wine arrived, Andreas lifted his glass. Everyone else lifted their soda. "Yiamas!" he toasted, and then turned to Lindi. "That means 'to our health'!" He drank from his wine.

"Yiamas," Stavros, Lindi, and Drea repeated and drank their beverages.

"This is so awesome, Dr. Karras," Lindi said. "Some time, I'll need to bring you all to an Irish pub. Bangers and mash and Guinness. And maybe some limericks and darts. Culture at its best!"

Stavros smiled and ate more food. The night was perfect. He could imagine that his mother was watching over them on a night like this, and she was satisfied that they all were happy.

At the end of the night, after they said goodnight to Drea, Stavros walked Lindi home. Before she went in, they sat on the front porch steps. The street was quiet and dark at this hour, and they were effectively alone. For the first time in eight weeks, they touched and caressed each other. And that's when Stavros noticed.

"Lindi," he said with awe, "your breasts are bigger. You were gone for eight weeks, and you came back with bigger breasts!" He checked again to make sure he was right. He was.

"Really?" Lindi asked. She looked down and then checked with her own hands, which nearly made Stavros fall down the stairs. "Yeah, I guess my bras have been a bit tight lately. But I hadn't really paid attention."

"That's okay," Stavros said, kissing her neck and continuing his investigation of her chest. "I can check for both of us. It's amazing. Wow."

Lindi giggled. Then she pulled away slightly and got serious. "Stavros," she said. She talked softly. "When you walk me home tomorrow night, we . . . we both will be different. Everything will be different."

Stavros nodded. "Yeah," he said. "Is that okay? Is it an okay different?"

"Yeah, I don't mind some things changing. Just as long as you don't, well, change the way you think about me. Like judge me."

Stavros shook his head. "Lindi, I would never judge you, any more than you would judge me. We're in this together. Equally. If anything, it will probably make me respect you even more. And love you. I mean, I don't feel like I can love you any more than I do now, but I'm guessing I can. I can't wait! So if I treat you any differently, it will only be because I love you more, okay?"

Lindi nodded. "Yeah," she said. "I know it will make us feel different. Good different. But neither of us will know what that's like until it happens. It's like torture to wait."

Stavros hugged her close. "I know," he whispered. "It will pass quickly. It will be here soon. I promise. And then, we'll know how it feels. And we can do it again. Whenever we can. And we'll be really good at it. You'll see."

Lindi smiled. "I'm gonna go to bed now so tomorrow comes faster." She kissed him. "I love you, Stavros."

"I love you, too, Lindi. Good night."

Stavros had trouble falling asleep that night. He thought about what Lindi said. Everything would be different when he went to bed tomorrow night. Nothing he did would be the same. Brushing his teeth would be different. Walking to school would be different. And as much as he resisted thinking about it, his relationship with his friends, especially Deanna, would be different. But they would all have to get used to it. Whatever changed, it would be worth it. Stavros felt restless but resisted doing anything to relieve his stress. He wanted to wait. He wanted to save it all for Lindi. Everything now was for Lindi. And that was okay.

Chapter 30

Dreams Come True

LINDI CALLED AT TWELVE THIRTY. "Are they gone?" she asked.

"They are," he said. "They took a shuttle to the airport. I'm here alone."

Lindi sighed. "I'm going to Deanna's in a few minutes. When I get back, I'll just need some time to get ready. Should I come over at six?"

"Five?" Stavros said hopefully.

"Five thirty," Lindi said with authority.

"I'm counting the hours," Stavros told her.

"I'm counting the minutes," Lindi told him.

He met his friends at the playground. They sat on the merry-go-round and twirled it around with their feet. Mario smoked a cigarette. He had taken it from his mother's pack. He thought it looked kind of cool. Stavros thought maybe it did, but it smelled awful. Alec and Mario were talking about Alec's crush, Felicia, and if Alec would get up the nerve to ask her out once school started. Stavros was listening but just barely. He was staring off into the distance.

"What's wrong with you, man?" Mario asked, and he attempted in vain to blow a smoke ring. "You're so quiet today. You usually have an opinion about everything."

Stavros shrugged. "Just thinking about stuff, I guess."

Alec looked up. "Didn't your dad and Drea leave today for Pittsburgh?" Stavros nodded. "And you're seeing Lindi later?" Stavros nodded.

A light appeared to go on in Mario's head. He laughed. "Oh, my God, Stavros! This is the big night, isn't it? This is when you go to the next level and become the trailblazer for all of us. Wow. Are you ready for this?"

Stavros sighed. He didn't want to get into too much detail. "Ready as I'll ever be, I guess."

Mario nodded. "It's a big move, Stav. Does Deanna know?"

"I'm guessing Lindi's telling her right now. I'm pretty sure girls talk about this stuff, right?"

Alec nodded. "I can hear my sisters talk about stuff all the time," he said. "Sometimes in more detail than I want to know. They're my sisters, you know? Gross."

Yeah, gross, Stavros thought. But he didn't think it would be gross at all. And he also didn't think he'd be telling his friends all the grizzly details. This was Lindi, not some conquest. It was bad enough that his friends knew they were going to do it at all.

When Stavros got home, he did some last-minute room cleaning before taking a shower. He put clean sheets on his twin bed. At five, the phone rang.

"Hello?"

There was a pause. "If you hurt her, I will kill you," Deanna said. "And I won't have any trouble picking a side. And one more thing. Don't you dare get her pregnant. Understand?"

"Yes."

"Good."

"Deanna?"

"Yeah?"

"I would rather die than hurt her."

There was a pause, then a sigh. "I know," Deanna said. "I'm happy for you both. I hope it's wonderful. I've gotta go. Bye, Stav." She hung up.

Stavros smiled. It was the first real blessing he'd ever gotten from Deanna. It felt good.

At five thirty, she was there. She looked beautiful. She was wearing a jean miniskirt and a hot pink tank top, tucked in, with a belt cinching her waist. He admired her, and then thought about how to get it all off of her quickly. He took her hand and kissed her.

"I think we should go upstairs now," he said, and his body agreed. "And then, I can make you dinner."

Lindi nodded. She looked nervous, but she smiled. He led her up the stairs to his room. They stood by the bed. They contemplated.

Lindi spoke. "How about we take our clothes off and get under the covers?" she said. "Is that okay?"

Stavros nodded. His heart was pounding, and his ears were ringing a little. They both went to opposite sides of the bed and started to undress shyly. Stavros was secretly relieved that he wouldn't have to figure out how to get her bra off.

They slid under the covers and faced each other. At first, they were afraid to get too close. Then Stavros reached out for her breasts. She moved closer. She caressed his chest. They kissed. Lindi dared to move her hand down his torso and below his waist. She touched lightly, unsure what to do. Stavros hoped she didn't do much because he was afraid this wouldn't last long. They kissed some more. Stavros felt dizzy.

"Are you ready?" he asked her.

She nodded. "I guess. I don't know what to do."

"Me neither," Stavros admitted. "But I know how to start."

He reached over to his nightstand and found the single condom he had put there. He made use of it. Then, he slid over her, and they kissed. Almost instinctively, he found the right place. But then he couldn't make it work, so he backed off. Then he tried again. But when he moved, he felt an awkward push, and again he wasn't where he wanted to be.

"Let me help," Lindi said softly. She used her hand to guide him, and after several seconds, they were met with success. They both made surprised noises. But by that time, Stavros wasn't able to wait. He tried to move slowly, but his control was gone. He barely had time to move at all, and it was over. It had felt good, but it was way too fast, and he had wanted it to last. He hadn't been able to do anything for Lindi.

He lay still and panted. "Lindi, I'm so sorry."

"That's okay," she said tentatively.

They lay there for some time, holding hands, alone with their thoughts. They had just lost their virginity, both to people they loved, and it was vaguely disappointing. Stavros caught his breath. He wasn't sure what to do next. So he went to his place of comfort.

"Let's get dressed and make dinner," he suggested.

"Okay," Lindi agreed.

They got dressed and went downstairs. "Do you want me to make something, or would leftover spanakopita be okay?" Stavros asked. "We can warm it up."

"I'm okay with the spanakopita," Lindi said.

Stavros preheated the oven, and then got them both glasses of water. He took out the leftover food and put it down on the counter. Then he sat down at the table with Lindi. She smiled at him.

"Are you okay?" he asked.

"Yeah," she said. "I'm good. It was just . . . different . . . than I expected."

Stavros felt his heart drop a little. "Lindi," he said, reaching for her hand. "I promise, that's not how it's gonna be. I just wasn't really prepared the way I thought I would be. I was too worked up. I wanted it to last longer, but I just couldn't. It will be better."

Lindi squeezed his hand. "No, Stavros, I'm not blaming you for anything. I guess that I've just watched a lot of soap operas, and I had an unrealistic view. But they're actors, and adults, and we're a couple of awkward sixteen-year-olds. But any time I'm with you, it's wonderful. And, yeah, we'll do it again, and it will get better."

Stavros gave her a smile. "You know, we can do it again today. Tonight. After we eat. I mean, the pressure is off now. We can do it as much as we want."

Lindi smiled. "I hadn't even considered that," she said. "Yeah. After we eat." She paused. "I don't know if you noticed or not," she said shyly, "but I was bleeding a tiny bit after. I think that's normal for the first time. But you'll need to be gentle, okay?"

Stavros had no idea that girls could bleed when they first had sex. There was so much to learn. "Are you sure it's okay?"

Lindi gave him a reassuring smile. "Yes, I'm sure. I want to do it again. I want to do it a lot. Stavros, I want to make you feel good."

"I want you to feel good, too."

After they ate, they went back upstairs. "Let's undress each other this time," Lindi said, and they did. And just as he expected, Stavros got caught up on the bra strap. Lindi laughed.

They kissed and explored standing up, with the lights on. Then they lay down on the bed. "Lindi," Stavros said softly. "When I'm alone sometimes at night, and I think about you, you know, I can do things to make myself feel good. Can girls do that, too?"

Lindi nodded. "Oh, yeah," she said. "Girls can do that, too."

Stavros nodded. "Show me how you do it," he whispered, "and I'll do it for you."

Lindi's eyes grew wide. "Really?" she asked. Stavros nodded. "Okay." She took his hand and guided it to where it needed to be.

"Right here?" Stavros asked.

"Almost," Lindi replied, moving his hand slightly. "Just right there. Now move it around. Smaller circles." She let out a moan. "Yeah, like that. Oh my God." She reached back several times to move his hand back to the right place. It was hard to find, but he was trying. He kept going while she moaned and whispered, "Yes right there. Keep doing that."

Stavros patiently continued while watching her face. She had her eyes closed but would open them and look at him. After what seemed like an eternity, her body stiffened, just like his would do when he was about to release. Then her moans got louder. He started to move faster, but she slowed him back down with her hand. Soon, her moaning became like a growl, then she let out a kind of low shriek. Her butt rose up, and then back down again. He kept going, until finally, she told him to stop. He reached over to get another condom, and this time, entering was easy. He stayed still for a moment, and Lindi went back to moaning.

"Oh my God that feels so good," she said.

Stavros started to move slowly, and now they were both making pleased vocalizations. Stavros felt like king of the world looking down at Lindi. She looked up at him like she adored every aspect of his being, and he felt the same way about her. He had always wanted to be even closer to her, and now he was. It was like a dream. He lowered his body so he was touching her in all places and kept moving. Then he moved faster. It was even better, and Lindi was not protesting. He was doing something right.

"Lindi," he finally said. "Lindi, I can't wait any longer."

She smiled. "Go ahead."

He thrust even faster and harder, and she moaned louder, and then he reached nirvana. It was nothing like the last time, or any of his times alone. It was like she had made him whole, and now he was sharing that with her. He felt like he went on for minutes, hours, but finally the feeling started to fade, and he realized that it was impossible to feel that good much longer than he did. It might have killed him.

He collapsed on top of her, and then they made eye contact. They both smiled and then started to laugh.

"Yeah," Lindi said, "that was it. That's how I imagined it. I mean, there's no way I could have known how it felt, but the feelings, oh my God. Stavros. Yes. That was amazing. I'm so glad we did it again. Yes. If we keep doing that, I'll be a happy girl."

Stavros smiled a smug smile. "Yes," he said. "That was very good." He looked down into her eyes. "I love you, Lindi."

Lindi closed her eyes for a few seconds. "Oh my God, it still feels good, and when you said you love me, I could still feel it. I thought it was over, but it just doesn't stop feeling good. I love you, Stavros."

Stavros was feeling the same thing. But after a while, he knew he had to move. He lay down beside her so their sides were touching and took her hand.

"Can you imagine," Lindi said, "if each time, it keeps getting better and better? We would never leave the bed. It would be our new life. Oh, I could live like that!"

Stavros laughed. He kissed her forehead. "That would be wonderful," he agreed. "Do you want to do anything now? We could go for a walk, or go get ice cream and then come back here and see if we want to have sex again. If not, that's okay, but it's on the table."

Lindi turned onto her side, facing him, and poked his nose. "I'll never say no to ice cream," she said. "And for that matter, from today on, I don't think I'll ever say no to sex."

They decided to walk to the neighborhood ice-cream shop, Frosty's. The nights were starting to get cooler, so Stavros loaned Lindi a sweatshirt. As they approached the door, Lindi went to open it and then released the knob as if it were on fire. She pulled Stavros back to the street.

"Oh, my God," she said. "My parents and my brother are in there!" She laughed. "I don't think they saw us, but I just can't see them right now. I mean, what if they ask us what we've been up to? Or what we're doing next? I would just die!"

Stavros took her hand, and they started to walk down the street. "Close call," he said, completely relieved that he didn't have to see the Leahys after just making love to their daughter and sister. He could just see himself saying something stupid to them and ruining the vibe of the evening. Their evening. So they made the longer walk to Friendly's.

There were some kids from school at Friendly's, but no one they knew beyond a polite wave. They sat at a booth and ordered large sundaes. When the ice cream arrived, they tasted better than any dessert they'd ever had. They both made moaning noises as they ate, and then giggled. Stavros looked around.

"This is the very booth I was sitting in when my mom told me that she and Pop were planning on having another baby," he said. "I remember being slightly upset about giving up my only-child role, but then, after a bit, I kind of gave her my permission to get pregnant. Can you imagine that kind of arrogance?" He laughed.

Lindi shrugged. "Maybe in some way, she did want your approval," she said. "You said she was always giving you choices and talking about free will."

Stavros nodded. "Yeah," he agreed. "She would give me choices about dinner, and books, and even when we bought clothes. It wasn't until much later that I realized that she was giving me choices between two things she had already chosen! So she was kind of sneaky that way. But it made me feel really powerful, you know? Like my opinion really mattered to her."

"She sounds so amazing, Stavros," Lindi said, reaching for his hand. "I feel like I know her from your stories, but I still regret that I didn't know her. I wish she was still here."

Stavros smiled. "It took me a long time as a kid to come to peace with her death," he said. "I asked a lot of questions and made a lot of people uncomfortable. Then I read a lot of books and talked with my dad about them. And I finally decided that you have to come up with your own ideas about what happens to someone when they die. Like there might be a heaven like they have in paintings at the museum, with angels, and old men with white beards, or maybe souls become energy. I don't know. But

I decided that my mother's soul was just too big to fade into nothing. So I imagine it being anywhere that people need strength. Sometimes, I feel like she's watching me. Kind of keeping an eye on me, keeping me honest. And sometimes I dream about her. Nothing too outlandish, she's just in my dreams. And it feels like she's just dropping in to say hi. Sometimes I get to hug her. Sometimes she's with her brother, David. And it sticks with me when I wake up."

Lindi nodded as she listened intently. "Wow. I can't even imagine what you went through. It's like too much to even think about. But I'm not surprised that it made you think. You're a deep thinker. You always try to get to the bottom of things. But I guess there's no bottom to this. It's just what you make it." She paused. "I think souls survive death, too. I don't know where they go, and I don't know if there's a God, but I would like to think that if there is, then people don't feel sad or angry or any pain after they die. And they don't become nothing. They're still a part of something."

Stavros smiled at her. "Where were you when I needed you with all that ten years ago? You just summed up everything I needed to hear back then, but everyone seemed afraid to tell me." He squeezed her hand. "How do you know me so well?"

Lindi looked at their hands clasped on the table. "I know you, Stavros," she said, looking up. "And now I know you inside and out."

They finished their ice cream and started their walk home. When they got there, they locked the door and pulled down the shades. Then they went back upstairs to Stavros's room.

They found new ways to explore each other's bodies and touch places new to them. They spent more time using their hands, and their mouths, and then finally came together in the end. They were already perfecting the beginning, middle, and end of their intercourse, and the third time was more intense than the second. They lay together on the bed after. It was only nine thirty.

"Do you want to sleep together?" Stavros asked. "I can set the alarm for midnight. I barely slept last night. Now I feel like I could just drift right off."

"Okay," Lindi agreed, curling up closer to him. "There was a lot of that not-sleeping going on in my room last night, too. I think a nap would be lovely."

Stavros set the alarm, turned off the light, and drew Lindi into his embrace. He felt light and content. Soon, he drifted off to sleep. In his dream, Rebel was eating ice cream in the shop, and then was talking about philosophy to a circle of classmates on the grass as she ate. Then she turned to Stavros and smiled. "I told you that you would do amazing things, my son," she said, and she reached out and touched his cheek.

He woke up abruptly to the alarm going off. Lindi stirred. It was time to get up. They got dressed and headed downstairs. Then Stavros walked Lindi home.

Chapter 31

Dance With Me

JUNIOR YEAR BEGAN, AND EVERYONE fell back into a routine. They all did their homework after school, hung out at night, and had fun on the weekends. Friday night was friend night, and Saturday night was date night, and everyone was having more and more dates. Alec was dating Felicia. Mario and Sandy were trying again. They had some sort of chemistry that sometimes fired and was sometimes inert. Deanna went on dates with different boys, but nothing had clicked just yet. There were sometimes double dates, and even one time, triple, but Stavros and Lindi savored their alone time.

They mapped out their families' schedules and were able to find times when either he or she had the house to themselves, and they made the most of those moments. Stavros got his license, and Lindi soon after, so they now used wheels instead of feet to get around. And in desperate times, the wheels became a mobile bedroom.

When winter came, they all went skating and took weekend day trips to ski in the mountains. Lindi had a strong arm, and was very accurate with a snowball, so snowball fight team captains always chose her first for their teams. They argued over whose mother made the best hot chocolate, and in the end, they agreed it was no one's mother; it was Stavros. So they went to his house, and with Drea's assistance and coaching, made cut-out holiday sugar cookies to decorate.

After the winter holidays, spring term began, and all thoughts turned to prom. It would be in early May, and it would be in the school gym. As the days passed and the event got closer, Deanna worried over whether anyone would invite her. Toward the end of April, she approached her friends at lunch with shock in her eyes and a dazed appearance.

"What's wrong?" Stavros asked, prepared to go kick someone's ass if they had offended her.

"Torrance Clark," she said.

Everyone looked at her. That wasn't enough information. "What about him?" Lindi asked.

Deanna turned to look at her and snapped out of her revery. "He just asked me to the prom!" she said, and she made a small, excited noise.

Lindi leaned in closer to her. "Torrance Clark?" she said with disbelief. "The same Torrance Clark who's on the basketball team and was in the play last year? The one who has a swimming pool in his backyard? That Torrance Clark?"

"Yes!" Deanna said. Now both girls made excited noises together.

Stavros turned to Lindi. "How come you know so much about this Torrance guy?" he asked her.

Lindi laughed. "Stavros," she said, "how come you *don't*? He's, like, the most popular kid in school. And he has a good chance of being prom king. All the unattached girls were hoping to be his date, but it's our Deanna! You said yes, right?"

"Of course I did! What, do you think I'm crazy?" Deanna exclaimed. "This is like, a once-in-a-lifetime opportunity! I just hope he didn't ask me on a dare or something."

Mario turned to Deanna and gave her a baffled look. "Deanna, have you looked at yourself in the mirror ever? You're really pretty! And you're no pushover. You don't kiss up to the popular kids. Torrance probably thinks that's refreshing!"

Deanna shot Mario a look. "You think I'm pretty?"

Mario looked at Alec and Stavros. "Back me up here, guys, okay? She's pretty, right?"

Stavros and Alec nodded. "I never really pay attention because I've known you since we were five," Stavros said, "but you're looking pretty hot these days."

Lindi shot him a look. He shrugged.

"I've always thought you were pretty," Alec said shyly. Alec was barely capable of speaking to Deanna because she intimidated him, so everyone knew he was being honest.

Deanna crossed her arms in front of her and nodded. "Okay, then," she said. "So I'm pretty. And I don't take shit from anyone. Alright. Maybe I'll end up as prom queen." She turned to Lindi. "You already got your dress, but you have to go back with me to get one. Can you go after school today?"

It was one of their empty-house afternoons, but when Lindi looked at Stavros, he nodded. This was Deanna. This was important. The other thing could wait for now.

"Okay," Lindi said. "It's a date."

The boys walked to the playground after school while the girls went shopping. The swings and seesaws were deserted due to earlier rain, but after shaking most of the water off the swings, the boys sat down anyway.

"I have a slight problem," Mario told Stavros and Alec. "Sandy wants to hang out with her friends before and after the prom. And I mean, it's only fair. She has a group of friends, too, and we're actually getting along pretty well right now, so I think I should just do it."

"Well, that sucks," Stavros said, pushing his feet off the ground and gaining some height on his swing. "I just assumed we'd all be together at prom, but I guess maybe next year, if you go with her again, you can say it's your turn."

"Yeah," Mario agreed, bending over so his elbows were on his knees. "I mean, I guess Jessica and Simon are okay. I don't really know the rest of them that well. But, you know, I might just get a shot at some alone time with Sandy if I play my cards right. Maybe soon, too. I don't know."

Stavros understood. Sometimes, you had to make sacrifices for a girl so you could win some points. Kindness was all good and fine, but you could go a long way with just being agreeable.

"So it will just be me and Felicia, and you and Lindi," Alec said, "'cause I'm gonna bet Torrance Clark's gonna want to hang out with his popular friends before and after prom."

Stavros knew that Alec was probably right. But no Deanna in their prom plans? That just didn't feel right. He didn't think Deanna would think so either. Maybe she hadn't thought it through yet.

Lindi and Deanna got off the bus near Stavros's house before dinner and knocked on his door. Drea answered and called for her brother. Then she went back to watching TV with her friend Susan.

Stavros came into the living room. "Hey," he said to Lindi with a smile as he bent forward to kiss her. "I wasn't expecting to see you tonight. Hi, Deanna. Did you get a dress?"

Deanna held up a plastic garment bag she had slung over her arm. "It's stunning on her," Lindi said. "She really might end up being prom queen."

Stavros smiled to see Deanna blush. It was a new look for her.

"Deanna, Alec brought something up earlier and I thought I should ask you about it. Is Torrance gonna want to do stuff with his friends on prom night? Because Mario's already gonna be with Sandy and her friends. I'd hate to lose both of you."

Deanna shook her head. "No," she said. "I talked to him about the plans. He clearly said he wants to hang out with my friends. I had to ask him twice and remind him who my friends were!" She laughed. "He said it was fine. He even said he'd contribute to a limo if we want to get one."

"Oh," Stavros said. "Well that's good, then. Nothing to worry about."

"I'm so glad," Lindi said. "It wouldn't be the same without you."

"It's too bad about Mario, though," Deanna said. "I may not be the biggest fan of Sandy and her whiny voice, but I'll miss having Mario there."

The girls hung out at the house, and they joined Drea and Susan by the TV. They both called home to ask if they could have dinner with the Karras family, and permission was granted.

"So what *are* we gonna do before and after prom?" Stavros asked the girls as they ate. "Where should we go for dinner?"

"You should go to Olympia's!" Drea said. "And then Papa and I can go and spy on you." Everyone laughed.

"Greek food may be kind of heavy for a night of dancing," Stavros warned.

"We could go to the Little Italy Café," Lindi suggested. "We'd need to see if we could get a reservation. It's my favorite Italian place."

"I like it, too," Deanna said.

"Italian food, huh?" Andreas teased. "Sounds like some tough competition!" The girls laughed.

"That's okay with me," Stavros said, always wanting to make Lindi, and Deanna, happy. "I know Alec will be alright with it, too. Deanna, ask Torrance if that's okay with him, and I can call to make the reservation."

"We'll have to rent the limo," Lindi said, "and then decide where to go after prom. My mom won't let me go to any hotel parties."

"Mine, either," Deanna said.

Andreas looked up. "Why don't you all just come over here?" he suggested. "Stavros, you can tidy up the basement. You're very good at tidying things. And then Drea and I can be upstairs so we won't bother you."

"Or I can see if I can stay over at Susan's," Drea offered. "It would be fun."

Stavros looked from Lindi to Deanna. "Sound good to you?" They both nodded. "Okay then. Thanks, Pop."

After dinner, Deanna headed home, and Stavros and Lindi went to the basement to look around. "This might work," Lindi said. "I can come over this weekend and we can clean up and organize everything. What would your pop think if there was some champagne?"

Stavros shrugged. "I think he'd be okay as long as we didn't get wasted and trash anything. And no one was driving."

Lindi smiled. "And look. Closets, if we want to play Seven Minutes in Heaven!"

Stavros laughed. "C'mon," he said, reaching to take her hand. "I'll give you a little tour of heaven."

The night of the prom arrived, and the group of friends, along with Felicia and Torrance, took the limo to Little Italy Café. It was not one of the more popular prom destinations, so the atmosphere was cozy and quiet. The group in their formal wear was conspicuous and received smiles from other diners and restaurant staff. They were offered free dessert by the owner. Torrance was gregarious, and conversed with each member of their group, asking questions and recalling things he knew about them from school. He was a true politician. Deanna smiled widely throughout dinner and glowed in her soft pink gown. Stavros had to admit to himself that his best friend was indeed very pretty.

But Lindi was exquisite. She was wearing a light blue strapless gown with matching high gloves that she took off to eat. Her hair was in an upsweep with rhinestone bobby pins inserted at various points. Her soft pink lips glowed with her lip gloss, and her eyeshadow made her blue eyes radiant. Stavros wore a black tux with a light blue bow tie and cummerbund, and together, they were a striking pair. Even small, skinny Alec was looking sharp in his tux, and he was all smiles next to Felicia, in an off-the-shoulder red gown.

They finished dinner and their free dessert and made their way to the limo. It was time for the prom. They entered the school gym as a group, and several other students called out to Torrance as he walked in. He held tight to Deanna's arm, and they all looked around at the decorations. Then they headed toward the punch bowl. Stavros located Mario, and the group moved over to where Sandy's group was standing. Mario looked relieved to see his friends.

After some milling around, the groups headed for the dance floor. They danced as couples, but within their groups. They started with several fast songs, and then Journey's "Faithfully" began to play. Couples put their arms around each other and swayed around the dance floor. Stavros pulled Lindi close. She rested her head carefully against his chest. Stavros placed his chin on the top of her head. Her hair smelled like flowers and hair spray. He looked around at his friends. They were all dancing close with their dates. He saw Torrance dancing with Deanna, but his eyes were fixed on Stavros and Lindi. He had a strange, intense look on his face as he watched them dance, which made Stavros feel vaguely uncomfortable. When Torrance saw Stavros looking, he smiled and turned away.

They all danced for several more songs, then decided as a group to take a break. It seemed the whole junior class had made the same decision. The tables filled up, and Stavros and his friends were forced to sit on the wooden bleachers. They sipped from their punch cups and chatted as they watched the die-hard dancers move. Lindi sat across Stavros's lap with her arms around his neck. They talked in soft tones and nuzzled their faces together and kissed.

Torrance came closer to the others. "Hey," he said as quietly as he could over the music, "my friend has some vodka. Does anyone want a shot in their punch?"

Alec and Felicia declined, but Deanna, Stavros, and Lindi nodded. Torrance went off for a moment and came back with an extra punch cup. He poured some clear liquid in their cups. Everyone sipped their drinks slowly. Torrance finished his and went back for more. He gave them all another round. Stavros could tell that it was going straight to Lindi's head. She promised him that she wouldn't drink anymore for the rest of the dance.

They all went back to dance feeling much looser. They laughed and twirled around, switching partners around the floor. Stavros was dancing next to Deanna when he noticed Torrance dancing close behind Lindi. Lindi was moving around and didn't notice him there. Then he saw Torrance's hand rest gently on Lindi's waist. Lindi smiled but didn't turn around. She must have thought it was Stavros. Stavros rushed over and took Lindi's hands. Torrance dropped his hand. Lindi hugged Stavros close and giggled. She had no idea what had just happened. Stavros wrote it off as Torrance having had a lot to drink but decided to remain close to Lindi.

The song ended, and the music stopped. Mrs. Francis, Stavros's English teacher and the faculty sponsor of the prom, went to a podium set up beneath the basketball hoop, and picked up a microphone.

"Good evening, ladies and gentlemen," she said. "Welcome to Junior Prom 1982!" The class erupted in cheers. "Thank you for coming and for being on your very best behavior tonight. I would like to announce the prom king and queen and their court. Starting with the king's court, second runner-up, Matthew Green!" Everyone applauded and Matt Green approached the podium. "First runner-up, Johnny Cohenour!" More applause. "And your 1982 Prom King is . . . Torrance Clark!"

Torrance looked surprised, like he hadn't been expecting this. He started to walk to the podium to massive applause, slapping raised hands along the way. Deanna stood in place, clapping, smiling, and bouncing on her feet. She looked at Stavros, and they smiled at each other.

Mrs. Francis cleared her throat, and the crowd went silent. "And now for your queen's court. Second runner-up, Jessica Fields!" Jessica shrieked and ran up to the front. "First runner-up, Deanna Collins!"

Deanna looked stunned. She hadn't really expected to be queen, but now she was a runner-up, and Torrance was the king. She put on a smile and worked her way to the podium. Everyone cheered her as she approached, and Stavros whistled.

"And now, the moment you've all been waiting for. Your Junior Class Prom Queen for 1982 . . . Miss Lindi Leahy!"

Lindi had been standing facing Stavros with her hands on his shoulders, and now she looked at him in confusion. "Did they just say I'm prom queen?" she asked. Stavros nodded. "Oh my God! I guess I need to get up there!" She hugged Stavros quickly, kissed him, then rushed to the podium. Mrs. Francis placed her crown on top of her head, and she reached up to touch it. She and Deanna hugged and looked at each other with puzzled looks. This was not what anyone had expected.

Stavros watched as Torrance stepped up closer to Lindi and said something. Someone stepped in front of him, so Stavros lost sight of them for a minute. He struggled to get closer. He saw Torrance reach out his hand, and Lindi reluctantly took it. He led her to the dance floor. Spandau Ballet's song "True" began to play, and the king and queen danced slowly, close and alone, on the dance floor. A little too close.

Lindi looked like she might tip over. Torrance was holding her up. The king and queen's court joined them on the floor and started to dance. Stavros could see Deanna dancing with Johnny Cohenour and watching Torrance and Lindi. Then Stavros turned his attention back to them, too. Torrance whispered something in Lindi's ear, and she shook her head emphatically. Now Torrance had his hand on Lindi's lower back and was slowly moving it down, down . . .

Stavros rushed into action and ran out to the dance floor. He tapped Torrance on the shoulder. "I'm cutting in," he said.

"No, thanks," Torrance said, and he started to turn away.

Stavros felt his adrenaline start to rise. "Torrance," he said in a louder voice, "I didn't ask you. I said I'm cutting in." His heart was pounding.

Torrance looked at him. "Okay, okay, fine," he said, letting go of Lindi and stepping back. "She's all yours. Lindi, I'll see you out in the hall when they take our pictures for the yearbook." He turned and walked in the direction of his own friends.

Lindi grabbed Stavros's hand. "Stavros," she said, "I'm a little drunk. Just a little!" She giggled. "Hold me, okay?" She put her arms around her neck and held on tight. Stavros danced her over to the edge of the dance floor.

Deanna followed behind them. When they got to the bleachers, she helped Stavros prop Lindi onto her seat. She looked at Stavros. "He gave her something in a cup right before they went to dance," she said. "And then he was groping her butt. She had no idea. Stavros, he was totally trying to get to Lindi. He might have put something in her drink. That is so wrong. He's not my prom date anymore." She took off her wrist corsage and threw it further up on the bleachers.

Stavros felt bad for Deanna, but he was mainly concerned about Lindi. "Dee, he was coming up behind her on the dance floor before and trying to touch her. I have to think he planned this. Oh my God, do you think he had his friends all vote for Lindi for queen so she'd win and they'd be king and queen together? Deanna, they take pictures of the court out in the hall. He almost got her into the hall. Then he could have just said she was drunk and needed some fresh air, and they'd be gone."

Deanna sat down hard on the bench. "This is why he didn't have any problem with hanging out with my friends."

". . . and why he was staring at me and Lindi while we slow-danced," Stavros said. "He could have done some real damage, Dee. What did he think was gonna happen? That I'd just let him walk off with my girlfriend?"

"Lindi," Deanna said softly to her friend, "do you remember what Torrance whispered to you when you were dancing?"

Lindi nodded. "He said I seemed like I might need some air. He said he would take me outside to get some. I said I would go outside to get air with Stavros, and he said Stavros said it was okay if I went with him. I told him that Stavros would never say that."

"Yeah, I would never say that," Stavros said in a controlled voice.

"I wanted to go find you, Stavros," Lindi went on, "but Torrance said we had to finish our dance. He was holding on to me so tight. But then you were there to dance with me, Stavros, so everything was okay." She giggled. "I don't know why I feel so woozy. I only had two drinks."

Now Deanna was furious. She stormed across the dance floor to where Torrance was standing with his basketball friends. Stavros couldn't hear what she was saying, but he could tell she was yelling. Torrance yelled back. Then it was Deanna's turn again. Torrance said something, and Stavros could hear Deanna gasp from across the room. Then her hand moved quickly and across his face. Deanna turned and stomped away while Torrance put his hand to his cheek.

Deanna came back to the bleachers. She was crying. "Let's get out of here, okay?"

Stavros nodded. He started to help Lindi to her feet. She looked at him sleepily and smiled. "I love you, Stavros."

Stavros started to help her down to the floor, and Alec came up and grabbed her on the other side. "I love you, too, Lindi," Stavros said. "We're gonna get you back to my house now, okay?"

Lindi laughed. "Are we going to bed now?" she whispered loudly.

Stavros brushed her loose hair back from her face. "Soon," he told her.

When they got to Stavro's house, Stavros climbed out of the limo first and ran ahead to find his father. He told him what happened. Andreas shook his head and followed Stavros back to the limo. Then he helped him get Lindi into the house.

"What did she drink?" Andreas asked as they placed her gently on the couch.

"She just had two shots of vodka with us, but then Torrance gave her something. We have no idea what it was or if he put something in it. Pop, I've only ever seen her drink once before, and she's a real lightweight. I'm gonna get her some water."

He went to the kitchen and filled a glass. He sat down on the couch next to Lindi and held the glass to her mouth. She sipped lightly and some spilled down her face.

Lindi smiled. "You're taking care of me," she slurred. "You really do love me, don't you? It's not just the sex, is it? You really love me."

Stavros looked at his father in horror. Andreas smiled at him. "Don't worry about it, son," he said. "People say crazy, mixed-up things when they drink."

Stavros looked at his father with gratitude. Deanna came over and sat next to Lindi. She ran her hand over Lindi's hair. "I'm so sorry, Lindi," she said through tears. "I just assumed he liked me for some reason. It was too good to be true; I should have known it wasn't. It's all my fault."

Andreas put his hand on Deanna's arm. "It's not any of your faults," he said. "It's Torrance's fault, no one else. Deanna, you're a victim here, not a villain."

Deanna nodded and wiped her eyes. She looked at Lindi. Lindi looked back at her and smiled. "I love you, too, Deanna," she said. "I'm the queen! Can you believe it?" She laughed. Then she stopped laughing and burped. "I need to throw up," she announced.

Stavros and Andreas dove toward her and quickly walked her toward the bathroom. They made it just in time.

Fifteen minutes later, they had Lindi stretched out on the couch, and she was moaning in discomfort. "I'm going to call the Leahys," Andreas said.

"What are you gonna tell them?" Stavros asked.

Andreas thought about it. "I'll just tell him that I'm going to have all of you kids stay over tonight if it's okay with them, and I'll be supervising. That way, we can let Lindi decide what she wants to tell them tomorrow."

Stavros nodded. "Thanks, Papa."

Deanna was sitting in Andreas's chair, and she was still crying. Stavros put his arms around her, and she sobbed into his shoulder.

"I'm so stupid," she said. "Why did I think I was so special? Why would Torrance have wanted to go to prom with me? I should have known that something was wrong, right away."

Stavros shook his head. "Dee, I'm so, so sorry. I'm just gonna say this once, okay? You're amazing. You've always been amazing. That's why you're my best friend. For eleven years, Dee. That's a long time. It takes someone pretty special to put up with me for that long." Deanna snorted with laughter through her tears. "And Torrance is an asshole. He couldn't have what he wanted, so he had to lie and cheat to try to get it. That's not someone special. That's a loser. He's fooled a lot of people. You're not alone. So stop beating up on my best friend, okay?"

Deanna pulled away. "But—"

"I said I was only gonna say it once, Deanna."

Deanna started to speak again, and Stavros shushed her. Deanna nodded. "Why didn't you ever fall in love with me?" she asked. "Eleven years, and you never fell in love with me."

Stavros looked at her carefully. "Is that what you would have wanted?"

She thought for a moment. Then her shoulders fell. "No. I would have rejected you. I would have broken your heart in a million pieces. The carnage would have been heartbreaking."

Stavros smiled. "Yeah, that's why I never fell in love with you. My fear of rejection." He gave her another squeeze. "I'm gonna go check on Lindi. Can you go downstairs and check on Alec and Felicia?"

Deanna nodded. "They had better not be making out," she said, and she headed for the stairs.

Lindi was still awake on the couch. The vomiting had sobered her up a little. Now she had a hand on her head. She looked at Stavros. "What train ran over me?"

"The Torrance Express," he said. "I'll tell you all about it tomorrow. But you're gonna be okay. You're gonna stay with me tonight."

"Okay," she said, closing her eyes. Then they popped back open. "Did I just hallucinate this, or did I tell you I knew you loved me and not just for sex, in front of your father?"

Stavros smiled kindly at her. "You did. But don't worry about it. He didn't hear a word."

Chapter 32

Repercussions

LINDI WAS OKAY PHYSICALLY THE next day, but she was understandably upset and felt violated. Deanna was subdued. When Mario heard what Torrance had done to his friends, he was furious. He came to school on Monday with a black eye.

"What happened?" Deanna asked at lunch.

Mario shrugged. "I paid Torrance a little visit."

"And he punched you in the face?" Stavros asked.

"Yeah," Mario said, "but not until after I slugged him in the mouth. I may have knocked a tooth loose." He grinned.

Deanna shook her head. "I can't believe you did that, Mario," she said with awe. "I guess, thank you?"

Mario looked her in the eyes. "No one treats my friends that way and gets away with it. If anyone ever hurts you, they're gonna hear about it."

Everyone was silent. Mario and Deanna maintained eye contact for several seconds, then both looked away.

As the weeks passed, things got back to normal, but Lindi had changed subtly. She'd lost some of her giddiness. She could smile and have fun with her friends, but now sometimes Stavros caught her looking quietly out in the distance, unfocused. He tried to draw her out and get her to talk about it, but she didn't feel it was necessary.

"I just need a little time," she reassured him. "I know everything worked out okay in the end, but it was still kind of a big deal. Just be patient with me, okay?" She smiled.

Stavros nodded, then hugged her. She was right. It was a big deal. Torrance had been stalking her. Lindi could have been really hurt. And he didn't want to think of what would have happened if Torrance had somehow managed to get her alone. It made him feel sick. He was glad Mario had punched him. Stavros vowed to be patient with Lindi and to be available if she wanted to talk.

Summer started, and Lindi was getting ready to spend another summer at camp as a junior counselor. Stavros spent as much time as he could with her, and they took full advantage of their empty-house opportunities. This year, Stavros had his license, and he had bought an old beater that he could drive up to New Hampshire to visit her on her nights off. The situation didn't feel as desperate as it had last year, but he knew he would still miss her being just four blocks away.

Stavros went back to his job at the grocery store; he needed gas money for his trips. He brought home phyllo dough and other ingredients to bake desserts with Drea. She was going to day camp, but now they had much more time together at night.

Stavros hung out with his friends most days, and Deanna spent time at the Karrases' house with Stavros and his family, just hanging out, baking, and watching TV. One evening, Stavros and Deanna were home alone while Andreas took Drea and a friend to a movie.

"So how's it going with Lindi being gone?" Deanna asked during a commercial break.

Stavros shrugged. "I've been able to go out there the last two weekends, and last week, she stayed over with me at my motel. It's way better than last year, but I like it better when she's home."

"Yeah," Deanna said. "I understand. I was talking to Mario the other day and we realized that next year, we're all gonna be getting ready to go to college, and none of us even knows where we're going, or where we'll get in."

Stavros thought about this. Then a thought occurred to him. "Wait a minute," he said. "You were talking to Mario the other day? We haven't gotten together as a group for like two weeks. When did you talk to Mario?"

Deanna squirmed in her seat. "I guess Mario and I got together recently and were talking, I don't know."

Stavros looked at her suspiciously. "You got together with Mario? What, was it like a date?"

Deanna shrugged. "I . . . I dunno. Maybe. We just hung out."

"Did the two of you . . . kiss?" Stavros asked.

"Stavros!" Deanna said. "What's gotten into you? So I got together with Mario. And yeah, maybe we kissed."

"Deanna," Stavros said, his eyes widening. "Did the two of you, like, make out?"

Deanna started tapping her foot on the floor. "There may have been some making out, I don't really remember." She paused. "Okay, yeah, there was some making out."

Stavros was quiet for a moment. "How long has this been going on?"

Deanna sighed. "Since after prom. After he got in the fight with Torrance. Stavros, he got in a fight to defend my honor. It was amazing. And he thinks I'm pretty! But yeah, that day, after school, I went to his house to thank him for what he did. I guess we both still had a lot of adrenaline going through us. We kind of just, like, fell together."

Stavros gasped. "You guys have been doing it, haven't you?"

Now Deanna was quiet, and she looked at her feet. "I guess we kind of have been. I mean, yeah. Like okay, maybe a lot. I wanted to tell you, but I was waiting for the right moment. It's kind of a weird thing to bring up. Like, 'Hey, Stav, I've been getting it on like a bunny with your friend for weeks.' It's just not an easy thing to bring up."

Stavros shook his head. "I'm not upset about that, Dee," he said. "No, I get that. But he's your first, right?"

Deanna nodded. "And don't tell him I told you, but I was his first, too."

Stavros was not surprised. But he was surprised that Mario hadn't told him.

"So, is this just about . . . sex, or is there something more to it?"

Deanna nodded. "Yeah, there's more to it. Can you believe that Mario has actually liked me since last winter break? I really like him, too. But I didn't see it until prom. He was so angry at what happened, but he was so kind and attentive to me. He promised me he's never been in a fight like that before, and he won't do it again, but I think we all agree that Torrance needed to be punched."

"Yeah," Stavros agreed. "He did. I wish there had been some kind of real consequence for what he did, but there wasn't. And Lindi's still dealing with the fallout." He inhaled and took Deanna's hand. "I'm really happy for you and Mario," he said. "You're my best friend, and he's one of my closest friends. I want you both to be happy. But I also want to let you know, if anything ever happens, I will always choose your side, okay?"

Deanna hugged him. "I know," she said. "And I know it's the same for you and Lindi. I've matured a lot since I said what I said about taking sides. It's not about me. And I'll always be your friend."

Chapter 33

THE FUTURE IS NOW

NOW THAT THE CAT WAS out of the bag, Mario and Deanna went public with their relationship. When school started again in the fall, they walked through the halls together holding hands. Deanna looked happy, and the incident at the prom was long forgotten.

It was time to start considering their futures, and Stavros had to decide what he wanted to do with his life after high school. He knew he was expected to go to college, and he accepted that fact. But he didn't know where, or what direction to go in. His father suggested he look at liberal arts schools, where he could take some time, try different classes, and see what interested him. Stavros took this advice and started to request catalogs through the mail. He also needed to consider schools where he could get free tuition due to his father's university job, and he had to figure out whether he wanted to stay close to home. And much of that last question had to do with where Lindi decided to go.

Lindi didn't know where she wanted to go yet, but she knew she wanted to focus her studies on early childhood education. She had been requesting brochures from schools close by and far away. Stavros was okay with that.

He wanted Lindi to find a school that would be good for her and where she would be happy. If they had to be apart, they would figure out the logistics. He wanted her to feel free to make the best choices for her, even if it would be really hard—and being apart would be. But he was thinking about their future, and he had some ideas that he hoped would make things easier for them.

The seniors took their SATs, and Stavros and his friends scored high enough to be accepted at most of the schools they were applying to. They completed applications and sent them in with essays and financial aid requests.

As spring approached, prom was announced, and Lindi decided she didn't want to go. Instead, she and Stavros would spend the evening together and go out for dinner and possibly a movie. Deanna decided to go to the prom, as she wanted to experience the event with Mario by her side. She knew if Torrance caused her any more grief, Mario would just sock him in the face and then kick him in the stomach when he hit the floor. Stavros knew the thought made her smile. Alec and Felicia would also be there, and the two couples would go together.

As prom got closer, acceptance packets started to arrive. Lindi got into Eastboro State, UMass, University of Denver, Arizona State University, and Baylor. Stavros was accepted at UMass, Boston University, Syracuse University, and Pittsburgh State College. They looked over their packets together and discussed the pros and cons of each school. Lindi was sure she didn't want to go to Eastboro or stay in Amherst. Stavros also didn't like the idea of going to school so close to home, but he did like the idea of being close to his Pennsylvania relatives.

By the end of the discussion, they had made their choices. Lindi was going to go to University of Denver, because she liked the idea of being around the mountains. Stavros would go to Pittsburgh State. They would be almost fifteen hundred miles apart, almost twenty-four hours by car and over three hours by airplane. Any way they broke it down, it was a long way. But it was where they needed to go.

Mario was going to UMass, and Deanna would be nearby at Mount Holyoke College. Alec had been accepted to Boston University but was considering deferring admission for a year so he could work. Felicia would be starting her studies at community college.

Prom night arrived, and Stavros and Lindi had a reservation at Little Italy Café. They dressed casually and were pleased to see no one there dressed in prom attire. They were seated at a table for two by the wall. Lindi watched the tea candle's flickering flame as they waited for their food to arrive. Stavros held her hand from across the table. Lindi's mind still wandered away at times, and he just stayed by her side and let her drift where she needed to go. Usually, after a minute or two, she would shake it off and look at him with a smile. He would smile back, but inside, he would be secretly cursing Torrance Clark and what he had done to break Lindi's spirit at junior prom. He just hoped that, with time and his complete support, eventually she would be able to move past her dark thoughts and be happy and carefree once more.

She was able to do anything she wanted, and they were spending time together, making love as they pleased, and professing their love to each other. But there was just this edge that wanted to cling to her, to make her doubt herself. Stavros longed to wrap his protection around her, to keep her safe, and to let her know he would never let anyone try to hurt her again.

Their food arrived, and they dug in, making conversation about their latest adventures. They kept the conversation light and easy and chose to see their time together as a celebration. Over dessert, they discussed their plans for the night. They were thinking of going to a movie, but neither of them were dying to see anything. They thought about going home to hang out, but both of them had family at home, and they wouldn't be able to be alone. Finally they decided to rent a motel room. They planned to make themselves at home and watch TV, and if they chose to, they could remove their clothing and partake in a little adult fun.

They got to the motel and registered at the desk. They would stay until midnight, and then drop the key in the box when they left. They went into the room, turned on the TV, and turned out the lights. Then, they cuddled together in the bed under the covers. Stavros could feel Lindi's body relax and slump in his arms. He kissed her head. About fifteen minutes later, she was sound asleep. Stavros set the alarm clock, held her closer, and closed his eyes. This was exactly the senior prom night that Lindi needed.

Chapter 34

WHAT I WANT

STAVROS KARRAS WAS A HIGH school graduate. He posed in his cap and gown for his father, his diploma clutched in his hands. Then Lindi joined him in front of the camera, and they both smiled and said, "Feta cheese!" Everyone came together in a group and hugged. It was a day long in coming, and it was the first day of the rest of their adult lives.

The Karras and Leahy families went out to dinner to celebrate. Lindi convinced her parents to try Olympia's, and they enjoyed their first foray into Greek cuisine. Lindi's brother complained that he didn't like olives. Andreas gasped, and Drea offered to eat them for him. He presented her with a plate filled with black olives.

"I can still taste them in my salad," Brian complained with a sour face.

"Brian, shut up," Lindi told him. "We can all go to McDonald's to celebrate if you ever graduate. The operative word being 'if'!"

"Lindi, that's enough," Mrs. Leahy told her, but she was obviously suppressing an amused smile.

After dinner, the friends all met at the playground. They stood on the merry-go-round and spun it around with their feet. Deanna yelled for someone to slow it down because she was gonna barf. Stavros put his foot down and dragged it on the ground until they slowed and came to a stop. Then they all sat on the merry-go-round floor.

"So we graduated," Alec said.

"Yes, we were all there, Alec, we remember," Deanna said. Felicia gave Deanna a dirty look. Deanna recoiled. "Sorry, Alec."

Alec shrugged.

"I'm leaving for camp in a few days," Lindi said. "I'll be a senior counselor this year. We go early to train the CITs. It will be my last year there."

Stavros grabbed her hand, looking to change the subject. "Hey guys," he said, "I got the job at Olympia's! I'll be starting next week for training. I'll start with bussing tables, but then I'll be able to do some kitchen work and wait tables."

"That's great, Stavros," Deanna said. "You've been going there for years! I bet that helped a lot."

Stavros nodded. "And my pop being a professor of Greek literature and knowing a little Greek myself doesn't hurt. And I hear I look the part, too."

Lindi squeezed his hand and smiled. "You do, Stavros," she said affectionately. "You look just like Apollo."

Mario chuckled. "Apollo Creed?" he said. Then he made some boxing moves.

Lindi rolled her eyes. "No, Mario. The other Apollo. The Greek god. He was very handsome and powerful, and very artistic. And he supposedly had curly hair." She reached out and caressed Stavros's head.

"I'm gonna work at the Gap," Felicia said. "I love their clothes, and I'll get a thirty percent discount, which is cool."

"I'm still waiting to hear from Spencer Gifts," Alec said. "It would be great, because it's right across from the Gap at the mall."

"What are you guys up to this summer?" Felicia asked Mario and Deanna.

The couple looked at each other and grinned. "Well, we have a few plans," Deanna said. "I'm gonna take a couple of classes to try to get ahead before school starts, and Mario's gonna work at his uncle's pizza place, but I guess the most exciting thing we're gonna do is go to Vermont."

She stopped and made sure everyone was looking at her.

"For our honeymoon!" she exclaimed. "Mario asked me to marry him earlier tonight!"

She held out her hand and showed her friends a small diamond ring.

"Obviously I said yes! So we'll get married in late August, and then we can move into married students' housing off-campus at Mount Holyoke."

"Oh, my God!" Lindi yelled, getting up on her feet and rushing to Deanna. "Congratulations! I am so happy for you! I can't believe it!" She hugged Deanna and then Mario. "Oh, this is amazing!"

She looked at Stavros. He was in a daze.

"Come here, Stavros," she said, motioning him over.

Stavros stood and joined them. "Wow, you guys. This is so unexpected! I barely know what to say! Congratulations! Wow!" He hugged them both, then stood back so Alec and Felicia could express their good wishes.

Stavros couldn't believe it. Two of his best friends, getting married. And they would both stay in the Amherst area for college. They would be happy, and together. He was happy for them, but he was also kind of envious. He had plans for himself and Lindi. He had a solid plan. But it wasn't time yet. He had to wait. It had to be just right. And not before she left town for more than eight weeks.

When Stavros and Lindi got back to Stavros's house later, they found his family had gone to bed, and his father had left a bottle of champagne on ice and two glass champagne flutes on the dining room table. Stavros popped the cork, and Lindi laughed. He poured some of the sparkling liquid into each glass and handed one to Lindi.

Stavros lifted his glass. "Yiamas, and L'chaim," he said.

Lindi raised her glass. "Sláinte!" she toasted. They clinked their glasses and took their sips. Then they put the glasses on the table and put their arms around each other's waists.

"Congratulations, Lindi Leahy," Stavros said softly, and he leaned in to kiss her.

"Congratulations to you, too, Stavros Karras." Now she kissed him. They stood in silence for a few moments. "I'm gonna miss you," Lindi said. "And not just when I'm at camp."

Stavros nodded. "Me too," he said. "But we'll have a few days when you come back from camp, and we'll spend every minute together. And we'll figure out how to make it work." He hugged her close.

"Thank you, Stavros," Lindi said, "for understanding. For knowing that I need to go. I think Denver will be good for me. All that fresh mountain air and the high altitude. I think I chose the right place."

Stavros nodded and kissed the top of her head. "I know," he whispered. "I only want the best for you." He pulled away and looked into her eyes. "But that doesn't mean I won't miss you every minute. *Every minute.*" He pulled her back into his embrace.

Lindi left for camp soon after, and Stavros started his job. The job was good, and Stavros felt he belonged there. But the time he wasn't working dragged by. He spent as much time as he could with his sister and father, and he made frozen meals for them to heat up after he left. He and Drea baked enough cakes, cookies, challah, and baklava to supply all of Amherst for a decade. He and Drea also went out for long walks and to talk. Drea would be starting seventh grade in the fall and was quickly making her way to becoming a teenager. He wanted her to know that he was there for her now, and would be later by phone, if she ever needed to talk. Sometimes, she would still hold his hand as they walked laps quietly around the park.

As the end of the summer neared, Stavros started to prepare himself for college. He decided what would go with him and what would stay behind. He went shopping for new clothing and items he would need for his dorm room. He started to pack all the belongings he wouldn't need for the next few weeks. When there was nothing left to do, he stopped. Then he approached his father.

"Papa," he said, sitting down on the couch next to his father's chair. "I need to let you know something, and I need you to let me say it all before you say anything." He took a deep breath. "Papa, I want to ask Lindi to marry me. And I don't mean to marry me now. I mean to marry her after we're done with college. But I want to ask her before we go. I want her, and me, to have something to hold on to when we're apart, something for us to look forward to, and I know what I want in the future is to marry her. So I want to ask her to marry me when she gets back from camp." He stopped and looked at his father. "Okay," he said. "I'm done now."

Andreas looked at him for a moment and nodded. Then he got up and walked out of the room. Stavros wasn't sure what to do. Should he just stay? Was Papa coming back? Was the conversation over? His heart was still pounding from anxiety about saying the words.

Andreas came back. He sat down on his chair. He looked at Stavros. "My son," he said, "you were worried I'd object. But I don't. I trust that you know what's right for you. I trust that you think things through before you act. I think that's why you're talking to me today before you do this. I think it's wise to talk it over. I remember talking to my papa before I proposed to your mother. I was so nervous. Not only was she not Greek, but she was also Jewish, and quite outspoken! So I didn't know what he'd say. But what he said, Stavros, was that he gave me his blessing. And now I give you mine. And I will give you something else."

He reached into his pocket and pulled out a box, which he handed to Stavros.

Stavros knew what it was before he even opened it, but still he lifted the top to look. It was his mother's engagement ring. He could close his eyes and remember it on her hand. He would twirl it around and around on her finger. And now it was in his hand.

"I . . . I can give this to Lindi?" he asked.

Andreas nodded. "If she will have you, she will have the ring. It's yours to do with what you want. And Stavros, I'm very fond of Lindi, as you know. I would be happy for her to join our family."

Stavros closed the box and put it on the table. He stood and went to his father. He leaned over and hugged him. "Thank you, Papa," he said softly. "I love you."

"I love you, too, Stavros," Andreas said. "And I'll miss you so much when you go. But I'm happy you will be so close to family. It gives me peace."

Chapter 35

HOW CHILDHOOD ENDS

LINDI WAS COMING HOME IN mere hours. Deanna and Mario were getting married in a small ceremony the next morning. And the day after, Lindi was leaving for Denver. He would ask her the night before she left. They would be alone. He would walk her to the playground, and they would go on the merry-go-round. He would get down on his knee, and he would ask her to be his wife. And God willing, she would say yes. And then the next morning, she would go, but it would be alright, because they would have a promise between them. They would go away, but later, they would be together forever.

She showed up at his door. He opened the door. She ran into his arms. He lifted her off her feet and squeezed. She felt so good. She smelled so good. He had been to see her at camp, but now she was in his house, in his arms. He had to savor every moment.

"Lindi," he said softly. He didn't say anything else. She took him by the hand and led him upstairs. They had the house to themselves, and Stavros suspected it was not by accident. They went into his room and closed the door. Then they came together, and they didn't part until they were satisfied. After, they still held each other tight.

"Tomorrow is a big day," Lindi said. "I can't believe our friends are getting married. It's so strange. We were so little when we met. We were Drea's age. Can you imagine? It makes me wonder, is there someone in Drea's circle of friends right now, two people, who someday will marry each other? Maybe one of them is Drea."

"Maybe," Stavros said absentmindedly. He knew the time had come. He couldn't wait any longer. He turned to her. "Lindi," he said, "I've spent a lot of time thinking of us being apart, mostly when we were apart, but even before that. And I know that being apart is what needs to happen. But I need something more. I need to know that we're gonna be together again someday and not have to be apart. Lindi," he said brushing her hair back from her forehead, "this isn't exactly how I planned to do this, but I'm gonna do it anyway."

He reached over to the drawer in his bed stand and withdrew the box. He flipped it open.

"Lindi," he said again, "will you marry me? I don't mean now, before we go away, but I mean when we're ready. When we can be together."

Lindi looked at Stavros and then at the ring. Tears came to her eyes. "Is that your mother's ring?"

Stavros nodded. "It is," he said. "My pop gave it to me. It's mine now, to use how I please. And I want to give it to you."

Tears were rolling down Lindi's cheek now. She sat up. "Stavros," she said. "My Stavros." She put her hand on his cheek.

He pulled his face back. "You're gonna say no, aren't you?"

Lindi squeezed her eyes shut as tears fell. She nodded. "Stavros, I can't," she said. "Not now. I just can't. . . ."

Stavros felt like he was going to vomit but instead he swallowed. "I don't understand. We've been together for four years. We've loved each other for so long. Why won't you marry me?"

Lindi tried to pull herself together.

"It's not that I can never marry you. It's just . . . we're going away from each other for a long time. We may see each other on the holidays and in the summer, but it's only going to be for short, intense periods of time. It's not like real life. Our lives are going to be at school now. It's not that I don't want us to be together. I do. But I can't commit to you right now for something we want to do four years from now. There's just too much that can happen between now and then. We're gonna grow, we're gonna change, and not when we're together." She paused. "Stavros, what happened to me last year, at the prom. I know it's over, and I know I wasn't hurt, and I know Torrance's master plan failed, but what if it hadn't? What if he had somehow gotten me out of the gym, and into another room? Did you ever think about that? Because I think about it every day."

Stavros nodded. "Of course I think about it," he said. "It haunts me sometimes. I think about what would have happened if I wasn't there. If I hadn't been watching. If Deanna hadn't seen—"

Lindi nodded. "Exactly. I think about that, too. But now, Stavros, you're not gonna be there. You're gonna be fifteen hundred miles away. And you're not gonna be able to watch over me. I'm gonna be on my own. So I need to be, to be on my own. I can't have that tether to you. No matter how much I love you."

Stavros shook his head. "So are you saying you want to break up?" Stavros hadn't cried for years. He tried to hold it back, but it was against his power. A tear dripped down his cheek and fell on the sheet.

"No, Stavros," Lindi said. "I'm not saying I want to break up with you. But what I am saying is that I'm not ready for us to talk about getting married. Not that I won't ever be. Just not now. Not yet."

"I don't know. It might be that being engaged is what I need, to be sure, to be able to stand us being apart. A tether, like you said. Only it wouldn't be a tether to me. It would be a lifeline."

Lindi's tears continue to fall. "I don't know what to do, Stavros. I don't want to lose you. I-I can't even think about losing you! It's too much right now. Please. Can we stop? Can we not talk about this right now?" She started to sob and covered her face with her hands.

Stavros pulled her toward him and put his arms around her. He held her tight. "Okay," he said softly. "We don't have to talk about it anymore tonight. Okay, we're okay." His tears fell on her naked shoulder and rolled down her back.

Stavros knew what was going to happen. Tomorrow, they would go to Deanna and Mario's wedding. They would celebrate with their friends.

Then tomorrow night, they would be together one more time, and they would make love. And they wouldn't talk about it. It would be the elephant in the room. And then, the next morning, Lindi would get on a big jet plane and fly away. And Stavros would get in the Volvo and go to Pittsburgh. And they would both be gone. And they would never talk about it. But their relationship would, effectively, be over.

And that's exactly what happened.

Part Five

Darlene:
Real Grown-Up Problems

"Both of my parents drove me to Ithaca," Darlene said. "They sat in the front seat. The trip took a few hours, and no one talked to me. They talked to each other a bit, but it was eerily quiet otherwise. So I ate all but one of the cookies Michelle gave me. They were good. She told me they were the same as love and I believed her."

Aspen nodded. "It was comforting for you," she said. "What happened when you got to school?"

"I was in a dorm called The Towers," Darlene said. "I was on the fifth floor. We lugged my things up to my room, and my roommate, Tina, was already there. After the tearful goodbye with my parents, I started to unpack my stuff, and I taped the pictures of my friends on the wall. I tried to talk with Tina, but she wasn't interested. I offered her the cookie. She just made a face and said she didn't eat sweets, and she especially didn't like chocolate. Then a little while later, she walked out and didn't come back for some time. It was dinnertime, and I had no one to eat with, so I went down to the cafeteria to eat by myself. And just as I'm walking in, I see Tina getting up from her table, where she had been eating, and she was all by herself. So she *would rather go to dinner by herself on the first night of school than ask me to go along with her. I knew right then we wouldn't be friends. It was a huge letdown."*

"That must have been so hard for you," Aspen said, "especially after being with such good friends for all those years. Were you able to make any friends in your freshman dorm?"

Darlene nodded. "Kind of," she said. "I made friends to go to dinner with, or to go out with, but they were never really people I thought I could confide in. I tried not to call my high school friends too much. I wanted them to think I was okay. And they had so much stuff going on, too. I didn't really want to bother them. But I did find one new friend that I couldn't have made it through without. It was a place called Dan's Cookies. They delivered warm cookies to your door. And you could also get milk, or a pint of ice cream. They had really good chocolate chip cookies. So whenever I was feeling isolated, or unloved, I'd call for cookies. And for a short time, I'd feel better."

Aspen smiled. "It was kind of like having a nice warm reminder of Michelle and her cookie love."

Darlene nodded. "That's exactly what it was. So eating cookies helped me along. And I guess, so did going to the bars with my dorm friends. A few ten-cent beers at Dimies on a Thursday night, and I didn't have any cares left to give. But there was only one problem with that."

"Just one?" Aspen responded. "What was that?"

Darlene looked at the floor. "On Fridays, I would be hungover. Not horribly, but just enough to not want to get up and go to class. So I deemed Friday classes optional. And you'll never guess what particular science lab I had on Fridays."

Chapter 36

OH, DARLENE, HOW COULD YOU?

DARLENE GOT A D IN biology. She hated biology. She hated every single little squirming cell under the microscope, even if they did come from swabbing her own cheek. She would go to class and watch the professor speak and try to understand, but her brain just wouldn't let her. And she rarely, if ever, attended labs. She did well enough on her exams to not fail, but she assumed that, because they were multiple-choice questions, it was just dumb luck.

Now it was Christmas break, and she was staying with her father while her mother was out of town. She hadn't told him about her D yet. She had only told Kim when she spoke to her over the phone on Christmas. Kim had known something was up, and she'd encouraged her to talk to her parents, to come up with a plan, but Darlene already had a plan brewing.

On the day her grades arrived, she intercepted the mail. She tore open the envelope from Ithaca College, and sure enough, bright as day, there was a big, huge D for Dummy next to the word *Biology*. She took the envelope to her room and put it in her dresser drawer.

When her father got home from work, Darlene had already made dinner for them. She had put a beer next to his plate.

"It stays cooler if you leave it in the fridge," her father said critically when he saw it. "Switch it out for a fresh one."

"Okay, Dad," Darlene said, and she replaced the beer with another one that seemed to be exactly as cold as the first.

They sat down to eat. Darlene listened attentively to her father talk about his day. She kept patiently quiet as he complained that his staff was inefficient and spent too much time socializing in the break room. She cleared off the dishes when they were done, and her father went to the living room to watch the news with a fresh can of beer.

Darlene sat in a chair, pretending to watch the news with him. She sat at the end of the cushion, the balls of her feet bouncing on the floor. When the news ended, her father looked at her.

"You're going to wear a hole in my carpet," he said. "Stop that infernal bouncing. You're making me seasick."

Darlene struggled to still her feet. "Dad, I need to talk to you about my grades."

She had Mr. Feinman's full attention now. "Grades arrived? I'd like to see them."

"I wanted to talk to you first," Darlene said, trying to keep her voice from shaking.

"What did you do, Darlene?" The volume of her father's voice started to rise. Not a good sign.

"I didn't do anything, Dad," she said. "I just didn't do well in biology. I tried, I really tried. I even went for extra help, but I still struggled. Dad, I got A's and B's in all my other classes, but I got a D in biology."

Mr. Feinman's eyes narrowed. "A D!" he exclaimed. "How is that possible? This is the one class you had to do well in, the one that really mattered! You must not have done enough! You'll take it again next term. You'll do better."

Darlene shook her head. "No, Dad, I can't," she lied. "I talked to my academic adviser. They don't offer the intro class next term. And she's from the biology department, and she says if I struggled this much with the intro class, I won't be able to make it as a biology major. She suggested very strongly that I look into other options."

"Other options?" Mr. Feinman said angrily. "What other options? You were intent on being a biologist. It's what you worked toward all these years. They want you to give all that up over one bad grade?"

Darlene felt she might be losing him with her lie. "Dad, it's not just that one grade," she said. "To be honest, biology is just not the right major for me. There's really nothing about it that makes me want to fight to stay in it. I found it confusing, and I had trouble keeping up in class. My adviser is right about me switching majors. And Mom agrees, too."

Mr. Feinman glared at her. "You talked to your mother about this already?" he asked, too quietly.

Stay strong, she told herself. She nodded. "I called her and told her. I let her know I was gonna take some other intro classes next semester and see if there's anything I was interested in learning more about. She thought that was a good idea."

Mr. Feinman was quiet for a minute. Darlene could feel her hands shaking. She sat on them. She had just thrown her mother under the bus. But she had no choice.

"I guess we have no choice," her father finally said, as if reading her mind. "Darlene, I am very disappointed in you. You failed me, and there's no excuse for that. I don't want this to ever happen again. If you get any more D's, I'm going to have to cut off your allowance. And if it keeps happening, maybe even your tuition. You don't want to be on your own, do you? Do you want to be flipping burgers for the rest of your life just to survive?"

Darlene felt a lump in her throat. She had to wait to speak. "No, Dad," she said. "I'm so sorry. I didn't mean to fail you. I really tried. I did."

"Not hard enough," Mr. Feinman scowled. "Go to your room. I can't even look at you right now. I'll tell you when it's time to come out." He went to the kitchen, most likely to get another beer.

Darlene, who was eighteen years old and in college, obediently went up to her room. And that's where she remained for the rest of the night.

Chapter 37

Going Out

DARLENE HAD THREE THINGS TO look forward to when she returned to school after winter break. First, even though she felt awful thinking it, she wouldn't have to see her father again for five months. Second, she would never have to see the inside of a biology classroom or lab again. She might have lost her father's respect and trust, but now she didn't really care. She was free from biology.

The third thing was a date with a guy named Phil. He had been in her math class the previous semester, and he had asked her out before break. She had never really noticed him before he'd approached her, but he seemed okay, at least for a date. He was kind of cute. He had dark hair and green eyes. He was thin, but not anywhere near as skinny as Charlie had been. He had a perfect nose, not too big, not too small, and proportional to the rest of his face. He was wearing a rugby shirt and acid-washed jeans the day Darlene had given him her phone number in math class, and now she was hoping he would call.

Her first day back in classes, Darlene attended Geology 105, English Lit 102, and Intro to American History. On the second day, she had Intro to Philosophy and Intro to Sociology. After attending her first sociology class, she was intrigued. She never knew there was a whole type of social science where you could learn about people and communities, and most of the research came from just observing people. Darlene was exceptionally good at watching people and learning their habits. She had to be. It was how she knew how to act when she was with them. She was excited about sociology.

There was a lot of dry reading for her classes, so she set to it right away. She liked to read in her room, but sometimes, especially when Tina was around and overtly ignoring her, she would go to the study centers on campus. The night the phone call came was a reading-at-home night. She was reading a chapter in a textbook about the philosophy of religion. She sometimes had to read each sentence twice to understand the concepts better, but it really wasn't as dull as she had thought it would be.

She picked up the phone on the first ring. "Hello?" she said, expecting to hear the voice of either Kim or her mother.

"Darlene?" a male voice on the other end asked tentatively.

"Yes?" she answered timidly.

"Hi, it's Phil Roth, from math last semester. How are you?"

Darlene hesitated. "Phil Roth?" she asked. "Like the author of 'Portnoy's Complaint?'"

Phil laughed. "Yes, just the same," he said. "But he wrote that book in 1969, and I was born in '68, so there was no way my parents could know. But trust me, all of my English teachers all through school thought it was hilarious."

"Oh, okay," Darlene said. "How was your break?"

"Not bad," Phil said. "It was weird having Chanukah start so late this year, the day after Christmas."

Darlene almost gasped. "I celebrated Chanukah with my dad this year," she said. "I didn't know you were Jewish!"

Phil laughed. "Roth?" he said. "It's almost as obvious as Feinman."

"Yeah, but my mom isn't Jewish," Darlene said, "so technically I'm half Jewish, and some people don't even consider me Jewish."

"Huh," Phil said. "As my grandfather says, 'A jew is a jew is a jew.' But whatever. Do you wanna go out this weekend?"

No beating around the bush with this guy. Phil was right on task. "Uh, sure," Darlene said. "What did you have in mind?"

"Some of us are going to Micawber's Tavern on Saturday night. Have you been there?"

"No," Darlene said, "but I don't have a fake ID or anything. It's pretty easy to get away with at Dimies, but I'm not sure I could get in anywhere else."

"Oh, Dimies," Phil said. "I went there once. Ten-cent drafts on Thursday nights. Terrible beer. You get what you pay for. But Micawber's does hand-stamping for under or over twenty-one, so you can get in. I have a good fake ID. I could probably get you drinks if you wanted."

Darlene felt a little unsure about going drinking on a first date, but she didn't want him to think she wasn't interested. "Uh . . . okay, I guess we could do that."

"Great!" Phil responded. "We'll probably go around nine. Want to meet us there, or should we come by to get you?"

"I . . . would prefer it if you came to get me," Darlene said. "I'm in West Towers."

"Okay, great," Phil said. "I'm in Upper Quads. I'll just swing over to get you in your lobby at about eight forty-five?"

"Okay," Darlene said. "That will be great!"

When she hung up the phone, she immediately called Kim. "I have a date on Saturday!" She knew this would make Kim happy.

"Oh, I'm so happy for you!" Kim exclaimed. "The guy from math class that you barely told me about?"

"Yes, his name is Phil. I would have told you more, but I didn't know anything yet. But we're going to a tavern. It may be noisy, but it should be fun."

"Ugh, yeah, noisy," Kim agreed. "Hard to have a conversation. But it's a start anyway." Kim grilled her on the details she did have about Phil. What does he look like? Is he cute? How tall is he? Does he seem nice? Then Darlene promised she would call Kim back on Sunday to let her know how the date went.

Just as Darlene got off the phone, Tina came in and silently sat on her bed, holding a book. She didn't say hello. Darlene tried to continue with her philosophy chapter, but she was too aware of the awkward silence between her and her roommate to be able to concentrate. She threw her textbooks into her backpack and went to study in the lounge.

Chapter 38

STAY THE NIGHT

DARLENE'S EXCITEMENT WAS MORE LIKE nervous energy. Her last real date had been the one where she broke up with Charlie and ended up sobbing and terrified on her bed. This was a whole new person, a whole new situation. But she hadn't really had much time to develop a crush, or any type of opinion yet about Phil like she had about Charlie before their first date. She was going to have to use their dates to get to know him and see if there was any chemistry.

But this was seriously scary, because while Darlene was getting to know Phil, he would be getting to know her, too. How would she even know how to act in front of him? She wished they had classes in things like this in college. That, and how to budget her money so she had enough left over for her phone bill every month.

She had no one to help her pick out her clothes and do her makeup, so she had to trust her own judgment. She almost laughed out loud when that thought crossed her mind. It was January, and they would be walking, so she needed to dress warm. She had learned her lesson about that on her skating date. She chose a long navy-blue sweater with a white turtleneck. She put on a denim skirt that reached her ankles with a long slit up the back. She fastened a wide white belt around her waist and puffed out her sweater. She blew back her wet bangs with her round hairbrush and hairdryer and sprayed them heavily with Aqua Net. Then it was time to tackle her makeup.

She lugged her makeup bag to the bathroom so she could look in the big mirror. There were a few other girls in there taking showers or fixing their hair and makeup for a night out. They all looked up at her as she walked in.

"Wow, Darlene, you look nice tonight," her next-door neighbor Paula told her. "I've never seen you in anything but jeans. Got a hot date?"

Darlene smiled as she pulled out her eyeliner. "I do," she said. She turned to the mirror and started to draw a thick line around her eye.

"Awesome," Paula said. "Where are you heading?"

"We're going to Micawber's," Darlene replied.

"Wow," Paula said, turning to look at her. "That's where the upperclassmen and townies hang out. I don't even think they have sawdust on the floor. Fancy!"

Darlene laughed but thought to herself that she might be dressed too young for Micawber's. But it was too late now. She was meeting Phil in the lobby in fifteen minutes. Well, she was eighteen. She might as well look the part.

She packed up her makeup and said goodbye to the girls. Then she went back to her room to get her coat and gloves.

She got to the lobby at 8:40 and stood by the door. At 8:50, Phil still wasn't there, but that was okay, it wasn't too late. Nine o'clock. Now she was getting worried he wasn't coming. At 9:05, she replayed their conversation in her head. They did say they were going to meet in the lobby, right? Not at the Tavern. Yes, she was sure.

There was a guy sitting behind a table checking student IDs when students walked in to make sure they belonged there. He'd taken his seat at nine. He was watching Darlene. She felt conspicuous. She started pacing around the lobby.

"You okay?" the guy asked.

Darlene nodded. "Just waiting for someone."

The guy shook his head. "Looks like you might have been stood up."

Darlene shrugged. "I'll give him five more minutes."

Phil arrived in six.

"Sorry," he said. "I got caught up watching a basketball game. I tried to call but you must have already come down. C'mon, my friends are waiting outside." He turned to walk back outside.

The security guy looked at Darlene, and she looked back. "First date?" he asked. She nodded. "Ever heard of a red flag?"

Darlene shook her head. "Gotta go," she said. "Bye." She pushed the door open and went out. Phil was standing there with two other boys and one girl.

"This is Mark, Kevin, and Grace," Phil said. "They live in my dorm. This is Darlene." They all looked at her and smiled. Darlene smiled back.

They walked to the Commons and lined up at the door for their ID checks. The three boys got in with red stamps on their hands to signify they were twenty-one and over, and Darlene and Grace were stamped blue for underage. The Tavern was crowded but not overcrowded. The music was loud. Mark pushed through the other patrons and found them a place to sit at a large, shared table. Darlene sat down, and Grace took a seat across from her. The boys went to get some beer.

Grace looked up at Darlene. "So how do you know Phil?"

Darlene stopped herself from saying that she really didn't know Phil. "We met in math class last semester. But this is our first time, like, hanging out."

Grace nodded. "He's really into sports. Pro sports, college sports, intra-mural sports."

"What kind of sports?" Darlene asked. "Football? Basketball?"

Grace nodded. "Yeah, both of those. And everything else. Ithaca Bombers, Cornell Big Red, New York Mets, New York Giants . . . several others. I think he hears cheers somewhere, and he just follows them to the game, whatever it is."

"Does he play anything?" Darlene asked. She knew almost nothing about sports. She never had to. Sally had all the sports knowledge in high school and usually explained what was going on during school games.

"No, not really," Grace said. "Well, we all play volleyball on an intra-mural dorm team, but it's the kind of thing where you drink beer as you play, so it doesn't really matter if you're any good. Do you like sports?"

Darlene shrugged. "They're okay. I like Boston teams. I've been to a few Red Sox games."

"Oh, your poor Red Sox," Grace said, shaking her head. "Our Mets kicked their asses in the World Series. Pretty embarrassing."

Darlene nodded. She had no idea who had played in the World Series, let alone who had won. At least now she knew in case Phil said something. Eyes and ears.

The boys came back with a pitcher of beer and five glasses. They passed out the glasses, and Phil poured some beer into Darlene's glass. "This is much better than the stuff you'll get at Dimies," he said with a grin.

Darlene smiled and took a sip. To her, it tasted exactly like the beer at Dimies. Phil was watching her expectantly. She nodded. "Yeah, it's good," she said.

Phil nodded. "So where are you from?"

"Eastboro, Massachusetts," she said. "About sixty miles from Boston."

"I've heard of Eastboro," Phil said. "It's not too far from the Centrum. Have you gone to concerts there?"

Darlene nodded. "I've seen a bunch. I saw Journey there a few years ago. That was probably the best one."

"Yeah," Phil said with approval. "Journey's pretty cool. You a Red Sox fan?"

"Yeah," Darlene said. She used the information she had gleaned from Grace. "I was pretty upset about them losing the World Series to the Mets."

Phil practically glowed. "Yeah. I'm from Long Island. I'm a Mets fan. It was too bad about what happened to Bill Buckner, though. That guy's never gonna live that down."

Darlene panicked. She had no idea who Bill Buckner was. She took a shot in the dark. "Yeah, I know," she said. "Too bad." She made a mental note to call Sally the next day and ask who the hell Bill Buckner was. But she seemed to have passed the test for now. Phil moved on to another line of conversation.

After they'd all had their fill at the Tavern, they started their walk home. They dropped the others off at their dorm, and then Phil walked Darlene back to her dorm. They showed their student IDs to the guy at the door, who gave Darlene a look. She turned away. They took the elevator to the fifth floor. Phil walked her to her room. For once, Darlene was hoping that Tina would be there. She'd had a few beers at the Tavern, and she was feeling both tipsy and groggy. She knew this was not a good combination.

She unlocked the door and knew instantly that Tina was not there. She had no idea where Tina ever went. She never told her. Sometimes she was gone for days. Phil looked around the room.

"Small room," he said. "Your roommate's not here. Can I come in?"

Darlene hesitated, then nodded. They stepped through the door. There was no place to sit but on the bed. They both took their jackets off. Phil looked Darlene up and down.

"You look really nice tonight," he said. "You were always so casual in class. I didn't know you had a body under there."

Darlene felt flushed. She wasn't used to compliments like this from a boy. Charlie had been stingy with his praise. "Thanks," she said shyly.

Phil cupped her chin with his hand and lifted her face slightly. Then he leaned in for a kiss. Darlene waited for her cue of what to do. But she didn't need it. Phil's kiss was wonderful. Just the right pressure, just the right placement, and no tongue in her mouth. She responded instinctively and didn't have to pull away. For the first time, she felt a tingling throughout her whole body and felt herself pull closer to Phil. He held her close with his arms around her waist, and she put her arms around him. The longer they kissed, the closer they got.

A little while later, Phil pulled away. "Are you on the pill?"

Darlene froze. "No," she said. "Phil . . ." She hesitated. "I-I've never had . . . sex before. I'm not ready for that. Not yet. Just give me some time to get used to the idea, okay? I'm not saying I won't, but just not tonight." She braced herself for his response. She hoped he wouldn't expect her to do . . . something else.

Phil nodded. "No, I get it," he said. "First date. We need to get to know each other better first anyway. That's okay." He looked at his watch. "But I'm gonna head out now. I'm going to a game at Cornell tomorrow, and I want to get up early to get ready and head up there. So I'll call you. Maybe we can get together next weekend?"

Darlene was disappointed. She was enjoying their kissing. She didn't want it to stop. If they'd had sex, he wouldn't be leaving so soon. But she couldn't. Not yet. She really wasn't ready, and she knew that she had to be. Even the old Charlie voice in her head was back, telling her to wait. But she wanted him to stay.

"You can stay here with me if you want," she said. "My roommate's never here. You could just stay and then leave early in the morning."

Phil smiled but still got up. "Thanks," he said, "but I think I'll just go. I had fun tonight. Thanks for coming out with me."

They walked to the door, and Phil gave her one last kiss. Darlene found herself giving him a small nibble on his lower lip. Then they said goodbye, and Phil was gone.

The Charlie person in her head was back. She couldn't ignore it. Now it wanted to make Phil happy, and it felt that Darlene had failed.

Next time, she thought. *I'll do whatever he wants next time. Then he'll stay. I'll make him stay. And then, maybe, he'll be happy. And then I'll be happy.*

"So the guy in the dorm asked you about red flags, but you didn't know what they were?" Aspen asked kindly.

Darlene shook her head. "No, I thought it might be a sports thing or something. I wasn't sure what he was saying, or how it applied to me."

"You know what it means now?" Aspen asked.

"Y-yeah," Darlene responded. "I mean, I guess so. But I never saw anything. Nothing that warned me. I mean, after the fact, I could see that maybe something didn't feel right, but it always felt like something that I was doing wrong. I always blamed myself for just not acting right, or doing enough to make the guy happy. I made them angry."

"Darlene," Aspen said inquisitively, "do you think you're a good person? I mean, basically, do you think you mean well?"

"Well, yeah," Darlene replied. "I mean, I've spent most of my life trying to make other people happy. That's gotta count for something."

Aspen nodded. "I agree," she said. "I think you're a good person. You focus so much on others, and you care greatly for your friends. So why do you think it was that the men in your life always got so angry? You were trying to make them happy."

Darlene squirmed in her seat. "Because I didn't try hard enough," she said meekly. "I couldn't do the right things."

"Darlene," Aspen said. "Think about that, and think about what you've told me about your dad, Charlie, and Phil. Was it really that you didn't try hard enough?"

Darlene contemplated. Then she slouched in her chair, and tears ran down her cheek. "No," she said. "I tried as hard as I could. But it didn't matter. No matter what I did, they would get angry at me. And I'd end up doing things I didn't want to do. But nothing I did could change that."

"Do you think that you were responsible for their anger?" Aspen asked.

Darlene took a tissue from the box on the table and dabbed at her eyes. "Yes . . . no? I don't know. Why couldn't they see that I was trying? Why didn't it work?"

Aspen nodded. "Darlene, there were signs. Signs that you couldn't see. You couldn't see the signs because they were a normal part of everyday life with your father. These are the signs that most people see as red flags."

Darlene nodded. "So if you see a red flag, it's some kind of warning."

"Yes," Aspen confirmed. "For most people, if they see red flags, they might reconsider being involved with someone. Let's talk about some red flags that might have been there with Charlie. Can you think of anything?"

"Um, I'm not sure," Darlene admitted.

"That's okay. I'll get us started from what you told me." Aspen looked back at her notes. "The first time you got together with him, when you went skating, you did a twirl for him. How did he respond?"

"He said something about it not being good enough for the Olympics."

Aspen nodded. "And how did that make you feel?"

Darlene lowered her head. "Not so good," she said. "I wanted him to say something nice. He said it was good, but then he had to go and say something not so nice and ruin it. He could have stopped with the nice."

"But he didn't," Aspen said.

Darlene shook her head. "No, he didn't. Red flag?" Aspen nodded. "He did a few other things that day that made me feel less than great. He commented on my clothes, and my lack of stamina. Then he just skated away when I got tired and wanted to stop."

"Did you have a good time that day?" Aspen asked.

Darlene sighed. "I thought I did. I told my friends I did. But it really wasn't that great."

"That's another red flag," Aspen said. "Lying to your friends about how you felt with Charlie and making them think it went well. A lot of girls would have decided not to see someone again after not having such a good time. Why did you decide to see Charlie again?"

"I blamed myself," Darlene said. "I could have spun better. I could have dressed warmer. I could have lasted longer. . . ."

"Before your date, did you plan out how you would dress, and what you would do with Charlie, like showing him a twirl?"

"Exhaustively," Darlene admitted.

"And still these things weren't enough," Aspen said gently. "So why did you agree to see Charlie again?"

"I . . . I didn't want to let everyone down," Darlene said. "I wanted every-one to like me, to be happy for me. And Michelle had met Joey, and I wanted to experience all of this with her, and I wanted my first kiss. And I didn't want Charlie to feel like I wasted his time."

"Okay," Aspen said. "I don't hear anywhere in there where you said you went out with Charlie again because you liked him, you were attracted to him, or wanted to get to know him better."

Darlene sat with the silence for several seconds. "Yeah," she said. "I didn't say anything about that, did I? I don't know. I'm not sure if I liked him. I think I was attracted to him at first, but then when he kissed me . . ." She looked at Aspen. "Another red flag?" Aspen nodded.

"Let me ask you this, Darlene," Aspen said, leaning in closer. "Was there ever any time, in all your dates with Charlie, that you, not Charlie, made any decisions on what you would do that night, or who you would do it with?"

"Well, no, not really," Darlene answered. "Oh! I just thought of another red flag! The action movie! He didn't like sci-fi. I liked sci-fi. He ignored that I wanted to see Starman, *and the movie he chose made me anxious. But I didn't want him to have a bad time,"*

"But you had a bad time," Aspen pointed out.

"Yeah, I did," Darlene said sadly.

"So why did you keep going out with him?"

"You keep asking me that," Darlene said. "I'm not sure why. I was scared not to. I don't know. It didn't really feel wrong, at least at first. It was familiar."

"How was it familiar?" Aspen asked.

Darlene didn't want to say it out loud. Everything in her body and mind told her to shut up. But she pushed through. "He treated me like my dad treated me," she said. "He made me feel like I was never good enough, and that it was all my fault. And I ate it up. It was who I was. I was the girl who tried to be good but could never be good enough. And Charlie just confirmed that for me. I deserved everything he said. I deserved it all." She paused. "But I didn't deserve what happened to me at prom," she said firmly. "He took it too far. He crossed a line. And when he looked like he was gonna shove me in the car when I broke up with him—my father would never hurt me like that. It was enough. That's when I knew it was over."

"So you do have a line that you're not willing to let anyone cross," Aspen observed.

Darlene nodded. "Yes. Apparently people can say whatever the hell they want to me. But somehow, I know my body belongs to me. That must be because of my mother. She's a strong woman. She would never let anyone mess with her that way. I think that's one of the reasons I've always wanted her to think I'm okay. I don't want her to know I'm not as strong as she is."

"Why are you so sure your mother is so strong?" Aspen asked.

"Because," Darlene said confidently, "she knew how to handle my father. And how to make him go away."

"I see," Aspen said. "Darlene, I'd like to keep working on where you draw that line. Maybe we can see if we can move it back, just a little, and help you to recognize those red flags while they're occurring. I'm going to give you a little homework assignment for next week. I want you to look back on your relationship with Phil. And I want you to consider what could have been red flags. And I want you to write them down. And next week, let's go over them together and talk about the choices you made after seeing, but not recognizing, the red flags. Does that sound okay?"

Darlene nodded. "I think I can do that."

Chapter 39

I Just Don't Like That

DARLENE AND PHIL HAD BEEN seeing each other for a few weeks, but they still hadn't had sex. Darlene couldn't bring herself to get to that point. They would kiss and touch in her bed until it got to that moment, and she just couldn't do it. Then he would leave. She didn't understand why he didn't want to stay. She just wanted him to be there with her. She longed to feel what that was like to sleep beside a boy, a man, all night. They were in college. They had no curfew. He could do what he wanted. And what he wanted was to leave. Darlene felt that if they spent more time together, maybe she would feel more ready. But it just wasn't happening.

It was February 28, and it was Kim's nineteenth birthday. Darlene wanted to talk to Kim, to ask her what she was doing wrong and why Phil wouldn't stay. She called her as soon as the time difference allowed, only to find out that Kim was sick. Really sick. Sick enough that her birthday was actually canceled. Carl couldn't talk because he had to take care of her. It was all Darlene could do to hold herself back from offering to fly out to take care of Kim herself. But she held back. Carl was plenty capable of looking out for his girlfriend.

Darlene really wanted to talk, though. She tried to call Michelle, but the phone just kept ringing and ringing. She thought about calling Sally, but Sally couldn't help her. James would never have left her side, even if she didn't want to have sex. James was one in a million. She even thought of calling Traci, but she hadn't spoken to her for a year and a half. They had only been writing letters. And Traci had no insight into Darlene anyway. She only saw a brick wall when she looked at her soul.

Darlene sat on her bed and pulled her knees up to her chest. She felt so lonely and alone.

When the phone rang, she dove for it. It was Phil. "I just came from playing volleyball," he said. "I was on fire tonight. You should have seen my serve. And I got one spike. We didn't win, but I don't care. I'm feeling all hyped up. I wanna take you out to dinner. Can you be ready in an hour?"

Darlene jumped up from her bed. "Yes. I'll be ready. Meet you in the lobby?"

She ran to the shower, washed her hair, and got dressed and made up with time to spare. She was so grateful that Phil had called. It was as if he somehow knew she was feeling down and needed cheering up. She made a decision.

Tonight, she thought, *I'll let him do whatever he wants. I'll let him see how much it means to me when he calls me, when he takes me out. I'll let him know that I appreciate him. And then he'll stay with me. That's all I want.*

She giggled. She had made up her mind. She was determined to lose her virginity that night.

Phil was ten minutes late, but she didn't care. He escorted her to the bus and paid her fare. They were going into town. She was excited.

"Where are we going?" Darlene asked.

Phil smiled. "Oh, there's this new restaurant I went to with my dorm friends a couple weeks ago," he said. "You'll love it. It's really cool. It's called Nori and Nigiri. It's a sushi bar."

Darlene instantly felt her face go pale. "Oh, okay," she said, instantly ditching her vow to never have sushi again.

Phil looked at her expectantly. "You like sushi, don't you?"

Darlene didn't want to upset him. This was going to be their night! She wanted it to go well. So she nodded. "Yeah. I've only had it once. Maybe you can help me order. I can try whatever you like."

Phil's grin reappeared. "Cool. They have really good California rolls.

They're good for beginners because they don't have raw fish. You'll like those."

Darlene nodded. She made sure to keep the smile on her face. Her stomach was already grumbling. She didn't know how she would get through dinner without gagging.

When they walked into the sushi bar, the smell hit Darlene as if she had been sprayed point-blank with a hose full of rotten fish parts. She pretended to cough and breathed into her hand. Phil didn't seem to smell it.

They sat at the bar, and Phil looked excitedly at the conveyor belt. Darlene had never seen anything like it before. She could see why Phil thought it was cool. It went around the whole bar, carrying little colorful plates covered with colorful sushi rolls. There were some other items, but Darlene had no idea what they were. Phil watched and grabbed specific plates off the belt as they went by. He put one in front of Darlene, and she looked at it. It looked like the sushi she'd had last time. He put two other plates next to the first. One looked like deep-fried shrimp.

"I think that's enough," Darlene said. She didn't want to have to choke down any more than three plates of sushi.

Phil pointed. "That's tempura. It's basically deep-fried shrimp. Then there's a California roll, and this is tuna maki."

Darlene didn't think tuna would be too bad. She tried the tempura first. It was okay, but the shrimp tasted and looked different than she was used to. Then she took a bite of the tuna roll. She suppressed a gag. This wasn't tuna! It was some sort of pink slime! She chewed and tasted salt. Her tongue tried to reject the flavor, but she forced herself to swallow it down and then took a gulp of water. Phil was thoroughly enjoying his sushi. *Maybe it's a New York thing*, Darlene thought.

"Try dipping the tuna in the wasabi," Phil said, pointing to a small container of green sauce.

"Oh, no," Darlene said. "I tried that last time. It burned the hell out of my mouth."

Phil laughed. "Wimp," he said. "Okay, try it with just soy sauce then. Try the California roll. It doesn't have fish, just avocado."

Darlene dipped the California roll into the soy sauce and took a bite. She smiled and nodded. But she hated it. It wasn't just the fish. It was the seaweed. And something in the rice. And it was just so darn salty! She forced the rest of her food down and drank three glasses of water. When it was time to leave, she burst out of the restaurant and took deep gulps of cold fresh air. Phil, who was walking behind her, took no notice.

The bus ride back to campus was bumpy, more bumpy than usual. And at every turn, Darlene felt waves of nausea. Phil talked about his volleyball game, and the upcoming NCAA playoffs. Darlene just kept nodding. She had to make it back to her room. She willed herself to be okay. But she had never felt such motion sickness in all her life.

When they got back to her dorm, she invited Phil up to her room. Then she told him she needed to go brush her teeth. She grabbed her bathroom bag and ran down the hall. She barely made it to the toilet before she vomited up her entire dinner and the three cups of water. She stayed where she was for a few minutes to make sure she was done. Finally, she got back to her feet and made her way to the sink to brush her teeth. Her neighbor Paula was there removing her makeup.

"Are you okay, Darlene?" she said. "Did you have a few too many with dinner?"

Darlene shook her head. "Sushi," she said as she put toothpaste on her brush. "I don't like it at all. I hate it. I ate it anyway."

Paula looked at her with confusion. "No, Darlene, don't do that. You don't want to get sick on sushi again. I'm so sorry. Why didn't you get something else?"

Darlene spit out her toothpaste and rinsed her mouth. "Phil wanted sushi. We got sushi."

Paula shook her head. "You're a better girlfriend than I'd ever be." She waved and walked out to the hallway.

Darlene washed her face. *I'm a good girlfriend*, she thought. *I make sacrifices. That's gotta be worth something.*

When she got back to her door, she put on a happy smile and turned the knob. Phil was sitting on the bed. He smiled at her. Darlene walked over to him. He had no idea how lucky he was about to get.

Darlene kicked off her shoes, maintaining eye contact with Phil. When she got to the bed, she sat down next to him, and they started to kiss. His mouth tasted like mint gum and sushi. She ignored it. She put her arms around him and pulled him closer. He ran his hands up and down her back and then reached for her front. She let him. He made his way up her shirt.

She didn't stop him. Her heart was pounding. She wanted it to go on, but she also wanted it to stop. No, she wanted this. She pulled away.

"Phil," she said softly. "Do you have a condom?"

Phil's eyes opened wider, and his breathing got faster. "Yes," he said. "I always bring a condom when I come to see you. I always hope—"

Darlene kissed him again. He worked her shirt up and pulled it over her head, and then she did the same for him. Then they helped each other out of their pants. Now they were just in their underwear. Darlene still felt nauseated from dinner, but she pushed past it. Phil worked the latch on her bra, and it popped open and slid it off. He touched her. She felt electric. Then he completely undressed her and looked her over.

"You are so beautiful," he whispered in her ear. She kissed his neck and then his lips. She hoped he didn't ask her to do the other thing . . . but he didn't. He pulled off his own briefs, and then laid her back on the small bed. He kissed her and worked her legs apart with his knee.

"What about the condom?" Darlene asked.

"I'll get it," Phil breathed. "In a second. As long as I have it in the end . . ." He entered her and started to move.

Darlene felt a sharp stabbing pain, and then it subsided. She moaned. He kept moving. Then he stopped. He pulled out and grabbed his jeans. He extracted the condom from his wallet and put it on. Then he came back to her and started again. Darlene felt stinging, but then she experienced something she had never felt before. It was a rush, a sensation of pleasure, making her want more. She moved with him, to try to make it last, to make it more intense, and then it was. She held her hands fast behind his neck and looked in his eyes. Then his eyes rolled back and he shut them tight, and then he made noises in the back of his throat, and he called out to her. It was powerful. Darlene fell back. Phil fell on top of her. They both panted.

Phil kissed her, then kissed her neck. "Thank you," he said. "Thank you for trusting me, for letting me do that. I know it was your first time. Are you okay?"

Darlene nodded. "Yeah," she said. "I'm good. Thank you. Yeah, that was nice."

Phil nodded. "Yeah. It was." He rolled off of her and lay next to her. They stayed that way for a few minutes. Then Phil checked his watch.

"Damn. I didn't realize how late it was." He kissed her one more time, then got out of bed.

Darlene was baffled. "You're not gonna stay with me? I thought you'd want to stay if we . . . you know . . ."

Phil pulled on his underwear and his jeans and started to buckle his belt. "No, I can't," he said. "I have to get up early tomorrow. I meet Grace for breakfast at the Commons on Sundays. She gets up early, so I do, too."

"Grace?" Darlene asked. "Grace from the Tavern? You meet her for breakfast on Sundays? Every Sunday?" She got her pajama top out from under her pillow and slid it over her head. She didn't want to be naked anymore. "Can't you reschedule this one time?"

Phil shook his head. "No, I already confirmed that I'd meet her. I don't want to go back on my word." He put on his shirt.

Darlene sat silently for a moment. "So . . ." she started. "What's the story with you and Grace?"

Phil pulled on his shoes. "We met at orientation. And then we found out she lived on the floor below mine. We've been friends since the first day I got here."

"Did you . . . did the two of you ever . . ." Darlene couldn't finish the sentence.

Phil shrugged. "Yeah, we did," he admitted. "A few times, last semester. But we don't anymore. It was never anything, really. Just sex."

"Just sex," Darlene repeated quietly.

Phil sat down and put his arm around her shoulder. "Yeah, we're just friends," he told her. "You've got nothing to worry about." He reached over and gave her a long kiss. "So I'll call you soon?" He stood and put on his jacket.

Darlene didn't stand up. "Oh, okay. I guess I'll talk to you soon."

"Bye, Darlene. Sleep well." Then Phil was gone.

Just friends, Darlene thought. *Just friends who have had sex. A few times. No big deal. But he couldn't stay with me because he needs to sleep so he can meet her early in the morning. Like he does every Sunday. I wanted him to stay. I thought if I gave him what he wanted, he would stay. It was my first time. He knew it. But he didn't stay.*

She got up, locked her door, turned off her light, and crawled into bed. Then she started to cry.

Chapter 40

Same Old Song and Dance

THEY KEPT UP THIS PATTERN for weeks. They would go out, alone or with Phil's friends, then go back to Darlene's room, have sex, and then Phil would leave. And he couldn't stay over on any other night either. Friday night was friend night, and Sunday was a school night—there was just no bargaining. Phil was a busy guy. He would occasionally meet her for lunch in the student center during the week, but otherwise, it was Saturday night. Date night.

Darlene figured that this was just what it was like. At least Phil was nice to her. He didn't hit her, or verbally abuse her, or cheat on her. Maybe that's all that mattered. But she felt lonely. And she hadn't seen Tina in weeks.

In mid-March, she got a visit from the Resident Adviser, Jennifer. She sat on her bed beside her and looked at her sympathetically.

"Tina won't be coming back," she said, and she took Darlene's hands. "I can't tell you the details, but she's really sick. She's been in the hospital, and her parents have decided to withdraw her from school. I don't know if the two of you talked at all . . ."

Darlene shook her head.

"Darlene, like I said, I can't really say anything, but I just want to let you know, if anything, well, strange or weird happened while she was here, it had nothing to do with you, okay? Tina's really ill, and hopefully she'll start getting better now that she's getting treatment."

"So will I get another roommate?" Darlene asked.

Jennifer shook her head. "No, it's so late in the year now. It's too late to put anyone in here. So you have a single now. Until next year. Will you be okay in here by yourself?"

Darlene shrugged. "I've been okay so far," she lied. "Not much I can do about it anyway."

Jennifer nodded and squeezed her hand. "Let me know if you need anything, Darlene. You can always just knock."

"Thanks, Jennifer."

Darlene sat on her bed with her hands folded across her lap. She knew what Jennifer was trying to tell her. Tina had a mental illness. She must have had a breakdown when she came to college. All this time, Tina was struggling. She would be gone for days. Where did she even go? Darlene felt sorry for her. Then she wondered how far she was from a breakdown herself. Maybe she wasn't so different from Tina. Maybe she just hid it better. An old quote came into her head, "There but for the grace of God go I." But what kind of grace would let something like that happen to Tina? Who chose who got the grace of God and who didn't? It was very confusing.

The semester went on, and now Darlene expected to be alone. She talked to people in class, she sometimes went out with her dorm friends on Thursday nights, and she saw Phil on Saturday nights. It wasn't ideal, but it was her life.

It was mid-April. One afternoon, Darlene was working on her sociology paper. She loved sociology. It was so interesting. She wanted to learn more. It was a kind of science. Her father would call it a "soft science." But maybe if she majored in sociology, it would be close enough to being a scientist. She would be a scientist, and she would still be surrounded by people. And she would be happy. Traci had been spot on. Darlene was glad.

The phone rang. It was Kim. They made brief small talk. Then Kim said something that would change their lives forever: Kim was pregnant! Darlene couldn't believe it. Kim, a mom? And Carl, a dad? This was humongous news! They talked for a while, and she determined that Kim was happy. That's all Darlene wanted for her. She would have Carl's baby. Oh my God.

Darlene would be going home at the end of the semester. She would see all her friends except Kim and Carl. That would be hard. They would all want to talk about Kim and Carl's baby. It would be especially difficult to not be with Kim while she went through her pregnancy. It actually made Darlene's stomach hurt to think about it. Her stomach hurt kind of bad. There were waves of pain. Maybe it wasn't because of Kim and Carl.

She ran to the bathroom. She couldn't go. It didn't help. She got ready for bed and crawled under the sheets. She tried to lie on her right side, then her left. It didn't make the pain go away. This was worse than the sushi. She got up and vomited into her wastebasket. The pain abated for a few minutes, but then it came back. It was on her right side. Maybe she had appendicitis. Scared, she called her mother.

"Mom, I don't know what to do," she moaned. "My stomach hurts so much. It's actually below my stomach. On the right. What should I do?"

Her mother paused. "I don't know, doll," she said. "Should you go to the infirmary?"

"Maybe," Darlene replied. She held her hand to her belly. It was just getting worse. "How do I get there, Mom? It hurts too bad to walk there."

"Doll," her mother said urgently, "go get someone. A neighbor or your RA. Tell them what's happening. Have them get you where you need to go. Please, Darlene, do it now." Darlene could tell her mother was worried. She might have even been crying. Darlene started to cry, too.

"Okay, Mom, I'll go get the RA. I'll call you back."

"Doll baby," Mrs. Feinman said, "should I come out there?"

Darlene tried not to vomit again. She didn't think her mother needed to come. But she gave in to her pain. "Please come, Mom," she pleaded.

"I'll grab a bag," her mother said. "I'll leave in fifteen minutes."

"Okay, Mom, thanks," Darlene said. She had to go. Otherwise, she wouldn't make it to the RA's room. "I've got to go, Mom. Find an RA when you get here, okay? They'll know where to find me. I love you so much, Mom." She was scared her mother wouldn't make it on time. But in time for what?

"Go, baby. I love you, too." She hung up.

Darlene half walked, half crawled to the end of the hall and pounded on Jennifer's door. Then she slid down the wall to the floor.

Jennifer opened the door.

"Oh, my God, Darlene, are you okay?"

Darlene was getting weak from the pain. "No," she said. "It hurts." She pointed to her belly. Then she closed her eyes.

She could hear Jennifer running back into her room and calling the emergency number and then the main dorm desk. She came back out and sat next to Darlene on the floor. "Help will be here soon, sweetie," she said softly. "I'll go with you. You'll be okay."

Darlene nodded and tried to smile. She hoped she wasn't interrupting something important. Jennifer probably had studying to do.

Soon, the elevator opened, and two paramedics came in with a stretcher. Other girls started to come out of their rooms to see what was going on. "Oh, my God, Darlene," Paula cried out, coming toward her. "Are you okay? Did she eat some sushi? Sushi makes her really sick!"

The paramedics came toward her and stretched her out on the floor. Darlene tried to curl back up. "It hurts," she moaned. The paramedics asked her questions about her health and allergies and started an IV. They took her vitals. They spoke over a radio. After what felt like an eternity, they finally got her on the stretcher, strapped her down, and wheeled her to the elevator. She could hear her floormates calling out their best wishes. She was loaded into an ambulance and Jennifer sat down beside her and held her hand.

"This seems like a big fuss for a stomachache," Darlene groaned. "I was just gonna go to the infirmary."

Jennifer shook her head. "No, Darlene," she said. "This is more than the infirmary can manage. They would have just called an ambulance for you." She paused. "I'll need to call your parents," she said.

"No, no," Darlene said. "I called my mom already. She's coming. She'll be here in a few hours. Please don't call my dad, okay? But watch out for my mom. Barbara Feinman." She closed her eyes. She was losing energy. She felt like she was going to pass out.

"Stay with me, Darlene," the paramedic urged. "We're almost there. You're gonna get help. Just keep talking, okay?"

Darlene nodded. "Okay," she said. She looked at Jennifer. "Kim's pregnant," she said. "Can you believe it?"

"Who's Kim?" Jennifer asked.

"She's my baby. I mean, my baby friend. My friend since babies. You know. She's having Carl's baby in California."

"Is that good?" Jennifer asked.

Tears dripped from the corners of Darlene's eyes. "She should come home," Darlene said. "She needs me. I need her. I need Michelle. Where's my mom?"

Jennifer squeezed her hand. "She's on her way, Darlene."

"We're here, Darlene," the paramedic said. "Get ready for us to move you out. You might get a bit jostled, but we'll try to give you a smooth ride. They'll take care of your pain real soon."

And then Darlene was in the emergency room. Her shirt was taken off, her pants were pulled down, and hands were on her abdomen. Doctors and nurses asked her personal questions about her health, and even asked if she had overdosed on alcohol or drugs. They drew blood. Then they pumped something into her IV. And suddenly her body felt heavy and light at the same time, and her pain, although still there, felt detached, like it belonged to someone else.

"Darlene," she heard someone say. "Darlene, we're going to take you down for some scans now, okay? You still with us? You feeling sleepy? Okay, Joe's gonna wheel you down, and they'll take some pictures, and we'll see what's going on with you. Then we'll do what we can to fix you up and make you feel better."

"I need to finish my sociology paper," Darlene said weakly. "It's about people."

"It's okay, Darlene, the paper can wait for now," the voice said. "You're in good hands. We'll see you in a bit."

Darlene could sense a change in the lighting overhead, and she could feel people walking past as they went down the hall. Then they stopped, and started again, and she could feel the floor fall out beneath them. They were going down in an elevator. And down. Then there was a ding, and they were again on the move.

Next thing she knew, there was another voice and a bright light. "Darlene, we're gonna do an ultrasound now to see what's causing your pain. It may feel a bit strange or uncomfortable, but it won't take too long. You're gonna need to stay really still for me, okay sweetheart?"

"Doll baby," Darlene whispered.

"I don't see a baby doll here, Darlene," the voice said. She couldn't tell if it was a male voice or a female voice, but it was soothing. "Okay, Darlene.

Here we go. Take a breath, please. Good. Keep it up. Take another one. Good. Just a little longer. You're doing great. We're getting some great pictures."

Darlene fell asleep. When she awoke, she was back en route to the emergency room. She was put back in her room, and for a brief time, it was quiet. Then there was a familiar voice.

"Darlene, can you hear me? It's Jennifer. How do you feel?"

"Groggy," Darlene replied. "Is my mom here yet?"

Jennifer sighed. "Not yet. But she should be here soon. It's been a couple hours. If she doesn't hit traffic, she should get here in the next hour. And they'll send her right here to be with you."

Darlene sighed. "Okay," she said. She let herself relax. It would be okay once her mother got there. She hoped Phil wasn't panicking, trying to find her.

Time went by. Jennifer was still holding her hand. Nurses checked in. Then they left. Her IV beeped, and it was checked. The doctor came in.

"Darlene," he said, "we think we know what's going on with you based on your blood tests and ultrasound, but we're getting a consultation with a surgeon. We think you might have a ruptured cyst on your ovary or fallopian tube, and we're monitoring you closely for now. We're trying to find out if we need to do surgery to fix you up. But it's nothing we haven't seen before. You're in good hands. I'll be back to check on you in a bit."

More time went by. Jennifer stayed by her side and held her hand. She'd have to have her mother get her a thank-you gift once this all was over. Her mother . . .

Then she heard her mother's voice. "Doll baby," she said. "I'm here now. You're gonna be okay. I'll make sure."

There was a rustling noise, and Darlene heard footsteps enter the room. "Darlene, we have Dr. Sanchez here," the original doctor said. Darlene couldn't remember his name. "He's a surgeon who specializes in gynecological issues. He's looked at your test results, and thinks that we need to take you to surgery."

Mrs. Feinman stood up. "I'm her mother," she said. "What's wrong with her? Why does she need surgery?"

The next voice Darlene heard must have been Dr. Sanchez. "Darlene, is it okay to talk in front of your mother?" he asked.

"Yes," Darlene croaked.

"So what we have here," Dr. Sanchez went on, "is an ectopic, or tubal, pregnancy. Darlene, do you know what that is?"

Darlene gasped. "I'm pregnant?" she asked. "No, Kim's pregnant."

"What?" Mrs. Feinman asked. "Darlene, you tell me later. Doctor, can you tell us more?"

Dr. Sanchez must have nodded. "So Darlene, yes, an ectopic pregnancy is similar to a pregnancy, but what happens is the cells implant in your fallopian tube before they can travel to implant in your uterus. And once that happens, the mass of cells will continue to grow, but it's not going to become a baby. It will grow until it becomes too big for where it is, and it can burst the tube, causing considerable damage and bleeding. So we have to perform surgery to remove it."

"Like an abortion?" Darlene asked.

"Yes, in effect," Dr. Sanchez said. "But you have to remember, this is not a viable pregnancy. It cannot grow into a baby. So the surgery is needed to keep you from being in serious danger."

"Okay," Darlene said. "Can you make it stop hurting?"

"We can make it stop hurting," Dr. Sanchez said, "but this surgery is not without risk. If there is already damage, or if there is a rupture, we may not be able to repair the fallopian tube. We might have to remove it. Which, you will need to understand, could limit your future fertility."

Darlene felt an increase in pressure on the hand her mother was holding. "Is there any way to treat her without surgery?" Mrs. Feinman asked.

There was a pause, where Darlene figured the doctor was making another head gesture. "I'm afraid not," he said. "The growth needs to be removed. And the sooner, the better. Darlene, we can get you up to surgery in the next hour. We just need to get your consent."

"Okay," Darlene said. "You can do it."

There was a flurry of activity soon after to get Darlene prepped for surgery. Her mother was allowed to stay with her for the time being. "Mom," she said, turning to face Mrs. Feinman. "I don't want Dad to know, okay? I don't want him to know that I could have been pregnant. That I did anything that could get me pregnant. Don't tell him, okay? Tell him something else. Tell him my appendix burst. Please, Mom."

Mrs. Feinman looked at her with concern. "Darlene," she said softly. "One of these days, you've got to explain to me what it is with you and your father. Please, tell me he never laid a hand on you." She looked as if she might cry, but she steeled herself and gave Darlene a serious look.

"No, Mom," Darlene said as her eyelids became heavy. "He never hurt me. I just don't want to let him down. I just want to be good. I need to be a good girl for Dad. Please, Mom?"

Mrs. Feinman sighed. "Okay, Darlene. I'll tell him you needed to get your appendix out. But please, doll baby, please know. You are good. You have always been good. Don't let anyone make you feel you're not good, okay? You don't have to prove yourself to anyone."

"It's time to bring her up," the nurse announced.

"Okay, Mom," Darlene mumbled. "I promise. I love you. I'm really sleepy."

"We gave you a sedative in your IV," the nurse explained.

"I love you, doll baby," she heard her mother say through an echo chamber. "I'll see you after surgery. You're my good girl. . . ."

"Darlene, can you hear me?"

She tried to open her eyes, but they felt glued shut. She tried to speak, but there was no air behind her words.

"You got through surgery great," her mother said. "The doctor was just here. They were able to take care of everything, and you're going to be fine."

"Tube," Darlene was able to say.

Mrs. Feinman was quiet for a few moments. "Doll, they weren't able to save the fallopian tube. They had to remove it. There was too much damage from the rupture. But you're gonna be fine. You just need to stay in the hospital for a couple of days so they can watch you and control your pain. And then I'm going to take you home for a week or two to recover."

Darlene felt tears rolling from the corners of her eyes. "So I won't be able to ever have a baby?"

She could feel her mother gently take her hand. "No, Darlene. You probably will be able to have a baby. It might just take you some time, and maybe some help from a doctor. But you still have your other fallopian tube. You still have a chance."

Darlene nodded. "Kim's pregnant."

"I know," Mrs. Feinman said. "I called Vee while you were in surgery to let her know what was going on, and she told me. That's really big news."

Darlene gingerly turned her head toward her mother. "Did you tell Vee what happened to me? The truth?"

"I did," her mother confessed. "But she's promised not to say anything to anyone, even Kim. Doll, I was so worried about you. Vee is my best friend. I had to talk to someone."

Darlene nodded. "I don't want my friends to know," she said. "I don't even want them to know I'm in the hospital, at least for now. I need to get my story straight."

Mrs. Feinman looked at her with concern. "Doll," she said softly, "I wish I understood what you were going through. Your friends will be there for you if you need them. You need their support."

Darlene shook her head. "Kim's pregnant. She's happy. She's telling people right now. This is her time. I don't want to ruin it." She paused. "Did you talk to Dad yet?"

Mrs. Feinman nodded. "I called him before you went into surgery. I told him they thought it was your appendix, but that I would know more after surgery. He's very worried about you."

Darlene nodded. "Okay," she said. "I know what we can tell him. They did the surgery, and they found a ruptured cyst in my ovary. They had to remove some of my parts due to the damage, so that will explain someday if I have trouble getting pregnant. And I can tell my friends the same thing. When and if I decide to tell them. Okay? So that's what you'll tell Dad?" She looked at her mother hopefully.

Mrs. Feinman bit her lower lip and nodded. "I'll do what you want me to do, Darlene. It's your story, not mine. But doll, I really am concerned about you. I wish you could talk to your friends. Confide in them. They can help you get through this. Doll baby, please don't take this the wrong way, but, have you ever thought of maybe finding someone else to talk to? Like a therapist?"

Darlene glared at her mother. "Mom, I don't need a therapist," she said. "I'll be okay. I just need to make sure we have our stories straight."

Mrs. Feinman smiled sadly. "Okay, doll." She paused. "Darlene, I need to ask you, who was it, you know . . ."

"Phil," she said with no emotion. "Phil Roth. He's kind of my boyfriend. He's probably trying to find me. We're usually together on Saturday nights. What time is it?"

"It's seven a.m., Sunday," Mrs. Feinman said.

"Oh," Darlene said, feeling deflated. "He has breakfast with Grace on Sunday mornings. He probably won't come."

"Darlene," her mother said, "if he's your boyfriend, he'll come. If he doesn't, then maybe he's not really your boyfriend. "

"If he comes, I'll see him," Darlene said. "But it's the same story. Ruptured cyst. I really don't want him to know."

"Darlene," Mrs. Feinman said, "were you being careful? You know, using protection?"

"We were," Darlene assured her. "But I don't think he was using it right. He'd always wait until the last minute. I kind of figured he knew what he was doing, but I guess he didn't."

"No, that doesn't work," Mrs. Feinman said. "I guess they didn't teach that in his sex ed class. But now you know. Don't let him do that anymore. Should we get you on the pill?"

Darlene tried to shrug, but it was too hard to move her muscles. "I don't know," she said. "I don't know if I want to do it anymore. At least for a while. Maybe later."

They sat quietly for some time, with nurses coming in periodically to check on her. At eight o'clock, a nurse came in.

"We have a young man who just showed up and wants to see you," she said. "His name is Phillip Roth? Could that really be his name?"

Darlene tried to sit up, but she didn't have the strength. She nodded. "Can I see him?" she asked. The nurse nodded. "But I don't want him to have any information about my condition."

The nurse nodded. "Not a problem. We don't share that kind of information anyway."

Two minutes later, Phil knocked on the open door and came in. "Oh, thank God I found you," he said, walking to her bedside. "Can I hold your hand?" Darlene nodded. "I got freaked out last night when I couldn't reach you on your phone, so I went to your dorm, and the guy working down there told me that you were at the hospital. No one knew what was wrong with you, except that they had to take you away by ambulance. Are you okay?"

Mrs. Feinman stood up. "I'll leave you two alone," she said. "Phil, I'm Darlene's mother, Barbara Feinman. I'll be out in the waiting room. Please come get me when you go."

"Okay, nice to meet you, Mrs. Feinman," Phil said. Then he sat in the chair she had vacated. "What happened, Darlene?"

"I'm okay now," she said to reassure him. "But last night, I had horrible pain in my stomach and called my mom to come. Then I got my RA, Jennifer, and I must have been in bad shape, because she called for an ambulance. It turned out I had a ruptured cyst in my ovary. It did some damage, so they had to do surgery. But I'm gonna be okay."

"Oh my God, I can't believe you had surgery!" Phil exclaimed. "That's a big deal. I'm so glad you're okay. Is there anything I can do to help you?"

"You can sit with me awhile," Darlene said hopefully. "Give my mom a break."

Phil looked at her apologetically. "I can't right now," he said. "I just needed to check to make sure you were okay. But Grace brought me over here, and she's down waiting for me in her car so we can go for breakfast. I can come back later though."

Darlene sat silently. "You're still going to breakfast with Grace today?"

Phil shrugged. "It's our routine. And she was nice enough to drive me over here. Oh, and she sends her best wishes to you. How long will you be here?"

Darlene had more to say about Grace, but now it felt awkward. "A day or two," she said. "And then my mom's bringing me back to Eastboro for a couple of weeks. I guess I'll use the time to catch up on my schoolwork and study for finals."

"You'll be gone for a couple of weeks," Phil said, "and then there's finals and then summer break. We're not gonna see each other much for a while. I'll miss our Saturday nights together."

Darlene nodded. "Yeah, me too," she said, "but it might be some time before I'm ready to, you know, again. I need to recover."

Phil nodded. "I understand. Well, I have to head out. I'm glad you're okay. You gave us all a good scare. I'll come back and see you this afternoon after the basketball game."

"Okay, Phil." Darlene said, trying to hide the disappointment in her voice. Phil gave her a kiss on the cheek, and he left. Even the two minutes she was alone before her mother returned seemed like an eternity.

"And then, Phil left, and my mother came back and thought that was strange, but I told her it was okay. 'Everything's always okay, Mom.'" Darlene paused. "Two days later, we went back to my dorm, packed up two weeks' worth of stuff, and let Jennifer know I would be gone for two weeks. She hugged me. I think I traumatized her a little. My mother gave her a box of chocolates from the hospital gift shop as a thank-you.

"We drove home, and my mom got me settled. Later, my dad showed up and came upstairs to see me. He brought me flowers. He was so sweet. He felt bad for what I'd been through. It's a good thing he didn't know what had really happened, or he probably would have blamed me for being too careless. But as it was, he was nice to me, and he offered to take me to Vale the following winter break to go skiing with him. I said yes. He seemed so excited about it."

"And Phil?" Aspen asked. "What happened with him?"

Darlene shrugged. "Next term, we saw each other sometimes, but not as often. I didn't want to have sex yet. I didn't want to have to deal with telling him what he did wrong with the condoms. I didn't want him to know it was his fault, sort of. So we'd kiss for a while, and then he'd leave. This went on pretty much through sophomore year, on and off, and then it ran its course.

I ran into his friend Mark during senior year, and he told me that Phil and Grace got an apartment together off campus, as a couple. They're probably married now, I don't know."

Aspen nodded. "Let's get back to what we talked about last week. Drawing the line on what is tolerable. You said you knew the value of your body, you learned that from your mother, and we were going to talk about drawing that line even further out, to other red flags you see. Were you able to do your homework?"

Darlene smiled proudly. "I was," she said. She took a piece of folded notebook paper out of her purse. "Should I just read it to you, or should we talk about it as we go along?"

"Why don't you just start reading," Aspen suggested, "and we'll stop if we need to."

"Okay," Darlene said, unfolding the paper. "The first one is him showing up a half hour late for our first date, but I almost think that one's cheating because someone else told me it was a red flag."

"But do you understand why?" Aspen inquired.

Darlene chose her words carefully. "If he liked me," she said, "he should have wanted to make a good impression and show me he was reliable. He would have prioritized being on time over watching a basketball game."

Aspen nodded. "Exactly," she said. "Respect for your time, and your safety. You were meeting in a public place. Okay, what's next?"

"Well, it was okay to take me out with his friends on the first date, and even to kiss me, but his expectations of having sex without getting to know each other . . . granted, it might have been okay for some girls, but it was definitely not my value. And then leaving. It made me feel like he left because I didn't put out."

"Good," Aspen said. "Red flags don't always mean that there's something bad about the person. It can be that you realize that your values don't align. You're really getting the feel for this."

"Next is the sushi restaurant." Darlene made a face. "I mean, he didn't consult with me at all about where I wanted to go, and he didn't pick up on my body language. If I had been consulted, I might have asked to go somewhere else."

"Yes," Aspen said. "Taking charge and making plans without consulting you. And not figuring out when you were feeling uncomfortable."

"This one is confusing," Darlene said. "He was very gentle and sweet when we had my first time together. He said nice things, and he made me feel good. But then, he ruined the whole thing by getting up to leave. Again. So he could get up early to have breakfast with another girl. It just felt wrong, even if they were just friends."

"Your idea of what was going to happen after sex was not your reality," Aspen said. "It felt weird for him to leave like that."

Darlene nodded. "Yeah, it hurt. He couldn't just cancel that one time. It was like he was more concerned about her feelings than mine." She looked up. "And the last one is very similar, but even worse. He left me in my room at the hospital to go to breakfast with Grace. I just had surgery! He should have stayed. I mean, Grace would have understood! I was never his first priority. It was sports, Grace, then me, it seemed."

Aspen smiled. "Darlene, that's a very thorough and insightful list. I think you're really getting red flags. So now we need to talk about what you do with red flags."

Darlene laughed. "Oh, you mean the real work. Okay."

"Think about the red flags with Charlie. Let's start with the ice skating. What might you do differently now, knowing what you know about red flags?"

Darlene thought about it. "I . . . don't think I would have gone out with him again," she said. "He wasn't very nice, but all I could think about was that he liked me and he was holding my hand. But if I hadn't gone out with him again . . ."

Aspen nodded. "When you catch the first red flag, it eliminates everything else that could happen after. It's a skill that we all develop, Darlene, so you don't have to beat yourself up over not doing it. The idea is to look forward and learn how to use the skills from now on. So if you did go out with Charlie after skating, and before the prom, what would you say would be your line now, knowing what you know?"

Darlene grimaced. "The kissing," she said. "It was bad. I didn't like it. It didn't do anything for me but make me want to vomit. There was no chemistry there. So now I have a guy who was not always very nice, and I don't even enjoy kissing him."

"Okay," Aspen said. "So now you know, when there's no chemistry, you don't need to keep going out with the person. No real attraction. In addition

to not really being very nice. So there's one line. Now how about Phil? What would be your line for him?"

"That one's harder," Darlene admitted. "He was nice, and mostly kind. And I could forgive the being late thing. I don't think I should have let it go, though. Often, he would change the subject before I could say how something made me feel. But I think the line should have been as soon as I felt weird about Grace. I should have said something to him about how that made me feel, and if he couldn't see why that upset me, that would be the line. Maybe, too, if I had asked him way before we even had sex why he wouldn't ever stay with me, he would have told me about breakfast with Grace, and that probably would have been enough."

"It seems that you're seeing a pattern in your behavior, too, Darlene," Aspen pointed out. "You can see that when something upsets you or confuses you, and you don't speak out about it, the other person doesn't change the behavior you don't like. Did I get that right?"

Darlene nodded slowly. "Yeah," she said. "I never said anything to Phil about how what he did made me feel, so he kept doing what he was doing. But if I had said something, he'd have had a choice. He could keep doing it, or he could stop or decrease his behavior to try to make things better for us."

"And then you have a choice, too," Aspen pointed out. "If he chooses to not change, you can decide if you want to keep or end the relationship."

"Wow," Darlene said. "It all makes so much sense when we talk about it in retrospect. It's probably not quite so easy in practice. But since Phil, there really hasn't been anyone else. At least not any relationships. I've had feelings and thoughts about guys sometimes, but nothing has ever happened."

"Tell me about those," Aspen encouraged.

"Well," Darlene said, sitting back in her chair. "Remember that Kim got pregnant. Well, later, she and Carl decided to get married. They went to the courthouse in California, but then came back to Eastboro at the end of sophomore year to have a ceremony with friends and family. I was the maid of honor, and Chris was the best man. Chris was still single, or was single again, I should say, and I thought about our kiss at the prom. So I considered pursuing that, now that we were older. But then over the weekend, it appeared that he and Michelle were spending a lot of time together talking and dancing, so I backed off. I thought they might hook up. But they didn't that weekend, or so I thought. I just I'd see how it went next time I saw him.

And there were some guys in my sociology classes—I took a lot of sociology classes in my four years at Ithaca, even more than I needed for my major—but nothing ever came of those crushes either. So I left college having had no relationships except with Phil. But it was okay."

"So you got your degree in sociology," Aspen said. "Tell me what happened after that."

Chapter 41

Grown-Ups

KIM AND CARL HAD TWO BABIES now, Drake and Elena. Kim was a group facilitator for a nonprofit agency. Carl was weeks from getting his electrician's license and had started classes at University of San Francisco. Sally and James were engaged and looking at houses. Sally was writing, and James was a chef. Chris got a job teaching at Randall Middle School. Michelle was working as a nurse in Amherst. Traci was an assistant manager at a women's clothing store.

Darlene was living with her mother in Eastboro and looking for a job. Apparently, there were no entry-level jobs in sociology. A degree could open doors, but Darlene didn't know which doorknobs to even turn. Her father had all sorts of "I told you so" expressions to share with her when she revealed she had yet to find a job. Her mother didn't care. She would be okay if Darlene stayed with her forever.

Sophomore year, Darlene had moved into East Tower with her friend Paula from her freshman floor. They got along well, and having company was a relief after Darlene's year of almost total solitude. Paula was a psych major and was doing an internship at a group home in Ithaca, helping adults with mental illnesses. She told Darlene stories about the residents and their symptoms, medications, and treatments. Darlene found it fascinating. She wondered if her old roommate, Tina, had ended up in a group home.

So when Darlene saw an ad in the Classifieds section for entry-level counselors for the group home setting, she applied. She received a call from human resources. They liked her résumé, but the full-time job was no longer available. Would she be interested in working on-call shifts? Darlene agreed. She had to tell her father she was doing *something*.

The interview was easy, and she knew all the answers to the questions. She was given a tour of the beautiful Victorian group home, which housed eight adults. When she met the residents, they all appeared interested in her, and some even tried to show off for her. By the time she was done with the tour, she was handed employment paperwork and asked if she could work the next night. She said yes.

She had two hours where she overlapped with another staff member for training before she was left on her own. Then all hell broke loose. Three of the residents went out. They said goodbye and just walked out the door before Darlene could ask them where they were going. She wasn't sure if they were supposed to do this, but the door wasn't locked, and she didn't have any way of stopping them. She didn't even know which residents they were. She was looking for a phone number to call to ask someone what she should do when another resident came into the office crying.

"My friends all went out and just left me here," she sobbed. "I was sleeping. They didn't wake me up!"

Darlene froze. She had no idea what to do, so she just sat down at the dining room table with the woman and talked. No, she didn't know where they went. No, she didn't know when they were coming back. And no, she didn't know if they were meeting up with anyone when they got there. There were several hypothetical situations posed to her.

"What if they left me on purpose?"

Darlene validated her concern, and they talked about it.

"What if my boyfriend went with them and didn't tell me?"

Darlene showed empathy, and this possibility was discussed.

This conversation went on for an hour. Darlene was exhausted. She hadn't learned any skills to deal with something like this in college. But she pushed forward.

Finally, the front door opened, and the three other residents returned.

They assured their friend that they didn't leave her behind on purpose, that they didn't go to her favorite club without her, and they didn't meet anyone where they went. Relieved and smiling, the resident said okay, and everyone went to their rooms.

Without the drama, it was eerily quiet. Darlene didn't know what to do. Eventually, she got up from the table, went into the den, and turned on the TV. After some time, one, then two residents joined her. Around nine p.m., the residents started asking for their medications. By nine thirty, everyone was medicated and had gone to their rooms. At eleven, the overnight staff arrived. Darlene was never so happy to see anyone in her life. She shared the story of what happened and was met with laughter.

"Oh, that's nothing," she said. "You wouldn't believe the stories I could tell you about things that go on at night here. But next time, if Angela approaches you, just tell her that everything's fine and she should go to her room and hug her stuffed monkey. That usually works. Otherwise, she'll talk your ear off, as you learned."

After two months on-call, Darlene knew all the residents' names, their diagnoses, meds, and habits. She knew what they found funny and what was offensive. They asked her questions about her private life, and she evaded and changed the subject. She laughed a lot at work and went home feeling like she'd helped.

Then a full-time counselor position opened, and Darlene was encouraged to apply. So she did. The first and second interviews went well, including a meeting with the staff she would be working with. But when it was time for the residents to grill her in a community meeting, she grew nervous. What if they didn't choose her? But they did. Then she found out that the resident meeting was just a formality. If you got the third interview, you were already chosen for the job. The other staff found it funny that she was more nervous about the residents choosing than she was about meeting with the CEO. Darlene felt silly.

Her shifts were three to eleven, and she quickly had to adjust her sleep pattern. She slept till noon, padded her way downstairs for a late breakfast, watched *Days of Our Lives*, and got ready for work. When she came home after work, she was too wired to sleep. She would stay up watching late-night TV. She worked some weekends, but on others, she got together with her coworkers or drove out to Amherst to visit Michelle. Sometimes,

Sally and James would come to town to visit their families and work on their wedding plans, and Sally would organize an outing for everyone who was in town. The wedding was coming up in April. Darlene would be a bridesmaid this time, and Michelle would be the maid of honor. Kim and Carl would be back with their kids. It was something to look forward to.

Darlene fell into a tolerable routine, and things felt like they were settling down. She was even able to enjoy short outings with her father. She was an adult now and supporting herself. She might not have become a biologist, but at least she was working and making money. She didn't have to depend on him anymore to support her. But she still didn't want to make him angry. It still wasn't safe.

She didn't date, and she wasn't interested in anyone. There were some male coworkers, but they were not prospective boyfriends for one reason or another. She did miss the physicality of a romantic relationship, but she didn't miss the stress and anxiety. She still held that little bit of hope for the future. There was always Chris of the senior prom kiss, and their other childhood friend, Pete. Pete had broken up with his longtime girlfriend in college, and Chris had been single since sophomore year. She could always pursue one of them. Kim and Carl and Sally and James had coupled up. It wouldn't be unimaginable for another couple to come out of their childhood friend group. Chris and Pete were like a warm, comfortable safety net in the back of Darlene's mind. Knowing they were out there made her feel not quite so lonely on the frigid winter nights.

The day of James and Sally's wedding was beautiful, and so was the bride. Darlene enjoyed her time with her lifelong friends, and especially seeing Traci. On her last day at McKinney High, Traci had asked her friends to please invite her to their weddings, and so far, the friends had come through. Traci was always up for anything. She and Darlene sipped contraband champagne at the dry reception, danced all night, and laughed uncontrollably when they got tipsy. They both eventually got tired and collapsed onto chairs at their assigned table. Darlene fanned herself with a loose wedding program and caught her breath.

"Traci," Darlene said, "I still can't believe you're here. It's like, when you're here, you never left at all except that you're older and you're beautiful!" She giggled. "Why are you here alone? You're too beautiful to be alone. There should be a line of guys just following you down the street like the pied piper!"

Traci laughed. "Darlene," she said, "the pied piper led away all the rats! Are you saying that men are rats?"

Darlene walloped with laughter and took another drink from the bottle of champagne she had swiped off of a caterer's stand after toasts and had hidden under the table. She stowed it back away when she was finished with it. "Rats!" Darlene said. "Yes! Men are rats! Do you have a rat back home?"

Traci shook her head vigorously. "No," she said. "No rats right now, but I did have a mouse until recently." She quickly put her hand to her mouth.

"A mouse?" Darlene asked, confused. The analogy had gotten away from her. "What's a mouse?"

"Shhh!" Traci said, leaning in closer to Darlene. "A mouse is a girl, but don't tell anyone, okay, because it's a secret!"

Darlene opened her mouth in surprise. "Traci, I didn't know you even liked mice. Have you always liked mice?"

Traci shrugged. "I don't know," she said. "I've always just liked people, and most have been boy people, but sometimes, there's an occasional mouse. I guess I'm just not that particular."

"Hmm," Darlene said. "I wonder if I like mice."

Traci shook her head. "No, you definitely go for the rats, Darlene. I know. I can tell. You may still have a brick wall, but I still can tell. And they've really been rats so far."

Darlene nodded. "Yeah," she said. "Rats. Can you still see the people in my head?"

Traci looked at her carefully. "I can't see the people, but I know they're still there. Not as many, but they're just as strong, and persistent. Do you know them?"

"A little," Darlene admitted. "But we're not on a first-name basis." She laughed. "That's a lie. Their first names are all Darlene!"

Traci smiled at her warmly. "I'm getting sleepy. It's probably the champagne and all the dancing. I'm gonna go turn in."

Darlene was disappointed. She wanted to spend more time with Traci. They rarely got to see each other, and something about Traci radiated love and safety. "Oh, okay."

Traci touched her arm. "Darlene," she said softly. "Come with me. Be my mouse tonight."

Darlene's eyes widened. "Traci," she said, "even you just said I'm a rat type of girl. I couldn't—"

"No, it's not like that," Traci assured her. "I wouldn't ever want you to do anything you weren't comfortable with. It's just . . . we could just get into bed together. And fall asleep. It just seems like we both could use that. And I really don't want to be alone tonight." She looked at Darlene closely. "You've spent far too many nights alone when you didn't want to be. Come with me tonight. We'll keep each other safe."

Safe. Darlene liked the sound of that word. She smiled at Traci, who could see her soul after all. "Okay. Let's go say goodnight to James and Sally, and then we can grab a shuttle back to the hotel."

When they got back to Traci's room, Darlene got shy. She wasn't sure what to do first. Traci helped.

"I always bring an extra toothbrush," she said, unzipping her toiletry bag. "You know, just in case." She handed the unopened brush to Darlene, and they went into the bathroom together. After they brushed, Traci gave Darlene some cotton balls and shared her makeup remover. Then, they went to the bed.

"I don't have anything extra for you to wear to bed," Traci said apologetically. "You can just sleep in your bra and underwear if you feel more comfortable."

Darlene looked down at her green bridesmaid dress. "Um, I'm not wearing a bra."

Traci gave her a warm smile. "Me neither. But I promise you, I really won't do anything to make you feel uncomfortable."

Darlene nodded. She didn't feel uncomfortable. She felt a sense of nervous anticipation. She was going to spend the night with someone. She was going to share their bed. And they weren't going to leave. She unzipped and removed her dress, facing away from Traci, and slid under the covers. Traci did the same. She turned the lights out.

"Traci," Darlene said, "I'm okay if we just, like, cuddle together."

"Oh," Traci said with surprise. "Okay. Turn away from me."

Darlene rolled on to her side facing away from Traci. Then Traci inched closer to her and pressed her body up against Darlene's back. Darlene could feel her soft breasts against her skin, and her belly up against the small of her back. Traci put her arm up over Darlene's back and put her knees against the backs of Darlene's knees. They were spooning. Darlene didn't feel scared. She felt peace. She reached out and took Traci's extended hand in her own. She closed her eyes. This was all she'd ever wanted. She felt safe. She fell into a deep sleep.

In the morning, Darlene woke up still entangled with Traci. She had a dry mouth, but she didn't care. She had gone to sleep with Traci, and when she woke up, Traci was still there. Traci's eyes opened when Darlene started moving around.

"Good morning, my mouse," Traci said with an affectionate smile. "Did you sleep well?"

Darlene smiled back. "That was the best sleep I've had maybe in my whole life. Thank you, Traci, for knowing what I needed."

"My pleasure." Traci reached over to kiss her on the cheek. Darlene turned her head and kissed Traci on the lips. Then she nibbled on her lower lip.

"What was that about?" Traci asked with surprise.

Darlene grinned. "I just wanted to kiss you. I still like rats," she confirmed. "But you're a special mouse."

Traci nodded. "Yeah," she said. "I think you made me feel a little too damn special, though. I'd better go take a shower."

Chapter 42

REUNION

DARLENE GOT A LOT OF mileage out of her interaction with Traci. She felt as if, for once, her gas gauge was on full. It was reflected in her work. The residents enjoyed sitting and talking to her and working together on their goals. She was volunteering to participate in training to learn new skills. She was learning a lot about mental illness, along with symptoms, treatments, and the stigma it created. She became a staunch advocate for her residents, and her motivation was not lost on her manager, Christa.

"I've been really impressed by your initiative lately, Darlene," Christa told her in their weekly supervision meeting. "Your teammates really appreciate your work and your attitude. And you really seem to enjoy what you're doing."

Darlene smiled. She was not used to accolades. It felt good. "Thanks. I really like our people. They're so much more than what's presented in their packets when they move in. I had no idea that Frida published a book when she was in her twenties! She knows so much about butterflies. Who would have even thought to ask her about that? She just lights up when she sees one or talks about them."

"I heard you took her for a butterfly walk at the arboretum last weekend," Christa said. "Nice touch. She hasn't had to take any extra medication for anxiety since then. That's not a small thing."

Darlene beamed. She was making a difference. "I'm gonna take Ramona to church again on Sunday," she said. "I was wearing jeans last time we went. She was so embarrassed. I told her that God doesn't care what you wear as long as you show up. But I'm gonna wear a skirt this time."

Christa laughed. "She'll like that," she said. "Darlene, I wanted to talk to you about something else, but it's related." She paused. "There's a position opening at Marina House next month, and I thought you would be a good fit. It's for the program supervisor."

Darlene's eyebrows shot up. "Me? As supervisor? But there are a lot of people who have been here a lot longer than I have."

"I know," Christa said, "but I'm not recommending them right now. I'm recommending you. I think you would be a good match for the program, and their manager. I would hire you in a minute here, but as you know, we already have a supervisor, and we love him. You don't have to apply, and if you do and you are offered the job, you can turn it down. It is a significant pay raise. But it's in Castor. So it would either be a long commute, or you would want to move closer."

Darlene thought about it. It was a thirty-minute drive to Castor. If she moved, she would need to leave her mom. But Castor was really close to Uxbridge, where Sally and James had settled into their new house. She could see them any time she wanted! But it would take her a half hour longer than it currently did to get to Michelle. It was a tradeoff. And she didn't want to live alone.

"And another thing," Christa went on, as if reading her mind. "There are two other women in the agency who have advertised at the main office that they're looking for an apartment and would like to find a third roommate. They both work pretty close to Castor. Maybe you could connect with them."

Darlene nodded. More money. Closer to Sally and James. Her own apartment with likeminded roommates. Showing her father how respected she had become at work and how independent she could be. "Okay," she finally said. "What do I have to do to apply?"

That night, Sally called and begged her to come to their five-year high school reunion in two weeks. Sally, James, and Michelle were going, and they were also trying to get Chris to commit to the event. Darlene hadn't been planning to go. She didn't think Charlie would be there, but there were still echoes of him in the high school hallways. But Chris would be there. She wondered if he was still single. She remembered their impromptu kiss at the prom. Chris had liked her kiss. Darlene thought it was almost as good as the kiss she shared with Traci, with the additional bonus that Chris was a man, and an attractive man to boot. Maybe, just maybe, he would be interested in kissing again. She hadn't been able to find a time that felt right to approach him to find out, but this was another good chance.

"I'll go," she told Sally.

"Yay!" Sally replied.

There were a lot of students from their class at the reunion, more than Darlene had expected. It was strange to be back in the old school gym, home of several homecoming dances and proms. Tables were set up around the room, and Darlene quickly found Sally and James sitting at one, talking to some acquaintances who stood beside them. Darlene approached, and they both stood up to hug her.

"It's so good to see you," Sally said. "I'm sorry we've been so busy since the wedding. It's like everything came down on us at once. And I just get in the zone when I'm writing. Jamie is kind of like acting manager at the Marriott now, so that keeps him on his toes. But it's good, because he wants to get the manager job at some point."

"Maybe not too far in the future," James said. "I think the manager is about to call it quits. I give him six months max before he throws in the towel."

Darlene held up crossed fingers. "I hope it works out, James. You'd be really good at that."

James gave her a warm smile. They had known each other since they were five. Seeing him was like coming home.

Soon after, Michelle and Chris walked through the door together. Sally jumped up to greet them and brought them back to the table. Darlene hugged them both. She intuitively knew something was off. They both seemed stiff. They were smiling, and talking about their work, but it was strained, which made Darlene curious. They had shared a ride to the reunion. She wondered if they'd had some kind of disagreement on their way over. It really didn't seem like a suitable time to approach Chris. He just didn't appear all that receptive. Darlene accepted this and moved on with her night. There would always be a next time.

But something was up with Michelle. She just wanted her to be happy. She went to the food table and brought her back a cookie. Michelle smiled as she took the cookie from Darlene's hand.

"Thank you, Darlene," she said warmly. "Cookies make everything better. I've been under a lot of stress lately, you know, but it's so good to be here and see you. I really miss you."

Darlene reached over and hugged Michelle. "I miss you, too," she whispered in her ear. "And I'm always just a phone call away if you want to talk."

Darlene looked at Michelle's face. For a moment, it looked like Michelle was going to say something to her, but then it passed. "I know. I appreciate knowing you're there."

The rest of the evening was uneventful. Michelle seemed to relax into the flow, and even Chris seemed to forget his tension as he caught up with James and talked about their antics back in school.

Finally, the night ended, and they all hugged their goodbyes. Darlene didn't know when she would see her friends again. There were no more weddings coming up, no events whatsoever. Darlene could usually depend on Sally to create something for them all to do, but now she was so busy. They would just have to talk on the phone. Darlene went home and called Traci to tell her about her night at the reunion. Traci asked her questions and held on tight to her every word.

Chapter 43

The Good, The Bad, The Ugly

DARLENE GOT THE SUPERVISOR JOB. She moved in with her two new roommates in a large apartment in an old house in Hopedale. It was a beautiful old town with a dilapidated mill next to a pond. The pond had trails that led to railroad tracks. It was easy to get lost, but getting lost was an adventure. It was summer, the skies were blue and bright, and warm breezes blew through the afternoons. Hopedale Center was quiet and rustic with old community buildings and old growth trees.

The only thing that got in the way of the 1938 feeling was the electric school bell across the street from Darlene's bedroom window that rang six times per day.

She was learning her new job. Of course, she was working with a different set of staff and a different set of residents, and they all treated her differently because she was the supervisor. She wasn't the boss, but she had the boss's ear. Darlene had to take on new roles. She was in charge of the schedule and the petty cash. If someone called in sick, she had to find a replacement or come in to work herself. She had to attend meetings with management at the main building. She had less time to sit and talk to the residents, to ask about what was important to them, what made them shine. Instead, she was called over if there was a crisis, and she was expected to know what to do. Sometimes, she knew. Other times, she went into autopilot. Autopilot was eerily similar to Neutral Darlene.

Two months went by. Darlene was getting used to the routine, but she wasn't totally convinced she liked it. It seemed so counterintuitive. You do really well at your job, so they tell you to go for the supervisor position. Then you get the supervisor position, and you don't get to do the job you love anymore.

She started thinking about other options. She wanted to talk to her roommates about their ideas, but although they were nice and friendly, they both worked opposite shifts than Darlene, and they all slept on different schedules. One night, Darlene came home and found a brochure on the kitchen table for Eastboro State College's Master of Social Work program. She turned it over. Her roommate had received it in the mail. Darlene looked through the brochure and read the blurbs. It was an eighteen-month program.

Graduate school. She had never even thought about that. And social work. Maybe that was the natural next step after a degree in sociology. If she got her master's in social work, she would be at a whole new level of working with people. And she would learn a whole new set of skills. She vowed to herself that she'd spend her next day off in Eastboro at the ESC campus where she could get more information.

But before she could even have a day off, she received a distressing phone call. It was Kim, calling from California.

"Darlene," she said, her voice strained. "Something awful happened. Carl's mother died. They found her dead of a drug overdose."

Darlene's hand shot to her face. "Oh my God!" she exclaimed. She sat down on her couch. "Kim! Are you okay? Is Carl okay?"

"We're all okay for now," Kim said, "but we don't know anything yet. All we know is she died in a group home she was at for drug treatment. The sheriff's office came to Gram's house last night to inform her. Gram is a wreck. I think we'll need to fly out there tomorrow. Can you come and be with me? I really need to see you, Darlene."

Everything else in Darlene's mind fell away. Kim needed her. That was all that mattered. She assumed her Kim/friend persona from elementary school. "Of course," she said. "I have to go to work tomorrow, but I can be there on Monday. Where will you be?"

"We're gonna stay with Gram Missy," Kim said, "but it seems like everyone's congregating at Cissy's house. Darlene, can you go over there tomorrow after work? Chris will be there, and Sally, James, and Michelle are coming by. Pete wants to come, but his car's in the shop. . . ."

"I can pick him up," Darlene volunteered. "Give me his number. I'll call him to arrange it."

Darlene picked up Pete after work. She was excited to see him. He had gone to Murphy High, so he hadn't been at the reunion. They hadn't seen each other since James and Sally's wedding. Pete was alone, so Darlene assumed he must still be single. They talked about their jobs and about their time in elementary school and junior high. They laughed when they recalled chasing each other around on the playground when they were in second grade.

"I can't for the life of me understand," Pete said, "why humans evolved to suddenly think that the opposite sex had cooties at age seven. I mean, aren't we supposed to guarantee the continuation of our species? It's like, hey, man, if you have cooties, just stay like twenty feet away from me. No propagating going on over here!"

Darlene laughed. She had forgotten how funny Pete was. He was still silly. And he was still the most handsome of all the posse boys. He was tall, lean, and muscular. And his smile . . .

They arrived at Cissy's house, and Darlene pulled up in front. She saw James's car in the driveway. She was glad she hadn't missed seeing him and Sally. Chris was also there. She didn't see Michelle's car, so she worried that maybe she had already left.

They went inside and found Sally and James sitting on the couch, and Chris and Michelle on the love seat. Everyone else was in the dining room. Her friends moved over to make room for the new guests. Sally and James stayed for about another hour and then had to leave. That left Michelle, Pete, Chris, and Darlene. Chris looked much less stressed than he had at the reunion, and Michelle looked like she was glowing with happiness, which was weird, since they were all there because Carl's mother had just died. But Darlene was going to find out why in less than a minute.

Michelle dropped the bomb: she and Chris were lovers. They were together as a couple. They had secretly been a couple for three years, since Kim and Carl's wedding, the day that Darlene had sensed there was something between them. They had hooked up that night after all. And many nights since then. They were in love. They were both ecstatically happy.

Darlene tried with all her might to throw Neutral Darlene from park into drive, but she failed. Her shock was evident. She was *floored*. Michelle, her first love, was in love with Chris, who she'd had a vague idea of being her next love. And Michelle was happy, happier than Darlene had ever seen her. Darlene shut up and let Pete talk, and then she was able to pull herself together and let Chris and Michelle know she was happy for them. She thought she might be. That was her role, right? To make sure everyone was happy. She had to shift gears again. Shift her thoughts away from Chris. Focus them on Pete. Pete was great. They had a long history, and he was funny, and they were friends . . .

Then Pete made an announcement. He had gotten back together with his high school sweetheart, Carolyn. Darlene felt as though the wind were knocked right out of her. She thought she might gasp, but she restrained herself. Pete and Carolyn. They were happy, and Pete didn't want to waste any time. He would probably propose to Carolyn soon. Everyone would be happy.

Sally and James. Kim and Carl. Michelle and Chris. Pete and Carolyn. They were all accounted for. Everyone was paired up now. Except for Darlene. They were always an odd-numbered group of friends. There was always the chance that one of them would end up alone. And now it had happened. And Darlene was the one.

She worked quickly. She searched through her head for just the right Darlene. She had to be happy for her friends. She had to show them how happy she was for them. She had to push the other Darlene away, the one that felt like she had just been hit by a car, and then trampled by a marching band. She pulled out the Darlene she used for her mom, her "everything is fine, and I'm really enjoying myself" Darlene, and they bought it. Everyone always did. Now she could breathe easily, at least until she got home.

Darlene completely forgot about the death of Carl's mother, about how much Kim needed her. It just didn't matter. Nothing really mattered. She was alone. She was perfectly and totally alone. She had Traci, who made her feel loved, and safe, and she had kissed Traci, but she had to be honest: she could never get what she needed from Traci. She couldn't be someone she wasn't. And Traci would know. Traci knew everything.

The phone rang. It was Traci. "Somethings wrong. What is it?"

Darlene paused. Where should she start? Then she realized that this was about Carl's mother, not about her. "Carl's mother died She overdosed on heroin. Kim and Carl are coming in tonight. We're all getting together tomorrow to support them."

"Oh, no," Traci said. "Oh God, poor Carl. Oh, that's not good. And I just know, there's gonna be so much more he has to go through before this is over. Please, let them know I'm thinking about them and sending my love. And Darlene." Traci paused. "I wasn't calling about Carl's mother, I don't think. I think my call had something to do with you. What else is wrong?"

Darlene ached to tell her. She wanted to open up her whole body and spill everything out to Traci. Then she wanted Traci to pick it all up and put it back in again the right way. But she couldn't. She just physically couldn't. When she tried, her throat constricted. No words could come out.

"Darlene? Are you still there?" Traci sounded worried.

Darlene took a deep breath. Then she pulled Neutral Darlene back into place. "I'm still here," she said. "I've just been struggling a bit with my new job. I don't really feel that satisfied with what I'm doing. I'm actually considering doing something else, like maybe going to graduate school for social work."

There was a pause. "You're lying to me, Darlene."

Darlene was taken aback. "No, I'm not! I'm really looking into it. I'm gonna go check things out at Eastboro State later this week!"

"No," Traci said. "That's not what I mean. What I mean is that you're lying to me about what's wrong. I think you should check into graduate school. I think you would be a great social worker. But I also think you should tell me the truth. The level of upset I get coming off of you is more than just from your job. Or from Carl's mom. Tell me."

Darlene opened, then closed her mouth. "No, Traci," she said. "There's nothing else. Really. I swear." She knew that Traci still wouldn't believe her.

Traci sighed all the way from Michigan. "You've always trusted my instincts. I'm right about a lot of things, and I'm right this time, too. You need to talk. Please. If you can't talk to me, you need to talk to someone. Before things get worse. Darlene, I'm worried. I feel that things are going to get way worse soon, and it will be too much for you to handle by yourself."

Darlene sat frozen for several seconds. *Worse.* How could things get any worse?

"I appreciate how much you care about me, and you worry, but I'm okay. But yes, I promise. If things ever get to be too much for me, I'll talk to someone."

"If you promise me," Traci said, "you can't back out, okay? You are bound by your promise."

Darlene closed her eyes. "I promise," she repeated.

Chapter 44

WHAT COULD BE WORSE?

KIM WAS PREGNANT AGAIN. SHE told Darlene the next day. This would be her third child. "And it will be our last child, too," she said quietly. "Don't tell anyone else, but Carl's gonna get snipped before we can have another. Three is enough. Three is plenty. I don't know how my mom handled five. She's a fucking saint."

Also, they had just found out that Carl was actually a tried-and-true genius, and he didn't even know it. "His parents kept it from him all these years," Kim told Darlene. "Carl could have gone to a special school if his parents had let him. Then we never would have gotten together. So in a way, I'm glad. His parents may have neglected him, but it sort of worked out in our favor."

Kim was all abuzz about Chris and Michelle. "Michelle and I are gonna be cousins. Can you believe it? She'll be Drake and Elena's aunt! Well, that's assuming they get married, but don't you think they will? I never imagined them together, but when you see them together now, you have to wonder why!"

Darlene couldn't help but smile. Kim was acting like the Kim of their childhood. And her level of effective gossip had now surpassed Darlene's, and maybe even her mother's. Darlene felt proud of Kim, yet again.

The group of friends spent that Monday together, supporting Carl and catching up on each other's lives. Everyone thought that social work school seemed like a great idea for Darlene. Carl was doing well in college. Kim loved her job. James was fast on his way to becoming manager. Sally had started graduate school. And Chris and Michelle and Pete and Carolyn . . . were head over heels in love.

At the end of the evening, they all said goodbye. Darlene figured the next time they would all be together like this would be for another wedding. And she would be a bridesmaid maid at least one more time.

Later that week, she went to Eastboro State College and got an application packet for social work school. She brought it home and spent her entire day off completing it and sending off requests for transcripts. Then all she could do was wait for a response.

Chris and Michelle got engaged the next week. Soon after, Pete proposed to Carolyn, and she said yes. Darlene went through every day as if in a trance. She got up and got ready. She drove to work, and she did her job. She came home and sat in front of her TV. Sometimes, she even turned it on. Sometimes she cried at night. Sometimes, she felt nothing and just shut down her body. She was alive, but she was not living. How could Traci think that things could get worse?

Darlene got into graduate school. She would start in January and finish at the end of the following summer. In December, Chris and Michelle got married. Darlene pulled out Fun Darlene and went to Michelle's bachelorette karaoke party the night before. She enthusiastically sang songs, toasted the bride, and spent time with Traci. Michelle was already radiant. Darlene couldn't help but love her even more than she already did. She was genuinely happy for Michelle and Chris. It wasn't their fault she was alone.

Darlene gave her notice at work. Her manager didn't seem surprised, which didn't shock Darlene. She couldn't even fake happiness at work. She just wasn't supervisor material.

She felt a small sense of excitement on her first day of graduate school. She packed her notebooks and pens in a book bag and packed her Darlene personas in her head. She would figure out which ones she would need later. There would be new people and new situations. She liked to customize when she could.

Her first day was interesting, but she mostly just learned everyone's names, then promptly forgot them. She ate her bagged lunch in the lunch-room with everyone else. She didn't speak unless spoken to. She went home after school and read her assigned chapters. It was a welcome distraction. Even robots thrived on fresh knowledge.

The first semester passed quickly. Her mother invited her for dinner that weekend to celebrate completing the term. They went to Luigi's. It was the only place Darlene felt she could handle the food. It was familiar.

"So tell me about the classes you'll take next term," her mother urged her as she sipped her wine.

Darlene took a sip of Sprite. She still had to drive back to Hopedale that night, and she wanted to stay sharp. "I'm taking a research class, a practice class, Intro to Mental Health, and Early Childhood Development. Next term, I'll be assigned to an internship. Next year, I get to apply for an internship of my choice. So far, it's been good. I like my professors and things seem to make sense."

"That's great, doll," her mom said. "Have you talked to your dad? I bet he's so proud."

Darlene nodded. "Yeah," she said. "He's proud." *As proud as he could be of such a soft science*, she thought. "He's helping me with tuition so I don't have to have huge loans, so that's great."

She stopped and tried to work up her nerve.

"Mom," she said, "I've been wanting to ask you: how would you feel about me moving back home for a while? Like until I'm done with school. To save money on rent and everything."

Mrs. Feinman smiled. "Doll baby, I'd love it if you moved back in with me. I like it so much better when you're there. The big old house feels so empty with just me there. Yes, you can move back in anytime you're ready."

Darlene felt a wave of relief. She didn't know how she was going to con-tinue to pay rent. She was also afraid that she would forget to buy food or fix herself meals. It was getting to be such a struggle to take care of herself. Being so many people every day was exhausting. Sometimes, it was all she could do to drive herself home after school, and then she would just fall exhausted into bed. Now, her mother could take care of her. She needed to be taken care of, at least for a while. She would be okay eventually. She wanted to be okay. She just needed a little time.

When they finished dinner, Darlene drove her mother home. She went inside to use the bathroom before driving home. Her mother went to check her phone messages. Darlene could hear a woman's voice coming from the answering machine, but she couldn't make out the words through the closed door. Then she heard her mother gasp and shout "Oh, God, no!"

Darlene flushed the toilet and ran out to her mother. Her mother was sobbing. Darlene had never seen her mother sob. It was a horrifying sight. "Mom, what is it? What's wrong?"

Mrs. Feinman looked at her daughter while tears ran down her face. "Oh my doll baby," she said. "Come, sit down. I need to tell you something."

And just like that, Traci's prophecy came true. Things got way, way worse.

Chapter 45

I Can't Do This Anymore

DARLENE STAYED AT HER MOTHER'S house. She couldn't leave. She couldn't get out of bed. She couldn't talk. Her friends called to check on her, but she wouldn't talk to them. She wouldn't see them. She couldn't eat. She couldn't sleep. She couldn't make herself care. Somewhere deep inside, she knew she couldn't go on like this. She had to pull out of it. But she had no idea how. She had no skills. She didn't know what to do. So she completely shut down.

After three days, nothing had changed. Her mother sat on the side of the bed and stroked her hair. "Doll," she said softly, "it's gonna be okay. I'll make sure it's okay. I promise you, I will do what I have to to make sure you'll be okay."

I promise, I promise. The words ran through Darlene's mind. *What was it? When you make a promise, something something. If you make a promise . . .*

"If you promise me," Traci said, *"you can't back out, okay? You are bound by your promise."*

She had made a promise to Traci, after Carl's mother died. She promised Traci that if she couldn't handle it anymore, if things got worse, if it was too much for her to take, she would find someone to talk to. Traci was depending on her to keep her word. If she didn't keep her word, Traci would be disappointed in her. And the last thing she ever wanted in the world was for Traci to be disappointed in her.

Mrs. Feinman patted Darlene's knee and got up to leave.

"Mom?" Darlene said softly.

Mrs. Feinman spun around and looked at Darlene expectantly. "'Yes, doll?"

"Mom, can you drive me somewhere?" Darlene asked. "And promise me, you won't ask me any questions?"

Mrs. Feinman smiled tentatively. "Of course I will, baby. Do you want to go now?"

Darlene nodded.

They pulled onto the main campus road, and Darlene directed her mother where to go. She had her pull up in front of the health center. "Mom, can you wait for me? I don't know how long I'll be. It could be a while."

Mrs. Feinman nodded. "I'll just pull into the lot back there," she said. "I'll wait as long as you need. I love you, Darlene."

"I love you, too, Mom."

She closed the car door and walked on wobbly legs into the health center. She walked past the front desk and followed the signs down the hall. She stopped at the reception area.

"I need to talk to someone," she told the receptionist. "Like right now."

The receptionist looked at her kindly. "Okay, honey, we'll get someone to see you as soon as possible. Can you show me your student ID?"

Darlene took out her ID and handed it over. She suddenly realized that she must look affright. She hadn't showered in three days. She had slept in the clothes she had been wearing. She wasn't wearing makeup, and her posture slumped. *Oh my God*, she thought, *I've become one of my old residents!*

The receptionist handed her ID back. "Darlene," she said, "you lucked out. We're not too busy this afternoon. We can get you in pretty quickly. But it might be a few minutes. Do you need someone to sit with you in the waiting area?"

Darlene shook her head. "No, thank you. I'll be okay."

She walked over to a chair and sat down. She looked around slowly.

There were a few other people waiting, reading magazines. One woman was staring at her child, who was crawling around an area filled with toys. She saw the others glance in her direction, and she wondered what they thought about her.

After ten minutes, a door opened to the left of the reception desk, and a young woman with short cropped blond hair and a business casual outfit stepped out. She looked at the waiting room. "Darlene?" she called out.

Darlene stood up and walked toward her. The woman smiled. Darlene thought she looked pretty. And friendly. And kind. Yeah, she would do.

"Hi, Darlene," the woman said as they stepped through the door and started down the long hallway. "I'm glad you're here today. My name is Aspen."

"Well, you know what happened next," Darlene said. "I took a leave of absence until the next semester. I moved in with my mom. I started seeing you twice a week at first, and once the crisis passed, once per week. My mom took care of me, which was something I finally let her do, and it was something I needed. She made me meals, took me out for walks, took me to movies and concerts, made sure I called my friends.

"Some big things happened with my friends. Kim had her baby, Amelia, and then Sally and Michelle both got pregnant, and then Michelle had her twins, Sadie and Julia, named after Beatles songs, just like her. Sally had her little girl, Jessica. I think they planned to have their babies at the same time. Pete and Carolyn got married. It was my first time at a wedding as a guest, not a bridesmaid, and Traci wasn't there, because she didn't really know Pete and Carolyn. James had been manager at the Marriott in Providence for some time, and he started making plans to open his own restaurant. Sally finished graduate school and found a publisher for her book. And most recently, I got the best news. Traci called me this week and told me she's moving to Eastboro! She's always wanted to come back, and now she has her chance. She's going to be manager of a boutique over by East Firehouse. I also suspect she's partially coming back for me because she knows I need her. I think she needs me, too."

Aspen smiled at the update. "And the other big news is how much you've learned and improved since beginning therapy," she said. "Darlene, you have a lot to be proud of. When you came to me that first day, you weren't able to take care of yourself at all. You had been on a downward spiral for months, if not for years. And look at you now. It's been a little over a year, you're back in school, you're developing an adult relationship with your mother, and you're letting your friends back into your life. You're really close to being done here. But there are a few more things I think we need to work on before that happens."

Darlene nodded. "My father," she said. "I need to figure out a way to come to terms with our relationship and figure out how I can forgive him and move on."

Aspen nodded. "But before we talk about that, let's talk about the progress you've made with your coping skills. Let's start with the skills you developed as a child. Eyes and ears. You distracted yourself by listening to other peoples' stories and conversations and passing them on to your friends. It got their attention. You learned this skill from your mom and Vee. Is this a skill that still helps you to distract?"

Darlene considered this. "No, not really. Now I think it's actually pretty invasive. With everything that's happened to me, I'd hate to think of myself being the subject of someone else's gossip."

Aspen nodded. "Eyes and ears served a purpose for you for a long time. It helped you survive many years of your childhood when you couldn't bear to focus on what was going on with you. So it's okay to say thank you to eyes and ears for what it did to help you, but then let it know that you don't need it anymore."

Darlene smiled. "I like that. That's a really nice way to put it."

Aspen glanced at her notes. "When you were really little," she said, "you would sway and move your feet and hear music in your head. What about that?"

Darlene smiled. "Yeah, I was doing that the first time Michelle approached me in kindergarten. She must have thought I was so strange. But I kept finding myself doing it over the years, even when I wasn't aware that I was. It was like I was dancing to my own private tune."

"Dancing," Aspen repeated. "You talked about dancing a lot. At the prom. At all the weddings. When you were dancing, you were happy. And you looked happy talking about it."

Darlene nodded. "Dancing makes me feel free, like I can fly. It's an amazing feeling, especially when I look around and see other people feeling the same way. It's like there is a moment in time when I can understand how other people feel. It's like magic."

"Do you ever go out dancing with your friends, when there isn't a wedding or a party?" Aspen wondered.

Darlene shook her head. "No," she said. "No one has ever suggested doing that."

"And you haven't suggested it either?"

"No," Darlene said. "Remember, I always went along with what everyone else wanted to do. I just wanted to be agreeable all the time."

"Let's talk about being agreeable all the time," Aspen went on. "Always deferring to the other person and what they want to do, to make them like you, and to make them happy, even at your own expense. Does that still work for you?"

"No," Darlene said quickly. "Not at all. It just led to hurt and pain. Going to Ithaca. Majoring in biology. Going to the cool sushi place." She shuddered. "What happened at junior prom. You know what? I need to start saying it out loud. What happened at junior prom. Charlie shamed me into performing oral sex on him when I clearly didn't want to. He made me think I owed him. I believed him. I ignored all the bells and whistles telling me to stop and run, just because I was afraid he would get angry. I thought doing that was better than him getting angry. But I was wrong. I should have been the one getting angry. And he would have deserved it, treating me that way. So yes, it's gonna be hard, but this has to stop. I need to start letting people know what it is that I want, even if it doesn't make them happy. And if it does make them happy, that's just an added bonus."

Aspen grinned. "Wow, Darlene," she said. "That was amazing. I'm really impressed. I hope you are, too. You know, this is the message that you need to give to your father."

Darlene nodded. "I know. But how?"

"You can go talk to him," Aspen suggested. "Or you can write him a letter. Or do both. He'll listen, Darlene. He has no choice. This is something that can free you."

Darlene nodded solemnly. "Yeah," she said. "This is what I need to do."

Chapter 46

The Letter

DARLENE WENT RIGHT TO HER room when she got home from ther-apy and started writing the letter to her father. She worked really hard to get it just right. She crossed things out and added things. She went to bed that night, and when she woke up in the morning, she wrote some more. When she was satisfied with the results, she copied the whole letter by hand onto pretty pieces of stationary paper she found in her mother's desk drawer, folded them, and put them in an envelope. Then, she got ready to go see her father.

Darlene got in the car and sat for a few minutes to prepare herself. Then she turned the engine and started to drive. She drove past the Drakes' house and the yard where she and Kim used to play as children. She drove past DeMarco Elementary school where she played on the playground every day with Michelle. She drove past the house she used to stay at with her father on their weekends together. She kept driving. She drove across town and past City Hall, with its statue of Jerome Farmer. Then she took a left turn. She followed the streets out of Eastboro and turned onto a side road. At the end of the road, she turned right onto a dirt road and went to the end. There, she parked her car and composed herself. She sighed. Then she grasped the letter in her hand and got out of the car.

It was dusk as she walked down the path in the cemetery toward her father's gravesite. She hadn't been there for over a year, but her feet remembered the way. When she got there, she noticed flowers in a mounted vase in front of the headstone, and several little rocks on top. There had been visitors, probably from her father's temple, and they had marked their place. Darlene scavenged around the area for a rock, found one she felt was just right, and put it atop her father's memorial stone. Then she greeted him.

"Hi, Dad," she said. "I haven't seen you in a while, but I have been thinking of you. I can't believe it's been over a year since you left. Sometimes it seems like years, and other times, it hurts just like it was yesterday. I wonder if it ever gets better. Anyway, I've been doing something you probably wouldn't approve of. I've been seeing a therapist. I just couldn't go on like I was any longer. I had to find a way to be happy. I would say 'happy again,' Dad, but I'm not sure that I've ever had a sustained period of happiness in my life. So now I want to be happy. I want to know what it's like. One of the things I never had a chance to do while you were alive was tell you how I feel about you, and about our relationship. So my therapist had me write you this letter." She held up the letter as if to show him. "So it might be hard to hear. It was really hard to write, but I think now it's time for you to know. So I'm just going to read it to you. I hope you're ready." She took out the papers, unfolded them, and cleared her throat.

Dear Dad,

Before I say everything I want to say to you, I want you to know that I love you. And I think you loved me too.

But things were never easy for us. I don't know when or why it started, but I was pretty young the first time you got angry at me. I was so scared. In that moment, I told myself that you didn't like me anymore, like you didn't like Mom anymore, and I became terrified you would leave me like you left Mom. I couldn't let that happen. So I learned to be good.

That was my downfall, and it followed me every day, for many years. I began to think that I only deserved love and affection if I was good, if I earned it. I was a child, Dad. I didn't know any better. So I was good. I found ways to be good for everyone, not just you. And being good was not the same for everyone I knew. I had to be different for every person I knew, so they would like me, so they would not get angry and leave me. So my mind split up into dozens of good little Darlenes who spent all their time trying to make everyone else happy.

This went on for years, Dad. Sometimes, it worked. But more often, it didn't. No matter how good I was for you, it was never enough, so I just kept trying harder. It was no use. I got myself into some pretty rough situations with boyfriends during that time, because I was so wrapped up in trying to make them happy that I lost my own sense of self. Those situations could have really ended badly. But I was lucky. I survived. And I never told anyone. I suffered in silence.

But I'm done suffering and being silent, Dad. It's a new era for me, one where I have to look out for myself, to find what works for me, what makes me happy. What would make me happy right now is if I could forgive you.

I think you did the best you could. I don't think you meant to break me. I think you loved me. I don't think you ever learned to really like me, though, for who I was. Your expectations were unreasonable, and they didn't align with mine. I recently came to the conclusion that it's possible you had a drinking problem. I'm not using that as an excuse, but it does explain a lot. You had a problem. Maybe it was your coping skill. I know a lot about those now. But at least now, I can try to understand and have empathy for you. I may have suffered, but you were suffering, too. Maybe we're actually kindred spirits.

I'll never forget the day that Mom got the message. It was the end of the first term of graduate school, and we had been celebrating. Mom got the message, and she broke down. She sat me down on the couch and told me.

You were at the City Club with your boss. You had just finished a round of golf. You went to the bar to have a drink. Suddenly, you clutched your chest, went pale, and collapsed on the floor. They called 911. One of the waiters started CPR. The ambulance got there, and the paramedics took over. They tried to shock you with the defibrillator, but it didn't work. They continued to try and transported you to the hospital. By then it was too late. There was nothing they could do. You were dead. You'd had a massive heart attack. Mom was still listed as your emergency contact with the hospital, so they called her, and I just happened to be with her when she heard the message.

I made it to your funeral, but after that, I was not okay. I kind of became catatonic. I couldn't get out of my bed. I really didn't care at that time if I lived or died. Mom was probably about to take me to the hospital to be admitted to the psych unit when I remembered a promise I had made to a friend and forced myself to go to the Eastboro State College crisis center. It was a decision that probably saved my life.

Dad, I would have loved to learn to forgive you while you were still here, but it took you leaving for it to happen. I regret that. So Dad, I forgive you. And I love you. And I hope that brings you some peace.

With all of my love,
Darlene

"How did it feel to read him that letter?" Aspen asked the next week.

Darlene sighed. "Good. And bad. But mostly good. Freeing. And it was good to go to the cemetery, too. I had been avoiding it since the funeral. I didn't even go to the unveiling of the headstone in May. My mom went. But I wasn't ready. I also got to see my grandparents there and put rocks on their headstones. That felt good. They knew I was there."

Aspen smiled. "You should be very proud of yourself, Darlene," she said. "You've come so far, and you're getting so close to finishing your MSW. We need to start planning wrapping up our work together. We can have a few more sessions and talk about a plan for you to continue to do your great work on your own."

Darlene looked at Aspen with a worried expression. "I don't know. It's scary. Do you really think I'm ready?"

"I really do. But there are some things you will need to do before we wrap up. There are some people you need to talk to, some people who need to, who deserve to, hear your story."

Darlene nodded solemnly. "Yes," she agreed. "Traci. Kim. Michelle." She paused. "My mom. She needs to know that everything was NOT always okay. She deserves to hear the truth."

"Yes," Aspen said. "And what is your plan to do all of this?"

Darlene considered. "Traci first. She's back now. I think that, as an adult, Traci is the closest thing I have to a best friend. So this weekend I'll talk to Traci. Then I have a week off from school, and I'm flying to California to visit the Bishops. I'll talk to Kim then. Then Michelle." Darlene sighed. "By that time, I'll be very close to graduation. And I'll probably be moving out of my mother's house. Before that happens, she and I will talk. We'll sit down somewhere, and we will talk about everything."

"That's a great plan, Darlene," Aspen said. "And remember, this is your story. You don't have to tell everything to everyone. It's up to you what you think is important for each of them to know. And for what you think is important for you to ask of them, too."

"Yes," Darlene said, setting her resolve. "When I get home today, I'm gonna call Traci. I'm gonna set the wheels in motion."

Chapter 47

TRACI

THEY WALKED THROUGH DARLENE'S BACKYARD and down the path to the woods. They pushed back the overgrowth and found the old trail. When they reached the clearing, they sat next to each other on a log and looked each other in the eyes.

"I'm ready to tell you everything," Darlene said.

"And I'm ready to hear it," Traci replied. "But first, I have to tell you something. It's gone. The brick wall. It's not there anymore. For the first time, I don't feel it. And the people . . ."

"They're gone, too?" Darlene asked.

Traci shook her head. "Not exactly gone," she explained. "More like, how do I explain this? It's like when the wall came down, they were no longer confined in their little rooms. They were allowed to roam free. And they found each other. And they came together. It's like they're still there, but they're also united. They're not alone anymore. They're not scared. Does that make sense?"

Darlene smiled. "Yes. And I'm going to tell you about the people now, so you understand. And then I'm gonna tell you what happened at junior prom."

Darlene explained the people. The prom trauma with Charlie. How her father bullied her into going to Ithaca to major in biology. She confirmed to Traci that she never wanted to be a biologist, how Traci had been right all along. She told her about Phil, and then she told her about her surgery, and what it was really for. Then she told her about Chris and Pete, and her overwhelming sadness and loneliness. She told her about her promotion, and what it took away from her. And she told her about how her father's death on top of all this had nearly killed her.

Traci was in tears by the time the stories were finished. She put her arms around Darlene and held her tight.

"Oh my God," she said. "Darlene, what I wouldn't give right now to go back in time, and save you, and hold you, and to let you know that you, just you the way you were, were just perfect! But I couldn't tell. It was as if you were a blank slate to me. I feel like I failed you."

Darlene swiped away her own tears. "No, Traci," she said. "You didn't fail me. If anything, you helped me. You let me know early on that something was off. My brick wall. I lied to you, over and over. But I also made you a promise, one I said I would never break. It literally saved my life. If it wasn't for you, I would have just died in my bed after my father died. The promise I made to you meant more to me than anything. I never want to let you down."

Traci shook her head. "You could never let me down, Darlene. I love you."

Darlene smiled. She reached over and kissed Traci on the lips and nibbled on her bottom lip. "I love you, too, Traci," she said softly. "You're my mouse. My one and only mouse. Yes, I am a rat girl, but you are my mouse." She paused. "Traci," she said, "will you come home with me? Will you stay with me tonight? To be my mouse, like at Sally and James's wedding? I would love that."

Traci nodded. "Yes," she said. "I would love that, too."

They went back to the house, and Darlene told her mother that Traci was staying over. They all had dinner together, and then they watched a movie on the VCR. Then Darlene and Traci went upstairs to get ready for bed.

"Do you have something for me to wear?" Traci asked as she stood beside Darlene's full-sized bed.

Darlene shook her head. Her heart was pounding. "No," she lied. "You don't need anything to wear to bed."

Traci looked confused for a moment, but then she looked into Darlene's eyes, and she smiled.

"I understand now," she said. "It's like a door has opened into your soul for me, and I can see you. Tonight, tonight is supposed to happen. We're supposed to be together. It's meant to be. We are meant to be each other's mouse. But just for tonight, Darlene. I can see it now. It's gonna happen for you, and it's gonna happen soon. A rat. A good rat. A man. He's gonna come out of nowhere, and he's gonna blow you right off your feet. And you're gonna rock his world. And this is gonna be it for you."

Darlene furrowed her eyebrows. "Really?" she asked. "So this is what it feels like, huh, when you can intuit something about me? You can really see me. It feels wonderful. But Traci, the rat can wait for now. Tonight, I want tonight to be the night we should have had at Sally's wedding. I want to make you feel good. I want to make you feel the love I feel for you in a special way. I have no illusions that we're going to be a couple, and I never want us to stop being close friends. But I'm learning to ask for what I want, and I know, right now, this is what I want. The rat comes later."

Traci walked around the bed to Darlene's side and gently lifted Darlene's shirt over her head. Then she kissed her lightly. Darlene started removing Traci's clothes. She felt an anticipation building she'd never experienced before. Traci stared into her eyes.

"Darlene, this is not just about making me feel good. This is also about me making *you* feel good. This is a give and take. It should always be a give and take. I think I'm gonna make you feel some things tonight that you never felt before, and I want to start now." She pulled her close and kissed her, and they moved onto the bed.

Later, Darlene lay on the bed feeling content and thoroughly satisfied. Traci lay beside her breathing hard. "So that's what it feels like to be with a mouse," Darlene said.

"No," Traci corrected. "That's what it feels like to be with a person, a person who cares greatly about you and thinks about how to make you happy."

Darlene felt tears roll down the sides of her cheeks. "Thank you, Traci," she said, "for believing in me."

"Always," Traci said. She turned on her side to face Darlene. "While we were, well, you know," she started, "I had another insight. For the first time in my life, I had an insight about myself. It's gonna happen for me too, soon, and it will be the real thing. And somehow, Darlene, you and I will always be connected after we meet our people. Beyond just being friends, which we'll always be. I don't know what the connection is. I can just tell that it's very strong."

Darlene smiled. She loved the idea of being connected to Traci in some way forever. "Rat or mouse?" she asked.

Traci shrugged. "I don't know," she admitted. "Person, I guess. But either one is okay with me. I think I'll know them when I see them." She grinned.

Darlene looked deep into Traci's eyes. "I'm happy for us," she said. "We're gonna find love, and we'll both never be alone again. And I'm happy now."

Traci reached over and caressed Darlene's hair. "And that's really all that matters." She leaned over to kiss her again.

Chapter 48

CARL WAS AT HOME WITH the three children, and Kim took Darlene to see the SCCC campus in Seska where she had gone to school for two years. The horticultural department had grown lush, beautiful gardens with paths for guests, and that's where the two lifelong friends explored. They found a bench in front of a patch of red and yellow tulips and sat down.

"I'm ready," Kim said.

So Darlene told her. She started with her parents fighting, and her attempts to block it out. She continued with how she became so divided in her head about how to be with people so they would like her. About her guilt over the way she treated Michelle and pushed her away. About trying to make Charlie happy, even though she didn't even like him. Then she told her about what happened at the party after junior prom.

Kim stopped her there. "Darlene," she said with tears in her eyes. "I had no idea. You told me a couple days later that you were thinking of breaking up with him, but you made it not seem like a big deal. What he did was so wrong. You didn't deserve to be treated that way. No one does. And it wasn't your fault, none of it. I was so wrapped up with what was going on with Carl that I couldn't even see beyond my own nose. I am so sorry! I should have been there to look out for you, to take care of you!"

"No," Darlene assured her. "You not knowing was part of my master plan, can't you see? Everything had to be okay, for everyone. I hadn't told anyone but my therapist until I told Traci last week. But Kim, I'm the one who should be sorry. About the Christmas party sophomore year."

Kim looked confused. "Why would you be sorry? You didn't do anything!"

Tears sprung from Darlene's eyes. This still felt so fresh, even after all these years. "I left you there, at the party. I should have made you come with us. Or had someone else bring Michelle home. It was my fault, what happened to you!'

Kim shook her head. "What happened to me?" she repeated. "No, that was totally on me! You couldn't have made me leave the party if you'd tried. Remember how stubborn I was? And Michelle needed you. You were being her devoted friend. No, what happened at the party is my fault and my fault only. Well, of course, it was Chris's fault, too."

Darlene's eyes widened. "Chris!" she exclaimed. "It was Chris Mahoney? All this time, it was Chris you had sex with at the Christmas party?" She gasped.

"Oh my God, Darlene, you really didn't know? No one ever told you?"

"No!" Darlene replied. "Why would anyone ever tell me? You refused to tell me. Oh my God, now it all makes sense! You were upset that it was Chris! Because of Carl! Oh, God, Kim. No wonder!"

Kim looked down. "There's a little more to it than that, Darlene," she confessed. "And I never told this to anyone." She paused. "It's possible I might have known what I was doing that night. I played it all off like I was drunk and stoned, and I was, but I just know. I saw Chris, and I'm pretty sure I saw a golden opportunity to do something to totally sabotage my life, and I jumped on it."

"Why, Kim?" Darlene pleaded. "Why would you do that? Why on Earth would you choose to sabotage yourself like that?"

"Because I thought it was my fault," Kim responded. She looked up at Darlene with tears in her eyes. "My dad. I thought his accident was my fault. I thought I didn't deserve anything good to ever happen to me because I couldn't stop it from happening!"

Darlene touched her arm gently. "You were a ten-year-old child. There was nothing you could have done! Why did you blame yourself?"

Kim nodded. "Yeah, I guess maybe I blamed myself for my father's accident for the same reason you blamed yourself for what happened to me at the Christmas party. We were stupid, fucked-up kids! Darlene, if only you and I had talked about all this back then. Just imagine. Would things have gone differently for us? Why was it all so fucked up back then? Why did we think we deserved to be so unhappy? Like you said, we were just children!"

Darlene wrapped her arms around her friend. "I don't know," she whispered in her ear. "Maybe we didn't deserve it at all. Maybe it really wasn't our fault." She sat up. "But on a positive note, it does make me feel better to know that I wasn't the only one who was so fucked up!"

They both laughed. Kim blew her nose and then sat up straight. "You have more to tell me, don't you?"

Darlene nodded. "I do."

She told Kim about everything that happened in college up until the death of her father. When she was done, Kim put her arms around her and held her tight, silently, for several minutes. She didn't ask any questions. When they let go, Kim dabbed her eyes with her tissue and offered one to Darlene. Then they started to walk back around the garden, holding hands.

Chapter 49

MICHELLE

"I KNOW ABOUT CHRIS AND Kim now," Darlene told Michelle. It was late July, and they were sitting out on the deck at Michelle and Chris's house on a rare cool midsummer day. The twin babies were at the park with their father, and Darlene and Michelle were sitting on reclining lawn chairs, sipping lemonade.

Michelle turned to look at Darlene. "How did you find out?" she asked.

"From Kim," Darlene admitted. "She thought I already knew. She and I had never talked about it after that one phone call the day after the party, and I just assumed no one knew. Now I know that everyone involved knew, and Chris told you before you got married."

Michelle nodded. "I'm sorry I never told you, Darlene," she said, "but I didn't think it was something you thought about anymore. I always blamed myself for what happened, because we didn't tell James to look out for her like we were supposed to, and I was worried that it was all my fault. But when Chris told me, I understood."

"You thought it was your fault?" Darlene chuckled. "I always thought it was my fault! For years! I thought it was my duty to protect Kim. But now I know, you can't really protect someone from themselves."

Michelle nodded slowly. "Darlene," she said, "what I really want to talk about was what happened in college. Your surgery. I can't believe you went through that and never told me. Or anyone! It must have been so hard for you. Do you ever, well, think about it now?"

Darlene nodded. "I do," she said. "Every time I have a period, I wonder if it's a real one or not. So, yeah, I guess I think about it a lot. Like what would have happened if that little cluster of cells had continued on its true path and embedded itself in my uterus instead? Like what would have happened next."

"I can't believe it was on the same day that Kim announced her pregnancy," Michelle said. "If you'd had a viable pregnancy, you might have had your babies at the same time."

"I've thought of that," Darlene said. "Maybe a month or so after Drake. But I don't know what I would have done if I had found out I was pregnant. My relationship with Phil wasn't at all stable, and I had been a total emotional wreck for years. I might have decided to terminate. And I probably never would have told anyone it even happened. As it is, my father never knew. I don't know. I'm just glad I didn't have to make that kind of decision."

Michelle nodded. "So in a weird, warped way, this was probably better for you in the long run. Only because you turned out okay. Are you worried, now, that you'll have any trouble getting pregnant? And is it hard to see us all getting pregnant and having babies all the time?"

Darlene shook her head. "I'm happy for everyone. I don't know what will happen. I think I want to have kids, and I hope I meet someone who wants to have them with me. According to Traci, that's supposed to happen really soon. Then we'll play it by ear."

Michelle reached out and took Darlene's hand. "I'm so glad you're talking about all this stuff now," she said. "There were so many things over the years, so much that makes sense now that you told me. And now, we can all be there for you, to help you any time you need it."

Darlene smiled gratefully. "Thank you so much, Michelle," she said. "And just to let you know, I'm done with gossip now. It just doesn't help me now like it did back then. So no more juicy stories." She paused. "Except for one about me, but you have to promise not to tell anyone, not even Chris."

Michelle looked intrigued. "Oh my God, Darlene. Spill it."

"Okay." Darlene took a deep breath. "I had mind-blowing sex with Traci a few weeks ago."

"What???" Michelle almost fell out of her chair.

Chapter 50

GRADUATION

"I'M SO PROUD OF YOU, Darlene," Mrs. Feinman said. "I can't believe you got your master's degree! The first one in our family! Your father would be so proud, too." She hugged her daughter.

Darlene nodded at her mother. "I know he would be, Mom," she said. "And I promise, I'm not just saying that."

Mrs. Feinman looked at Darlene and furrowed her brow. "What does that mean?"

Darlene sighed. She knew the time was right. "Mom," she said, "sit down. You've always wanted to know what it was between me and Dad. And now I'm gonna tell you."

Mrs. Feinman sat down cautiously. Darlene sat by her side, their thighs touching lightly.

"It all started before kindergarten," she said.

Fifteen minutes later, Darlene sat hugging her mother, both in tears. "If I had known any of this," Mrs. Feinman said. "If I had known what Charlie did to you . . . maybe it's better that I didn't. I might have killed him with my bare hands. Oh, Darlene. I just don't understand. All of these things, starting with the time I left you with your father and you spilled his beer. Why did you always tell me everything was fine? Why couldn't you tell me? I wouldn't have gotten angry at you. I would have tried to help you. I always thought we were close, but now I'm thinking that I missed so much of what was going on! Why did I always believe you when you said everything was okay?"

Darlene pulled back. "Aspen said that it's possible that when I told you those lies, I actually believed them myself at the moment, so they probably sounded true. But I think that it's also what you wanted to hear. Mom, remember when you and Vee were going to Atlantic City before I started kindergarten, and you took me and Kim to Friendly's? I remember it like it was yesterday, and I don't know why. When you told me I would be staying with Dad for five days, you and Vee looked at each other and you both looked worried. I never knew what it meant. Then when you came back and I told you I didn't want to go to Dad's house anymore if you went away, you pulled the car over and asked me if something had happened. Mom, were you expecting that something would happen?"

Mrs. Feinman shed new tears. She shook her head. "I didn't want to leave you alone with him," she admitted. "I didn't think he would physically hurt you in any way, but I just didn't know if I could trust him with you for that long. But Vee and I had to go on that trip. It's not my story to tell you, so I can't say why, but we had no choice. We had to go right then. He was the only one who could watch you. Doll baby, after you were born, your father changed. I was never sure why, but I had my suspicions. Before that, he was a loving and attentive husband, generous and fun. We had a good marriage. But when it went bad, it went bad fast. I kept hoping it would pass, and things would get back to normal, but they never did. I tried to shield you from the fighting, but I failed. There was just too much fighting. And finally, one day, I'd had enough, and I told him I wanted a divorce. And that was our biggest fight ever. Do you remember when he left for good?"

Darlene nodded. "I remember the last big fight," she said, closing her eyes. "I tried to block it out. I got good at that. But I could hear things anyway. I heard loud banging. I think I heard something shatter. I got scared. I ran to my door. I heard words."

She stopped, the images and sounds getting clearer in her mind. Now that all the people in her head had gotten quiet, the memories were much more vivid.

"And you told him to get out. There was silence. Then there was his voice. When his voice got really quiet, that was when it was the scariest. I had to strain to hear. He said, 'I hate you, Barbara. I don't think I ever loved you.' I couldn't believe he would say something like that to anyone! You were crying really loud. That just made him go on. Then he said, 'You've always loved Darlene more than me. She ruined everything. I wish she had never been born.' Then he went out the door. Then the door slammed, and he drove away.

"I went back in my room, and I started to sway. That's what I did back then. It was my anxiety dance. I was swaying, and rocking, and singing in my head, and then the music got louder and louder. Then I sang out loud. Over and over, I kept singing. Until it went away. And I forgot what he said, until right now. I don't know how I forgot. Now I don't know how I remember. When I went downstairs, you must have cleaned everything up because everything looked normal again. You saw me, and you looked happy and you were smiling. You asked me what I wanted for dinner. And that was that. Like it never happened."

Mrs. Feinman was openly crying now, and the tears were running off her face and onto the front of her skirt. "I . . . I never knew you heard all that," she said softly. "He didn't say it very loud. It was almost a whisper. I remember being relieved that at least he didn't say it in front of you. I never dreamed that you heard."

Darlene nodded. "I heard. I may have forgotten, but I heard. My daddy didn't even want me to be born. My daddy hated my mommy. So it made sense when I stayed with him that he got mad at me. It wasn't that he just didn't like me. It was that, deep down inside, I also knew that he didn't love me. You never said anything, because you didn't think I heard, so I just thought that it was okay with you that my daddy didn't love me. Oh, Mom, I was so wrong. All this time, I thought you left me with a man that you knew hated me. And I didn't want to let you know that you were right. I just wanted you to think everything was okay."

Darlene stopped talking and hung her head. Then she started to sob.

Mrs. Feinman put her arms around her daughter. "Oh, doll," she said.

"He didn't hate you. I promise. He loved you very much. He was just so, so angry at me. He wanted to say something that he knew would hurt me to the core. If he knew that you had heard, he would have been mortified. No, baby, your daddy loved you. I could hear it in his voice all the time when he talked about you. Yes, he didn't like me much in the end, but that had nothing to do with you. Baby, your daddy, well, I think, no, I know he had a drinking problem. It started around the time you were born. I thought it was just the beer, but it wasn't. It was his work, and that club. They would all hang around that club, smoking cigars and drinking scotch. And your dad, well, he couldn't handle that scotch. He got mean. I think that's what started it all, looking back. It wasn't you being born like I had thought at first. I thought he didn't like being a father. But no, it was that he was up for this promotion, and they kept giving him that damn scotch, even at the office!"

Darlene looked up. "S-so when he went to the club to go golfing, or go to lunch all those times?" Mrs. Feinman nodded. "So he *was* an alcoholic. And when he couldn't drink . . ."

"He'd go through withdrawal," Mrs. Feinman answered. "It wasn't pretty. I think his drinking is what eventually caused the heart attack that killed him. His body just couldn't handle the years of drinking."

Darlene stared at the living room wall for several seconds, but she didn't see anything. "So my daddy did love me," she said softly. "He was just fucked up, just like everyone else."

Mrs. Feinman looked at her daughter as if shocked by her words. Then she burst out laughing.

"Oh my God, Darlene," she said. "Truer words have never been spoken. You hit the nail right on the head!"

Darlene stared at her mother and watched her laugh. Then her lip quivered, and she snorted.

Mother and daughter sat laughing together for several minutes. Then they hugged for several more before it was time to prepare for their celebratory night out.

"Congratulations on your graduation," Aspen said.

Darlene laughed. "Which one?"

"Both," Aspen said. "You and I now have matching degrees. But I have another certificate for you, too." She reached over to her desk, grabbed a stiff piece of paper, and handed it to Darlene. "As I said, happy graduation."

Darlene looked at the certificate and read the words out loud. "This is to certify that Darlene Feinman has completed exemplary work on her own self, and hereto and henceforth and all other forths will have one, and only one, Darlene in residence in her head at any given time. Signed today, August 27, 1993, by Aspen Wright, Official Head People Shrinker, LCSW." Darlene laughed. "Very funny. Don't quit your day job to write greeting cards, okay, Aspen?"

Aspen laughed. "So what's next, Darlene?"

Darlene smiled. "Now, I find a job. A job I will love. Then a place of my own. And something really, really cool is that my friend James is having a soft opening of his restaurant this weekend for friends and family, and all my friends will be there. I'm going with Traci. My friends have been so awesome to me. I can't wait to see them. And Aspen." She paused. "Thank you. It's like thank you isn't even near enough. You have listened to me, and heard me, and helped me to help myself out of a giant abyss I had thought

I was bound to die in. You've given me something to strive for in my own practice. All I'll have to do if I get stuck is think, 'What would Aspen say?' And the answer will be right there in front of me."

Aspen smiled, and Darlene thought she saw the start of a single tear in the corner of one of her eyes. This wonderful therapist who knew all of her deep parts and secrets. Darlene knew absolutely nothing about her private life. "Thank you, Darlene," Aspen said. "That's probably one of the nicest things anyone has ever said to me. You are going to make a fantastic social worker."

Darlene stood. "Is it within your comfort zone to let me hug you?" she asked. "Because if it isn't, I'll respect your boundaries."

Aspen stood and embraced her briefly. "A great social worker," she repeated. Then she walked Darlene out the door and down the hall. "Goodbye, Darlene," she said, "and good luck." They waved at each other, then Aspen disappeared behind the door.

Darlene looked at the receptionist. It was the same one who was there the day that she had first come in. She raised her hand to her.

"Goodbye, Millie."

Millie looked up and smiled. "Goodbye, Darlene. Be well."

And Darlene left the counseling center for the last time.

Chapter 51

And So It Ends . . . Or Begins

TRACI PICKED UP DARLENE IN her red Ford Mustang. "Have you given any more thought to moving into my house with me?" Traci asked as they pulled out of Darlene's mother's driveway. "You know I have the room. And you don't have to pay any rent until you've gotten a job."

Darlene smiled. "I have been thinking about it a lot," she replied. "I was thinking, if we're somehow going to be connected together forever in some way like you said, it might make sense for us to be roommates. As long as we maintain our boundaries, especially if we're going to be meeting the people of our dreams someday soon. But yes, I will move in with you."

"Yay!" Traci exclaimed. "I'm so excited! It will be so fun. And I'll give you plenty of personal space. And I've been thinking about putting in a swimming pool next summer."

Darlene's mouth dropped open. "Are you fucking serious?" she asked. "Oh man, if I had said no before, I'd totally be changing my mind around now!"

They arrived at James's new restaurant. There was a large sign outside that stated its name: MILO AND GINGER'S. Darlene had to laugh.

Those were the names of Sally's childhood cats. It was such a Sally thing to do. She and Traci got out of the car and headed toward the door. Darlene immediately saw James's brother, Howie, standing in the hostess area with his boyfriend, Kevin. "Hey guys," she said. "You remember Traci, right?"

"Of course!" Howie replied, and he came over to hug them both.

"This place is so great!" Darlene said. "Such a nice space! I'm so happy for James and Sally. By the way, where are they?"

"James is supervising in the kitchen, naturally," Howie said, and he pointed to a dining table, "and there's Sally right there, sitting with Michelle and, oh, that's James's business partner, Steve."

"Business partner?" Darlene asked. "I didn't know he even had a business partner." She looked at the table. And there he was. James's business partner. Steve.

She walked over to the table with Traci. Sally stood and hugged them both. "I'm so glad you guys made it!" she said. "Steve, I want you to meet our friends. This is Steve, James's partner and friend from culinary school. This is Darlene and Traci, some more of our friends from high school."

Steve stood. He looked at Traci and smiled. "Hi, Traci," he said, and he shook her hand. He turned to Darlene. "Hey, Darlene," he said, and he reached for her hand. His hand was warm, and strong, and seemed to radiate some sort of electrical current directly into Darlene's body. They maintained eye contact for the count of four inside Darlene's now non-crowded head. Then they both looked away. "It's nice to meet you both," Steve said.

Darlene heard someone clear their throat behind Steve. "Oh, I'm so sorry," he said. A gorgeous young woman with light brown hair had just stepped up next to him. Darlene's heart fell. Steve's wife. "Traci, Darlene," Steve said, "this is my little sister, DeeDee. DeeDee, this is Traci and Darlene."

DeeDee came forward to shake their hands. "Sorry about my rude, much older brother," she said. "It's nice to meet you both."

Traci smiled. "Nice to meet you, DeeDee," she said. She grasped Darlene's arm. "Darlene, we've got to wash our hands before we eat. Let's go find where they're hiding the ladies' room in this place, okay?"

"Oh," Steve said. He pointed to the back right corner. "Right over there, down the hall."

"Thanks," Darlene said, and she smiled at Steve. "We'll be right back."

She and Traci walked calmly to the ladies' room, and as soon as they got inside, they turned to each other and made quiet shrieking noises.

"Oh my God!" Traci yelped. "He's your rat! He's got to be your rat!"

Darlene nodded enthusiastically. "I know," she said. "And he has a sister, Traci, a beautiful sister. I think we may have found your mouse! My rat and your mouse might be brother and sister! There's the connection!"

They looked at each other again, then grabbed each other's elbows.

"Oh my God!" they said together.

Stavros: Hitting Rock Bottom

Chapter 52

Nature's Way of Telling You

DRINKING MADE THE PAIN GO away. At least for a while.

Stavros learned this very early in his college career. It was so easy to get drinks in college. It was as though no one paid attention. There were bars that let students in if they were eighteen, and there were parties at fraternities and sororities. Sometimes, his dorm mates had parties in their rooms. He didn't know where they got the beer, but he didn't complain. Beer made the pain go away. At least for a while.

His pain was always present. It was there the day he arrived at Pittsburgh State College. It moved into his dorm room with him. He decorated his walls with it. It came with him to classes, to the dining hall, and to his first trip to Stanley's Pub. There, he drank his first college beer, and then his second. The pain started to lessen, at least a little. So he drank another. And another. By the time he got back to his room that night, his roommate had to pile him onto his bed and pull the covers over him. He was wasted. He either fell asleep or passed out, he never knew which.

When he woke up, he had a raging headache and nausea. And the pain was back.

He was eighteen years old. He was eight hours away from home. And Lindi was gone. It felt as though one of his arms had just dropped off his body without warning. He looked complete on the outside, but inside, he felt shattered. He had only felt this level of loss once before, and, really, how could he compare his breakup with Lindi to the death of his mother? But it was there. He remembered when Rebel died. He kept wanting to talk to her, to ask her what to do next, how to make it okay. And now he felt the same way about Lindi. Before, he wanted comfort from his mother. Now, he wanted it from his best friend. But she was gone.

Stavros drank beer on weekends until the pain left, and then he drank more for good measure. He wasn't deterred by the hangovers. But soon, the pain got worse on weeknights. So he would drink beer so he could sleep.

He went to classes, but he found it hard to concentrate on the lectures. He'd go back to his dorm and read his textbooks. Somehow, that would keep him afloat. He passed his tests, but not by much. After his exams, he would crash and go out with his dorm mates for some more beers.

Winter break was approaching. Stavros was going to take the bus home. He called Deanna.

"I'm coming home for two weeks," he told her. "I don't think I can see her. I just don't think I can take it."

"Oh, Stavros," she said sympathetically. "You don't need to worry about it. Lindi's staying in Denver for the break." She paused. "I . . . think she feels the same as you do. She won't be coming home until summer."

"Oh," Stavros responded, feeling both relieved and disappointed. "Alright. So I don't need to worry about running into her."

"Stav, are you okay? You just don't sound like yourself."

"It's been hard," he told her. He could feel tears coming, but he pushed them back. "But I'll be okay. It'll be good to see you and Mario and Alec. And not to have to worry." He knew every single thing in Amherst would remind him of Lindi.

"Okay, Stav," Deanna said. "Let's get together on Sunday, okay? Just you and me. And then we'll hang out with Mario and Alec. But I think you and I need some time together alone."

"Yeah," Stavros said, "that would be good." He wanted Deanna to tell him everything she knew about Lindi, how she was doing, what she was thinking, if she was in as much pain as he was. If she would ever change her mind and agree to be his wife. But he knew that if that were the case, Lindi would have told him herself by now. He couldn't ask Deanna anything about her. It would hurt too much to know.

When he got off the phone, he planned to join his friends at the pub. But it was just too much. He couldn't even get himself to leave his room. So he opened his mini-fridge and took out a beer. And he drank it alone. And then he drank another.

Chapter 53

WINTER BREAK

THE BUS RIDE HOME WAS long and unpleasant. The man in the seat across the aisle smelled like perspiration and rotten teeth. It was raining, and the morning skies were dark and gray. Someone was playing music on a boom box, and the bass was turned up way too high. Stavros had a headache and his temples were throbbing. He was worried he would vomit. He closed his eyes and pretended to be asleep, and at some point, he actually drifted off.

When he awoke, he checked his watch. There were still five hours left in his journey. The music was still playing, and strangely, it sounded like the same song that had been playing as he fell asleep. At least the rain had stopped, and he could see blue breaks in the clouds. His headache had abated, so he pulled out his book. He was able to lose himself in his reading for over an hour. He nibbled on his snacks and popped open a can of Coke. He had been avoiding drinking anything because he didn't want to have to brave the bus bathroom. But he was thirsty and was sure he was dehydrated from drinking the night before. The Coke helped.

Stavros wondered how he would get beer in Amherst, but he knew this was a stupid way to think. He couldn't get wasted in front of his father and Drea. He couldn't let his sister see him like that. But he'd need to figure out another way to get through the days and nights.

The bus finally pulled into the station in Amherst. Stavros peeled himself out of his seat and grabbed his bag from the overhead rack. He pushed up to the front of the bus, eased down the stairs, and remembered to thank the bus driver.

He walked into the station lobby and Andreas was there. His father embraced him. "It's so good to have you home, my son," his father said. "How was the ride?"

"Long and smelly," Stavros admitted. "Where's Drea?"

"She stayed at home," Andreas told him. "Her friend Violet is over. I think they may be baking something for you." Andreas grabbed Stavros's bag and started to walk toward the exit.

Stavros smiled. Baking was the way he and Drea showed love. He wanted to see Drea, but not while in the state he was in. He would run upstairs when he got home, wash his face, and change his clothes. Only then could he face his sister.

Violet joined them for dinner, and the conversation remained light. Stavros told them all about his dorm and his roommate. He gave them a rundown of all of his classes, and the places he would go around campus, except for the Pub. He didn't tell them about the Pub.

After dinner, Drea brought out a freshly made baklava. Stavros smiled at her in gratitude. It was her first attempt at making one without him, and it was delicious. She served it proudly with vanilla ice cream. Stavros knew now that he was home.

That night, Stavros lay on the bed in Drea's room with her, telling her the stories, the ones that never got stale. She listened attentively, sometimes saying the words along with him as if they were singing the lyrics to a classic song.

"Stavros," Drea said after he finished his last story, "it's not the same without you here. Papa hired a lady to come make dinners for us. He doesn't know how to bake, and he doesn't have time to learn, really. And it's not his fault." She paused and looked at him with her eyes wide. "Stav, it's like I finally know what it's like to not have a mom. It's like, all this time, you've been my mom."

Stavros felt his heart sink. He thought of all the time he had been griev-ing his loss of Lindi like a death, and at the same time, Drea had been actually grieving for their mother, for the first time. He was speechless.

"Stavros," Drea said, barely above a whisper. "Did I kill Rebel?"

The words hit Stavros like a brick to the face. "What?" he said. "No, of course not, Drea! Why would you even think that?"

Drea shrugged. "This kid in my class overheard me saying that my mom died when I was born, and he asked me what it felt like to kill my own mother."

Stavros could feel his heart rate increase. "What did you say to him?" he asked her.

"I didn't say anything," Drea responded. "Susan did. She told him he was a big stupid jerk to say something like that. Then she pushed him."

"Oh," Stavros said, feeling glad that someone had pushed the boy. "Drea, no, you had nothing to do with Mom's death. You were just a tiny little baby growing in her uterus. But Mom's body just couldn't handle the pregnancy. It doesn't matter if it had been you or twenty different babies. There was nothing you did or could have done to cause her to get so sick. Sometimes, pre-eclampsia happens to other pregnant moms, too. Some-times, they get better after the baby's born, and that's what we all thought would happen with Mom. But later, we found out that she had an aneurysm in her brain. It might have stayed there forever and not done anything, but the stress from the pre-eclampsia and her surgery was just too much. Drea, she wanted to have you so badly. I was there when she was holding you for the last time. I could see how much she loved you. Looking back, I know she knew she didn't have much time left. She was trying to memorize your face, to remember every little bit of you, as if she could bring the memory with her where she was going. Maybe she did."

He looked up at Drea. She had tears running down her face. Stavros couldn't remember ever seeing Drea cry over their mother. He didn't know if this was a positive or negative thing. He reached out and stroked her hair. "You okay?"

Drea nodded. "Yeah," she said. "My mommy loved me. Rebel loved me, even before I was born." She turned to face him. "I miss her, Stavros. How can that be? I don't even remember her, but I miss her."

Stavros put his arms around her and let her cry on his shoulder. "I know, Dray," he said. "Sometimes these things don't make any sense. I've spent your whole life telling you Rebel stories, every night. And now I'm gone. It must be like she's gone, too." He pulled away and looked at her. He had tears in his eyes, too. "Maybe," he said, "we need to make a plan, where we talk on the phone a few times a week, and I tell you the stories. Do you think that would help?"

Drea nodded. "Yeah, I think it would," she replied. "Stav, I miss you so much. I wish you didn't have to go back to college. I wish you could always be with us."

"I know," Stavros said. "But someday, Drea, you'll go away to college, and I'll need to have something to do with myself. So I have to go to college to learn to do something. But Dray, I miss you, too, every day." He hugged her again. "I'm really tired. I need to get ready to go to bed. I'm going to see Deanna tomorrow. I'll bring her back over here to say hi. Tomorrow night, I'm gonna see the guys, too. Let's go brush our teeth, and then we'll both get some sleep, okay?"

Drea sniffed. "Okay, Stavros."

Chapter 54

THE LONG NIGHT, THE DAY AFTER

AFTER STAVROS GOT READY FOR bed, he crawled under the fresh, clean sheets in his childhood bed and closed his eyes. He was exhausted, but sleep wouldn't come. He tried changing positions, but nothing helped. Then it hit him: the first wave of pain. It felt like a stabbing in his heart. Her face appeared behind his closed eyes. *No*, he thought. *Not now. I need to sleep. Let me sleep, Lindi, go away.* She would not comply.

It was one in the morning. Andreas and Drea were sound asleep. Stavros got up and made his way to the bathroom. He opened the medicine cabinet and looked around. There had to be something in there to make him numb, to help him sleep. An old prescription bottle of sleeping pills, some expired Benadryl, anything. He couldn't find anything. He went downstairs to see if there was any chance that his father had suddenly developed a taste for mixed drinks and was stowing a bottle of alcohol on one of the pantry shelves. Or some wine in the refrigerator. Or even some ouzo from ten years ago. Flat, leftover champagne from graduation. He didn't care. Just something. He couldn't find anything. His heart was pounding. His head was aching with memories. It was too quiet. It was like Lindi was in every cell of his body.

He went back to bed and got under the covers. It was no good. He turned on the light and read for a while. When he was feeling sleepy, he turned out the lights again. He closed his eyes and could still feel the motion of the bus from earlier in the day. He tried to let it lull him to sleep while he told himself Rebel stories, and when he finished them all, he recalled the stories of the Greek warriors. Then he started to count in Greek. He didn't know how long this went on, but the next time he opened his eyes, light was slipping through the gaps in the window shades. It was morning. He had no idea if he had slept. He got up anyway.

His father was up, reading his Sunday paper with his mug of coffee. "Good morning, Stavros," he said with a smile. "You're up early. I thought for sure you'd sleep in. Did you sleep well?"

"Yeah, Pop," he lied. "Did you make a pot of coffee? Is there any for me?"

"I didn't know you drank coffee now," Andreas said. "I made a pot, and there's a bit left, but it's yours if you want it."

"Thanks, Pop," Stavros said. He went into the kitchen and poured himself the rest of the coffee. He sipped it. It was bitter and unpleasant. He didn't like coffee, but he knew he'd need it to get himself through the day. He added two tablespoons of sugar and some milk, and it made the coffee slide down his throat with ease. He checked the clock on the oven. It was 8:45. He would give Deanna until 10, and then call her to plan their day. He grabbed a box of Frosted Flakes and a bowl and brought them out to the dining room. He went back for his coffee, the milk, and a spoon and then sat down and fixed his breakfast. His father watched him from his armchair.

"So Stavros," Andreas said, "how did you like your classes this semester?"

"Um, they were good," Stavros said between mouthfuls of his cereal. "They were interesting, I guess."

"Which was your favorite?" Andreas inquired.

Stavros thought about it. "I guess I liked psychology," he said. "They're all intro classes, so it's hard to say, but psych was good."

Andreas nodded. "So how do you think you did in the classes?"

Stavros froze. He didn't know if his father was getting at something specific, or if he was simply curious about how things went. Stavros was going to assume it was curiosity. "I'm not sure yet, Pop," he said. "Grades should be mailed home this week. I guess we'll see."

Andreas nodded again. "But you must have some idea of how things went."

Stavros put his spoon down. "Well, Pop, I just don't know," he said, a little louder than intended. He made an effort to tone it down. "I mean, it was my first semester. I'm not sure. There was a lot to get used to, you know? So maybe, my grades might be okay, but maybe not as great as they could be." He looked at his cereal but left his spoon on the table. His father would see his grades when they arrived. There was no use lying about them.

"Okay, Stavros," Andreas said. Stavros was sure his father was reminding himself to be kind inside his head. "So we'll drop it for now, and we'll talk about it again when your grades arrive, okay?"

Stavros squeezed his eyes closed. "Okay, fine, Pop." He stood up. "I'm gonna go take a shower." He walked to the stairs, abandoning his remaining cereal on the table, along with the carton of milk. He could feel Andreas's eyes following him as he went up each step.

At ten, Stavros called Deanna. They planned to meet at the apartment she shared with Mario near Mount Holyoke. She gave him the address and directions, and they ended the call.

Chapter 55

FRIENDS AT HOME

STAVROS ARRIVED AT MARIO AND Deanna's apartment a little after noon. The building looked like a dorm, and when Deanna let him in, it had a certain familiarity. It reminded him of the apartment he lived in with his parents at the university before they bought their house. The memory was faint, but the smell of industrial cleaner was an unmistakable part of his past.

Mario was visiting his family and would be back in the evening. The three of them would have dinner and meet up with Alec after. Deanna gave Stavros a tour of the tiny apartment, and then they both sat on the loveseat.

"How are you doing, Stav?" Deanna asked. "To be honest, you look like shit."

"Thanks, Deanna," Stavros said sarcastically. "That means a lot coming from you." He scratched the back of his neck. "I didn't sleep well last night. I haven't slept well in a long time. I might have forgotten how to sleep."

Deanna looked at him with concern. "Is this still about Lindi?" Then her hand went to her mouth. "Oh my God, I'm so sorry. I didn't mean for that to come out like that. I mean, if you're still struggling about Lindi, that's okay. It's just that I want you to feel better. I want you to be happy again."

"Well, D, you can't always get what you want, you know?" Now Stavros regretted his choice of words. "No, I mean, yeah, it's been hard. I can't stop thinking about her. D, she was my whole life for four years. When I was happy, it was because of her. And then it was just over, and not because we stopped loving each other. It would have been okay to be apart for school. We were always apart in the summer for camp, and it was hard, but we knew we'd see each other again, and it would be totally worth it. But this, this isn't worth anything."

He stopped. He knew he was doomed to start crying again if he kept this up. But it was too late.

"I still don't understand why. I mean, I do, but I still don't. Why couldn't she have just said yes? I would have been so good to her."

He felt his whole body shake as the sobs started yet again. But this was the first time he had seen Deanna face to face since that fateful night. It had to come out.

Deanna's tears streaking down her face. She wrapped her arms around Stavros. "I just don't know, Stav," she said softly. "I don't even think Lindi knows, really. She just knew it was what she needed to do. I was really rooting for you two. It's still so hard to believe. I can't even imagine how hard it is for you." She pulled away slightly. "And now I'm gonna have to get to know you again in some ways, too. It was four years of the two of you together for all of us. It's an adjustment. But like I told you that one time, I won't take sides. It's not about sides."

Stavros nodded. "I know," he said. He took a couple of deep breaths to compose himself. "I know she's your friend. I know she needs you, too. I'm glad she has you. But it's hard to deal with the fact that you know things about her that I don't. It would be easier if you didn't."

"I'll respect both of your privacy," Deanna said. "I'm not gonna talk about her to you, or you to her. That just wouldn't be cool. I really don't want to be in the middle. So don't ask me to be, okay?"

"Okay," Stavros promised. "I won't."

Deanna stood. "C'mon," she said. "Put your jacket and hat back on.

We're gonna walk to campus, and I'm gonna give you a tour. And we can get something to eat at the campus center."

Stavros and Deanna took a brisk walk around the snowy quad. Deanna pointed out all of the sights relevant to her, including her student mailbox. Then she brought him upstairs for lunch.

"This is the Blanchard Campus Center," she said. "It's the only place on campus where you can get Doritos. They also have concerts here. And there's an apparel store if you want to get a T-shirt or something to bring back to school to show where you went during break."

They went through the line in the cafeteria, and both got sandwiches, Cokes, and Doritos. They sat down at a small table by a window.

Stavros chugged down his Coke, hoping for some instant energy. Deanna watched him in awe. "I don't know if those come in kegs," she said, "but maybe we can find you one."

Stavros laughed. "I just need a bit of artificial energy to get me through the rest of the day. I started drinking coffee at school. I don't like it. It's a necessary evil."

Deanna watched him for several seconds. "So what do you do at PSC, when you're not in class or lying awake in your bed?"

Stavros shrugged. "Not much," he said. "I study. I read. I eat. I go to the pub."

"Have you made any friends?"

Stavros thought about it. "Friends. Hmm. I guess so. I have my roommate, Brad. He gets me beer and makes sure I don't fall out of bed. Then there's Caleb, who goes to the pub with me if no one else wants to go. There are a couple other guys on my floor that I guess I could call friends."

"I see kind of a pattern here, Stav," Deanna said. "It seems like you spend time with your friends and beer. Typical freshman."

Stavros grinned. "Yeah, typical."

"Have you had any, y'know, hookups since you've been there?" Deanna wondered.

Stavros was about to take a bite of his sandwich, but now he held it suspended in the air in front of his mouth. "Deanna," he said. "What do you think?"

Deanna shrugged. "I don't know. Maybe you become a big slut when you drink. I've never really seen you drink that much, so what do I know?"

Stavros took a bite of his sandwich, chewed, and swallowed. "No, Deanna," he said. "No hookups. Would you hook up with some guy who smells like a brewery and looks like he got his clothes out of the bottom of his laundry hamper?"

Deanne made a face. "Ew. Yuck. Even the thought of hooking up with you is gross. But Stav, maybe a hookup would help. You need to get laid."

Stavros nearly fell out of his chair. "Deanna! You've been around Mario far too long. Stop talking like that. I'm fine. I just need time, that's all." *And amnesia from the last six years*, he thought.

"Well, whatever," Deanna said, taking a sip of her Coke. "Can't say I didn't try." She handed Stavros the rest of her Coke, and he immediately downed it. Then he belched.

"Thanks," he said. "Let's go to the apparel store so I can get a T-shirt for Drea. And then let's head over to my house and take her to a movie or something. Lord knows she could use some fun about now."

Mario came back to the apartment near six, and the two old friends greeted each other. Stavros thought Mario looked relaxed and content, and he and Deanna were so at ease in their interactions with each other. He felt a small wave of grief just watching them together, but he pushed it back and smiled.

"What should we do for dinner?" Mario asked.

"We should get some gyros from the new sandwich shop," Deanna suggested. "We can show Stavros how they do Greek over here in South Hadley. They have a good Greek salad, too."

Stavros nodded. "I'd go for that," he agreed. "I haven't been able to find a good gyro place near PSC, so it's been a while."

Deanna called in their order, and Mario and Stavros walked down to get the food.

They braced themselves against the biting western Massachusetts winter wind. "So, Mario," Stavros said as they walked. "You got any beer? Or maybe we can get some?"

Mario shook his head. "Sorry, man, I'm fresh out. We drank the last two last night, and the package stores are closed on Sundays. You know that. Blue laws."

"Oh," Stavros said, frowning and looking down at the street in front of him. He had no idea how he was going to sleep that night. It was all he could think about. He could ask his father to get some beer for him on Monday, but then there would be the looks, and maybe the questions. "Would you be able to get some tomorrow?" he asked. "I don't have a fake ID."

Mario shook his head again. "I don't have one, either, and they're really strict around here. The guy who buys for me went home for break, so we're out of luck." He walked a little closer to Stavros. "I do have a little bit of weed, if you want it," he confided. "Not much, but every now and then, Deanna and I like to smoke a little, you know, just to help us . . ."

Stavros put up his gloved hand. "I get it, you don't have to paint a picture." He thought about it as they reached the crosswalk. "I guess I could stand a little weed," he said. "Does it help you sleep?"

Mario shrugged. "Sometimes," he said. "But it always makes me feel good. If I'm having a bad day, it makes it all float away. It's nice every now and then."

"Okay," Stavros said. "I'll try some."

After dinner, Alec and Felicia arrived, and they spent the evening talking and eating cookies. Alec had decided to defer college for the year and was working at a textile mill, loading and unloading boxes. He had put on some muscle and had picked up some confidence from working with the other laborers. He could no longer be intimidated by Deanna. But he was looking forward to starting school the next fall so he would never have to do that type of work again. Felicia was taking classes at the junior college and working at a real estate agency answering the phones in the afternoons.

At the end of the night, Mario brought Stavros into the bedroom and showed him how to roll a joint. "There's enough in here for another joint if you want it," he said, handing Stavros a package of rolling papers. "You don't have to bring it back if you don't use it. We can get more."

Stavros took the baggie, the papers, and the joint and put them in his pocket. "Thanks, man," he said. "Where do you even get this stuff?"

"There's a guy in the building who gets it for us," Mario said. "I just give him the cash, and later in the day he appears with a little bag. Easy."

Stavros nodded. He'd never purchased any drugs before, and it seemed kind of seedy to him. But he kept this knowledge close to the front of his brain, just in case.

By the end of the night, Stavros was more exhausted than he'd ever been, and his stomach was tied in knots from all the caffeine he had consumed. He said good night to Andreas and Drea and went into his bedroom and closed the door. Then he waited. At eleven o'clock, he heard Andreas come upstairs. He heard the water running in the bathroom, and several minutes later, the master bedroom door closed with a click. Stavros knew his father had gone right to bed and was usually asleep within five minutes. He waited fifteen to be sure. As soon as he could hear his snores, he gently pushed up the window next to his bed. He raised the screen a few inches. He lit the joint. His heart was pounding. He took a drag, exhaled out the window, and held the joint out the window in the chilly air. He took another drag, and then another. Then he felt a wave of sensation flow through his body. He stopped to pay attention to it. It started in his chest, and radiated down his limbs, and then up to his head. His head felt slightly enlarged, like it had been filled with cool air. It felt lighter. He took one more drag, then stumped the joint out. He needed to conserve what he had in case he had another night with no beer.

Stavros lay down on his bed. He found his book and tried to read, but the letters became blurry. He tried squinting. Nothing changed. He laughed. Life was stupid, all of it. Everything was so stupid.

He put down his book and turned off the bedside lamp. He faced the ceiling in the dark with his eyes open until they adjusted to the light filtering in the window from the street. He tried to think of what to do next, but he was stumped. Then the thought crossed his mind to close his eyes, so he did. The room seemed slightly atilt at first until he got used to it, and then it was morning.

"What the hell," he said out loud. He had no hangover. He felt awake and alert. It was ten o'clock. He had slept through the night, and more, for the first time in months. He had also left his window open, and now he was freezing. He got up, closed the window, and put on his sweats. He was ready to face the day.

Chapter 56

DISHONOR ROLL

TUESDAY WAS CHRISTMAS. ANDREAS WENT to church the night before for the two-hour Christmas Eve liturgy. Stavros and Drea, as per their holiday tradition, opted out, using the fact that they were half Jewish as an excuse.

Stavros, who had now slept well for two consecutive nights, was ready to bake with Drea. They made Kourabiedes and Melomakarona cookies, and the house filled up with the aroma of sweet spices. Stavros put together a Spanakopita and a salad, and Andreas brought home a precooked roast beef and dolmades. It was just the three of them for dinner, and they ate way more than their fill.

Andreas and Stavros packed the leftover food into storage containers to be consumed over the twelve days of Christmas. The holiday would culminate with the Epiphany on January 6. After dinner, they made calls to the aunts, uncles, and cousins in Pittsburgh to send them holiday cheer. They sang the kalanta, the traditional carols, together over the phone. It was as traditional as an American Greek family could get on a windy, snowy December night in Massachusetts.

Stavros smoked himself to sleep that night, but it was the last of the weed. He had to make a plan to get through until he could get some more, or maybe some beer. He liked the weed better. It didn't make him feel bloated or hungover. But he had to figure out his next move.

On Wednesday, things returned to as normal as they could get, and the mailman came early. When Stavros got up, his father sat in his armchair with his book, a piece of open mail sitting on the table beside him.

"Come here, Stavros," he said, motioning toward the couch. "Let's talk for a minute."

Stavros walked slowly to the couch and sat down. "What is it, Papa?" he asked innocently, although he was already fairly sure what his papa was going to say.

Andreas lifted the piece of paper. "Your grades came in the mail," he said, handing them across to his son. "Take a look."

Stavros took the paper gingerly, making sustained eye contact with his father. He opened the folded document and looked down. Then he closed his eyes. Two Bs, two Cs, and one D. It was worse than he'd thought.

"So, Stavros," Andreas said softly, "what do you think happened? It appears as if maybe you had some challenges at school."

"That's a bit of an understatement, Pop," Stavros replied. "So, yeah, I guess I didn't do too well in my classes. But I did get two Bs."

"Congratulations on the Bs," Andreas said genuinely. "It probably would have been acceptable to get one C in your first semester. But Stavros, I know at the university, Ds don't even get counted on your transcript. You'll need to retake that class. And the Cs will greatly decrease your grade point average. Do you have any sort of plan for how you'll remedy this next semester?"

Stavros ran his fingers through his mass of messy curls. "I don't know, Pop," he said. "I guess I'll just have to try harder and do better."

Andreas stood up and came over to the couch. He sat down next to Stavros. "Son, I'm just not sure it's as easy as that. You've gotten yourself into a little hole at school, and now you're going to have to do something deliberate to get yourself back on solid ground. If you like, I can help you come up with a plan. I'm pretty good with things like this, you know."

Stavros squirmed in his seat. "It's okay, Papa," he said. "I can figure it out myself. I just need to get more serious about my studying, and maybe ask for help from my professors or something. I can do this."

Andreas didn't look reassured. "Stavros," he said. "You like to bake,

I know. Maybe you can think of this challenge as a recipe. You need the right ingredients to put in the bowl in order to get the best results. But it's not just the ingredients. Sometimes they have to be added in a certain order. And you have to stir a certain number of times. You must grease the pan and make sure it's the right size. And you have to bake it for the allotted amount of time. If everything goes as planned, you get a delicious dessert. If not, you get a mushy mess. Do you see what I'm saying?"

Stavros nodded. "Yeah, Pop, I get it. It's a good analogy. My grades were a mushy mess. I'll remember that. Can I go get some breakfast now?"

Andreas sighed and nodded. "Okay, Stavros. Go eat. We'll keep checking in about this." He got up and went back to his chair. "Oh, and one more thing," he called out as Stavros headed to the kitchen. "I found your bedroom window open yesterday morning. It's very cold outside. We don't want to try to heat the entire neighborhood. Try to remember to keep it closed, okay?" Stavros nodded. "It's not a great idea to sleep with the window open in this weather. I think it went as low as fifteen degrees last night."

"Okay, Pop, thanks," Stavros said. He went into the kitchen, braced himself against the counter, and took a deep breath. This was getting to be too much. He could have failed some of his classes. He could have gotten kicked out of school. He had to do something. Maybe it was the beer. Maybe it kept him from being able to concentrate. Maybe he had to change what he was doing. Maybe it would be better if he just switched to weed. He had to figure out how he could get more weed.

Chapter 57

A little Help

MARIO AND DEANNA WEREN'T HOME, so Stavros waited. He called at the top and bottom of every hour. Finally, at nine o'clock, Deanna picked up.

"Hey, Stav," she said. "We just got back from Mario's nana's house. Christmas leftovers party. How was your Christmas?"

"Great," Stavros told her. "Very Greek. Lots of food. Hey, maybe we can get together tomorrow to hang out. Then we can make plans for New Year's."

"Yeah, we'll be here tomorrow," Deanna confirmed. "When do you want to come over?"

"Uh," Stavros said, "I'm not sure yet. I've got to take care of some stuff first. I'll let you know later. Is, uh, Mario around?"

"Yeah, he's in the bedroom. Let me get him. Mario! Stav's on the phone! Pick up!"

Stavros heard a click. "Hey man, what's up?" Mario said cheerfully.

"Did Deanna hang up?" Stavros asked.

"Deanna, are you there?" Mario asked quietly. There was no response. She was gone. "What's going on, Stav?"

"Uh," Stavros started. "I was wondering. Is that guy, you know, the one you told me about with the weed? Is he around during break?"

"Yeah," Mario replied. "I saw him at the mailbox earlier today. Why? You want me to ask him to hook you up?"

"Y-yeah," Stavros said. "I guess. If it's not too much to ask. I don't know anyone else who could get some for me. I just need a little help for those nights I can't sleep. That stuff really helps."

"Yeah, bro, no problem," Mario assured him. "I can go knock on his door and see if he can help you out. When do you want it?"

"I was hoping for tomorrow," Stavros said. "I was just talking to Deanna about coming over tomorrow, so that would be convenient." He didn't tell Mario that he had only planned his visit for the next day so he could get the weed.

"Okay, man, I'll ask him tonight," Mario said. "And then we can give you your Christmas present, too. Why don't you just come over around three?"

"Okay," Stavros agreed, realizing he didn't have a gift for Mario and Deanna, and he'd have to get something before three tomorrow. "So if you can pay for the stuff, I'll pay you back later, okay?"

"Yeah, man, that would be cool," Mario said. "I've got your back."

Stavros asked his father for some money to get presents for his friends. He spent half the money on the gifts and used the rest to reimburse Mario. He promised himself that he would pay his father back when he could. He couldn't let his father pay for his drugs. It just didn't feel right.

Chapter 58

THE LONG HAUL

WHEN IT WAS TIME TO go back to school, Stavros steeled himself against the horror of the ten-hour bus ride back to Pittsburgh. It would be endless. But he had made a decision. After Andreas and Drea said goodbye and left him at the bus station, he went behind the building and smoked a joint. Then he quickly boarded the bus and found a seat near the back. Within fifteen minutes, he was either asleep or pretty close to it.

He later recalled dreaming, or it could have been memories. There were images of Drea opening a present, Drea in tears about their mother, Drea telling him a story about her life, and then Drea saying goodbye at the bus station. He could see her in the distance as the bus pulled away. She was reaching out to him, and he reached back, but he couldn't touch her. She faded to black. "How could you let me down like this?" Andreas asked, shaking his head back and forth. "I had such high hopes for you. You were supposed to be the future. Is this the future that you want?" Then Andreas started to laugh, but it wasn't a joyous sound. "What would your mother think, Stavros? She was depending on you to fix the world."

Stavros's eyes popped open. He heard the steady sound of rubber tires on a wet road. He could feel the vibration beneath him. The other passengers on the bus were silent, some asleep, some reading, some staring straight ahead. Stavros felt his head clear, and he remembered. It was all true. He was supposed to be a catalyst for change. He was supposed to avenge his uncle's needless death in Vietnam by working toward peace and knowledge. And he was supposed to help Drea learn and grow so she could walk beside him on this journey. This was the quest that Rebel died for. He couldn't let her down. He had to do better.

By the time he arrived in Pittsburgh and caught a cab back to his dorm, he was determined. He would change. He would do better. He would improve his grades and show his father how serious he was. He would lead Drea in the right direction. He wouldn't let her see him crash and burn.

He got to his room and dropped his bag on the floor. He sat down on his bed without turning on the light. Brad was already asleep in his bed. Stavros wanted to read, but he didn't want to wake his friend. His heart started to pound. He started to sweat in his down jacket. Lindi. He remembered Lindi. He reached into his pocket and withdrew the little baggie inside. He removed his jacket. He opened his window a crack and lit his joint.

Just tonight, he thought. *I just need to get through this one night.*

And that was the message he gave himself every night for the next five months.

School came easier now. He didn't have to go to the pub to get relief anymore. Now he could spend more time in his room studying. It was easier to focus in class now that the morning headaches were gone. The concepts all made more sense.

Brad told him about a guy he knew on another floor that could get him weed, and they became good friends. Sometimes they got high together, but Stavros preferred to get high alone and go to sleep. It was his escape. He started his own small business, typing papers for his classmates for money. He used the money to buy more weed. He had everything down to a science.

As the end of the term neared, Stavros was confident that his grades would be better this semester. His father would be able to see that he turned things around. He wouldn't have to make excuses anymore. This would make everything better.

But his next call to Deanna was a brutal reminder. Lindi would be coming home for summer break. Lindi would be in Amherst for three months. And she should be. It was her home. She shouldn't stay away just because it was his home, too.

He started to panic. He couldn't see her. But there was no way he could avoid it. Amherst was small, and they shared all the same friends. But he wasn't ready. It still felt too fresh even after almost a year.

Shouldn't it be easier by now? he thought. *It still hurts just as much as the last day I saw her. I thought time was supposed to make everything better.*

He needed a plan if he was to get through the summer. He could still smoke weed to sleep, but there would be no justification for being high all day, every day. He knew there were limits.

The thought hit him as he walked across campus that day and saw a sign on the bookstore window: Help Wanted. That was the answer. He could stay in Pittsburgh for the summer. He could ask his Bubbe and Zayde if he could stay with them, and he could get a job. He wouldn't have to face the bus. He wouldn't have to face the reminders. Most of all, he wouldn't have to face Lindi.

He put in an application at the bookstore, and then completed several more at stores and restaurants. Then he called his grandparents.

"Bubbe, I'd like to stick around Pittsburgh for the summer," he told her, "and I've applied for jobs. I'm wondering if it would be okay to stay with you while the dorms are closed."

"Stavros, we would love to have you," Bubbe replied. "You know we have lots of room. Have you talked to your father about this? What does he think?"

Stavros paused. "I haven't talked to him yet," he admitted. "I wanted to work out the details first, so he can see that I'm capable of planning something like this on my own. So if it's okay with you, and I get a job, I'll let him know. I think he'll be okay with it."

"Zayde will be so excited to have you here," Bubbe said. "He always enjoys talking to you. He thinks of you as an equal and he values what you have to say. Well, talk to your father, and let me know, so I can clean out your room for you and put clean sheets on the bed. And I'll have to fill up the refrigerator. I know you're still a growing boy."

Stavros interviewed at the bookstore, a pizza place, and a fast-food restaurant. The fast-food offer came first, but he declined. It was hot and greasy in the kitchen, and it would be a long, sweltering summer in Pittsburgh. Flipping burgers just didn't sound appealing. The bookstore was very sorry, but they were looking for someone with any retail experience. Stavros had none. When the pizza place made an offer, he jumped on it.

Paulo's Famous Pizza was close to PSC, and a fifteen-minute drive from his grandparent's house. Probably twenty-five minutes by bus. He would learn to make the pizzas and use the cash register. But first he would start by chopping vegetables for toppings. Paulo's had a delivery car with a sign on top. Stavros would have to learn his way around the streets of Pittsburgh.

The call home was hard.

"Can you tell me why you want to stay in Pittsburgh?" Andreas asked. "Last time I heard, we have pizza shops in Amherst where you could work. Or you could come home and take the summer off."

"Pop," Stavros started, unsure of how he would finish the sentence. "There's a lot of reasons. The bus ride for one. It's horrible. And Bubbe and Zayde aren't getting any younger. I'd like to spend some real time with them. And with your family. And, you know, get the full experience of being in Pittsburgh, not just for school. I mean, you and Mom grew up here."

Andreas paused, and Stavros could tell he was considering his words. "Those are some compelling reasons, Stavros. But it seems to me that maybe you want to avoid coming to Amherst more than you really want to stay in Pittsburgh."

Stavros sighed. "Well, yeah, Papa," he admitted. "Sure. I mean, Lindi will be there."

"Ah," Andreas said. "I see. Well, I understand, my son. It seems like you've already set this whole process in motion. Who am I to get in the way of your progress? Fine, you have my blessing to stay in Pittsburgh for the summer, but maybe we can look into flying you back next time, instead of the bus, since the bus is so stressful for you."

Stavros exhaled deeply. "Thank you, Papa. That means a lot."

"And you'll have to talk to Drea," Andreas went on. "She won't understand, Stavros. She has been looking forward to you being home. You'll have to explain."

Stavros was silent. In all of his planning and worrying about what his father would say, he hadn't even considered Drea. That wasn't like him. Normally, everything was about Drea. He felt a tightness in his chest. "Okay, Papa," he said. "I'll talk to Drea. Should I do it now?"

"She's upstairs," Andreas said. "I'll get her. And Stavros—"

"I know, Papa," he interrupted. "Always be kind."

"Hold on a minute."

Stavros felt his heart palpitate. He knew this would hurt, both for him and Drea.

"Hello?" Drea's tiny voice came over the line.

"Hey, Dray," Stavros said. "It's me. What's new?"

"When are you coming home?" Drea asked right away. "I have a new cookie recipe I want to try with you. It has cinnamon and nutmeg."

Stavros felt a wave of nausea. "Drea," he said softly. "I just talked to Papa. I'm going to be staying in Pittsburgh for the summer. I got a job, and I'll be staying with Bubbe and Zayde. So I won't be home until Christmas break."

There was silence. "Why, Stavros?" Drea asked, and Stavris could tell she was crying. "Why don't you want to come home? Did we do something last time you were here so you don't want to come back? I won't bother you, you know, if you don't want me to. We don't have to bake. We can do other things. Or you can just hang out with your friends."

Stavros considered his reply. "Drea, this doesn't have anything to do with you or Papa, I promise." He decided to go with the truth. "It's just that Lindi will be home, and to be honest, I can't see her. I won't be happy knowing she's so close by. It still hurts a lot, Drea. I'm just not ready."

Drea sniffed. "Does that mean you're never gonna come back at all if Lindi is here?" she asked. "Because her parents live here. She could be here a lot."

"I just don't know, Dray," Stavris replied. "I think it won't always be this way for me. At least I hope not."

"Can we come to Bubbe and Zayde's house to see you, then?"

Stavros thought about this. "You'll need to talk to Papa about it, but it's okay with me. I really want to see you. Tell you what. I'll see if I can get them to invite you, and maybe you can come stay for a while. Maybe if Papa doesn't want to stay very long, you can stay and fly back by yourself. You're old enough now."

"Okay," Drea said. "But I still want you to come home, Stav. I really do."

"I know, Dray," he told her. "Just make sure if you do come here you bring that new cookie recipe."

Chapter 59

Summertime Blues

STAVROS HADN'T TAKEN INTO ACCOUNT the heat from the pizza ovens. He was not allowed to wear shorts to work, even when the temperature went over 90 degrees outside. It was stifling. He welcomed the days that he was assigned to delivery duty. The delivery car was old, and it often stalled at intersections, but it had a functioning air-conditioning system. Sometimes, the crew would draw straws to see who would get to have car duty for their shift.

Andreas called Stavros two weeks into the break. He had received his grades in the mail, and he wanted to offer his congratulations. Stavros got an A, three Bs, and one B-. It was a huge improvement. Stavros had been informed by his advisor that the D he had received in the fall would be dropped from his transcript, but the tuition for the class would not be refunded. If he received another D, he would be facing academic probation. But for now, there was cause to celebrate.

Stavros had gotten onto a comfortable routine with his grandparents. On the days that he worked, he would eat for free at Paolo's, come home after ten, and make sure everyone was asleep. Then he would take a few drags off his joint out the window and go to sleep. In the morning, Bubbe would make him breakfast, either eggs and toast or oatmeal, depending on whether or not she needed to go to the grocery store. Zayde would have had breakfast hours earlier, but he would sit with Stavros and chat while he feasted. Bubbe's coffee was rich and excellent and required very little alteration to be tolerable.

One morning Zayde looked perplexed. "Stavros, have you been smelling anything strange in the house lately?" he asked. "For the last couple of weeks when we have the fan on at night, I've noticed a strange, earthy kind of smell coming in the window. It's not altogether unpleasant, but it's got me wondering if maybe the neighbors might be burning something, like sage or incense. Have you noticed?"

Stavros froze. He thought he had been so careful. Did Zayde not know what weed smelled like? He had raised three teenagers during the 1960s and '70s. Could he really be that naive? Or did he know exactly what he was smelling, and this was his way of letting Stavros know he was on to him?

"Uh," Stavros pretended to think back. "I don't think so, Zayde, but I usually fall asleep pretty quickly once I get into bed. I might just not notice."

Zayde nodded. "Okay, Stav," he said. "Just keep a lookout, would you? Maybe it will go away on its own. Let me know if you notice it, okay?" Zayde picked up his newspaper and started to read.

"Okay, Zayde," Stavros said.

That night, after he got off at his bus stop, Stavros took a long walk around the block, sneaking in several drags of his joint as discreetly as he could. He looked around him often to make sure no one was behind him, and every time a car passed, he was sure it would be the cops. When he finally let himself into his grandparents' house and went upstairs, he didn't feel his usual sense of relaxation and calm. He felt jittery and nervous. This was not how he wanted to feel before trying to go to sleep.

He sat on his bed and thought. There must be some other way than sneaking around. He didn't like feeling like he was being so dishonest with his grandparents. And he didn't like feeling that wired. He also had another problem. He was almost out of the weed he had brought from school, and he had no idea where to find more. That meant he had to ration what he had left until he had some other option. This was getting way harder than it should be. The weed was supposed to be helping him cope, not making his life harder. At least he wasn't perseverating over Lindi. Until he started thinking about how he wasn't thinking about her. Now the thoughts returned.

Andreas and Drea would be coming in August. It was mid-July. He needed to work this out soon. He had to be present for Drea. He had to make Drea more important for him than he was making weed. The thought that he could prioritize drugs over his little sister terrified him. *Am I addicted to weed?* he thought.

Stavros sat on his bed and considered. He had been drinking beer every night, and it became a problem because he couldn't access it easily and it gave him a hangover. So he switched to weed. It was easier to get, took up almost no room, didn't need to be refrigerated, and it didn't make him feel sick in the mornings. He had somehow convinced himself that this was a solution to his problems. He could smoke weed and still live his life, and he could just go on this way forever. Then why was he so stressed out when he didn't know how he was going to get his next high? And why was he working so hard on keeping it a secret? It just didn't feel right.

Stavros thought about how he had solved problems in the past. Mostly, he had talked to his father. Andreas had a certain wisdom within him that was soothing and left Stavros feeling like everything would be fine. But this wasn't something he could talk to his father about. He had to take care of it himself. So what would Andreas say, if he did talk to him? He thought back on the past when Andreas had offered him advice and counsel. He remembered the first time. It was when he wanted, or needed, to know what happened to a person's soul after they died. After getting no help from anyone else, his father had suggested they go to the library.

The library! The library had books about every conceivable topic. There had to be information there to help him. Stavros would go to the library on his next day off. Until then, he would have to just tolerate the walks around the block and monitor what he had left in his baggie. For now, he would go to bed and pray that he could get some sleep.

Chapter 60

Make It Better

IT WAS TWO WEEKS LATER, and Stavros's family would be arriving in a couple of weeks. He had been to the library twice and taken out six books. He read them in his room at night and stowed them in a bag in his closet during the day. He hoped his Bubbe didn't get too curious when hanging up his laundry. He had learned several things. One of them was that he was heading down the long road of addiction. Another was that he had a chance to turn it around before it became too serious. He needed to do two things: stop using the drugs, and get support from other people who were also committed to stopping. All of the books said so. It was proven by research. Research didn't lie.

He didn't know where to go for support. Pittsburgh was so big, and there were so many people. He didn't want to walk into a support group meeting and be face to face with fifty-year-old recovering addicts. He wanted to be around people closer to his own age. He looked at the resource lists in the appendices of his books. Many of them listed college counseling centers. He called the counseling center at PSC. They were open for the break. He asked about support groups for addicts. He was told there was a Men's Recovery Group on Tuesday nights at seven.

On Monday night, he smoked the rest of his weed in the local elementary school playground. He sat alone on the merry-go-round, spinning it around with his foot. It was nighttime, and he recalled that in junior high, Deanna and Lindi's parents didn't let them go out after dark in Amherst. They were afraid they would be approached by unseemly strangers. Stavros had to laugh. He had become the unseemly stranger.

On Tuesday, he borrowed Bubbe's car, telling her he was going to meet a friend. He parked in the counseling center lot and started his trek to the door. When he got inside, there was no one in the waiting room, and he worried he had come at the wrong time. Then a man behind the counter called out. "Men's Recovery?"

Stavros nodded.

The man pointed to the right. "Down that hall, last group room on the left. Number seven. Just go in. No need to knock."

Stavros waved his thanks and headed down the hall. He could hear male voices coming from the group room. The group appeared to be the only activity at the clinic that night. He opened the door slowly, and several heads turned to look at him. There were about twelve young men sitting in a circle. One of them smiled at him and gestured to an empty seat.

"Welcome," he said. "Have a seat. We're just about to start."

Stavros sat and looked around. He didn't see anyone he recognized from school, and he was relieved. The chair he sat in was made of rigid plastic, and he squirmed around to get comfortable.

"Okay, let's get started," said the man who had spoken earlier. "Welcome to the Men's Recovery Group. I'm glad you're all here. I see a couple of new faces tonight. Everyone will have a chance to speak if they choose, but first, I'll just say a few things about the group. My name is Jack, and I'm a graduate student in the counseling program. I am also in recovery. My last use was four years ago. I started my journey by attending this very group as an undergrad. This is not Alcoholics Anonymous, although we do encourage everyone to attend those meetings, since we only meet once a week. I want to remind everyone that anything said in this group, stays in this group. If you see a group member on campus, no talking about the group. No talking to others about who is in the group. This is a safe place where you can feel free to share your stories and experiences. When others speak, they have the floor, and we respect their time. We offer positive and constructive advice and feedback. No judgment. With that being said, I would like to again welcome the new group members. You're welcome to introduce yourselves and tell us why you're here tonight. If you don't feel comfortable talking, please just let us know your first name, and we can go on to the next member. Any volunteers?"

Stavros shot his hand up before he had a chance to change his mind. Jack acknowledged him, and it was his turn to speak.

"My name is . . . Steve," he said, suddenly wanting to use the English translation of his Greek name.

"Hi Steve," everyone said.

Stavros cleared his throat. "So I have a problem with weed," he said. "It started with beer when I couldn't sleep last year, but then I started to do really bad at school, and feel sick all the time. I was getting wasted every weekend. I think I blacked out a few times. I was letting everyone down. And then I couldn't get any beer over winter break, and my friend hooked me up with some weed. I thought it solved all my problems. I could sleep, do school work, and my grades went up. I didn't think there was anything wrong with it at all. Until I realized that I was worrying all the time about running out, and where my next weed would come from. I started trying to make money just to pay for the weed. I was hiding my use from my family. Then, last week, I realized I had no way to get any weed for the rest of the summer, and I panicked. That really scared me. This was supposed to be what helped me, but it was freaking me out. So I read some books, and realized that I might have an addiction. The books said to get some support, so that's why I'm here. I last smoked weed last night. Now I'm out. I won't have any tonight, and I'm terrified I won't sleep. And when I don't sleep, I think about my high school girlfriend, who broke up with me after I proposed, just two days before we left for college. And the feelings are so strong, it feels like it just happened yesterday. My father and sister are coming to visit in two weeks. I don't want to be a total mess when they get here. I need some help to get through this. I'm sorry, I just went on and on. I hope that's okay. This is the first time I've ever said this stuff out loud to anyone."

Jack gave him a warm smile. "That was great, Steve," he said. "Thank you for sharing. You are definitely in the right place. You and I can talk after group to discuss some of your immediate concerns, and hopefully you can learn something tonight from the other members of the group that will help you. I'm glad you're here."

The rest of the group applauded. Stavros sat back in his chair. He realized he was done. He still felt scared, but his body felt lighter. He listened as others told their stories. Then the focus turned to excuses. The group gave examples of excuses they used to continue their use and their addiction behaviors. Many of the examples rang true for Stavros. He had no idea that he was justifying getting high to make it seem normal. It was as if he thought he was immune to any of the effects of addiction. Now he realized that was not true.

After an hour, the group wrapped up, and the other members started to file out of the room. Jack asked Stavros and another student to stay. Once everyone else was gone, Jack turned to Stavros.

"Steve," he said, "I think you did the right thing by coming here tonight. I want to let you know, you're not alone in this anymore. You have a team behind you that will help and support you." He gestured to the other student. "Steve, I would like you to meet Kurt. Kurt has volunteered to help our new members through the first few days or weeks of recovery if they need it, and it sounds like you could really use some extra support right now. Kurt will be available by phone, or in person if you arrange it. I thought maybe the two of you could chat real quick right now to make a plan."

"Yeah, that works for me," Kurt said. "Can you stick around a few minutes, Steve?"

Stavros felt slightly detached, hearing people call him by his alias. "Sure," he replied.

Jack smiled. "Steve, I hope to see you back here next week," he said. "There are lists of AA meetings and other support groups you can attend before then on the table in the lobby. Please pick one up. I'll leave you two to talk now. Take care."

"Bye Jack," Kurt said. He gestured for Stavros to sit down. "So, Steve, you're kind of the first person I'm doing this with, so we've gotta figure this out together, okay? I've been sober for six months now. For me, it's alcohol. I can't touch the stuff. It's like poison to me. Like, not even a beer at a football game. I work nights doing security at a warehouse. Eleven to seven. So I'm up all night. What do you think would help you tonight?"

Stavros shrugged. "I have no idea," he admitted. "I'm assuming I won't be able to sleep tonight, that's for sure. From what I've read, I shouldn't have any physical withdrawal from weed. It's more of an emotional addiction. But I can't even remember the last time I tried to sleep without using something. Luckily I'm not working tomorrow, so that's helpful."

Kurt nodded. "I'll give you my work number before we go," he said. "You can call me any time during the night when you need to talk. I can think of a few things that might help, though. Like, don't go to bed if you're not tired. And if you lie down and can't sleep, get back up and do something. It's no good just lying there thinking. That just makes it worse. Watch TV, read, or do some pushups. Do you ever run?"

"No," Stavros said. "I really don't do much of anything."

"Yeah," Kurt said. "I remember those days. Low motivation to move your body. I go running in the mornings. Maybe in a couple of days, when you're feeling up to it, we can go running together. I'm really not that fast, so I know you can keep up." He paused. "You said something when you introduced yourself, and it reminded me of what I went through. I started drinking after my father died when I was seventeen. I was somehow able to make it through the rest of my senior year and my first year of college, although I'm not sure how I managed. But I can tell you this, when I finally made the decision to stop drinking, it was like the grief was still so fresh in my mind. I tried to talk to my brother and sister about it, but they had already gone through their grief, and they just didn't understand why I wasn't doing better a year and a half later. When I started in the group, Jack pulled me aside after, like he did with you tonight, and explained it to me. I guess when you're going through something hard in your life, like a death or a breakup, and you start doing something like drinking or using drugs to cope with it, it kinda freezes you in time. It's like taking the pain and pushing back, but then it keeps trying to push back up front. Every time you use, you push it back again. It never gets to express itself, you know? So when you first get sober, the pain can finally come up front. And it's just as bad as it was the first day you felt it."

Stavros felt chills run down his spine. "Yes," he said. "That's exactly how it feels. Everyone thinks I should be starting to move on by now, but I just can't. Every time I think about Lindi, it feels too bad, and I feel like I need to make it go away, and fast. I can't sleep because when I close my eyes, she's the only thing I can think about, and I can even see her face. It's been almost a year since we ended it. I don't want those feelings to be there anymore."

Kurt nodded. "Yeah, that's exactly how I felt," he said. "But the bad news, or maybe it's good news, is you have to go through the pain to get rid of it. So just to let you know, this could be hard for a bit. I go to AA meetings, if you want to come with me. There aren't any Marijuana Anonymous groups around here, although I hear they're starting them up around the country. But I think you could relate to AA. Addiction is basically addiction. And you might want to look into getting some counseling. It's free here."

Stavros thought about it for a moment. "I can go to a meeting tomorrow," he said.

Kurt smiled. "Great! I go to the one at the Elks Club. It's men and women, so I hope that's okay. Let's get the list in the lobby and I'll show you where it is so you'll have the address."

They walked to the lobby, and Kurt found the list. He circled the group listing with a pen and handed it to Stavros. "So come a few minutes early, and I'll meet you before we go in. That way, you'll already have a friend there. And seriously, Steve, if you need me tonight, just call. It's so slow at the warehouse, and I doubt there will be any action tonight. I'll just be at my desk, reading."

Stavros nodded. "I might just do that. Thanks so much, Kurt. I appreciate your help."

Kurt shook his hand. "It's my pleasure, Steve."

Stavros grimaced with embarrassment. "It's Stavros," he told him. "I don't know why I said Steve. I just panicked, I guess."

Kurt laughed. "Stavros," he said. "It suits you better. You aren't the first person to panic here. I'll walk you out to the parking lot."

Chapter 61

&MERGING

THE FIRST NIGHT WAS HELL, but not as deep in the abyss as Stavros thought it would be. He took Kurt's advice. He stayed up late. He read. He watched TV. When he felt sleepy, he went to bed, but he couldn't sleep. He got up and read some more. He tried doing some pushups but could only make it to ten. He cleaned his room quietly so he didn't startle his grandparents. It was three o'clock.

He called Kurt. Kurt answered on the first ring and talked him through it. He distracted him by talking about movies and politics. Stavros had strong opinions about politics. Kurt had him talk about his family, and then he told Stavros about his. They talked for an hour. Now it was four o'clock. Stavros felt wide awake.

"Do you feel safe enough in your neighborhood to go out for a walk?" Kurt asked.

Stavros snickered. "I think I was the only dangerous person walking around my neighborhood late at night this summer," he said. "It was the only place I could smoke a joint. I can try to go for a walk."

"Look around you while you walk," Kurt suggested. "Look at the houses, and the trees. Look for lawn gnomes. See if you can smell anything out there. Just hope it's not dog shit. Make sure to pay attention to the details. This is stuff my therapist tells me to do. I would never have thought of it on my own. I could just walk around with my thoughts and not notice anything about my surroundings. Remember, this is the present. This is where you are now. You don't have to walk around in a cloud of the past."

"Okay," Stavros agreed.

After they hung up, Stavros pulled on his clothes and quietly crept out of the house. He walked his usual route toward the school yard, but this time, he watched where he was going. He kept his hands jammed in his pocket as he looked at each house and noticed its color, its shape. He actually saw a lawn gnome and had to smile. He felt tired, but he pushed through. When he got to the school yard, he took a deep breath. He could smell wood fire smoke and pine needles. The merry-go-round had its own smell, the smell of children at play, reminding him of when he was in grade school. It was a pleasant memory. He looked at the school building and noticed it was one-story tall, and the ceilings inside most likely would seem low to him. The school was closed for the summer, but inside, it waited patiently for its students to return in the fall. Stavros spun a few times on the merry-go-round, and then continued his walk.

When he got home, it was nearly five o'clock. He read for fifteen minutes, and then turned out his light. He was sure he wouldn't fall asleep but accepted that was his fate on his first night of sobriety. He closed his eyes, and to his surprise, he soon felt himself starting to drift off.

He awoke with a start at eight. He got out of bed. He was done with sleep. He'd gotten fewer than three hours of sleep, but he had slept. He saw this as a victory. He got dressed and headed downstairs. His Bubbe was in the kitchen. When she saw him, she smiled and took the eggs out of the refrigerator.

He went to the meeting that night with Kurt, and they attended several more that week. Every night was challenging, but he got through them one at a time. By the end of the first week, he slept five hours in one night. He was exhausted, and he struggled through each work shift. But he kept it up. He had to keep going. To stop was to give up. Any improvement was welcome. His family was coming in one week. He hadn't smoked weed for seven days. When he attended the Tuesday night group, the members applauded him. No one gave him any grief when he revealed his actual name. Kurt gave him a big smile. But Stavros knew he was not out of the woods yet.

As he left work on Friday, Stavros noticed some of his coworkers who had also just gotten off shift. They were standing in the parking lot in front of an old Chevy Malibu, and Stavros could smell the familiar aroma of weed wafting toward him in the wind.

"Hey Stav," Joe called to him. "You want to come hang out with us tonight? We're going to Ned's house after this."

Stavros took a deep breath and savored the scent. It was so welcoming, and it promised freedom, relaxation, and a good night's sleep. He was tempted. He didn't want to go to Ned's house, but he wanted a drag. He could almost feel the smoke going down his throat and resting in his lungs before the exhale, the first wave of the high . . .

Lawn gnomes. The image and the words appeared unbidden in his mind. Lawn gnomes? Yes, he had seen one on his walk that first night. That first night was so hard, but he had gotten through it. Three hours of sleep had been such a victory. Weed could give him a solid eight, maybe more, but then, he wouldn't notice the lawn gnomes. It was a strange thought, but he recognized why it was there. It wasn't just the lawn gnomes. It was the houses, the trees, the school yard. And it was Drea.

"No thanks," he yelled to Joe. "I'll see you guys tomorrow." He walked the last steps to the bus stop and welcomed the smell of diesel fuel over that of weed. He got on the bus and went home. He went to bed thinking about lawn gnomes and slept six and a half hours that night.

Chapter 62

FAMILY TIME

ON FRIDAY, ANDREAS AND DREA arrived. Zayde and Stavros picked them up from the airport. They parked and went in to meet them at the gate. When Drea's head appeared at the end of the jetway, she saw Stavros standing there waiting. Her face lit up with a huge smile, and she ran toward him and into his arms. He held her for what felt like an eternity.

"I missed you so much, Stavros," she said through tears.

"I missed you, too, Drea," he said, stroking her hair and smiling at his father in greeting. He took Drea's backpack from her as she hugged Zayde, and together the small group progressed to baggage claim. Andreas talked about the flight, and how nice it was to not have to drive.

"Stavros, I am definitely getting you plane tickets when you come home next time," he promised. "This is much better. And maybe you will be much better rested if you don't have to spend ten hours on a bus." He grabbed his suitcase from the moving belt and watched for Drea's bag.

"Thanks, Papa," Stavros said. "Yeah, I'm hoping next time I come home, I'm gonna feel a lot better."

Andreas would be in Pittsburgh for a week, and Drea would stay for two. During the first week, they visited Andreas's brothers, sisters, nieces, and nephews and feasted on traditional Greek food. They visited their Aunt Sarah and her family. They went to the graves of Yaya and Papou to pay their respects. They went as a family to see Rod Stewart in concert at the Pittsburgh Civic Arena. They visited the Carnegie Museum of Natural History and the Art Museum. During down time, they rested at home with Bubbe and Zayde as they told Drea and Stavros stories about their mother.

"She was always fighting injustice, even as a child," Zayde said. "In the 1950s, girls weren't allowed to wear pants to school. Rebecca didn't think this was fair, since the winters were so cold and skirts did nothing to keep her and her friends warm. So she would wear dungarees in protest, and she would be sent home from school to change. This happened a few times before she was finally told she would be suspended from school if she didn't wear a skirt. So the next day, she went to school in a skirt. Worn over her dungarees! Oy, the principal learned pretty quickly to choose the correct words when giving Rebecca instructions!"

"She loved her baby brother David," Bubbe recalled with a sad smile. "She was almost twelve when he was born. When she wasn't in school, she was with David. She would read to him, and take him for walks. As he grew up, she would look after him, and teach him about the world. It was so hard on both of them when Rebecca left home. But it was her time to go, to find her true place. They stayed close, but when Rebecca and your papa moved to Amherst, David was distraught. It got better as he got older, and they would speak on the phone and write. And David had good friends to keep him busy. The day that David died, I think a piece of your mother died with him. It made her redouble her efforts to fight to end the war. And to do what she had in her power to make the world a better place." Bubbe smiled. "And that's why she had you, Drea."

Drea smiled meekly. "I know those stories," she told her grandmother. "Stavros told me all about them. Rebel told Stavros to teach me the stories, to help me to learn. And he has. I could probably tell the stories in my sleep!"

Andreas stood up. "It's getting near time to turn in," he announced, stretching his arms over his head. "'But I think I'll take a little walk first. I have a long journey home tomorrow. Stavros, would you like to join me?"

Stavros nodded and stood up. He followed his father to the door. It was a warm and clear August night. The crickets were chirping under a starry sky, and there were few people on the streets in the Squirrel Hill neighborhood of Pittsburgh. Both Stavros and his father immediately turned right toward the school.

"Are you coming home for Christmas?" Andreas asked. "I know it's not for several months, but I'd like to have some idea what's going on, so I can tell Drea when the time comes."

Stavros walked quietly for a moment. "Yeah," he said. "I'll come home. I can't just stay away forever."

Andreas nodded. "And what if Lindi's there?"

Stavros shrugged. "I'll have to figure that out when it happens, Pop," he said. "I can't let what she does rule my life. I mean, it would be hard to see her, but it's gonna have to happen sometime, right?"

"Yes," Andreas agreed. "But you let me know if there's anything I can do to help, okay? That's why you have family, to help you through the tough times. I'm glad your grandparents let you stay here this summer so you could have some time, but I'll also be happy to have you back at home."

They walked quietly into the schoolyard and made their way around the periphery. "It's hard to imagine Mom coming here as a little girl," Stavros said. "I come here a lot and sit in the playground and think about it. I wonder what games she played with her friends during recess."

Andreas laughed. "I don't know," he said, "but I'm sure whatever it was, she was in charge and made the rules!"

Stavros laughed with his father. "Papa," he said slowly, "do you still miss her?" They stopped at a bench and sat down.

"Oh yes," Andreas answered softly, nodding. "I think about her every day, and every time I look at you or Drea. Sometimes, when no one is around, I talk to her and ask her for advice. I like to think that she watches over the three of us and guides us to do the right thing."

"Yeah," Stavros said. "I think that, too." He paused. "Pop, would you ever consider being with someone else? Another woman?"

Andreas considered. He scratched his ear. "I think about it," he revealed. "I have been on a few dates, usually friends of colleagues, but it's never gone beyond the first meeting. I'm not closed off to finding love again, but I don't want to become involved just for the sake of not being alone. If I find someone I'm interested in, I won't hold back. I am human, after all."

Stavros nodded. "I don't have any problem with it, Pop," he said. "I think it would be great if you found someone. I know Mom would want that." He sighed. "I'd like to find someone else someday, but for now, it would still feel like I was cheating on Lindi. And that wouldn't be fair to the new person, either. I have to be ready. And I'm just not."

Andreas put his hand on his son's shoulder. "You'll know when it's time, Stavros," he assured him. "It will feel right, and you won't even think about Lindi. You will just go forward with your life, and you won't have to keep looking back. I know that seems impossible now, but just give it some time." He looked at his watch. "Let's head back now. I need to be up early to catch the shuttle to the airport." They stood up and started walking. "You take good care of Drea this week, and the two of you have fun. And let her talk to you if she needs it. She hasn't been talking much. I don't know if it's just her age, or if she's struggling with something. But if she is, she might talk to you."

"I will, Pop," Stavros promised. "I'll take her to the zoo. That's always a good place to talk."

Chapter 63

Sisters Are Forever

STAVROS WAS GOING BACK TO school shortly after Drea left for home, so he quit his job a week early so he could spend all of his time with his sister. First they went to Monongahela Incline and rode the freight car to the top depot. Then they walked along the streets of the Mount Washington neighborhood and treated themselves to ice cream. The view of the city from the top of the incline was spectacular. They rode back down and took pictures of each other with the picturesque background.

On Tuesday, they went to the zoo. Drea loved the zoo. She would watch the animals quietly and then talk to them softly. It always seemed that they heard her and responded to her words, even the polar bears in the tank. Drea seemed at peace around animals.

They stopped in front of the giraffes, and Drea looked up at their gigantic faces with wonder. "Do you think I'll get tall?" she asked Stavros.

Stavros shrugged. "Mom was about five-foot-four, and Papa's five-foot-nine, so you won't be as tall as a giraffe, but I think you still have a few inches to grow."

"Are you still gonna grow?" she asked.

"I don't think so," he answered. "I think I'll always be five-eight and three quarters. I would like to be taller than Pop, but I might be done."

"Do you think I'll be as beautiful as Rebel?" she asked, tilting her head to the side. She was wearing one of Rebel's headbands to hold her long, light brown hair away from her flawless skin, and her blue eyes sparkled in the sun.

Stavros nodded. "I think you're already as beautiful as Rebel," he told her, looking directly into her eyes. "Maybe even more so."

The corner of Drea's lip turned up slightly. "You have to say that," she said. "You're my brother."

"No I don't," Stavros assured her. "Most brothers wouldn't say that. But I only say things I mean, so you can trust me."

"Stavros," Drea said softly, "do you ever worry about being alone? Like forever?"

The question made Stavros slightly uncomfortable. "I think everyone does sometimes," he told her. "We don't know the future. We can't see who will be with us, so sometimes that picture looks empty. But what's more important is what's happening now."

Drea nodded. "I guess," she said. "Sometimes even now I feel alone, but only when I am alone. Does that make sense? I mean, I don't feel lonely when I'm with my friends. But it's like you said. I don't know what's gonna happen next, so sometimes, I get scared."

"I know what you mean," Stavros said. "It's hard to be alone." He put his hand on her shoulder as they approached the tiger enclosure. "Is there anything specific that's making you feel sad and alone lately?"

Drea shrugged. "No, not just one thing," she said. "Sometimes I think of a lot of things, all at once. I think about Mom, and I think about you, and sometimes I think about what things will be like when I'm older. I worry that I won't find someone who I'll love. Or if I do, they won't love me back. And I don't want to meet someone, and then get hurt, like . . . well, you know." She looked at her feet.

Stavros nodded. "Like me and Papa," he finished for her. "You've seen us hurt, and it's scary to watch, I know. But there's no reason to think your story will be anything like mine. We're very different people. We have different experiences. And there's no reason to think that there will be no one who will love you, Drea. Any guy would be lucky to have you in their life."

Stavros thought he saw something dark pass by Drea's eyes but it was gone in a flash.

"Yeah," she said. "I mean, there's someone for everyone, right?" She walked forward toward the cheetah. Stavros followed behind her, and they watched the big cat bask in the sunlight in silence.

They baked with their Bubbe and took walks to the school yard. They played Sorry! and Yahtzee and told stories to their Bubbe. On Drea's last full day in Pittsburgh, the four of them went to Three Rivers Stadium to see the Pirates play the Mets. They ate hot dogs and peanuts and watched the Pirates win the game, 7-1.

On Thursday, Drea said goodbye to her grandparents, and Stavros drove her to the airport. Since she was still thirteen, she needed to be escorted to the gate and presented to an airline representative. She was given a pin that resembled wings to wear on the flight. Andreas would meet her at the airport at home.

Before they said goodbye, they stood by the jetway. "Stavros," Drea said, "are you coming home for Christmas?"

Stavros sighed. "I told Papa I would."

She grabbed his hands. "Stavros," she said sternly. "Promise me. You need to make a promise. And not back down from it."

Stavros could feel the intensity of this demand. He pulled his hand free and wrapped his arms around his sister. "I promise, Dray," he whispered in her ear. "I promise I will come home for Christmas."

Chapter 64

Take Two

STAVROS WAS FACING COLLEGE FOR the first time without the support of substances, and he was scared. He was living with Brad again, and Brad liked his beer. He had to hope that Brad would understand that things had changed. They had to change. Stavros was sleeping seven hours a night now. He would take that. He didn't want to ever go back to where he was.

When he moved into his new dorm room, Brad was already there. They talked about their summers, and the classes they would be taking in the coming semester. Stavris arranged his belongings and put up pictures of his friends and family. As the day turned to evening, the roommates went down for dinner. They attended a floor meeting and met some of their new floormates. Then they went back to their room.

"Do you want to go to the pub?" Brad asked. "Tom and Stu are going, and I thought we could go meet them for a beer. Not a late night or anything, though."

Stavros froze. This was his first test. He had to handle it with care. "Uh," he started. "I don't think so. I'm gonna stick around, maybe hang out in the lounge and get to know everyone. Maybe watch some TV. Yeah, I think I'm gonna try to keep it lowkey this term. I kinda overdid it last year, and I paid for it with my grades. So, yeah."

Brad nodded. "That's cool, man," he said. "We can hang tomorrow if you're around. Like I said, I won't be too late. But don't wait up, okay?"

Stavros nodded. "Yeah, tell Tom and Stu I said hi."

After Brad left, Stavros breathed a sigh of relief. That had been easier than he thought. He sat on his bed for a while and read, and then joined his floormates in the lounge. Then he went to a late meeting with Kurt.

The semester had a different feel without the weed or beer, but it wasn't unpleasant. Stavros went to class, went to the library, had dinner with Brad, and hung out with his new dorm friends. He went to meetings and groups four times a week, more if he felt he needed it. He called Kurt whenever he needed to talk. They became good friends. Brad and his old friends still asked him if he wanted to go to the pub, but he politely declined. He lost his old dealer's phone number and never saw him on campus. He was taking interesting and challenging classes, and he finally felt like he had arrived at college.

Lindi was still there in his head, but she no longer stood in front of everything and everyone else. She would sometimes surface late at night just to remind him that she was still there, but he would just acknowledge her and turn onto his other side. He was sleeping seven and a half hours a night.

Midterm grades came in, and Stavris was doing well. If he kept it up, he would have all A's and B's by the end of the semester. He joined classmates for study groups and worked with them on projects. He considered what major he might want to declare junior year, but he still couldn't narrow down the field. He decided the decision would take care of itself in time.

In November, Andreas purchased plane tickets for Stavros to come home for winter break. He looked forward to sleeping in his old room and seeing his friends. It had been a year since he had seen Deanna, Mario, and Alec, and he missed them. This time, he wouldn't be so preoccupied with finding somewhere to get beer or weed.

He hadn't been on a plane in years, and it was worlds better than the bus. The bathrooms were clean, and smiling attendants brought him things to eat and drink. The other passengers smelled clean and were on their best behavior. Some were even dressed up for airline travel. Stavros basked in luxury.

Dinner was hot and ready for him when he got home. Andreas and Drea had made Souvlaki and salad, and it was delicious. They both smiled widely while Stavros feasted and made approving noises. Drea had made cookies for dessert.

At bedtime, it was time for stories. Stavros let Drea take the lead while he rested on her bed. He looked around her room as he listened. Not much had changed. She still had posters of horses and dogs on her walls, and bookcases filled with her favorite novels. He didn't notice any pictures of teen idols or pop bands. Her old stuffed animals lay in a line at the side of the bed, and her zebra was still by her pillow. It was like Drea had been frozen in time at age twelve.

When Stavros was ready for bed, he went into his room. The window was tightly shut, and the air was toasty warm. The last time he had been there, he slept with the window open because he was too high to remember to close it after smoking his joint. His father must have known something was going on. But at the time, Stavros had thought he was fooling everyone.

As he closed his eyes, he remembered that this bed was the place where he had proposed to Lindi—and where she had said no. He turned away from the nightstand and promised himself that tomorrow he would find an AA list and go to a meeting that night. He needed the support. Someday, he would feel ready to tell his father. But this was not that day.

He fell asleep, and slept seven hours. After breakfast, the phone started ringing. It was Deanna. She wanted to see him. She asked him to come over to visit. They were still living in the same place, so after his shower, Stavros headed over and spent the afternoon with Deanna and Mario. Alec was now attending UMass and working part time, but now that he was on break, he was working extra hours, but he joined them for dinner.

Deanna served them baked chicken and rice with broccoli. After the entree, she brought out brownies that she had baked while Stavros went out with Mario to run errands. Once everyone was served, Deanna looked at them all quietly and started pulling at her fingers. Mario kept looking at her out of the corner of his eye. Deanna started tapping her foot.

Stavros watched all of this with curiosity. "What's going on, you guys?"

he finally asked. "You're acting all squirrelly. Do you have other plans later or something?" He thought instantly about Lindi and regretted his choice of words.

Deanna and Mario looked at each other for about five seconds. Then Deanna turned back to Stavros and Alec. "No," she said with a shaky voice. "We're just kind of nervous, that's all. We need to tell you guys something and we're just being big, huge wimps."

Stavros felt like there was lead in his stomach. They were going to tell him something about Lindi and they were afraid he wasn't going to be able to handle it. Was she engaged? Married? In trouble?

"Just say it, you guys, okay?" he demanded.

Deanna took a deep breath and then let it out.

"Okay, here it is." She paused. "I'm pregnant! Surprise!"

She sat down on her chair and let her head sink down toward her lap. "Okay, I said it, Mario," she said from under the table. "Now you talk."

Mario nodded. "Okay," he said. He smiled. "Deanna's pregnant. And I'm the father!"

Deanna picked up her head. "You moron," she said, shaking her head. "That's totally not in question. Of course you're the father. Idiot."

"Wow," Stavros said, his eyes wide. "Whoa. Pregnant? D, my God, are you doing okay? Congratulations!"

Alec joined in. "Yeah, wow, you guys. Congratulations! Oh, man, I wish Felicia was here for this! This is awesome!"

Deanna nodded. "Thanks, you guys. I'm fine. I've barely been sick. But I've for sure been craving brownies." She bit into the one in her hand. "But yeah, I'm due at the end of June. So we have a long time to go. But we are the worst at telling people, you know, and everyone hugging us and shit, so no hugging, okay? Well, maybe one hug would be okay."

Stavros and Alec hugged both Deanna and Mario. Mario looked like he was going to burst.

"Can you believe it you guys?" he asked. "Me, a dad? Man, when we were kids, I never thought a girl would ever let me close enough to get her pregnant, but now I have a wife and we have a kid coming. We're, like, grown-ups!"

Stavros smiled at him. He wasn't sure yet how he felt about Deanna being pregnant, but he was relieved that the news wasn't about Lindi.

He would have to figure out a way to be with Deanna without worrying about what she might say about Lindi. He would have to talk about it at a meeting—

A meeting! He had forgotten to find a list of meetings. He had been distracted by Deanna's call that morning, and he hadn't even found a place to get a list yet. He would do it the next morning. He needed his meetings. Especially now, being back home. He couldn't do this by himself.

After dinner, Mario cracked open a can of beer and gave one to Alec. He offered one to Stavros, but he waved it off. They sat around and talked for another hour, and then Deanna started to yawn.

"Sorry, guys," she said. "I've been going to bed at eight lately. But let's get together again soon, okay?"

When Stavros got home, he told Andreas and Drea the news. Drea was excited. "Maybe they'll let me babysit!" she exclaimed. "That would be totally awesome!"

Stavros smiled. It would be awesome. Drea would be great with a baby. She was so patient and soothing. He was absolutely floored, though, at the fact that his teenage sister could end up babysitting for his best friend's baby. It was kind of surreal. He wondered if Lindi knew about the baby yet. Of course she did. Deanna probably called her right after finding out. Girls were like that.

Thinking of Lindi reminded him about finding meetings. He went to the kitchen to find the yellow pages and looked up Alcoholics Anonymous. He wrote the number on a slip of paper and put it in his pocket. He would call when he got a moment alone in the morning.

The next morning, Drea was up and ready by the time Stavros came downstairs. "Stav, can you drive me and Susan to the Hampshire Mall to go Christmas shopping? Her brother was gonna bring us, but he's sick."

Stavros sighed. He had not gotten his full seven hours of sleep and he was still feeling groggy. But he didn't want to let Drea down. "Okay," he said. "Just let me have some coffee first, then I'll get dressed."

"You'll need to stay there with them," Andreas told him. "I don't want them getting stuck there in the crowd and not being able to get in touch with us. Is that okay?"

"Yeah, I guess so," Stavris said. He drank his bitter coffee and went upstairs to get dressed.

Later that night, when he changed his clothes for bed, Stavros found the slip of paper with the AA number on it in his pocket. "Shit," he said, sitting on his bed, holding the paper. He vowed to do better the next day. For now, he was tired and wanted to get to sleep.

He called the next day and got information on where to go to a meeting that night and also got a list of other meetings. He made plans to go, but then his father got stuck at the university and couldn't get the car back home in time. Stavros couldn't explain why he needed the car so desperately, so he made a run for the bus stop. He missed the bus he needed by two minutes, and the next one was running late. It was too late now to get to the meeting.

Stavros felt his heart pounding from stress when he dragged himself home from the bus stop. This was almost as bad as trying to get weed the previous year. He felt stuck. He decided to call Kurt to get some support. He had to shoo Drea off the phone with Violet, and then he went into his father's room and shut the door to make the call.

"I'm sorry," a woman at the other end of the phone told him after he dialed Kurt's home number. "He's out for the night with his brother and sister, and then we're all leaving in the morning to go see family for Christmas. Does he have your number? I can tell him to call you the first chance he gets."

Stavros left his number and hung up. He sat on his father's bed for a few minutes, staring at a wedding picture of his mother hanging on the wall. Finally, he got up and went back downstairs to watch TV. He was still tired, and now Lindi was starting to creep back into his conscious thoughts. He needed distractions. Tomorrow would be Christmas Eve, and the next day, Christmas. There would be no way to get to a meeting those two days. He slumped in his seat and closed his eyes. He took two deep breaths. He tried to relax his muscles. He could get through this. This was just a bump in the road. He was getting stronger. He could ride it out. He just had to remember the things he had learned in meetings and groups. He needed some sleep. And he needed to remember to keep breathing.

Andreas was going to the Christmas Eve liturgy as usual, but this time, Stavros asked to go with him. His father recoiled in disbelief but agreed to take him to the service. Drea didn't want to be left home alone, so she grudgingly came along, pouting the whole time. Stavros felt bad for Drea.

He didn't want to drag her into his misfortune, so he offered to take her and a friend to a movie after Christmas. Drea brightened up for a few minutes after that, but then sat sulking through the entire service.

He took Drea, Violet, and Susan to see *Gremlins*. Drea couldn't choose just one friend, and both of her friends wanted to hang around with Stavros. These were thirteen-year-old girls. Violet and Susan giggled a lot in the backseat. Drea rolled her eyes.

Stavros paid for their tickets and bought them popcorn and candy. Then they went into the theater. While the previews were playing, Drea suddenly realized she had to go to the bathroom, and she didn't want to go alone. Stavros followed her out of the theater into the lobby, and then leaned on the wall outside the ladies' room with the other waiting men. He looked around at the coming attraction posters, but then the sound of laughter drew his eyes back to the concession stand. His eyes rested on its source.

Lindi was in line for snacks along with Deanna, Mario, and another young man and woman their age. They were chatting and smiling, and then Lindi reached out and touched the man's arm with her hand. She said something to him and he laughed. Stavros felt his stomach turn. He became lightheaded and dizzy. Drea came out of the ladies' room and he looked at her. She started back toward the theater, and he followed her mechanically. They found their seats and sat down.

Stavros couldn't concentrate. The movie started, and he didn't know if Lindi was in the same theater. He couldn't turn around to look. So he sat still and assumed she was there. He could almost feel her gaze on the back of his head, but he knew this was not logical. She might not even be there. He needed to watch the movie. That's why he was there. But it was Lindi. He had seen Lindi. And it seemed that maybe she had moved on.

They left the theater without seeing Lindi or her friends and headed home after dropping the girls off. Drea sensed something underneath Stavros's silence.

"Stav, are you okay?" she asked. "You kind of look like you've seen a ghost."

Stavros glanced at her as he drove. He wasn't sure if he should tell her. But he decided he could tell her a little. "Lindi," he said. "I saw her in the theater, buying popcorn while you were in the bathroom. It's the first time

I've seen her since . . . well, it was just hard to see her." He omitted the part about her touching the strange man.

Drea opened her mouth a little and looked at him. She pulled her eyebrows together. "Did she see you?"

"No," Stavros said. "She was with Deanna and Mario. None of them saw me."

Drea nodded. "I forgot the thing with Deanna still being her friend. I'm so sorry, Stavros. That really sucks."

Stavros almost smiled at his sister using a cuss word. She was thirteen. It was normal. "I'll be okay," he assured her, hoping to reassure himself. "It had to happen at some point. I knew it wouldn't be easy."

Drea reached across the seat and took his right hand. She held it in silence as they drove down their street. Sometimes Drea seemed like a sullen teenager, and others, a little girl walking with Stavros in the park and sleeping with her stuffed zebra. At that moment, Stavros needed the little hand-holding girl, and there she was.

That night, sleep did not come easily. Stavros lay still in bed and breathed. He tried to visualize himself at a support group meeting. He pictured himself sitting in the circle, and Jack talking to the group. He listened to the words in his head and repeated them to himself. If his mind drifted back to Lindi, he brought it back to the words, to his breath. Eventually, he fell asleep. He slept five hours. It was a step backward but not all the way back. He drank coffee in the morning and faced his day.

That afternoon, Kurt called. Stavros almost cried when he heard his voice. He closed himself in his father's room and told Kurt everything that had happened.

"Have you gotten to a meeting?" Kurt asked.

"I haven't," Stavros confessed. "It seems like every time I try, something gets in the way and stops me."

"Stavros," Kurt said. "I know you're feeling tired and sad, and like everything's going against you, but you can't forget, every day is a reset. Things don't really pile up. It's a different day now, man. When you hang up with me, you call that number again and you find a meeting tonight. Plan to take the bus just in case, so you're ready. No excuses, Stav. Just do it, okay?"

Stavros paused. "I'll do it."

They talked a little longer, and then hung up. Stavros called the AA number and found a meeting, and then found the bus route. Luckily, Andreas was home that evening and handed him the keys when he asked. He drove to the Presbyterian church, parked, and walked into the building. He followed the signs and entered the group room. He looked around and saw his people. His shoulders relaxed, and he inhaled deeply.

Before he left that night, he obtained a list of other local groups. He could make it to another two meetings before heading back to school after New Year's. He would plan it out in advance. That night, he slept for six and a half hours.

The day before his flight, Stavros got together one last time with his friends. They went out to dinner and afterward went back to Mario and Deanna's apartment.

"Next time we see you," Deanna said, "I'm gonna be gigantic! Can you even imagine? I can't. You'll probably be able to roll me around from place to place!"

Stavros laughed. He looked at Deanna and had mixed feelings. He wanted to stay with her and watch her grow, but he also wanted to stay away forever and never see Lindi around town again. Deanna had kept her word. She had never said a thing about seeing Lindi or if she had a new boyfriend. It was impossible not to know, but it would have been just as impossible to know. Stavros hugged his friends and said goodbye, and then went home for his last sleep in his own bed.

Chapter 65

Springing Back

SPRING SEMESTER STARTED OFF POORLY. Stavros was exhausted. He just wanted to sleep. He was sleeping five to six hours a night, but it wasn't enough. He went to meetings and groups, but he couldn't stay focused. He went to classes and took notes, but sometimes dozed off and wrote nonsense in his notebook. He brought his books to the library, but the overhead lights hurt his bloodshot eyes. And Lindi was always there. He couldn't make her go away. He had been so close to moving on before break. Things had been going so well. But now, he felt like a failure. He would fail all of his classes and let Andreas down. He didn't want to use alcohol or weed; he just wanted to escape into sleep. He resisted using everything but coffee to wake him up in the morning.

Kurt became concerned. "Stav," he said, "it's great that you're not using, but you're not living either. I'm worried about you. I think you need to talk to a therapist. You can't go on like this. You're gonna crash and burn. You need help."

"Okay," Stavros agreed, but he was too tired and distracted to follow up.

The next week, Kurt was more insistent. "Man, you're gonna die if you don't do something. Tomorrow, I'm gonna come get you and bring you back here to meet with someone. It's time. I'll be there at ten. Don't go anywhere, just wait for me. I promise I'll be there."

"Okay," Stavros agreed. He didn't have the strength to argue. He would do whatever Kurt told him to do. For now, he went back to his dorm room and sat on his bed.

Fifteen minutes later, Brad came in with Tom and Stu. "Hey, Stav," he said. "It's Tom's birthday. We're gonna take him to the pub and buy him a birthday beer. Why don't you come along? You can get a Coke or something. You don't have to have a beer."

Stavros nodded. He would go with them and have a Coke. It was better than spending the rest of the night in the room alone. He grabbed his jacket and followed his friends out the door. The last thing he remembered that night was standing in line at the bar in the pub.

The next thing he knew, he woke up with a dry mouth and a throbbing head, in a bed that didn't feel like his own. And his hand was resting on warm flesh that also didn't belong to him. He opened his eyes and tried to focus. He saw a Bon Jovi poster on the wall. He saw a jewelry box on top of a dresser. He had no idea where he was. He moved his head slowly to get a better look. He could see a mass of messy light brown hair on the bed next to him, and as he shifted slowly, he could see it was attached to a sleeping naked woman.

"Fuck," he said softly.

He had been clean and sober for seven months.

He walked around campus to clear his head. He couldn't remember a thing about the previous night or the girl he had woken up next to. He had looked in her wallet when he had gotten up. Her name was Lori Smith. There were probably fifty Lori Smiths at PSC. As he left her room, she called out groggily to him, "See ya, Steve." He walked out of her dorm and had no idea where he was. It took him fifteen minutes to find the library so he could orient himself.

He sat on a bench in the quad with his head in his hands and sulked. He'd blown it. All that work, all of those meetings, for nothing. He was right back where he started. Now he was going to fail all of his classes, let his father down, *and* he had gotten wasted. Why was this any different from before? Kurt had been right. He needed more help than groups and meetings could give him. He needed to try—

Kurt! He looked at his watch. It was eleven thirty. Kurt was supposed to come get him at ten to go to the counseling center. Now on top of everything else, he had blown off Kurt, the one person who wanted to help him the most. Stavros jumped up off the bench and started back to his dorm. Maybe Kurt waited. Maybe he'd still be there.

He wasn't there. The hallway was empty. Stavros let himself into his room and sat on his bed. Brad wasn't there. He was alone. He had never felt more alone. He thought about Drea, who thought about being alone a lot. Another person he had let down. That's when he started to sob.

He let the sobbing run its course. He had no idea how long he cried, but his pillow case was damp, his eyes ached, and his nose was stuffed. And he knew what he had to do. He picked up the phone.

"Hello?" he heard Andreas say on the other end of the line. Stavros felt the knots in his stomach start to loosen when he heard his father's voice.

"Papa," he said softly.

"Stavros, what's wrong?"

"Papa," Stavros repeated. "Please, come get me. I need to come home."

Stavros stayed with his grandparents that night. Andreas arrived the next afternoon. That night, Stavros attended his last Men's Recovery group. He told the group what was happening with him and that he needed to take some time to heal. At the end of the group, the other students shook his hand and wished him well. Jack and Kurt gave him hugs, and Stavros promised to stay in touch with Kurt to let him know how he was doing. The next day, Stavros and Andreas drove back to the dorm, packed his belongings, and loaded them in the car. Before he left, Stavros sat down with Brad to tell him the truth about what had been going on and to say goodbye. Then he went to inform his RA he was leaving. The last stop was the registrar's office to file for a leave of absence. Then they hit the road to Amherst.

On the trip back, Stavros told his father everything, starting with his first beer in college and ending with his last beer earlier that week. Andreas nodded and listened as he drove.

When Stavros finished, they rode in silence for a few minutes. "I'll help you find a counselor," Andreas stated. "Someone who knows about this delayed grief, and about addiction. We'll call together tomorrow and try to get you an appointment for next week. And then we'll do whatever we need to do to help you. Stavros, I knew the breakup with Lindi was hard for you, but I never suspected it was this hard. I imagine it can't be easy to lose the two people you love the most in one short lifetime. There must still be grief for your mother that makes every loss harder, and having to deal with everyone else's grief, as well. I underestimated how much one young man could handle. I'm sorry, Stavros. I won't do that again."

Stavros sunk deeper into the seat of the Volvo, and his shoulders dropped in relaxation. "Papa," he said, "no one can fake it better than an addict. You couldn't have known. I mean, maybe some things looked off, but not enough to give me away. I made sure of that. I thought you had me nailed on the open window that one time, but I guess it was just my own paranoia."

Andreas shook his head. "There were clues," he admitted. "I just didn't put them together. I thought you were just finally rebelling against me."

Stavros laughed. "Yeah, I could see how you would think that." He paused. "Pop, I need to tell Drea the truth. I think it would be good for her. And for me. And I just feel like there's something going on with her, like you said over the summer. Maybe if I tell her what's happening with me, she'll come clean about what's going on with her. Maybe we can help each other."

"I support you telling your sister the truth," Andrea told him. "She knows you're struggling, and that's why I came to get you. She wanted to come, too, but I wouldn't let her miss school. We'll pick her up at Susan's on the way home. We all need to be together now."

They talked for a long time, then stopped for lunch and to fill up the gas tank. After a few hours, Stavros wadded up his down jacket and wedged it between his head and the window. He closed his eyes and concentrated on the sounds of the road. He found himself fading out. The next thing he heard was his father saying his name softly.

"We just entered Massachusetts," he said. "We'll be home soon."

Stavros checked the clock. Three hours had passed since he had fallen asleep. He felt awake now and ready to face his sister. Once he was settled, he would have to talk to his friends. That would be hard. But he knew without a doubt that they would support him.

Stavros walked to Susan's door and knocked. When Drea came out, she threw herself into his arms. "You're okay?" she asked into his jacket.

"I'm okay," he reassured her. "We'll go home and we'll talk, okay?"

Drea pulled away and nodded.

When they got home, they went to Drea's room and lay on her bed. Stavris told her everything, except the details of his one night stand. Even he didn't know those.

"Stavros, you're gonna get better, right?" Drea asked when he was done.

Stavros nodded. "I am. Papa's gonna help me find someone who can help me get better. But right now, I need to be with you and Papa. I need to be home. And I need you both to understand that I *want* to get better. So I'll also have to go to meetings a lot, at least for a while, because the people at the meetings have been through this, too. And when new people come in later, I can help them by talking about my experiences."

Drea folded her hands together on her belly and stared at the ceiling. "It's so great that you can talk to some people who understand you," she said. "I bet that really helps you feel less alone." She turned to face him on the bed. "I'm so glad you're home, Stavros. I'm glad that you wanted to be with us. I don't think I would be okay knowing you were having such a hard time so far away, and we couldn't help you, or just hug you."

Stavros nodded and closed his eyes. He was glad to be home, too. And he knew something else that he hadn't told Andreas and Drea yet. He was not planning on ever going back to PSC.

Chapter 66

WE NEED EACH OTHER

THE NEXT DAY WAS FRIDAY, and Andreas called his insurance company. He obtained a list of therapists that would be appropriate for Stavros. They called each number and found two that were taking new clients, one who could get him in the next week. They made the appointment. Then they called AA and found a meeting for that night.

Saturday was a day to settle in. Stavros cleaned and rearranged his room, so his bed was no longer in the same place where he proposed. Then he and Drea baked a cake. Later, they all went to Olympia's for dinner and watched movies until bedtime. Then they had nightly story time.

Andreas and Stavros sat in the living room on Sunday morning, Andreas reading his newspaper in his chair, and Stavros stretched out on the couch reading *The Color of Magic* by Terry Pratchett. He had just discovered the world of fantasy fiction. He liked the way the stories took him away from himself, into a distant world, where he didn't need to think about himself and his problems, which were small in comparison to the scope of the entire universe, fictional or not.

Drea came downstairs in her pajamas just before noon. She padded into the kitchen and poured herself a bowl of Apple Jacks. Then she sat at the dining room table and ate in silence. After she put her dishes away, she came back out to the living room, switched on the TV, and sat on the couch close to Stavros.

After a while, Andreas put his paper down and stood. "Well, I need to run to the market and get us a few things for the week. Drea, do you need me to get you anything?"

Drea continued to face the TV. "Can you get me some Oreos, Papa?" she requested. "The double stuffed ones."

"It shall be done," Andreas said. He grabbed the keys to his Volvo from the table. "Stavros, would you like to join me?"

Drea looked up. "Papa, there's a show coming on that I wanted to watch with Stavros. Stav, can you stay here with me?"

Stavros looked at Drea. Her eyes were pleading with him to stay. "Pop, I'll go with you next time, okay?"

Andreas nodded. "Okay," he said, opening the front door. "I'll see you both later."

As soon as the door closed, Drea stood and turned off the TV. Then she sat back down next to her brother. She had obviously been waiting for Andreas to leave so she could talk to him. She had something serious to discuss. "Stavros," she started, "I have a crush on someone who was in my class last year."

"Really?" Stavros couldn't believe that Drea was old enough for her first crush. But she was almost fourteen. That's how old he was when he first kissed Lindi. He smiled at her supportively. "Tell me about him."

Drea hesitated, and Stavros could see she was struggling with her next words. "It's . . . well, actually it's a girl," she revealed.

Stavros was stunned. He had not been expecting this. He didn't know how to respond. He resisted the urge to say, "Are you sure?" He knew he needed to say the right thing. *What would Mom say to Drea to make her feel supported?* he thought.

"Okay," he finally said. "So she's a girl. So tell me about *her*."

"Oh, okay," Drea said, looking at him cautiously. She readjusted herself in her seat. "Her name is Catherine. She's tall, well, for an eighth grader, and she's really pretty. She has brown hair and blue eyes. She helped me in the school yard last year when my bead necklace broke. She actually got down on the ground and helped me find all the beads." By the time she finished her description, Drea had the start of a smile on her face.

Stavros felt confident that he had said the right thing. He had encouraged Drea to keep talking. Now he considered his next words. "That's great, Dray," he said. "Does she like you, too?"

Drea paused. "I-I don't know," she said. "I mean, I know she's nice to me, and friendly, but Stav, I think of what it would be like to touch her face, or to kiss her. And I don't know if that's the kind of thing she thinks about when she thinks about me, or any girl. I don't even know how to find that kind of thing out. I mean, all the girls talk about boys. No one talks about liking girls. I might be the only one. What if I'm the only girl in my school who thinks about kissing girls, Stavros? Does that mean I'll never find anyone who likes me, and I'll be alone forever? That can't be fair."

Suddenly Stavros understood why Drea had been so preoccupied with being alone all the time. "Dray," he said, "You're an amazing person. I don't think you'll end up being alone. But I really don't know how you find out things like that. Maybe you just pay attention. You just watch, and listen, and pick up cues. But I know that's hard. I went two years having a crush on Lindi, and I never knew she liked me."

"Yeah, Stav, but that's different," Drea said. "If you told Lindi you liked her, and she didn't like you back, you would have just been sad. But if I tell Catherine I like her, and she doesn't like me back, then she knows I like girls, and she might tell her friends about it. Then everyone would know. And they'd probably treat me differently. And my friends . . . they might stop hanging out with me. I don't know what to do."

Stavros knew his sister was right. She had discovered something about herself that could make her life so much harder. That's what she had been dealing with all this time. She would have to make decisions that he never had to make, and she wouldn't always know who to trust.

He took Drea's hand. "I know there are other girls out there who like girls," he told her. "I promise you. And some day, you'll find one who you like and she likes you back. But you might have to take some chances to find out. She's probably not gonna be wearing a sign that says, 'I like girls.' I really don't know, Drea. I know there are places you can go when you're older to meet other girls, like bars or clubs, and you'll know that they feel like you do, but until then, it might be hard." He thought about it. "Maybe we can find a grown-up for you to talk to about this, someone who went through the same thing as a teenager. I bet Papa knows someone. Or maybe we can check out if there's someone at Smith or Mount Holyoke. They're both all-women's schools, and I know there are a lot of women who go there because they like other women and feel safe to be themselves there."

Drea looked at Stavros in surprise. "Really?" she asked. "I didn't know that. I always wondered why anyone would want to go to a school with no men, but now it's starting to make more sense. So you think I should tell Papa?"

Stavros nodded. "I think you should. You and I won the lottery when it comes to great papas. He'll want to help you. He won't judge you or be upset. Look how he's helping me. He's worked at the university for years. He's seen everything. If you want, we can talk to him together."

Drea nodded. "Yeah, I think I'd like you to be there." She paused. "So does this mean I'm a lesbian?" she asked softly.

"I think it might," Stavros said. "Some people like both boys and girls, and they're called bisexual. Do you think you like boys, too?"

Drea shook her head. "I don't think so," she admitted. "When I look back, I think that I've always felt kind of different than the other girls about boys. I just wasn't interested in liking or not liking them. Or even talking about them. And going way back, I think I might have even had different feelings about Sasha when I was seven. I just didn't have the words for it then." She sighed. "So I guess I'd better get used to the word," she said. "Lesbian. I'm a lesbian."

Stavros nodded. He had to admit to himself, it sounded weird and uncomfortable. He would have to get used to it, too. But it was part of who Drea was, so he would deal with his own feelings. He would help her. He felt sad for her, that she would have this new challenge in her life, but he knew that if she found the right people, things would be easier, and someday she would find love. For now, she just needed him and their father.

Stavros reached over and hugged his sister. "Dray," he said quietly. "I'll always be here for you, you know that, don't you?" He pulled away, and Drea nodded. "We'll talk to Papa tonight, okay?"

Drea nodded again. "Stavros," she said, taking his hand. "Is this okay? Can you handle dealing with my problems when you're dealing with so many of your own?"

Stavros met her eyes. He nodded. "I'll be fine, Dray," he said. He squeezed her hand. "We're both gonna be okay. Remember, both of us are part rebel . . ."

"And part Greek warrior," Drea finished. "I know, Stav. We'll be fine. I just don't think it's always that easy to be a strong person. Sometimes, being strong is scary."

Stavros sighed. "That's probably the most grown-up thing I've ever heard you say, Drea Adira Karras." He leaned over and kissed her cheek. "But if either of us gets scared, we just have to remember that we're never alone."

Drea stood up. "I'm gonna go take a shower and get dressed before Papa gets home," she said. "We can talk to Papa after dinner tonight. Thank you, Stavros. I love you."

Stavros smiled. "Dray, I love you more than all the love in the universe."

Chapter 67

CHANGE BEGINS

STAVROS STARTED THERAPY THE NEXT week. His counselor's name was David, and his name alone helped to start the conversation about his childhood loss and grief. They met twice a week at first, and David also encouraged Stavros to attend recovery groups as part of his treatment. David led two groups per week, and his colleagues led others. For the first four months, Stavros attended four groups per week and ninety AA meetings in ninety days. He talked to David about his mother and sister, and recalled the love and loss of Lindi. They discussed processing grief in a healthy way, without pushing it back or completely submerging in it.

As the months went by, treatment was Stavros's full-time job. He spent his days learning how to get well, his nights at meetings for support, and his time off watching Deanna's belly getting larger as her pregnancy progressed. As summer approached, Andreas asked him what his plan was for returning to school.

Stavros sat opposite his father's armchair on the couch and took a deep breath. "Papa," he said, "I'm not going back to Pittsburgh."

Andreas stared at him with no expression. "Go on," he said quietly.

Stavros sighed. "I knew I didn't want to go back when I left," he revealed, "but I didn't want to make that decision right away. I kinda wanted to see how things played out." He paused and shifted in his seat. Then he sat up straight. "Papa, I don't think college is the right place for me right now. I didn't feel like I could really connect with any of my classes. I couldn't find an interest in anything I'd want to major in. I think it would be a huge waste of time to pick a major in something just because I have to, if it's not something I'd really like to pursue."

Andreas nodded. "I understand," he said. "But I worry that if you don't return to school, you'll greatly limit your options for the future. Stavros, you're twenty now. You're an adult. You'll have to find a way to support yourself. I'll help you until you find your way, but that won't be forever. I don't want you to have to be dependent on anyone, or have to take a job that doesn't challenge you just to survive. You're very intelligent, Stavros. I don't want you to have to settle for something out of desperation."

Stavros nodded. "Papa, I hear what you're saying, but I don't think it'll be that way. I think I'll find something I like to do. But it won't be in Pittsburgh. I'm not ruling out going back to school at some point, but only when I have a plan for what it is I want to learn. In the meantime, I'll start looking for a job. I think I'm ready now. And I won't let it get in the way of my recovery, I promise."

Andreas considered this. "And you've talked to David about all of this?"

"I have," Stavros assured him. "He agrees. I need to be doing things that are meaningful to me. I've already put an application in at Olympia's. I'm pretty sure they'll take me back. I left on good terms. I liked it there. It's a good place to start until I decide my next move."

"It sounds like you've thought this through pretty thoroughly," Andreas said. "We'll have to contact PSC to let them know you'll be withdrawing from school. And I'll need to check with my insurance company to see if you'll still qualify under my plan if you're not an active student. If you get a job offer, you should discuss if health insurance is available. I don't want you to lose your ability to see your therapist. We will pay out of pocket if we need to."

Stavros felt a wave of warmth though his body. He couldn't believe that his father not only didn't get upset about him leaving school, but he was also being supportive of his choice and offering to help. Stavros thought that his father must be very atypical. From what he had heard from his friends, most fathers weren't always as understanding as his. He had helped Stavros when he was in the worst place in his life, and he had comforted and supported Drea when she came out to him as a lesbian. Now, he would assist Stavros with finding the path that truly worked for him. If he had any other father, this might not have worked out quite as well.

Chapter 68

Next Steps

DEANNA AND MARIO HAD A healthy baby boy in June. They named him Theodore and called him Teddy. Stavros brought Drea to the hospital to see the newborn. She sat in the recliner holding baby Teddy and talking to him softly as Stavros visited with his friends. Deanna assured Stavros that she would definitely be utilizing his sister for childcare services in the near future.

Stavros started work at Olympia's. Most of the staff had turned over since he was last there, but the management and ownership remained the same. He was trained by George Markopoulos, the manager, who was the son of Christos, the founder and owner of the restaurant. Stavros would be waiting tables and assisting in the kitchen, depending on what was needed each shift.

Stavros loved the Markopoulos family. They were open and friendly, and Christo's wife, Olympia, reminded him of his Aunt Alexis. She would come to the kitchen and show the staff new recipes she had found or developed—and make sure they knew that the ingredients of her meals were eighty percent food, twenty percent love. The staff would stay after hours to partake in her cooking, many of them drinking ouzo and toasting for hours. Stavros often found himself sweeping up shards of plates smashed against the wall with love at the end of those nights.

As the months passed, Stavros took on more and more responsibility at the restaurant. George showed him how to open and close the cash registers and to account for the daily profits. He was trusted to make runs to the bank to make deposits after his shifts. He was often dubbed sous chef when the need arose, and he learned more and more about cooking massive quantities of multiple food items for a demanding audience. As Christos retreated more from the business end of the restaurant, George pulled Stavros further and further in. He was learning about operating a busy restaurant, including managing staff and marketing their product. By December of what would have been his junior year in college, he was named assistant manager and given a pay raise.

Stavros was starting to feel something he hadn't felt for quite a long time: happiness. He was enjoying himself. He was working at a job he loved, he was living with his family, and he was spending time with his best friends. He was watching Teddy as he grew and learned new skills, and he was observing Drea become closer to Deanna as she worked for her as a mother's helper. He had never seen Drea seem so animated and purposeful.

Days went by when he didn't think about Lindi. She still popped in his head from time to time, and he would feel the pull to let himself sink back into the depths of despair, but now he had skills he could use to bring himself back to the present and all the progress he had made. It helped that she hadn't come home for the summer. He wondered sometimes if Deanna had told her about Stavros's troubles in school the previous year. He hoped that if she did, she also told her that he was doing much better now, and his life was good.

Before Christmas, George brought Stavros back to his office to talk. Stavros immediately thought he must have done something wrong. He dismissed that as being his old way of thinking and sat down across from George at his desk.

"Stavros," George said, "you have become indispensable to me. I don't know how I ever ran this place without you. With that being said, I'm going to encourage you to leave."

Stavros sat up and stared at George. "Why?" he asked, shaking his head. "Things are going well. You just said so yourself."

George smiled. "I don't want you to leave right away," he clarified. "What I want is for you and me to talk about what comes next. Stavros, you are part of the Markopoulos family now. I watch you with my mother when she is creating new dishes, and I see you making suggestions. And I see you brighten up when something works. You are a natural in the kitchen, and I think someday, you should have a kitchen of your own. I think you should consider going to culinary school."

"Culinary school?" Stavros asked. He had never thought of going to school to learn more about the hobby he had enjoyed since he was a very young boy. "I don't know," he said. "I'll have to think about it. Where would I even go? Is there a school in Amherst?"

George shook his head. "Not the last time I checked. There are some particularly good choices closer to Eastboro and Boston if you want to stay in Massachusetts. I personally went to Johnson and Wales in Providence. I completed their four-year program and left there with an MBA. I've worked in restaurant management for years, and my education and experience have greatly benefited my family. Stavros, you're a very bright young man. I think you could go very far with the proper tools. Think about it. And if you decide to go ahead and apply for a program, I'll do whatever I can to help you. And you will get a strong recommendation letter from me. Oh, speaking of things you'll get from me…" George opened his top desk drawer, and Stavros could hear him rustling through some papers. "Aha!" he exclaimed as he pulled out an envelope. He handed it to Stavros. "Merry Christmas."

Stavros opened the envelope and looked at the check inside. He gasped. George laughed. "Christmas bonus," he said. "It was a very fruitful year, Stavros."

When Stavros got home that night, he told his father what he and George had spoken about. Andreas thought for a moment, then nodded.

"So what do you think?"

Stavros smiled. He knew his father would never give his own opinion until he knew what Stavros had considered.

"I think it's an interesting idea," he said. "I love to cook, I love to work in the restaurant, and it's something I'm already good at. I never considered being a chef or having my own restaurant as possible careers. I mean, it's something I've always just done. Something that's part of me. I guess, why not?"

"Yes," Andreas replied. "It is something you're good at. And you've gotten an endorsement from someone who knows what he's talking about. I think it's something worth learning more about. You could request information from some schools."

"George says there are some not far from here," Stavros said. "One or two hours by car. That's good because I don't want to be that far away. And I like the idea of getting an MBA. Maybe I could transfer my credits from PSC. I finished three semesters there. Oh, and here." Stavros handed his father the check he had received from George. "I might be able to get myself a new old car so I can come home whenever I want."

Andreas's mouth dropped open. "This is your Christmas bonus?" he asked. Stavros nodded. "Okay, then," Andreas said. "Maybe the restaurant business isn't such a bad idea after all."

Stavros laughed. It was a rare thing to see his father looking shocked. He would have to take a mental photograph so he could remember it later.

Stavros discussed his thoughts with Drea, who loved the idea of him being a professional cook. She agreed that it was a profession tailor-made for his needs. She also liked the idea of being able to visit him at school and having him drive home on the weekends. Stavros requested applications to three schools and sent them in. He was accepted to all three. After mulling over his decision and discussing the pros and cons with his family and friends, Stavros chose Johnson and Wales because of the MBA option. He would start in the fall of 1986.

Chapter 69

FOOD FOR THOUGHT

Stavros spent the rest of his time at home working, socializing with his friends, and hanging out with Andreas and Drea. Drea turned fifteen. She had leveled out at a slim five-foot-five, and her figure was starting to fill out. She maintained strong friendships with Susan and Violet but had not yet revealed her sexual preference to them. Susan had a boyfriend, and Drea tried to relate as best she could to her stories of their dating exploits. She tended to smile and nod a lot when she didn't know how else to respond. She had developed a friendship with Renata, a friend of Deanna's at Mount Holyoke who had gone through a similar experience in high school and was always willing to commiserate with Drea about her thoughts and concerns. Stavros was glad that his sister had found an ally.

School was starting after Labor Day. Stavros spent the last couple days of August making the rounds in Amherst, saying goodbye to his friends. He spent the last night at Olympia's with his work and home families. They indulged in Greek appetizers, entrees, and dessert, along with ouzo and Retsina for those who wanted to imbibe. There was music, singing, dancing, and the smashing of many ceramic plates. Drea danced with Olympia and her granddaughters and smiled wide under her rosy cheeks. Andreas sipped his drink and practiced his rusty Greek with George and Christos. Stavros ate and watched and did a little dancing himself. He knew that goodbyes were hard, but this was the send-off of a lifetime.

He stood in the driveway with Andreas and Drea the next morning, hugging and making sincere promises to stay in touch frequently. Stavros felt a tug on his stomach as he walked away from his father and sister and got in his car. He sensed them watching him as he backed out onto the street and headed toward the highway. He was on his way to the next chapter of his life.

It took him fewer than two hours to get to Providence and navigate the streets to Johnson and Wales College. His next stop would be his dorm, Culinary East.

He found a place to park and started unloading his car. He located his room and discovered he had arrived before his roommate, Andre. He made four trips to and from the car before he let himself sit on the small bed and rest for a moment. He could see other students walking back and forth down the hall through his open door, and he could hear snippets of conversations they were having with their friends or parents. He saw one guy with light blond hair walking along hand in hand with a pretty brown-haired girl, talking to each other in hushed tones. He was looking forward to meeting his neighbors that night at their floor meeting. It would be nice to talk to some new people. He was determined to find the non-drinkers and then go on a quest to find the closest AA meetings.

Andre arrived shortly before dinner with his arms filled with hifi speakers. He was with an older man who was carrying an ancient turntable. They all said hello and introduced themselves, and then Andre and his father headed back out for more belongings. Stavros hoped that his roommate had brought some good albums. He liked most music, but heavy metal sometimes made him feel a bit uptight right before bedtime. He wasn't sure how much studying he would need to do in his room, but instrumental music always went well with reading.

Andre and his father returned to the room after several trips, and they hugged their goodbyes. Stavros knew that he might be older than most of the other students, but Andre looked so young, vulnerable, and small after his father departed.

"You hungry?" he asked him.

"I could eat," Andre responded in a soft voice.

They walked to the cafeteria together and brought their trays of food back to an empty table. Stavros noticed the blond guy sitting with the brown-haired girl in a secluded corner and watched briefly as they ate and maintained strong eye contact. They looked like they were getting ready to part for the first time and neither wanted their time together to end. Stavros turned his attention back to Andre.

"Where are you from?" he asked.

Andre finished chewing his food and swallowed. "I'm from Fall River." He took another bite.

Stavros nodded. "I'm from Amherst," he volunteered. "I guess both of us are pretty close to home, anyway."

Andre nodded. "I've never been away from home before. It feels pretty far away."

"Yeah," Stavros said. "This is my second time being away. The first time was hard, but it got easier. Probably a lot of the guys here are away from home for the first time."

Andre gave him a weak smile. Then he ate some more. After a few minutes, he spoke again. "My letter from the school said your name is Stavros, but you told me and my dad that your name is Steve."

Stavros nodded. "Yeah, sometimes I go by Steve. Stavros is Greek. Sometimes people don't remember it as easily as Steve."

"I know what you mean," Andre said. "My brother is Demarcus and my sister is Lashawndra. Everyone always gets both of them wrong. I'm only Andre because it was my great-grandfather's name."

Stavros smiled. "My Pop's name is Andreas. You wouldn't believe some of the Greek names I've heard. I worked with two guys named Yiannis and Konstantinos. They went by John and Kostas. I guess Stavros isn't all that bad!"

Andre laughed. Then he went back to eating in silence. After dinner, they went back to their room, and at seven, they walked together to the floor lobby for the meeting. Stavros sat down on the couch next to the blond guy.

"Hey," he said.

"Hey," the blond guy said back.

"Your girlfriend left?" Stavros asked.

Blond guy shook his head. "She's waiting in my room. Sally's starting at Providence College. I'm gonna drive her over after the meeting and help her unpack. We drove here together from Eastboro. I'm James." James put out his hand.

Stavros shook his hand. "Steve."

"Nice to meet you," James said. "I'm pretty psyched to get started here. I kind of want to get my hands dirty."

"Me too," Stavros said. He introduced James to Andre, and soon after, the meeting started. When it was over, one of the other residents organized a floor trip to a pub. Several others agreed to go, but some stayed back. Among them were James, Andre, and Stavros.

"Don't like beer?" Stavros asked James, fishing for other people in recovery to accompany him to meetings.

"I just don't drink," James said. "And I've got to take Sally to her dorm. But yeah, I don't like to drink or be around bars. My brother's in recovery, and Sally and I decided a long time ago that we weren't drinkers."

Stavros smiled. "I may be sharing too much too soon," he said, "but I'm in recovery, too. Can't touch the stuff. I can't even risk going to a bar."

James nodded. "I respect that. I know how hard it can be to stop. My brother had a rough time. Maybe we can hang out sometimes. And not drink."

Stavros laughed. "My favorite activity."

Stavros and Andre followed James down the hall. They stopped at James's room and were introduced to Sally. Then James and Sally headed back toward the elevator, and Stavros and Andre went back to their room.

"How old are you?" Andre asked as they both unpacked their clothes into their dressers.

"I'm twenty-one," Stavros responded. "Why do you ask?"

Andre shrugged. "You said you're in recovery, and this is your second time leaving home. You just seem kind of young to have gone through all that. All the alcoholics I've ever known were like fifty."

Stavros smiled. "Anyone can become an addict," he explained. "Addiction doesn't ask your age. But yeah, I started kind of young. I was in college in Pittsburgh, and I let beer and weed take over my life. I've got things under control now. But I still need to go to meetings and keep an eye on things. Recovery's an ongoing thing."

Andre nodded. "That's cool," he said. He walked toward his stereo. "Do you mind if I put on a record? These belonged to my grandfather."

"What do you have?" Stavros asked.

Andre pulled an album from the milk crate he had used to carry them in.

"Are you okay with Miles Davis?"

Stavros grinned. "I'd really like to hear some Miles Davis," he told Andre.

Chapter 70

GETTING SCHOOLED

STAVROS, ANDRE, AND JAMES BONDED over their lack of alcohol use and spent many late nights together listening to jazz and classic rock on vinyl. Sally often came to visit and joined them in long conversations and movie-watching marathons. They took their classes seriously, and the two years went by in the blink of an eye. The three friends were all going to continue on for two more years to obtain their MBAs. Stavros and Andre found an off-campus apartment to share along with their classmates Jeff and Eugenio. James and Sally moved in together in a small apartment near Providence College.

The MBA program was challenging. The friends had to work hard to complete their studying and projects. Stavros continued to drive home once a month to visit his family, and Drea, who was a senior in high school, was now able to drive to Providence to visit Stavros. She was interested in the University of Rhode Island and spent some time visiting the campus while she was there.

Stavros was still single and was still attending meetings a few times per week. He had a tight band of friends who he spent most of his time with, but he especially valued his first Johnson and Wales friends: Andre, James, and Sally. He thought Andre and James were incredibly talented and would make great chefs, and someday, fantastic business owners. Stavros knew that he would be returning to Amherst after graduation and that he would miss seeing his culinary school buddies. He hoped they would all remain in touch and keep up on each other's successes. He especially hoped they would all have a reunion at James and Sally's eventual wedding.

Graduation day finally approached. The day before, James appeared at Andre and Stavros's door. "You guys know I won't be at graduation tomorrow," he said. "I have to take that one class I had to miss when I had mono this summer, and I'll be going to Sally's graduation at PC. But I wanted to let you know." He exhaled loudly. "I'm proposing to Sally tomorrow night at dinner with our families."

Stavros grinned. "Congratulations, James!" He embraced James and clapped him on the back. "I'd tell you I'm surprised, but I don't really think anyone will be surprised!"

James smiled weakly. "I hope Sally's surprised, at least a little. Look, I have the ring." He took the box out of his pocket and showed his friends.

"Wow," Andre said. "That's some rock. Nice job, James."

"It's got a backstory," James said. "One of the small stones comes from the necklace I gave Sally in high school. It was a promise type thing."

"Crap," Stavros said. "I don't think anyone is ever gonna be able to out-romanticize you on this, James. Wow. You're gonna blow her away. You actually planned this in high school?"

James looked at his shoes. "Well, yeah," he said. "I knew back then that Sally was the only one I ever wanted to be with. It didn't really seem like I was risking anything. And I knew she felt the same. I guess I just got really lucky."

"I hope I can get that lucky someday," Andre said.

Stavros thought the same thing. Someday, he wanted to be as sure of someone as James was of Sally. He had felt that confidence only one time before, but he had been dead wrong. He hoped that next time he would see things more clearly, that he would have no doubts at all. That he'd find a woman who made her feelings about the future clear, and who made him feel like their relationship was the center of her universe.

"I've got to go," James said. "My brother and his boyfriend are staying at the Marriott for the weekend. I'm gonna go bring him the ring to hold on to for me. I'll give you guys a call on Sunday? Maybe Sally and I can stop by before everyone heads out, to say goodbye."

Andre and Stavros nodded. "Yeah, that would be great," Stavros said, starting to miss his friends already. "Good luck tomorrow night. I guess that ring will be on Sally's finger the next time we see you."

Now James's smile was broad. "Yeah," he responded. "It's gonna be pretty cool."

Chapter 71

HOMECOMING

STAVROS WAS BACK IN AMHERST. Drea had just moved into a dorm at Mount Holyoke College. She was starting her sophomore year. She and Stavros had spent the summer together, going to the movies, going for walks, telling each other stories. The Karras family took a two week vacation in East Falmouth on Cape Cod, basking in the sunshine on the beach and feasting on lobster and steamers. At the end of August, Stavros helped Drea pack her belongings to go back to school. And at this school, she had a girlfriend.

"I can't believe Gemma and I will be in the same dorm this year," she told Stavros. "No more cold nights walking across campus to see each other. Now I just have to walk up a flight of stairs. I don't even have to get out of my pajamas or put on shoes!"

Stavros laughed. "That's so awesome," he said. He really liked Gemma, but she lived in Arizona and had gone home for the summer. Stavros worried about what would happen if they were still together when they graduated. He wanted Drea to be happy, but he would hate it if she ended up moving so far away.

Andreas had offered to support Stavros financially over the summer so they could all spend time together, but now it was time for Stavros to start his career. He was in the midst of interviews with several restaurants in the Amherst area. Olympia's wasn't hiring, and Stavros was okay with this, as he wanted to try his hand at different cuisines. He didn't want to be typecast in Greek food. He loved Greek food, but he wanted to diversify. It was good for his résumé. He was waiting to hear back from Chez Jaques and Rotini's, the two restaurants that had most piqued his interest.

In the end, Rotini's made the most attractive offer, and Stavros started work as head chef at the new Italian restaurant in September. He liked the idea of getting in on the ground floor and having a say in the development of the menu. The owner was an Italian immigrant in his fifties, and the manager was his thirty-five-year-old cousin. Most of the hostesses and waitstaff were between seventeen and twenty-one, so Stavros decided early that his social life would not revolve around work.

Mario and Deanna were expecting their second child. Alec and Felicia were living together but had not gotten married. And Lindi was living in Aurora, Colorado. She would not be coming back to Amherst, except for occasional visits with her parents. Stavros had to admit to himself that this did make his life in his hometown much easier for him.

Stavros enjoyed working at Rotini's. He liked it when the owner, Sergio, and his cousin, Franco, were on site. They were jovial, and both enjoyed singing opera loudly in Italian, or as Sergio would say, "the one true language of opera." Stavros would watch the kitchen staff move like choreographed dancers to the music, and it made the work in the kitchen flow. The waitstaff had fun and felt valued. The mood each evening was light and airy. This was the type of restaurant that Stavros would like to open on his own one day, when he was ready to take on that type of responsibility. But for now, he just reveled in the merriment and actually looked forward to going to work.

The invitation to James and Sally's wedding arrived in the mail the same day as an invitation to the nuptials of his cousin Daphne in Pittsburgh. Stavros had to make a decision. He hadn't seen Daphne since he had stayed the summer with his Bubbe and Zayde, and Sally and James were just an hour away.

"Go to your cousin's wedding," James told him when he called with his dilemma. "We'll plan to get together later in the spring. We'll be able to spend more time together then anyway. The wedding's gonna be really hectic for us, and we won't be able to socialize much."

"Yeah, I guess," Stavros replied. "I hate to miss it, though. I never get invited to weddings, and now I'm invited to two on the same day. That sucks. I appreciate your understanding. Are you still enjoying the Marriott?"

"I am," James said. "My manager is getting ready to bail at some point, though, so I'm hoping I'll be up for the position. I'm really ready for the next step, you know? And more money."

"More money's always good." Stavros was still enjoying living at home with Andreas, but he knew eventually it would make sense to get his own place, to really become an adult. More money would definitely help the process along.

Chapter 72

Let's Meet

STAVROS ENJOYED GOING TO THE wedding with Andreas and Drea and seeing the entire Karras clan gathered in one giant hall. Everyone danced and sang along to classic Greek tunes. Small children ran around the room in formal partywear, chased by older cousins. Waiters and catering staff hurried around the venue, cleaning up shards from broken plates so that dancers wouldn't impale their feet. Stavros wondered how much all of the broken dinnerware would cost the bride's family after the event.

After two exhausting days of revelry, Stavros and his family flew back to Massachusetts and went back to their daily routines.

Stavros visited James and Sally at their new house in Uxbridge in late May. He was impressed by the quiet suburban neighborhood and the old growth trees. He didn't envy James for the lawn he would have to mow weekly in the coming summer, but he did envy the couple's life together. They just looked happy.

James caught Stavros's wistful expression. "Are you seeing anyone?"

Stavros laughed. "Do you mean therapist or woman?" he quipped.

James smiled. "Woman," he clarified.

Stavros shrugged. "I've been on a few dates here and there, but nothing serious. The girls at work are always trying to fix me up, but nothing ever goes beyond a first date."

James and Sally looked at each other. "I'm really good at fixing people up," Sally said. "I don't know of anyone offhand, but if I think of anyone, would you want to maybe give it a try?"

"I guess," Stavros said.

"I have one friend I'd love to hook you up with," Sally went on. "She's in some weird relationship right now, but I don't think it's going anywhere. If anything changes, I'll let you know."

"Are you thinking about Michelle?" James asked. Sally nodded. "She actually lives in Amherst. She went to UMass. Yeah, you'd probably like her. She's cute, and she doesn't take any shit from anyone."

"And she's a nurse," Sally said. "She's really caring and nurturing. She's my best friend from high school."

"She sounds great," Stavros agreed. "Let me know if she becomes available. With my luck, that will happen sometime in the next century."

Sally smiled warmly. "Stavros, you'll find the right person. It will happen. Good things take time. They're worth waiting for."

He waited until August, and then he got the call from Sally. "My friend Michelle said she'd like to meet you. She's not seeing anyone now. I can give you her number."

"Okay," Stavros said.

He called her the next week. They were both busy with work and decided to get together later that month. Stavros called Michelle before the last weekend in August.

"Do you maybe want to go check out the arboretum, and then have lunch?"

"That sounds like fun," Michelle agreed. "I haven't been to the arboretum before. I hear it's beautiful."

"How about Saturday?" Stavros suggested. "I could pick you up at ten thirty?"

"Sounds great," Michelle said.

Stavros allowed himself to get excited about the date. This was Sally and James's friend. She must be a good person. She sounded nice over the phone. When he went to bed on Friday night, he thought about how the date might go. It had been a long time since he'd kissed anyone. He wondered if he would kiss Michelle tomorrow when he dropped her off at home.

In the morning, he took a shower and started getting dressed when the phone rang. It was Michelle.

"I just got a call that my friend Carl's mother died last night," she said. "I have to go to Eastboro to be with everyone. James and Sally will be coming, too. She died really tragically. I am so sorry, but I'm gonna have to cancel. I'm sorry it's so last minute, but I literally just found out. This is one of my friends since I was five. I have to be there."

"I understand," Stavros said, his shoulders slumping. "You need to be with your friends. I'd do the same thing. Why don't you call me after everything blows over and we can try again? I'm so sorry about your friend's mother."

"Thanks," Michelle said. "Me too. And thanks for being so understanding."

Michelle never called back.

But Sally did, two weeks later. "I'm so sorry, Steve," she said. "Our friend's mother died, and while we were there consoling him, we found out that the guy Michelle was seeing before was one of our close friends. They ended up getting back together. And to be honest, they just got engaged this week. I'm kinda glad you didn't end up going out with her. I think them getting back together was inevitable. If I had known, I'd never have tried to set you two up in the first place."

Stavros sat down on his bed. "Engaged? Oh, okay. Well, good for her." He paused. "I guess this is a hit to your matchmaking statistics, huh?"

Sally laughed lightly. "Steve, I'm sure there'll be someone else. I do have one friend, but she's really too wrapped up with stuff right now to be available. But don't give up, okay? You're such a great guy. Someone's going to take a chance on you, I know it."

"Thanks, Sally," Stavros said. He got off the phone and sighed heavily. Then he called Deanna, and they made plans for dinner.

The big news the next month was that Franco, the Rotini's manager, had decided to move back to Italy to marry the sweetheart he had left behind. That left an open position that needed to be filled. Sergio looked immediately to Stavros.

"My friend, you should apply for the job," Sergio told him. "You would be my preference to replace Franco. You have an MBA and experience with management at Olympia's. George raved about your skills when I checked your references. Are you interested in helping run this place?"

Stavros gave the proposition some thought. He had prepared for this type of work. He had poured two years into business management. A management position could lead to other possibilities in his future. He told Sergio he would consider applying, and then went home.

Andreas gave it some thought and suggested that the manager position would be a positive move for Stavros if it was what he wanted to do.

James, who was now managing the Providence Marriott food service, encouraged him. "You would be fantastic at that job," he said.

Andre agreed. "I'm not quite in that place yet," he admitted, "but you would be right at home in management."

Stavros decided to go forward. He completed the application, submitted his résumé, and to the surprise of no one, he was offered the position. He assumed the role immediately and was put on the task of hiring a new head chef.

Stavros became accustomed to his new role, and the restaurant thrived. He was a reasonable manager, and his employees respected him. He focused on marketing and brought in many new customers, including those from surrounding towns. College students brought their parents there when they visited. Prom-goers made it a favorite stop before their festive events. Sergio was happy, and Stavros had strong job security.

Drea graduated from college with a degree in early childhood education, the same as Deanna. Gemma moved back to Arizona, and Drea stopped talking about them as a couple. She got a job working in a child-care center and moved back in with Andreas.

The seasons passed. James and Sally had their first child, a little girl named Jessica. Andre met and married a woman named Jacque and moved to Cambridge. Stavros found an apartment in Amherst that was walking distance from work, and a five-minute drive to his childhood home. It was his first time living alone, and it was a challenge. When he got lonely at night, he would go to a meeting. Sometimes, he would go on a date that went beyond a first kiss, and his apartment was a welcome place to explore new limits of intimacy.

Stavros enjoyed being a manager but realized that his one true passion was working with ingredients in front of the stove. He relished the times when he would cover for the head chef for vacations and sick time and basked in the revelry with the kitchen staff. Going back to his office felt empty after those occasions, but once he engaged himself back in his work, he would push these feelings away and concentrate on keeping Rotini's the best-rated Italian restaurant in Amherst.

That winter, Stavros got a welcome call from James. "Steve, I'm gonna do it. I'm gonna start planning to open my own place. I'm ready to be on my own, and to be done with the Marriott. And my family's backing me up."

Stavros smiled. "That's awesome, James. What's the timeline?"

James sighed. "That's the holdup right now. I think I could get things moving and aim for an opening early next fall, but I've got one issue." He stopped.

"What is it?" Stavros asked.

"I think things would move along much faster and easier if I had a good, dependable business partner. Steve, I want you to come on board with me. Like fifty-fifty. To develop a business plan and get things going. I think we'd make a good team."

Stavros was stunned. He hadn't been expecting this. He paused to think and determine what to say next. "Where would this restaurant be?"

"I'm thinking in Eastboro," James replied. "It has the best potential for customers and is a central location. And I'd like to try to come up with something different from what's already offered there. Something new. I think Eastboro is ready for something unique. And since we both have experience in all areas of restaurant work, I think we could make our place a huge success. Think about it. We would be our own bosses."

Stavros loved the idea immediately. He could help build the business. He could be part of developing a new and exciting menu. He could be part of the action. And if the restaurant became successful, there was the chance that he could improve his cash flow. He wanted to do it.

"Let me think about it," Stavros said, determined not to make a snap decision. "Have you written up any kind of proposal yet?"

James laughed. "Said like a true businessman. Yes, I have something for you. I can send it to you by fax if you don't mind getting it at work."

"No, that would be fine," Stavris said. "Just call me first so I'll be by the machine when it comes in. Yeah, I'm excited to take a look at it, James. I'm honored that you even thought of me for this project. It would definitely be fun to work with you on this. Can you give me a week to mull it over?"

"A week?" James asked. "I was thinking you might need longer. No, a week would be great!"

"Okay then," Stavros said. They stayed on the phone for a few minutes to talk about other aspects of their lives, and then James promised to call tomorrow to send the fax.

When Stavros hung up the phone, he sat on the couch and went over the conversation with James. Barring anything outrageous in the proposal, Stavros already considered himself in. He was ready. It was time for him to have his own place, and being a co-owner with James would be ideal. Stavros was feeling elated. He wanted to celebrate. So he went to an AA meeting.

Chapter 73

You Named It What?!

ONCE STAVROS JUMPED ON BOARD with James, things went quickly. He informed Sergio of his plans and agreed to stay on at Rotini's until August. He traveled to Eastboro to scout locations with James and Sally. He and James developed a plan and applied for a small business loan. They spent hours over James's dining room table and stove discussing and creating possible menu items. Sally and Jessica were their test audience. During downtime, they thought about names for the restaurant.

"James and Steve's Bistro," Sally suggested.

"Why does James come first?" Stavros teased. "Or we could take a Greek route: House of Stavros."

James laughed. "I never knew it could be so hard to find a name for a restaurant. We want something with a hook, but not too jargony or silly. And it has to sound sophisticated, but not pretentious."

Stavros shrugged. "I've heard of people naming restaurants after their kids or pets."

"Jessica's?" James suggested.

"There's already a Jessica's in Framingham," Sally said. "Plus, once we have other kids, it wouldn't be fair to them if Jessica got all the attention. What about Ringo's?" Ringo was James's dog when they first met.

"The surviving Beatles might not be too happy about that," Stavros said. "Plus, people might think it was a nostalgic bar or something. Any other pets?"

James lit up. "I've got it." He looked at Sally. "How about Ginger and Milo's?" These were Sally's childhood cats.

Sally wrinkled her nose. Then she smiled. "Milo and Ginger's!" she exclaimed.

James and Stavros looked at each other, and they both nodded.

"If anyone objects," James said, hovering a pen over their application for a business license, "speak now, yadda yadda yadda."

"I'm all in," Stavros said. Sally nodded. James wrote the name on the line.

James looked up and smiled. "Welcome to Milo and Ginger's!"

Chapter 74

OPENING DAY

"THANK YOU," MICHELLE SAID TO James as she and Chris walked into the restaurant, pushing a double baby stroller. "Glad to finally be here!"

"I'm gonna go take the girls to the bathroom and change their diapers," Chris said. "They want to be at their best for their first fancy dinner party." He leaned over and gave his wife a kiss. "Be right back, Chelley."

After Chris walked away, Stavros came out of the kitchen and approached James and Sally. James made introductions. "Steve, this is our friend Michelle. Michelle, Steve."

Stavros looked toward the redheaded woman sitting in front of him. "Michelle?" he asked. "Michelle from Amherst?"

Michelle laughed. "Oh my God, you're *that* Steve?"

She looked at Sally and James, who obviously had forgotten about the setup a few years earlier. They both looked slightly horrified.

"Steve," Michelle went on, "I guess this is my chance to apologize to you for canceling on you back then. I'm so sorry. I never even anticipated things would go the way they did the few weeks after that. I always felt bad about not calling you back. But Chris and I ended up getting married, and that double stroller you just saw rolling toward the restrooms was carrying our twins."

Stavros smiled and sat down next to Michelle. "Hey," he told her, "you can't get in the way of destiny." He looked over toward where Chris had gone with the babies. "Twins. Huh. You can probably guess I won't be asking you out again."

Everyone laughed, and Sally sat down on the other side of Michelle. James remained standing. "I'm gonna go check up on the kitchen staff," he announced. "I think one of us should check in every now and then. I'll be back in a few minutes." He walked toward the back of the restaurant.

Stavros, Sally, and Michelle talked for several minutes until they saw a young woman with light brown hair walk through the front door. Stavros stood up and walked over to her. "Dray!" he called.

Drea looked up at him and smiled. She gave him a hug. She looked around. "This place looks great, Stav. Is Papa here yet?"

Stavros shook his head. "Not yet. Don't forget, Dray, everyone here knows me as Steve. It would probably be better if you called me that while you're here."

Drea nodded. "Okay, *Steve*," she said emphatically. "In that case, why don't you call me *DeeDee*. It's what the kids call me at work. I'm just trying it on for size. Let's see if it sticks."

"Okay, DeeDee," Stavros agreed. "C'mon, I'll introduce you to these ladies."

After Drea met Sally and Michelle, she excused herself to use the bathroom. Soon, the front door opened, and two women walked in. Stavros had no idea who they were, but he immediately noticed they were both beautiful. He couldn't stop staring. Especially at the dark-haired one. She was stunning. She stopped to hug James's brother Howie, who then pointed her to the table where he was sitting.

Sally saw the women and stood up to greet them. She introduced them to Stavros as Darlene and Traci. The woman with the dark hair was Darlene. He stood up, shook her hand, and looked into her eyes. He looked too long and had to look away. Then he heard Drea approach behind him. She cleared her throat. He made hasty introductions.

"Traci, Darlene," he said, "this is my little sister, DeeDee. DeeDee, this is Traci and Darlene."

Drea came forward to shake their hands. "Sorry about my rude, much older brother," she said. "It's nice to meet you both."

Traci smiled. "Nice to meet you, DeeDee." She grasped Darlene's arm. "Darlene, we've got to wash our hands before we eat. Let's go find where they're hiding the ladies' room in this place, okay?"

"Oh," Stavros said, hoping he didn't look too disappointed that they were going away, even just for a few minutes. He pointed to the back right corner. "Right over there, down the hall."

"Thanks," Darlene said, and she smiled at Stavros. "We'll be right back."

Stavros stared after the two women as they walked away. Then he heard his sister whisper his name. He turned to look at her. She was staring at the two women, too. She pulled him closer.

"When they come back," she said urgently, "I want you to introduce me to Traci again. This time, tell her my name is Drea. I really want to hear Traci call me Drea."

DARLENE & STAVROS:

OF MICE AND RATS

Chapter 75

OPENING DAY

STAVROS LOOKED DIRECTLY AT TRACI. "I was mistaken," he said with a smile. "My sister informs me that she no longer goes by DeeDee. I would like to reintroduce her. Darlene, Traci, this is my sister, Drea."

Traci smiled and reached her hand back out to Drea. "Nice to meet you, Drea," she said. Drea beamed.

James came back to the table with Chris and his identical twin toddlers. "I'm gonna give a kitchen tour," James said. "People are still shuffling in, so we're gonna wait to start serving food, but some folks have asked to see where all the action takes place. Anyone else want to join?"

"I'd like to see the kitchen," Traci said.

Drea immediately stood up next to her. "I'd be up for a tour, too."

Michelle joined Chris, and Sally trailed behind her husband. Stavros and Darlene were left alone at the table.

"You didn't want a kitchen tour?" Stavros asked.

Darlene shook her head. "I'd rather go when there are fewer people in there. Maybe you can show me later."

"I'd love to," Stavros said. "Maybe when things quiet down a bit."

They looked at each other, then both looked away. Then they looked back. "So," Darlene said to fill the silence. "What was that whole DeeDee–Drea thing about?"

Stavros laughed. "My sister is the most interesting person I know," he told her. He paused and considered his next words. "And I'm pretty sure she likes Traci."

Darlene let out a huge sigh. "Oh, thank God," she said. "I have it on very good authority that Traci likes Drea, too." There was a silence. "You know, in a twenty-second conversation, you and I probably just eliminated the need for Traci and Drea to do that long tap dance where they try to figure out if the other likes women. Now they can just skip that part and get down to the really good stuff."

"Yeah," Stavros agreed. "I know that sometimes Drea has a hard time picking up the signs. That must be hard. I can kind of relate, sometimes."

Darlene looked right into his eyes. "I like men," she said, and then she looked down at the table and shook her head in embarrassment.

Stavros grinned. "Good to know,"

There was a short silence. Then Darlene spoke. "Do you live in Eastboro?"

"I live in Amherst right now," Stavros said, "but I'm considering moving closer to Eastboro, perhaps down the road, because of the restaurant. Drea and our father are in Amherst, and we're all very close, so I don't want to go too far away."

Darlene nodded. "I can understand that. My mom is here in Eastboro. I want to be close to her, too. I've been staying with her since I finished graduate school, but now I'm planning to move in with Traci at her house."

"You two seem really close," Stavros observed.

Darlene smiled. "Traci's my best friend. She's been a lifesaver for me. I went through some hard stuff after my father died a year and a half ago, and she was really there to help me."

"I'm really sorry about your father," Stavros said gently. "I lost my mother when I was six, right after Drea was born. It's so hard. I went through a hard time recently, too, but I know what you mean about your friends helping you through." Stavros saw some motion by the door and looked up. "Speak of the devils."

Deanna came in, holding the hand of seven-year-old Teddy, and Mario followed close behind carrying their younger daughter, Crystal. Next came Alec and Felicia, and in the rear was Andreas, carrying an umbrella. They all saw Stavros stand up at his table and approached him.

There was much hugging and congratulations, and Stavros introduced his friends and father to Darlene. She smiled shyly and shook hands with everyone. They all sat down, and Crystal jumped off her father's lap and climbed up onto Stavros. He put his arms around her and looked at Darlene.

"Crystal's my goddaughter," he explained. "We're pretty tight." Crystal smiled up at Darlene when she heard Stavros's approving tone.

Darlene leaned in close. "Why are your friends calling you Stavros?" she asked.

"Oh!" Stavros replied. "I wasn't even paying attention to that. Yeah, my real name is Stavros. I go by Steve in my chef life."

Darlene laughed. "Does everyone in your family have an alias like you and Drea?"

Stavros grinned. "Not my Pop, but my mother was named Rebecca, and she went by Rebel. She really was one. It fit her. Do you have any aliases?"

Darlene thought about it. "My mom calls me doll baby. I have never really known why. I mean, doll, Darlene . . . I guess I can see how it might have morphed. I love it when she calls me that."

James came by and gathered the next group for the kitchen tour. Everyone got up except for Stavros and Darlene. Darlene's friends were all huddled around a table covered with appetizers, with Drea and Traci to the side, speaking animatedly.

"Alone again," Stavros said to Darlene.

"Yeah," she replied. "That kind of keeps happening." She was starting to feel a little less shy.

"I'm probably gonna have to start helping James with the dinner soon," Stavros said, "but I'd love to continue our conversation some other time, like, maybe over dinner?"

Darlene felt her heart start to pound. "Yeah," she said. "I'd like that."

Stavros nodded. "I know of this great sushi place over on Main Street. They got great reviews in the *Examiner*. Do you like sushi?"

Darlene hesitated. This was her chance to make her needs known. It was actually kind of a powerful feeling, knowing she could assert herself. "Actually, no," she said, making a face. "I don't like sushi. I think I might be allergic to the taste."

Stavros laughed. "That's okay," he said. "It's not really for everyone. I can always make Drea go with me another time. What kind of food would you like to get?"

Darlene reveled in the fact that she was being given a choice, and she had made this happen by asserting herself. It was the first time a man had ever asked her for her input about what to do on a date. "I really like Italian food. Do you?"

Stavros nodded. "I love Italian food. I worked in an Italian restaurant in Amherst for years as a chef and manager. What's your favorite place in Eastboro?"

Stavros was making this so easy. He was listening to her, curious as to what she wanted. It made Darlene want to hug him. That, and that hair of his. And those shoulders . . .

"Luigi's is my favorite place," she said. "My friends and I go there a lot."

Stavros smiled when he recognized the name. "That's the place where James used to work," he remembered. "I've never been there. I'd love to see what all the hype is about!"

Darlene smiled. "They have the best chocolate cake."

James poked his head out of the kitchen and motioned for Stavros to join him.

"I've got to get back to the kitchen," Stavros said with a slight frown, "but I guess that's why we're all here tonight. To open our new restaurant." He grinned. "We're living the dream."

Darlene smiled wide. "Yes, and congratulations. I can't wait for dinner!"

Stavros nodded. "It should be good. And speaking of dinner, would tomorrow night work?"

Chapter 76

TICKET TO RIDE

DURING THE DRIVE HOME, DARLENE and Traci had so much to say that neither one wanted to go first. Finally Traci broke down. "I hope Drea likes mice."

Darlene nodded excitedly. "She likes mice!" she revealed. "And just about now, Stavros is probably telling her that you do, too!"

Traci shrieked. "Are you kidding me?" Then she looked confused. "Who's Stavros?"

"Steve!" Darlene explained. "Steve is English for Stavros, which is his real name. Kind of like how DeeDee turned out to be Drea. They're Greek."

"Yeah, I know," Traci said. "Drea told me." She shivered. "She actually asked me if I would like to get together for a Greek dinner. I was worried she was just trying to be nice because I kept asking her all these questions about Greek food. But maybe she was actually asking me out!"

"Stavros was positive she liked you. Did you get her number?"

Traci shook her head. "But I gave her mine! Yikes! Maybe she'll call me!"

"Traci, she is one hundred percent going to call you." She paused. "Stavros asked me out to dinner tomorrow night."

Traci took her eyes off the road for a second to look at Darlene. "So you said yes, of course."

"I did," she said. "He asked me if I liked sushi and I said no!"

"Oh, Darlene, that must have felt so great!" Traci said, giving her a warm smile. "So where are you going?"

"Luigi's," Darlene said. "It's a safe place. I know I'll feel comfortable there." She sighed. "It's hard for me to know how much to reveal to him, you know? Like, maybe I should wait a day or two before I tell him I almost had a total mental breakdown not that long ago."

"Darlene," Traci started, "you legitimately went through a lot. But you dug your way out, kicking and screaming. You're strong because of it. He'll see that. Just tell him what feels right. You'll know."

"I hope so," Darlene said. "He seems so nice and genuine. I don't want to do anything dumb. I don't want to miss any signs this time. But I also don't want to be all paranoid, you know?"

Traci nodded. "I know. It will be okay. You're not the same 'people' you were those other times. This singular Darlene will make good choices. You'll see."

Darlene smiled. "Did you see that curly hair?" she said, looking out the window and recalling the image in her head. "I mean, who even has hair like that! And those shoulders . . ."

"Thanks for letting me stay and ride back with you, Stav," Drea said. "I was having a good time. I didn't want to have to go back early with Papa."

Stavros smiled. "I could tell you were having fun. Traci seems pretty cool. And she's really pretty."

Drea beamed. "Do you really think so? I got her number, but I think she just wants to get together because I got her all excited about trying Greek food." She frowned. "I just can't tell."

"What if I told you," Stavris started, "that Traci is not only excited about Greek food, but I also confirmed that she's really excited about the fact that she'll be eating it with you?" He glanced over at Drea with a sly smile.

Her mouth dropped open. "Really?" she said. "Darlene told you she likes me?" Stavros nodded. Drea made excited noises. "Oh, now I'm totally gonna call her. Would tonight be too early for me to call her?"

Stavros laughed. "Dray, you do whatever feels right. If you're excited about Traci, and you want to call her tonight, just do it."

Drea turned to look at her brother. "So are you gonna call Darlene tonight, then?"

Stavros sat quietly for a moment. "It's that obvious, isn't it?" he asked. "God, I feel like I have electric currents running through my whole body right now. I haven't felt like this, well . . . maybe I never have! She just walked through that door tonight—"

"And right into your heart, right?" Drea asked. "It was like the two of them just dropped down in front of us like a gift from heaven." She paused. "Or maybe a gift from Rebel," Drea contemplated.

Stavros nodded. "I wouldn't put it past her. She's probably out there somewhere saying 'I want grandchildren already. Get off your lazy asses and get me some grandchildren!'"

Drea laughed. "Well, I can't physically make her any grandchildren with all girl parts," she lamented. "But I would love to have my own family someday. Including babies. And it would be nice to have someone to do it with."

Stavros reached out for her hand. "If there's a will, my sister will find a way." He continued to hold her hand. "I haven't had anyone in my life for a really long time. I wonder how she'll feel about the fact that I'm in recovery."

Drea shrugged. "Better in recovery than actively using," she pointed out. "She might have questions the first time you turn down a glass of wine at dinner, but you're always so good at explaining it to people. Just be honest. If she's the right one, she'll understand."

"Yeah," Stavros said. "I hope so. I'm taking her out for Italian food tomorrow night. She'll notice the wine thing for sure. Drea, you're so wise. I'm sure you got that from growing up around me,"

Drea laughed. "Can't you drive any faster?" she pleaded. "It's getting late. I need to get home so I can call Traci before she goes to sleep."

Chapter 77

GETTING READY

"SHE CALLED ME LAST NIGHT, Darlene!" Traci exclaimed.

"What?" Darlene asked, sitting up in her bed. It was 9:48. It seemed a little early on a Saturday morning for Traci to be calling her.

"Drea! She called me when she got home last night! We talked for two hours! She is so amazing. She works with kids. And she loves animals. She's really soft spoken, but when she talks about something she's excited about, she gets all animated. It's so cute!"

"Traci," Darlene said, shaking the sleep out of her head. "Did you stay up all night? You sound way too energetic this morning."

"Darlene," Traci said solemnly. "You need to get excited with me. A girl I like, a beautiful, interesting girl with a brother you're going on a date with tonight, called me as soon as she got home from meeting me. She really likes me, Darlene! I feel like I'm in high school again! I wish I could ask her to the prom!"

Darlene smiled, despite the early weekend hour. "Traci, I am really excited for you. I'm pretty certain these two are the lifetime connection you saw for us. I can't believe another one of your intuitions came true!"

"I know!" Traci replied. "I'm gonna drive out to Amherst on Friday so she can take me to this Greek place there called Olympia's. She said Stavros used to work there before he went to cooking school. She said it's really authentic. I hope I like it."

Darlene laughed. "You've had baklava before, Traci. You liked it. You'll like the food. So what should I wear on my date tonight?"

"Um . . ." There was a pause. "Wear jeans. Those midnight blue ones you have. Those are really sexy on you. And didn't you get a peasant shirt when we went to the mall? That would be cute. Especially for Luigi's. And wear real shoes, no sneakers."

"Perfect," Darlene agreed. "Hair up or down?"

"Oh, totally down," Traci said with conviction. "Darlene, always wear your hair down. Trust me. I know. Yikes."

Darlene got up, ate breakfast, and took a shower before sitting down to make a call.

"Kim," she said when her friend picked up the phone in California. "You'll never guess what happened to me and Traci last night!"

Stavros spent the morning and into the afternoon at Milo and Ginger's with James. The soft opening had gone well. The staff were prepared, and they were precise and professional. The meal went down without a hitch. The grand opening would be the following Saturday night. They already had reservations booked. This was becoming real. There were still several details to work out, though.

Stavros was distracted. His mind drifted away while James was reading him a list of numbers. "Steve," James said.

"Yeah?" Stavros said automatically without really hearing anything but his name.

"Steve, man, where are you? You're definitely not here with me right now." James looked at him slightly impatiently.

Stavros blinked his eyes a few times. "Uh, sorry, James," he said. "Where am I? More like when am I. I guess I'm sometime tonight, at Luigi's."

James laughed. "This is so weird, Steve," he said. "You know I've known Darlene since I was five. She's been one of my closest friends since high school. It's totally bizarre to see you going all ape shit over her after meeting her one time. Man, if I had known this would happen, I'd have fixed the two of you up years ago!"

Stavros shook his head. "No," he said. "I wasn't ready. No, this is the perfect time for me to meet her. Everything's lined up. I know what I'm doing for once."

James nodded. "Yeah, that probably worked out the best for Darlene, too, after everything she's been through."

Stavros made eye contact with James. "Everything she's been through?" he asked. "I know her father died not long ago."

"Yeah," James said. "It was really hard on her. They had a really fucked-up relationship. She never got to tell him anything she wanted to say while he was alive. But she's so much better now. She's great, as a matter of fact. And you're actually the perfect person for her. She needs someone who will treat her well, listen to her, and treat her like a queen. I know she'll get that from you."

Stavros stared out the window. "Yeah, James," he told him. "I think I've been training my whole life to prepare to meet Darlene. I'm pretty sure I know exactly the way I'm supposed to be with her."

"Yeah," James said. "But right now, I kind of need you to be one of the owners of Milo and Ginger's. I promise you, at five o'clock, you can be anyone else you want."

Stavros laughed. "Okay, okay," he said. "I'm all yours." He turned his attention back to the list of numbers

Chapter 78

Dinner for Two

DARLENE HAD NEVER BEEN TO Luigi's on a real date before. It was always as a group or with a friend. After she introduced Stavros to her mother, they headed out in his car to the small and intimate Italian restaurant. When they got to their table, Stavros pulled her chair out for her. She couldn't help but smile as she sat down. He sat down across from her and looked at her expectantly.

"So you need to tell me what's good here," he said. "I'm a big spaghetti and meatballs guy, which I guess is pretty weird for a chef, but, hey, you like what you like, right?"

Darlene laughed. "Yeah, I guess you do." She looked down at the menu. "I like chicken, so I usually get the chicken parm or picatta. The garlic bread is really good. I know Sally likes the eggplant parm if you're into vegetables. And our friend Carl loves the spaghetti and meatballs here. I won't think any less of you if you decide to go with that."

Stavros smiled. He looked at the menu for a few minutes and then nodded. "Yeah, you know, I think I will go for the meatballs. Why kid myself?"

Darlene nodded. "And I'm gonna get the chicken parm. You're right. Nothing beats comfort food. I think I'll get a glass of wine, too."

The waiter came over and they gave their orders. Stavros ordered a Sprite.

"You don't drink wine with dinner?" Darlene asked. "I would have thought you'd know all the pairings. Now you really don't seem like a chef!"

Stavros grinned. "I know, you would think that, wouldn't you? But no, I don't drink."

"Oh," Darlene said. "So that's probably how you and James became friends in cooking school. He and Sally were famous around our high school for their lack of drinking and drug use. I think in most other schools, it's the other way around!"

Stavros nodded but said nothing else about drinking. "Yeah, James and Sally and I spend a lot of time together in school," he said, adeptly changing the subject. "We also had a friend named Andre. The three of us were pretty tight. That's why it's so awesome that James and I have gone in together on this restaurant. I was really missing those two, and now I get to see Jessica grow up."

"That's really nice," Darlene agreed. "All of us from high school are near here now except for our friends Carl and Kim, who live in California with their kids. But we still see them and talk on the phone all the time. Have you ever heard about the Bishops and the Farmers?"

Stavros indicated that he had not, so Darlene told him the story of Chris and Carl's famous family, whose patriarch was the mayor of Eastboro about eighty years earlier. Then she told him about Chris and Carl's identical twin grandmothers, and how Chris and Michelle's twins had been such an amazing and unexpected coincidence.

"And I hear you almost went out with Michelle," she said.

Stavros nodded. "Yeah, I guess James and Sally are really into fixing people up. But that one didn't work out too well."

Darlene nodded. "You should have seen everyone's faces when we heard that Michelle and Chris had been sneaking around behind our backs for three years. We were all floored. I'm not surprised James and Sally had no idea."

"What were James and Sally like in high school?" Stavros asked.

Darlene laughed. "They were absolutely ridiculous in love. It was like a fairy tale. They fell in love about a week into junior year, and the rest is history. They've been glued to each other's sides ever since. I guess you could say it was love at first sight." She stopped, continued to look at Stavros for a few more seconds, then looked at the table.

Stavros considered her words and her reaction. He felt a tingling in his stomach. "Yeah . . . that's pretty amazing, just to walk into someone's life like that, out of the blue. Like you didn't know what hit you."

The waiter appeared with their food, and Darlene was grateful. She had no idea what to say. She was a firm believer in love at first sight. The thought had just occurred to her for the first time ever the night before: Stavros had blown her off her feet.

Stavros took a bite of his meatball and chewed it slowly. Love at first sight. He hadn't been considering it, but now it was right in front of him. He had spent the whole previous night with Darlene when he wasn't in the kitchen, and he'd thought about her on the drive home and as he prepared for bed. The image of her face was like a pacifier. He had slept like a sedated elephant the previous night, falling asleep thinking that he would see her again the next day. And here she was. Darlene was totally rocking his world.

After dinner, they shared a piece of chocolate cake and sipped on decaf coffee. They talked as the tealight in front of them burned and until they were both ready to stand up. But they weren't ready for their night to end.

"Have you been to Twin Bridges Park?" Darlene asked.

Stavros shook his head. "No. Is it nearby? I'm guessing it's a park with a couple of bridges."

Darlene laughed. "Yeah, it's close by, and you have to drive by my old high school to get there. Want to go there for a walk?"

Stavros felt a wave of relief. He would delay dropping her off for as long as she was willing to spend time with him. "I'd love to."

They walked around the park and continued to talk. Stavros told Darlene about Rebel and the stories she would tell. Darlene told Stavros about her friends and their many exploits in high school. They both avoided any dark topics, keeping the conversation light. Eventually, Darlene could no longer suppress a yawn.

"I'll take you home now," Stavros said. "I need to drive back to Amherst anyway. But would it be too forward of me to ask you out again? I mean, I guess the right thing would be for me to call you in a couple of days and ask you out, but I don't see the need to keep you guessing if I'll call. And I don't want to have to wait to guess if you'll say yes."

"I'll say yes," Darlene answered quickly. A thought occurred to her, and she smiled. "Stavros, do you like to dance?"

"Dance?" he asked. "Like what kind of dancing? I hope you don't mean tap or ballet."

Darlene laughed. "No, I mean just moving around to music with other people. Just letting yourself go. Just hearing and being the music."

Stavros thought about it. "I haven't been to a dance club or anything," he said, "but I have been to a lot of Greek and Jewish family weddings. There was a lot of dancing at those, and plate smashing. I'd love to go dancing with you if that's what you'd like to do next time."

Darlene smiled. "Yes, that is what I'd like to do, Stavros. I would like to go dancing." She paused. "Jewish family weddings? Do you have Jewish family?"

"Yes," Stavros told her. "I'm half Jewish. My mother was Jewish. So according to Jewish law, I'm actually considered a Jew. But I wasn't raised in either Judaism or Greek Orthodox, per se. I mean, I know the traditions, foods, and holidays, and I can bake a mean challah, but otherwise, I would say I'm a free agent."

"Wow," Darlene said. "I'm half Jewish, too. My father was Jewish. You might have guessed by my last name. So according to the same Jewish law, I'm not considered Jewish, but I think I'm more Jewish than anything else. If I was gonna be anything, that is. So between the two of us, we're one whole Jew!"

They laughed together, and then walked to the car. Stavros drove Darlene home. Darlene's heart started pounding. She didn't know what was going to happen when they got there. She was a little scared, and she was feeling very timid. When they got to the driveway, Stavros turned to look at her.

"I had a really good time tonight," he said softly. "I can't wait to see you again and to go dancing." He paused, looking at her face. "But I'd better head out now. I'll watch you walk to the door to make sure you get in safely. Would it be okay if I call you, maybe, tomorrow?"

Darlene nodded. "I'd really like that, Stavros."

Stavros smiled. "I like that you call me Stavros," he said. "It just sounds right." He reached out and touched her arm for a moment. Then he pulled his hand away. "Good night, Darlene," he said. "I'll talk to you tomorrow."

"Good night, Stavros," Darlene said gratefully and got out of the car.

As she walked toward the door, she realized what had just happened. Stavros was watching. Stavros was paying attention to her, to what she was saying without words. He could tell she was feeling uneasy about the end of the date. He probably wanted to kiss her, but he could tell she was feeling unsure. So he let her go with a touch on the arm. She turned around and waved at him after she unlocked the door and then she stepped inside. She walked up to her room as if in a trance.

She had found someone who actually cared about what it was that *she* wanted.

Aspen would be proud.

Chapter 79

THE STORIES

STAVROS SPENT THE TIME DRIVING home going over everything Darlene and he had talked about the whole night. Every word, every movement and gesture. Every one was meaningful. He had wanted so badly to kiss her in the car. He wanted to hold her in his arms and feel her lips and her body against his, but he could tell it wasn't time yet. There was something there in her eyes, something telling him to go slow. Darlene was wonderful, and open, and beautiful, but he could tell she was haunted. He was okay with that. He was haunted, too. He had to play this right. He had to earn her trust before he could go any further. He would do whatever he could to show her that he would be kind, and gentle, and never hurt a hair on her body. And maybe at some point, they could share their stories, the stories that must be told.

An hour later, he made the decision to go to his father's house instead of his own apartment. It was late, but he could see Drea's light glowing from behind the drawn shades in her room as he passed by. She was awake. He wanted to see her. He turned his car around and parked in the driveway.

He let himself in the front door and walked up the stairs quietly, but not quietly enough to make Drea feel like he was sneaking up on her. He approached her closed door and knocked lightly. She called out for him to come in. It was one in the morning, but she was on the phone.

"Traci, I need to go now," she said into the receiver. "Believe it or not, my brother just walked in. He was out with Darlene tonight. I'm sure I'm about to hear all about it. Okay. I can't wait. Bye, Traci. You too." She hung up.

"How long this time?" Stavros asked, sitting down on her bed, and then letting himself fall back on her extra pillow.

"What time is it?" she asked.

"One o'clock," he answered.

Drea gasped. "One? Holy shit, Stav. I was on the phone with Traci for three and a half hours! Hold on, I really have to go to the bathroom." She jumped off the bed and ran out of the room. Stavros laughed.

"So how was your date?" she asked when she got back and settled in.

Stavros closed his eyes and sighed. "I'm dead meat," he told her. "She's fantastic. I can't believe I got to spend my night with her. And she seems pretty into it, too. I don't know what the hell is happening to me, Dray."

Drea smiled. "I do. I think you're falling in love with a girl you just met for the first time last night. And you know what?" She fell back on the bed next to him. "So am I!"

"I think they came directly from some kind of witch ritual or coven before dinner last night," Stavros quipped. "They did some sort of magic spell. The first people they saw when they walked into Milo and Ginger's would fall madly in love with them. Isn't that what it feels like?"

"It totally does," Drea agreed, staring at the ceiling. "Did Darlene tell you about Traci's intuition?"

Stavros rolled over to look at his sister. "No. What intuition?"

"Well," she started, "Traci has some sort of ability to know things. It's not like ESP or anything. She can tell things about people, just by looking at them. She thinks maybe she can see their auras. She and Darlene are really close; they have been since high school. Traci says until recently she couldn't see anything in Darlene's aura. But recently, she started to see things. Like she knew something bad was going to happen to Darlene not long before her father died, and she made her promise to get help if she needed it. And just a few weeks ago, she got another feeling. This time, it was about her and Darlene. She had a strong feeling that both of them were going to meet the person of their dreams, and in some way, the people they met would connect them together for the rest of their lives. They didn't know how, but Stavros, it's pretty clear now, isn't it? We're brother and sister! How much closer could we be connected? Isn't that amazing?"

Stavros nodded and thought about what his sister said. He didn't know if he believed that Traci had some kind of gift that made her able to tell what was going to happen, but he also didn't close his mind to these sorts of ideas. But he had to admit, she had been right on. So Traci and Darlene believed they had met the people of their dreams. Either it was destiny, or it was a self-fulfilled prophecy, but either way, Stavros didn't care. He and Darlene had seen each other from across the room the night before and made eye contact, before she even knew he had a sister. She had no way of knowing. So he knew they had a connection, and he wouldn't question why it was there. He was simply happy it was.

"Did Traci tell you about the Bishops and the Farmers?" he asked Drea.

"No," she replied. "Like bishops from a chess game? What do they have to do with farming?"

Stavros laughed. Then he relayed Darlene's story about the famous Eastboro family to his sister, but as was his way, he embellished a few facts along the way to make it more exciting for his sister.

Chapter 80

Dance the Night Away

DARLENE KNEW OF A DANCE club right outside of Eastboro that was known for clientele that enjoyed their dancing more than the idea of getting wasted and making fools of themselves. There was a bar, but it was not the focal point of the club. Darlene ordered a white wine spritzer, and Stavros got a Coke. They wandered around the periphery of the dance floor and found an unoccupied round table with two chairs. They sat down to enjoy their drinks.

"So the grand opening went well then," Darlene said.

Stavros nodded. "Yes, it was a full house. We had a couple of newspaper critics, and the reviews this morning were pretty decent. They said we were a place to watch. The diners all seemed happy when they left. We'll see if they come back again. James seemed happy. I think it was great. And James was pretty generous to give me tonight so I could go out with you. It helps that he's pretty fond of you."

Darlene smiled. "Yeah, I'm pretty fond of him, myself," she said. "You should have seen his little blond head when we were in kindergarten. And then we used to chase him and his friends around the playground in second grade!" She laughed. "I'm glad no one has cooties anymore. That was a rough time!"

Stavros laughed. "I bet you were a cute little kid."

Darlene bit her lower lip. "I bet you were quite a sight with your curly little head," she said. "I bet the little old ladies at the grocery store were always trying to touch your hair."

"They were," he confirmed. "And my mom just let them. It made them happy. She was all about peace and happiness." He took a sip of his soda. "Let me know when you're ready to dance."

Darlene swallowed her sip of wine. "Oh, I'm ready," she said. "I don't need to finish my drink."

Stavros stood up and held out his hand. Darlene took it and followed him to the dance floor. They started to move to the music, and Darlene grinned. They danced song after song, and when slow songs came on, they danced, close, but not too close. Darlene could smell his citrus-tinged cologne. It was understated enough that she hadn't noticed it before. It suited him.

They danced and talked for two hours, and then decided to go to get dessert. They drove to Denny's, the only place open at that late hour, and ordered a warm brownie à la mode. They shared it across the table.

"So you had some interviews this week?" Stavros asked.

Darlene nodded. "Yeah, I interviewed at a few counseling centers. I'll need to work in a place where I can be supervised. Oh, that sounds so funny, like I'll be running amok or something!" She laughed. "No, but I need two years of supervision so I can get a social work license. Once I get it, I can go into private practice if I want to. I'm not sure that's what I'll want to do, but it will be nice to have an option."

"I think it's pretty cool that you're a therapist," Stavros said. "I have a lot of respect for the field. I spent some time seeing a therapist, and he really helped me figure stuff out."

Darlene looked at Stavros with respect for his honesty. "I did, too," she said. "Therapy was a real turning point for me. And my therapist, Aspen, gave me something to strive for in my own career."

They sat silently for several seconds. Neither of them volunteered any more information about why they had sought therapy. It wasn't time yet. But they had opened the door to start the conversation.

"So Drea and Traci went out on Friday," Darlene said. "I hear from my camp that it went well."

Stavros nodded. "That's what I hear, too. Drea's just beside herself. She really likes Traci. I've never seen her so excited about a woman before. It's nice, because she had a girlfriend in college, and it kind of ran its course. I'd love to see her happy. Maybe I can stop worrying about her all the time."

Darlene looked at him enviously. "I wish I had a brother or sister," she said. "It would have been nice to have someone there all the time, someone to play with when I was alone. I had my best friend Kim, and she was great. But an older brother to look out for me . . ." She sighed. "Drea is really lucky to have you."

"Thanks," Stavros said, looking her in the eyes. She had found his soft spot. He hoped she wouldn't exploit it.

They left Denny's and drove back to Darlene's house. Darlene was hoping that they would share more than a touch on the arm, but she wasn't sure what. She wanted to touch him, but she didn't want to lose control. After he pulled into the driveway, he turned off the engine and got out of the car. He walked her to the door. They looked at each other silently for several seconds, sizing the other up. Then Darlene reached out to hug Stavros. They held on for the count of ten inside Darlene's head. Then they pulled away. Then Stavros leaned toward her and kissed her on the cheek. His lips were soft and warm.

"Next weekend?" Stavros whispered in her ear.

"Yes," Darlene whispered back, enjoying the sensation of his breath on her skin.

"I'll call you tomorrow?"

Darlene nodded.

"I had a great time tonight, Darlene," he said. "I'd love to take you dancing again sometime. I love your happy smile."

Darlene smiled in response. "Thanks," she said shyly. "I had a great time, too. I'll talk to you tomorrow. Drive safely going home."

"I will," Stavros said, and he stayed to watch her go inside. Then he got in his car and started back toward Amherst. His heart was pounding. He had wanted to kiss her so bad; it was all he could do to hold back one more time. He felt like he might die if he didn't kiss her soon. But he knew the wait would be worth it, both in establishing trust and in building suspense. And the suspense was killing him.

Darlene went to her room and called Traci. She was still up. "Traci," she said. "What am I gonna do? I think I'm in love."

"Darlene," Traci said. "Just go with it. Just let it happen. He's crazy about you. Drea says you're all he talks about. I think he's in love with you, too."

Darlene felt flushed. "How can we be in love?" she pleaded. "It's only been two weeks! We've been on two dates!"

"Darlene, if it makes you feel any better," Traci said, "Drea is thinking of moving to Eastboro so we can be closer to each other, and I'm all for it. Sometimes, you just know."

Darlene considered this. "Traci, do you still want me to move in with you? What if you and Drea end up wanting to live together?"

Traci laughed. "Darlene, if Drea moves in with me, then I will live in a house with you and Drea. I think that would make me happy. And Stavros can join us, too, if he wants!"

Darlene laughed. "I don't think I want to think about that yet," she said. "We haven't even kissed yet."

She heard a clunk. "What???" Traci exclaimed. "Darlene, you have to kiss him! You've heard people say sealed with a kiss, right? I think that's kind of what it means. Next date, you need to kiss him!"

"Have you kissed Drea yet?"

There was a pause. "Darlene, Drea and I have already slept together. I don't see how you and Stavros haven't!"

"Oh my God, Traci," Darlene said. "On your first date? Okay, I'm not gonna judge you. I'm happy for you. Maybe I'm just jealous. Okay, I'll kiss him. Next date. And on Sunday, I will move into your house."

Traci sighed. "I can't wait."

Chapter 81

$\mathcal{T}$HIRD/$\mathcal{F}$OURTH $\mathcal{D}$ATE

"I HOPE YOU HAVE A great time with Stavros, doll baby," Mrs. Feinman said. "I'm just gonna stay at Vee's for the night. I'm taking my stuff with me. But I'll be back by noon tomorrow to help you with the move. What time are your friends coming over?"

"Around noon," Darlene said. She was bouncing with anticipation. Stavros was coming over and bringing Greek food from Olympia's. He wanted to cook for her, but things were too hectic at the new restaurant, so he decided to just introduce her to his favorite local cuisine. Then he would come back the next day to help her move to Traci's house. Her new house. And he would get to spend time with her and her friends. It would be a new experience for Darlene, hanging out with a new boyfriend with her friends. She was excited.

"Okay, doll," her mother said. "Are you ready? Do you need me to pick up any more boxes for you on my way home?"

Darlene shook her head. "I really don't have that much," she said. "And the only things I have left to pack are the things I need to use until tomorrow. I'm good to go. I can just relax and enjoy my date."

Mrs. Feinman smiled. "I really like Stavros," she said, "and I can tell you do, too. I think this relationship is good for you. I catch you smiling all the time, even when you're just sitting there watching TV or eating. This is new for you, Darlene. I'm very happy for you."

Darlene smiled. "I think he's good for me, too. Thanks, Mom."

Mrs. Feinman stood up with a sigh. "Okay, then, I'm heading to Vee's." She gave Darlene a tight hug. "I love you, doll," she said. "I'll see you tomorrow." She grabbed her bag and headed for the door.

"Bye, Mom. I love you."

After her mother left, Darlene scurried around the house doing last-minute cleaning. She set the table and chose CDs to play during dinner. Then she took a shower. She managed to somehow wash and condition her hair, although her mind wasn't on her tasks. Her mind was on Stavros's lips and what it would feel like to kiss them. She mechanically got out of the bathtub and dried herself off.

She would kiss him tonight. It was the right time. But that's all they would do. They would kiss, and then they would stop. She had it all worked out in her head. The third date was for kissing. Fourth date, anything goes. So she had to stay focused and in control. She couldn't let herself get too wrapped up in the moment. She couldn't let herself get pulled in by the desire to please him, to do whatever she thought was needed to make him stay. Stavros would be back. She could tell. He would come back, again and again. And it would happen. It was just a matter of the timing being right. And it would be, soon.

It seemed like it was an eternity until six o'clock. Darlene sat as patiently as she could on the couch, waiting for Stavros to arrive. She focused on her breath. *You've got this*, she told herself. *You're strong, and you know what you want. What you want is just as important as what he wants, even more so. Just keep breathing.*

The doorbell rang at 6:05. Darlene stood up slowly and walked to the door. When she opened it, Stavros was there, and he smiled.

"Hey," he said.

"Hey," Darlene said back. They hugged briefly, and Stavros came inside. He was carrying several brown paper bags filled with food. He took everything out and placed it on the table. The room filled with the aroma of meat and spices, along with something sweet.

"I stopped along the way to get some vanilla ice cream," Stavros said. "The baklava is homemade by Drea. She made it for Traci and was nice enough to share." He opened some containers while Darlene went to get serving spoons. "Just so you know," he went on, "I taught her to make baklava, so in a way, I kind of indirectly made this for you."

Darlene laughed. She loved baklava, and the fact that Stavros appeared to want to impress her with his ability to make it was endearing. They both sat at the table. Stavros served the food and gave a brief explanation of each dish.

"I know you don't like sushi," he said, "so I wasn't sure if you would like dolmades. The grape leaves can be kind of salty, like seaweed. So you don't have to eat them if you don't want to. I like them, so if you don't eat them, they won't go to waste."

Darlene wanted to try the dolmades, so she asked him to put one on her plate. She took a bite and made a face. "Yeah," she said, grimacing. "Salty. But I like the stuffing. Is it okay if I take the inside out and just eat that?"

Stavros laughed. "Darlene, you can do whatever you want. I'm just happy you were willing to try it." After she removed the outer leaves, he took them from her plate with his fork and ate them. "Yum," he said, and Darlene laughed.

They ate in silence for a while, and Darlene enjoyed her food. There were mixes and spices she never would have thought to put together, but they made sense in these dishes. When they finished, Stavros jumped up to clear the plates while Darlene got small plates from the cabinet and spoons for the baklava and ice cream.

As they ate the baklava, Darlene smiled. "Mmm," she said. "I hope you brought enough for seconds!" She could see Stavros smiling at her response. She adored his smile. When they were done, they went to the couch to watch a movie. Stavros had told her that he had never seen *The Princess Bride*, and Darlene had found that tragic. She had rented it at the video store earlier that day. She started the movie, and they watched intently.

Toward the end of the movie, they both watched as the two main characters shared what was described as one of the most perfect kisses in history. As the credits rolled, Darlene turned to Stavros. "I love that scene," she said. "It just makes the whole movie perfect."

Stavros nodded. "It was a really good movie. I can see why it's become such a classic. I wonder if there is such a thing as a perfect kiss."

Darlene's heart thumped. She forced herself to laugh lightly. "When I kiss," she said, "I have this weird habit."

Stavros was intrigued. "What is it?"

Darlene smiled. "Well, at the end of the kiss, I nibble on the other person's lower lip. I mean, gently. Not like I'm trying to bite them or something."

Stavros laughed. "No one has ever complained that you hurt them?"

Darlene shook her head. "No complaints."

Stavros nodded slowly. "Do you think, maybe, you could show me how you do that?" he asked softly.

Darlene nodded. Then, she leaned in closer to Stavros, and they met in the middle. Their lips touched. They moved their lips to various positions and applied just the right amount of pressure. After about a minute, Darlene started to pull away, and she nibbled on his lower lip.

They stared at each other. "Okay," Stavros said. "I get it. I can see why no one complained. But . . . maybe . . . can we try that again? You know, I just want to kind of get a better feel, you know, for the sake of research . . ."

They came together again, and this time, everything else was forgotten. Darlene felt as if her insides might explode with desire. She moved her hands to his shoulders, and then to the back of his head to push his lips even closer. She entwined her fingers in his mass of curls. His hands crept to her waist and around to her back and pulled her body against his own. Darlene moved her hands under his arms and explored his chest and back. Stavros let out a guttural sound, and Darlene shivered. This went on for several minutes, and then Darlene pulled away.

"Oh," she said. "Okay." She took a deep breath. She wanted him. She wanted him bad. She had to apply the brakes. This would be too much all at once. "Wow," she said. "Okay."

"Yeah," Stavros agreed, his hands still touching her waist. "I agree."

"I have to move tomorrow," Darlene said. "It's getting late. And you're going to be helping me move."

Stavros nodded. "Yeah," he said. "And I have a long drive home. I guess I should head out."

Darlene stared at him as her thoughts ran in circles. Then they became clear.

"That doesn't make any sense," she said. "I mean, for you to drive all the way back to Amherst tonight, just to have to turn around and come back here tomorrow to help me. Why don't you just stay here? I mean, you know, to sleep. So you don't have to drive home. You can stay with me, in my room, or if you don't feel comfortable doing that, I can sleep in my mom's room and you can have my room. I mean, it just makes sense, right?"

Stavros had to admit to himself that it did make sense. And he didn't want to leave. He wanted to stay with Darlene, even if it didn't lead to sex. He just wanted to be near her. He nodded.

"Okay," he said. "But I want to stay with you. In your room. We can keep our clothes on. We don't have to do anything else. We can kiss, but that's all. I want to make sure you feel comfortable with that."

Darlene nodded. She couldn't believe that she had asked him to stay and he had agreed. And sex wasn't even on the table.

"Okay," she said. "Well, then, let's go upstairs and get ready for bed."

Darlene went into the bathroom and changed into a nightshirt and sleep boxers. She removed her makeup and brushed her teeth. Then she found an unopened toothbrush in the medicine cabinet and gave it to Stavros. He took his turn in the bathroom and came out wearing boxer shorts and a white undershirt. Darlene turned on her bedside lamp and turned off the overhead light. They crawled under the sheets and comforter. They turned to face each other.

"This is the first time," Stavros confessed, "that I'm going to spend all night in a woman's bed without being wasted and waking up lost and confused with a headache."

Darlene's eyes widened. "Really?"

Stavros nodded. And then he told her everything.

He started with the story of Lindi, about what happened to her at prom, and how she had broken his heart. Then he moved on to the story of his addiction. The beer, and then the weed. The fear and anxiety about getting his next high. His eventual foray into recovery. His fateful relapse his sophomore year and dropping out of college. Coming home and devoting his entire life to recovery and therapy. He told her about his delayed grief for his mother, and how the loss of Lindi had triggered a cascade of feelings he couldn't face, so he drowned them out with substances. Then he told her that everything was good now, and that he still went to meetings for support. He had no intention of ever go back to using, but he had to continue to do the work.

Darlene stared, fixed on his every word. She couldn't believe that this perfect man was sharing this story with her. That he trusted her to the point where he felt he could tell her the most intimate details of the lowest point in his life. It made him more perfect in her eyes. She asked him questions and listened intently. When he was done, there was a long silence. Darlene dared to fill it.

"I had kind of a mental breakdown after my father died," she shared. "But the ball had already been rolling toward that for a long time before his death." She started from the beginning. Her parents fighting. Her desire to block it all out. Her intense need to try to make everyone happy. The multiple Darlenes in her head for every occasion. Her trauma with Charlie. Her forced decision to go to Ithaca, and her failure to become a biologist. Her time with Phil. Her surgery, the true story. And how she hadn't been with anyone since. She left out the part about Traci, for now. She told him about the grief of losing the job she loved when she got promoted, and how that along with feeling alone, and the ultimate death of her father, and remembering the time he said he wished she'd never been born, sent her into a tailspin that she would never have been able to get out of on her own. She credited Traci for saving her life. And Aspen for helping her learn to be whole again.

As Stavros listened to her story, he felt the waves of grief for Darlene's losses, but as she told him about her recovery, he felt hope. They were kindred spirits. They had both fallen to the bottom, but then climbed their way back to the top, still working hard to stay there, and still feeling vulnerable in a world that was so much easier for many others. They were survivors. And the miracle of it all was that they had found each other.

They talked for hours, neither of them daring to admit they were sleepy and wanting to turn out the lights. As the hours passed, the physical space between them closed, and their legs were pushed together, their feet entwined. Finally, Darlene looked at the clock.

"It's five o'clock," she said. "We've talked all night."

Stavros looked at her ruefully. "Crap. And you have to move in a few hours. Maybe we should try to get some sleep."

"No," Darlene said, shaking her head. "You don't understand. We had a date last night. It was our third date. But now, it's Sunday, and it's a whole new day. Wouldn't you say that that means that this is a new date? Like, this is our fourth date?"

Stavros shrugged, not understanding what she was getting at. "Yeah, I guess so," he said. "This can be our fourth date."

Darlene smiled brightly and put one of her hands on each of his shoulders. "Do you know what that means?"

Stavros shook his head. "No, not really," he admitted.

Darlene decided to show him rather than tell him. She grasped his neck and pulled herself closer. Then she kissed him. She kissed him hard and urgently. And then she reached down to the bottom hem of his T-shirt and ran her hands underneath, up his belly to his chest, and caressed his nipple.

Stavros pulled his head away slightly and opened his eyes. "Oh," he said softly. "I see. So I think I understand the significance of the fourth date now." He kissed her some more and started to reach for the bottom of her night shirt. Then he pulled away again. "Darlene," he said, "I need to make sure you know, I wasn't expecting this. I didn't stay because I wanted you to think we had to do this. If you're not ready for anything, please, let me know."

Darlene looked up, then kissed his neck and behind his ear. "Stavros," she whispered. "Thank you for saying that, but I don't feel pressured. I know what I want. I really know. What I want is to be with you right now. I want to be with you completely."

She kissed him and pushed hard against his mouth. Stavros pulled her shirt up over her head, and then kissed her breasts. Darlene moaned softly. Her heart was pounding, and the rest of her body was on fire with yearning. She worked his shorts down off of his legs and touched him. Then she was overcome with a thought. She began to slowly kiss his chest, then his belly.

He stopped her. "Darlene," he moaned. "You don't have to. This is perfect, even if you don't."

Darlene shook her head. "No," she insisted. "I want to. This is what I want if it's what you want. I'm not afraid. I promise."

Stavros lay back on the bed and allowed himself to let her continue. He closed his eyes again and lost himself to the sensation. She worked slowly, and meticulously, exploring and learning the terrain. He ran his fingers through her hair and made soft noises of pleasure. He wanted the whole thing to last, so he stopped her. He kissed her and then rolled her over on her back. Then he reciprocated her actions.

Darlene wanted to surrender. She wanted to let everything go. She wanted to let go of the precipice she had been clinging to forever and fall, fall, fall into the endless pleasure, so she did. She focused on her breath and felt the full impact of his soft, skillful tongue on her skin. It was almost too intense. She moved her body to accommodate the sensation. And then it peaked, and her whole body convulsed. She cried out and grabbed Stavros's head. She ran her fingers through the strands of his hair and pulled lightly as her body continued to spasm, and then she lay still, panting. Stavros looked her in the eyes, and then he climbed on top of her, maintaining his gaze. She could feel him moving closer, until she felt the pleasure mounting, and he was moving fast. Then he slowed down and caressed her face.

"Darlene," he whispered. "You feel amazing. Your body is amazing. You are so beautiful. You're making me feel so good."

He continued to move and talk softly to her. The entire experience was the most intimate she had ever felt with another person, and she almost felt like they had joined their spirits, for at least a short time. She kept expecting it to end, but it went on, and she relished every moment.

Then Stavros looked at her. "Are you doing okay?" he asked. She nodded. "Then how would you feel about getting on top now?" Darlene nodded again slowly. She had never been on top.

He dismounted and rolled onto his back and helped her into position. She didn't think anything could feel any better than how she had felt so far, but she was so wrong. She felt it to her core. It felt like feathers tickling her in her most sensitive places deep inside. She moved in an attempt to make the feeling spread, and it did. Stavros was making intense eye contact with her now, and she didn't dare to turn away. She was locked in. Finally, she could see a change in his expression.

"Kiss me now," he said quietly. She leaned over and kissed him, desperately, and he pulled her head closer. He thrust harder, and then he started to moan. "Oh God, Darlene," he said out loud, and then he became very still. She could feel all the muscles in his body tighten. She felt the tickle increase, and then Stavros made a loud groan. Darlene felt another wave of pleasure through her body, and it lingered. Then they both collapsed in exhaustion.

Darlene laid her head on Stavros's chest. She was feeling lightheaded but didn't want it to end. She didn't make a move to roll away. They stayed still silently, regaining their breath, both deep in thought. Eventually, Stavros rolled her to his side, and she cuddled up against him.

"That was like nothing I've ever experienced," Darlene told him. "You made me feel things I didn't think possible. It's like you already knew my body. How did you already know my body?"

Stavros laughed. "I've been thinking about you, about all of you, since the day I met you," he told her. "I've imagined this night, what it would be like. I guess my body knew what to do. Darlene, you made me feel things, too. Healing things. You make me feel whole."

Darlene stared into his eyes and knew immediately that he was right. They were each other's missing part. They fit together like puzzle pieces.

"Stavros," she said, "I think . . ." She stopped. She wasn't sure if she should go on.

Stavros pulled his brows together. "What do you think, Darlene?" he asked. "You can say anything. I promise."

Darlene nodded. "Remember I told you how I learned about red flags?"

"Yeah," Stavros responded, now worried that he had said or done something that concerned her.

"Well, I'm scared," Darlene went on. "I want to say something to you, but I'm afraid that it might be a red flag for you."

Stavros pulled closer to her. "Darlene," he said softly. "A few hours ago I confessed that I'm a recovering addict. If that wasn't a red flag for you, I can't imagine there's anything you could say to me that would be a red flag."

"Okay," Darlene said. She sighed. "Stavros, I think I'm falling in love with you."

Stavros froze. He was expecting another confession, another story of something that had happened in her past. He was not expecting a declaration of love.

Darlene grimaced. "It was too much, wasn't it? I'm so sorry. It's too soon. I don't want to scare you away. Just forget I said that."

"No," Stavros said.

Darlene blinked. "No? You—you don't . . ."

"No, I don't want to forget it. Ever. Darlene, I wasn't quiet because what you said scared me, I swear. It was just that I can't believe it, and I'm so glad you had the nerve to say it first."

"You are?"

"Yes. Because I'm pretty damn sure I'm falling in love with you, too. I guess I was scared that you wouldn't feel the same way."

Darlene shook her head. "Stavros, I felt something the first time I looked at you, but I knew I couldn't trust just a look. I had to get to know you first before I could let myself feel anything. I've never loved anyone before, and I wanted to be sure. But Stavros, what I've gotten to know about you makes me want to love you even more. Even before you knew my story, you were so kind, and gentle, and understanding, as if you knew that I needed to be handled lightly. And you were so patient. I don't know how you did it. It almost killed me to let you walk away without kissing me last time, but I knew it was right. I knew you did the right thing. I needed to know you were a safe person. And you are. You are more than safe. You are accepting, and interesting, and funny, and so loving. I saw you with Drea. You are amazing. I have never seen anyone so protective, but also willing to step back and let her take risks, even if she fails. That's what I need in my life, and that's what you are to me. I guess the truth is, I'm not falling in love with you, Stavros. I already love you. I love you."

Stavros was struck dumb by her words. He could hear it over and over in his head. *I already love you. I love you. I love you.*

Finally he spoke, and he knew what he was saying might be a red flag in any other situation, but not this one, not now.

"Darlene, I'm gonna start looking for an apartment in Eastboro on Monday. I don't want to be so far away from you anymore. I love you."

Darlene felt her eyes tear up. "Oh my God, Stavros, I can't believe you would do that! But what about your family? You're so close. Won't it be hard to be so far from them?"

Stavros laughed. He was genuinely happy. Darlene wanted him to be close by. She wasn't scared of his words. She wasn't Lindi. She was just concerned about his feelings.

"Darlene, I was planning on moving here eventually to be close to the restaurant, and I have the feeling that when I'm in Eastboro, I'll be seeing Drea even more than I have been in Amherst. She's at Traci's all the time now, and she's looking for a place of her own. And my pop's gonna be retiring soon. He wants to sell the house. He doesn't want to be out there all by himself. He and my mom moved to Amherst for his job all those years ago. I think they did expect to grow old together in that house, but obviously, that's not gonna happen. I think that maybe I can talk him into finding a small house or condo in Eastboro. He'll want to be near me and Drea. And Drea and I will be wanting him to get to know you and Traci, too. It's kind of a win-win situation."

"Stavros," Darlene whispered. She leaned toward him and kissed his cheek. "That would be so amazing. Maybe you can find something near the lake. You'll love it here. It's so beautiful in the summer, and we can skate in the winter . . . if you like to skate, that is."

"I like to skate," Stavros said.

Darlene smiled. "I do, too. I would love to skate with you." She looked at the clock. "It's seven o'clock. Should we try to get some sleep? Everyone's coming at noon. We'll have the U-Haul until four."

Stavros didn't think he would be able to sleep, but he nodded. "I think that's a good idea. We're gonna be tired anyway, but I guess it will be a good tired!"

"I don't start my job until next Monday," Darlene said, "so at least it won't matter if I'm dragging on Monday. But you have a restaurant to run."

She turned her back to him so he could spoon her. He obliged, and she settled in.

"Stavros," she said quietly, "that was the best fourth date I ever had. And I didn't even need to get out of bed for it!"

Stavros laughed and closed his eyes, expecting to lay awake for some time. Both he and Darlene were asleep within five minutes.

Chapter 82

MOVING DAY

THEY WERE AWOKEN BY THE ringing of the doorbell. "Go away," Stavros mumbled from his pillow. Darlene glanced up at the clock.

"Shit," she said. "It's 11:45." She threw the covers back and got out of bed. She walked, naked, to the window and looked out. "It's Traci's car, thank God. I'm gonna go let her in." She put on her bathrobe and headed for the stairs.

Stavros sat up groggily and rubbed his eyes. He looked around, and he smiled. He had spent the night with Darlene. He was in her childhood bedroom. And they'd had sex. And the sex was so good. He felt free of the tension he usually felt upon waking and getting up. He climbed out of bed and found his boxers. Then he slid into his jeans and put on his shirt. He started down the stairs. Traci and Drea looked up at him as he descended.

Drea laughed. "Oh, look what the cat dragged in!" she said. "So why is it that Darlene came down in her bathrobe and you just greeted us fully dressed?" She looked at him again. "Wait a minute. Where are your shoes?"

Darlene flushed. "I need a cup of coffee."

"I'll help you," Stavros said. They walked to the kitchen.

They stopped at the sink and looked at each other. They both started to laugh. "Oh my God," Darlene exclaimed. "We are so busted! And by your sister!"

Stavros smiled. "Think about it, Darlene. They came here together, in one car. Drea is famous for never getting up before ten on weekends. That girl didn't come here from Amherst this morning. She came from Traci's house, and that's probably where she's gonna be after we move you today, too. Better get used to seeing my sister around!"

He came up behind Darlene and wrapped his arms around her. He kissed her neck.

"I don't care who knows it," he said. "I had sex with a beautiful, intelligent, amazing woman last night. That's something to be proud of!"

Darlene grinned, then turned around in his arms and kissed him, the coffee forgotten. The door to the kitchen opened and Traci came in. "Oh come on, you guys! Enough already!" But she was smiling.

Darlene went upstairs to get dressed while Stavros made a pot of coffee. Soon, Mrs. Feinman, Sally and James, Chris and Michelle, and Pete and Carolyn arrived. It was a large group for such a small move, but it was the first time they had all been together for a long time, and they were treating it as a special occasion. James and Pete left to get the U-Haul, and Michelle went in the backyard to watch her twins and Sally's little girl.

Darlene went back to bring some outdoor toys to Michelle. Michelle looked closely at her face. "Darlene," she said, "your cheeks are really rosy today, kind of like maybe you've been kissing someone with a five o'clock shadow."

Darlene absentmindedly reached for her cheek. It was a bit sensitive. "Oh, really?" she asked. "Oh, I'm not sure what that's all about."

Michelle stepped closer and embraced her. "Darlene, I'm so happy for you. Steve seems so great. He looks at you like you're the pot of gold at the end of the rainbow he's been following. And you just look so happy and relaxed. I think you might be on to something here."

"I love him," Darlene said.

Michelle's head jerked back a bit. "Good God, Darlene," she said. "You keep saying things like this to me. I'm beginning to think you're just doing it for the shock value! But you love him? Have you said it?"

Darlene nodded. "Last night."

Michelle circled her hand in front of her in a gesture of impatience. "And . . .?"

Darlene nodded. "He loves me, too." She smiled at Michelle. "He's going to move to Eastboro. Soon. He wants to be closer to me."

"And you're feeling okay with this?" Michelle asked with concern. "You don't feel like it's moving too fast?"

Darlene shook her head. "We talked about it," she explained. "We talked about red flags. We talked about everything. He's been so respectful of my needs. I'm not worried."

Michelle nodded. "Okay," she said. "I trust your judgment. But I don't want you to ever feel like you're letting anyone down if you change your mind. I'm not saying that you're going to change your mind, but just remember that this is about you, not everyone else, okay?"

"Okay, Mrs. Mahoney," Darlene stated obediently. She was actually glad that Michelle was checking these things out with her. She needed to know that her friends had her back, no matter what.

After everything was loaded in the truck, Mrs. Feinman called in an order for pizza for everyone from the parlor on the corner. Traci and Drea went to pick it up. When they left, Sally pulled Darlene aside.

"What's the story with Traci and Drea?" she asked. "They seem to have become awfully close since the soft opening. They weren't friends before, were they?"

Darlene suddenly realized that her high school friends didn't know about Traci. She had not come out to them. She wasn't sure what to do. She needed some guidance. "Sally," she said. "I need your help on this." She sat her down on a kitchen chair. "Traci and Drea are dating. Traci is bisexual. She's in love with Drea. It's pretty serious."

Sally looked shocked, but then she smiled. "That's awesome that they found each other. Isn't it weird, though, that she and Steve are brother and sister, and you and Traci are so close?"

Darlene laughed. "That's the weird part? Sally, you really have nothing to say about the fact that our close high school friend is gay? And has a girlfriend?"

Sally shrugged. "I don't know," she said. "I mean, maybe in high school if I had known, I might have reacted differently, but now it just seems so normal, you know? Like, when a guy talks to me about his boyfriend now, I don't even have to think about it for it to make sense. Maybe it's because of Howie. I don't know. But I think that by the time Jessica is in high school, all of that will be a nonissue. I guess the only reason it would surprise me is because I've seen her with boyfriends, in high school and at Kim's wedding. But I guess if she's bisexual, that explains it."

"Do you think she needs to come out to everyone?" Darlene asked. "I mean, our friends? Or do you think they'll just figure it out?"

"I don't know," Sally admitted. "Maybe she thinks you've already told people. But if not, I'd just leave it up to her what she wants to do. Coming out is a person's personal choice. Someone else can't make it for them."

Darlene nodded. "Okay, well, I'll ask her when she comes back so I know what she wants me to say if anyone else asks me about them. Thanks, Sally. I hadn't even thought about it before now. And yes, it's kind of weird that we're all together. I'm a little concerned that at some point, we'll all end up living at Traci's house together! As it is, I'm fairly sure we'll all be sleeping over there a lot at the same time."

"Yeah," Sally said. "Weird. I think I'd want to poke my eyes out before accidently walking in on my brother, Nate, having sex with his wife in my house. Ew."

Darlene laughed. "In this case, I think we'll all be busy enough on our own to not be paying attention to what's going on in the other bedroom. At least for now."

Traci and Drea came back with the pizza. They put the boxes on the dining room table in front of their friends, and then sat down on the couch. They immediately sat close, held hands, and smiled at each other. If everyone didn't know before, they all knew now. Darlene exhaled and enjoyed her pizza.

Chapter 83

Moving Night

AFTER THE MOVING CREW LEFT, it was just Stavros and Darlene, and Drea and Traci, left at Traci's house. They all sunk into the couches in the living room and chilled out. Traci was lying down with her head on Drea's lap, and Stavros had his arm around Darlene, with her head on his chest. He and Darlene were exhausted after getting fewer than five hours of sleep the night before and then following that with a day of hauling boxes and furniture. They were happy to be sitting in front of the TV with a bowl of popcorn and their favorite people.

Drea finally broke the silence during a commercial break. "So you guys had sex last night, huh?" she said to Stavros and Darlene.

"Drea!" Traci said, sitting up.

Stavros laughed. "Drea's bluntness is okay with me if it's okay with Darlene," he said. "We aren't your normal brother and sister. We talk about everything. Not usually in front of other people, but yeah. So Darlene, I'll let you decide how you want to answer Drea's question."

Darlene leaned her head deeper into Stavros's chest and grinned. "Drea," she said, "I'm in love with your brother."

Drea gasped, and her hands flew to her mouth. "In love? Oh my God! You two! I can't believe it! I'm assuming that if you're telling us this that he has said it back."

She looked at her brother, who nodded. Stavros smiled to himself at the way Darlene had gotten out of answering Drea's private question. Drea could make up her own mind about what went on the previous night.

"Well, I'm psyched for the two of you! This is amazing!" Drea cuddled closer to Traci. "We've been talking about some serious stuff, too," she went on. "Have you two ever heard the term U-Hauling?"

"I've heard of U-Hauls," Darlene said. "I rented one today, remember? Is U-Hauling the act of moving things in a truck?"

Traci laughed. "Don't worry, Darlene. I never heard of it until this weekend, but now it's like my very favorite thing. It's kind of a joke in the lesbian community. The joke is, what does a lesbian bring on a second date?" Stavros and Darlene shook their heads. "The answer is a U-Haul! Apparently, it's quite common to move in together pretty quickly." She paused. "So Drea and I are thinking of U-Hauling, and I wanted to see what you both think about that."

Stavros shrugged. "I think it's great," he said. "I mean, I assumed Dray would be over here all the time anyway, and you might notice that Darlene deliberately chose a bedroom not right next door to Traci's. We figured a buffer zone might be a good idea." They all laughed. "But I mean, as long as there are boundaries, I think it's a great thing. And I'm gonna start looking for an apartment nearby tomorrow, so hopefully I'll move soon. And Pop won't be far behind us; I'm guessing when he retires next spring. Drea, I'm just glad we won't be so far apart."

Drea nodded. "I don't want to be far from you ever again, Stav," she said. "It's too much. I don't think I'm over Pittsburgh yet. If you go, from now on I will follow. Well, I guess I'll need to consult with Traci now, but you know what I mean."

Darlene looked from Stavros to Drea and back. Their connection made her feel warm inside. She looked at Traci, who smiled at her. Traci was happy with Drea. Darlene was happy with Stavros. It was a perfect moment. Then she yawned audibly. Stavros squeezed her shoulders.

"I'm gonna take you to bed now," he said quietly. He looked up and saw Drea and Traci grinning at him. He shook his head. "I'm going to put her to bed," he clarified, "you perverts. And then I'm gonna lay down next to her." He helped her to her feet, and they started toward the stairs. "Good night," he called back.

As they climbed the stairs, Darlene looked up at his face sleepily. "You're going to put me to bed?" she asked with a grin.

Stavros shook his head. "No," he said, as they walked into Darlene's new room. "I lied to them. I'm gonna take you to bed, and I am going to take off all your clothes, and I am going to make love to you until you feel more love than you have ever felt, and then I'm gonna hold you all night until you wake up, and then I'm gonna make love to you again. And by then, I'll probably need to take a shower."

He looked over at Darlene. She was crying.

"What is it?" he asked, sitting her down on the edge of the bed and taking seat next to her. "Did I say something wrong?"

Darlene sniffed, and then smiled. "No," she reassured him. "You didn't say anything wrong. It was all just right. I've never had any man make love to me ever until last night. I mean, yes, I've had sex, but it wasn't making love. And now that you've made love to me, the idea of doing it again is like adding an extra layer to an already delicious cake."

Stavros smiled. "I know a thing or two about cake, Darlene. After all, I'm a chef."

Darlene laughed, but then her face got serious. "I don't know how I got so lucky! How did we manage to be at the same place, at the same time, and to look up at the same moment, to meet each other's eyes and make a connection? How does the universe work, that things like this can happen? Is it science? Is it magic?"

"Yes," Stavros answered softly. "It's magic. That's the only thing it can be. Whatever it is between us, it's magic, and I believe in it with all of my heart."

Darlene swallowed and looked away. "But . . . what if this is just some sort of trick of the imagination? What if it all disappears? What if I did go crazy last year after all, and this is all a delusion? I'm not crazy, Stavros, that's not what I'm saying. But what I need to hear you say, and what you keep saying, is that you're here, and you're real, and you're not going to disappear. I just need you to keep telling me that, to reassure me that you're not going to go away. And if you are going away, don't just disappear. Be honest about it. Talk to me. Tell me everything. Don't keep secrets from me. Just love me the way you have already. Love me every day."

Stavros sat, breathless, listening to her words. They were jumbled, and rambling, but they made perfect sense. And he was willing to do everything she asked. He was willing to do it every day, for the rest of his life. He could barely contain himself, but he took a breath. He put his hands on both of her cheeks and looked into her eyes.

"Darlene," he said softly, barely above a whisper. "I love you. I have loved you since the beginning of time. I will love you until the end of time. If anyone tries to pull me away from you, I will fight them with all my strength. I will never leave you. And I will remind you of this anytime you need me to, even if it's the first thing you need me to say to you every morning, or the last thing before we go to bed."

"Stavros," Darlene said quietly.

He pulled her to him and kissed her hard. She put her arms around his neck and kissed him back, and they fell back on the bed. His face was getting damp from her tears, and he could taste the salt on her lips, but he kept kissing her. Finally, he pulled away and looked back into her eyes.

"I want to take things slow, Darlene. I want us to learn about each other. I want to know every inch of you, and see you in every situation, in every season. I want us to make latkes together, and teach you about Greek cuisine. I want to take you to my mother's grave, and go to see your father. Maybe someday, I'll go to see him by myself and ask him permission to marry you, if that's what we decide we want."

Darlene put her hand to her mouth and laughed. "Oh my God, Stavros!"

Stavros smiled. "So we'll be together for all the seasons, and if we still feel this way, and I know we will, we'll know that this magic trick was the best trick ever cast by any magician in the history of magic."

"How do you come up with this stuff?" Darlene asked, looking at him in awe. "It comes out of your mouth like an epic poem. I open my mouth, and a jumble of words pours out in random order. But you speak like an ancient poet. It's like verbal music. You are amazing."

Stavros grinned. "You have to remember," he told her. "I was raised on romances and tragedies, epics and lyrics. My mother read me poetry while she nursed me. I've been hearing stories on a daily basis since I was still in the womb. I have a lot of words inside me, Darlene. Rebel gave them to me because she knew I could use them. And now I can. And I want to use them on you."

Darlene wiped her eyes with the sleeve of her shirt. "Magic, huh?" she said. Stavros nodded. Darlene nodded back. "Okay, I can accept that. So we have magic. So show me some more of your magic now. I'm ready for it."

Stavros felt as if his tether had been untied, and his lips were on hers, his hands on her body immediately. They made love until they exhausted themselves, and then they slept for hours.

Chapter 84

SEASONS CHANGE

IT HAD BEEN A YEAR since Milo and Ginger's had their soft opening.

"I made us a reservation for tonight at six," Stavros told Darlene. "We're closing early tonight for a private party at seven, an engagement party. We're not taking any reservations or walk-ins after six."

"I can't believe it's been a year since the day we met," Darlene said, shaking her head. She embraced Stavros and buried her face in his chest. "It's been the best year of my life."

Stavros closed his arms around her and held her tight. "Mine, too," he said softly. Then he pulled away. "Okay, we need to go to work. So I'll plan to meet you at the restaurant at six, then."

They walked out to the driveway of Darlene, Traci, and Drea's house and said goodbye with a kiss.

Darlene arrived at the restaurant at 5:55. She was not surprised to see Sally there with Jessica, and her new baby, Naomi. "Stavros is still working in the kitchen," Sally told her. "He asked me to show you to your table."

Darlene followed Sally and the kids to a table for two against the wall by the kitchen door. Sally sat down in the other chair, shifting the baby to make room for Jessica on her lap.

"Remember that night last year, when we opened?" Sally asked. "It was the start of so many things, for all of us. I can't believe how fast time flies by. It seemed so slow when we were younger."

"That's true," Darlene said. "A year for the restaurant, and a year with Stavros. Everything seems so perfect, but I'm afraid to jinx it by being too happy!"

Sally smiled warmly. "I know you and Stavros believe in magic," she said. "You just need to keep believing in it. It will take care of you. Just trust it. You'll see."

Stavros came out of the kitchen, dressed in his work khakis with a dark polo shirt. He approached the table. "Good, you made it," he said, leaning over to give Darlene a kiss. "I was worried some client would have a crisis right at the end of the day and keep you from me on our special anniversary night." Sally stood up, and Stavros sat down across from Darlene. "I already put our regular orders in with the kitchen, and they'll bring things out one at a time. That way, we don't need to worry about interruptions." He took her hands across the table and smiled. "Remember last year, when you came in through that door and we saw each other for the first time?"

They spent the next hour eating food that was created from the mind of Stavros and reminiscing about their year together. They laughed at their silliness and recalled arguments that were settled by using kindness and makeup sex. When their dinner dishes were empty, they were cleared and replaced by dessert. They shared warm baklava with vanilla ice cream.

As they were finishing up, James came out of the kitchen and approached the table. "Hey Darlene," he said. "I've got to grab Steve for a second in the kitchen to check on some last-minute details for our private party. Could you excuse us for a sec?"

"Sure," Darlene said. "One of the hazards of having dinner at your own restaurant, I guess."

Stavros laughed. "I'll be right back," he told her and leaned down for a kiss.

Darlene finished the last bites of her dessert and then dabbed her mouth with her napkin. She dropped the napkin on the floor and bent down to pick it up. When she sat back up, there was a woman standing beside her. She gasped.

"Kim!" she exclaimed. She jumped up from her seat and threw her arms around her lifelong friend. "Oh my God! What are you doing here?"

Kim pulled away and smiled. "Carl and the kids and I flew in this morning. We were invited to a big party for one of our friends, but I knew I had to come here first to say hi to you. I wanted to surprise you."

"Where are Carl and the kids?" Darlene asked.

Kim bit her lip and tilted her head. "They're right over there," she said, pointing to an area behind where Darlene was standing. Darlene turned around slowly.

And there was Carl with the kids. And next to him was Michelle and Chris and their three children. And Pete and Carolyn. And Drea and Traci. Deanna and Mario. Alec and Felicia. Andreas. And Darlene's very own mother, standing with her best friend Vee. Darlene was baffled. "What the hell is going on?" she said, spinning around to face Kim.

But Kim was no longer there. Now, in front of her, was Stavros, and he was looking up at her, perched on one knee. He had changed his clothes and was now wearing a suit jacket and a tie. He was holding a small velvet-covered box in his hand. Darlene gasped, and her hands shot up to cover her mouth.

"Darlene," Stavros said softly. "Last year, you walked through that door and directly into my heart. I knew there was something magical about us the first time I saw you. And now, we've spent 365 days together. That's 52 weeks, 12 months, and four complete seasons. And the magic is still with us every day. Last year, you asked me to tell you that I would never leave you, and I have, but now, I want you to have this ring as a symbol of my promise to you that we will be together forever. All you have to do is look at this ring, and you can be assured, I will never leave you." He paused and opened the tiny box, revealing Rebel's engagement ring. "Darlene Renee Feinman," he said, his voice shaking with emotion, "will you marry me?"

Darlene's eyes opened wide, and she opened her mouth. She had forgotten how to speak, but now she knew she must. She tried again. "Yes," she said. "Yes, yes, yes!" Then she sank down to the floor on one knee. "And you, Stavros Karras," she said through tears. "Will you marry me?"

Stavros smiled through his own tears. "Yes," he answered. Then they both knelt on both knees and reached for each other for a kiss. They heard applause behind them. Darlene pulled away and looked up.

"Stavros," she said. "I can't believe you got all of our friends and family here! This is perfect! But don't we have to clear everyone out soon for the private party? You said there was an engagement pa—" She stopped and looked into his eyes. "The engagement party is for us, isn't it?"

Stavros smiled at his future bride and nodded. "Thank God you said yes, huh? That's how confident I was that you would say yes," he told her. "And if for some reason you didn't, I would have made up some story about Drea and Traci or something. But you did say yes. Thank you, Darlene, for saying yes."

They both stood and embraced again. Then their guests started to approach, and the room became loud with conversation and congratulations. Darlene could not stop her tears. She was surrounded by so much love and support. Everyone was there for her because they wanted to celebrate her happiness. For a moment, it became too much. She pushed through the kitchen doors and rushed to the open back door to get some air.

Moments later, Traci found her and stood beside her. "You're still afraid it's not real, aren't you?"

Darlene nodded. "What if the spell wears off? What if things go back to the way they were? What if one day, Stavros wakes up and looks at me, and wonders what the hell he's gotten himself into? Traci, can someone really promise to never leave you? I mean, we can't see the future." She paused. "When my mom and dad got married, they promised to love each other forever."

Traci nodded. "I know," she said. "It's all so confusing. We don't have a crystal ball, even with my intuition. Do you know, I have not had even one intuition since the day I met Drea? Maybe, Darlene, whatever magic I had all that time, maybe some of it was transplanted that night last year when we met Stavros and Drea. Maybe that's the magic that we both feel." She paused. "Our night together, over a year ago," she said quietly. "You and I shared the magic. I think that's how it started. And then we gave it to Stavros and Drea. It's love, Darlene. You can trust this love. It's very, very strong."

Darlene looked at Traci as the tears rolled down her cheeks. She reached for her and held her tight. "I love you, Traci," she said. "And you'll always be magic to me."

Traci let go and handed her a napkin, and Darlene wiped her eyes. The door to the kitchen opened, and Stavros spotted Darlene across the room. He approached her. "Traci, can you give us a minute?"

Traci smiled, then embraced Stavros. "Congratulations, you two," she said, and she crossed the kitchen and returned to the dining room.

"Darlene," Stavros said. "In all the excitement and confusion, I forgot something very important." He pulled the velvet box from his suitcoat pocket. "I never gave you the ring."

Darlene laughed. "Oh my God, you didn't!"

Stavros opened the box and Darlene examined the ring.

"It's so beautiful," she whispered. "I can't believe it's mine! Was this Rebel's ring?"

Stavros nodded. "It was. And she would be so thrilled to have you wear it, I know. She would have loved everything about you." He removed the ring from the box and slipped it onto Darlene's finger.

"It fits!" she exclaimed.

Stavros laughed. "It better," he said. "You have no idea what it took for me to figure out your ring size. I got it sized. Again, that's how sure I was that you would say yes."

Darlene grinned. "As if I would have ever said anything else!" She stared for several seconds at her sparkling new ring. Then she and Stavros grabbed hands and went back out to their engagement party.

Chapter 85

Making Plans

THE NEXT SEVERAL MONTHS WERE a flurry of activity. With the restaurant gaining success and popularity, Stavros was there most of the time. He and James were doing well enough that they could splurge on hiring a general manager and a weekend manager. They would continue to work in their offices at the restaurant, but the day to day activity would be handled by people who knew what they were doing. And Stavros and James would have the weekends off, barring any crises.

Darlene and Mrs. Feinman were busy planning a wedding. They were gathering brochures in a large binder and making calls for estimates. Darlene knew she wanted a traditional wedding, but she wanted certain aspects from the Jewish and Greek Orthodox faiths. They had chosen September 14 as their wedding day, as it was Stavros's name day, but it was also the day of the celebration of the Exaltation of the Holy Cross, an especially important Greek Orthodox remembrance. They chose the fifteenth instead. They would wear Greek wedding crowns and stand under the chuppah. The couple would step on a glass after being pronounced married. Olympia's would cater the wedding, but Stavros would also make a giant challah for the guests to make blessings over before the meal was served. And there would be dancing. Lots of dancing. The guests would have access to many ceramic plates. There were other minute details, but Darlene couldn't keep them all straight. She was glad her mother was there to help keep her sane.

Stavros, Darlene, Traci, and Drea drove to Amherst on the Monday of Memorial Day to help Andreas pack up his house. He had bought a cottage on the shore of Carson Lake and would be progressively moving his belongings over the next two months. He had officially retired from the university at the end of the school year and had been given honors at the graduation ceremony the day before. He was ready to be close to his children again and not to be bogged down by such a large house.

By five o'clock, Drea began to complain of starvation, and she wanted Chinese food. They all chose their orders, and Drea called them in. Then Stavros and Darlene headed into town to pick up the food.

They had half an hour to wait, so they decided to walk around. They held hands as they window-shopped and pointed to items they would love to have when they bought a house together that coming summer. They approached the CVS and Darlene stopped. "Can we go in here real quick?" she asked. "I need to get some Advil. I forgot I used the last one the other day, and I'd hate to be out if one of us needs one."

"Fine by me," Stavros said, and he opened the door for her. They walked to the back of the store by the pharmacy, and Darlene found what she was looking for. They started back toward the front to check out when a woman came speeding around the corner, and they had to stop quickly to avoid running into her.

"I'm so sorry, excuse me," the woman said as she shuffled around them in a rush.

"Lindi?" Stavros called out.

The woman stopped short. She turned around slowly. "Stavros?" she said with disbelief in her voice.

Stavros took a step closer, not letting go of Darlene's hand. "Wow, Lindi," he said. "I haven't seen you since, well . . . You look good. What are you doing in Amherst? I thought you were living in Colorado?"

Lindi glanced at Darlene, and then back at Stavros. "I was. I mean, I am," she said. "But my mom's been having some heart problems, so I came home while she's having some tests done, to support her. I just stopped here real quick to pick up her prescription."

Stavros nodded. "Oh," he said. "Well, I hope everything works out for your mom. So are you still in Aurora?"

Lindi nodded. "I'm working as a science teacher in an elementary school, just like I always wanted. I love my classroom. We even have a guinea pig. What have you been doing with yourself?"

"I own a restaurant in Eastboro with a friend," Stavros said. "I'm a chef now. And before you ask, no, it's not a Greek restaurant!"

Lindi laughed, and then turned to look at Darlene.

Stavros remembered his manners. "Lindi, I'd like you to meet my fiancée, Darlene Feinman. Darlene, this is Lindi. Is it still Leahy?"

Lindi nodded. "Yeah," she said with an awkward laugh. "Still Leahy." She reached out her hand toward Darlene and smiled warmly. "It's nice to meet you, Darlene," she said. "Deanna had mentioned that you were engaged, Stavros, and that they really like your fiancée. I'm really happy for you both." She glanced at Darlene's left hand.

Darlene felt a rush of empathy toward Lindi. She looked a lot more human, and fragile, than she had expected. She wanted to make this less awkward. One part of her wanted to just walk away, but another almost wanted to invite her to dinner, to hear more about her, to see what she had been doing all these years away from Stavros. But instead, she lifted her hand. "Would you like to see?" she asked.

Lindi nodded gratefully and took Darlene's hand gently. She smiled. "It's Rebel's ring," she said. "It's so beautiful." Darlene could see a tear in the corner of Lindi's eye. "Treasure it, Darlene," she said softly. "Treasure him. You found yourself a great guy."

Darlene squeezed Stavros's hand, and he squeezed back. "I know," she said.

Lindi blinked a few times. "Well, I've got to go. Mom's out in the car waiting." She looked directly at Stavros. "I wish you all the happiness in the world, Stavros," she said.

Stavros nodded. "Thanks. That means a lot. You too. It was really good to see you."

Darlene smiled. "It was really nice to meet you, Lindi. Take care."

They walked in opposite directions. Darlene made her purchase, and she and Stavros left the store. They headed for the Chinese restaurant to retrieve their food.

Darlene stopped before they went inside. "Are you okay?" she asked him.

Stavros nodded. "Yeah" he said. "Yeah, I really am." He pondered for a moment. "There was a time in my life where I couldn't even see myself having a life without Lindi. I just didn't see the point. God, it was so intense, so real. But once I went through recovery, I realized what her loss represented to me. I had made her so much bigger than life when we were together. Everything was about Lindi. About being with Lindi. I didn't have any place for just me. I think Lindi was supposed to fill a hole in me left vacant by my mother, but she wasn't my mother, she was just this young, vulnerable girl, trying to survive into adulthood. But now," he took both of Darlene's hands in his, "now I have someone in my life who completes me. You don't have to save me, Darlene, you just have to be by my side. We're partners, and we're heading in the same direction. I forgive Lindi for what happened when we were eighteen, but I also thank her for saying no. If she had said yes, everything would have been different, and not in a good way. But you said yes, and that's all that matters."

Darlene nodded, and then reached out to hug Stavros. "Yes, I did say yes," she whispered. "And I would say it again. I have no doubts, no second thoughts. You are my partner. We are in this together. We both have an equal say. And right now, I say that your sister is starving and we'd better get this food back to her."

Stavros laughed and gave her one more squeeze. "Let's get some food to Drea," he said. "And then we can think about heading back home."

About the Author

Debby Meltzer Quick is a full-time social worker in Portland, Oregon. She has been writing for fun since age twelve. Growing up in Massachusetts, she became a huge fan of Boston sports, especially the Red Sox and the Patriots, and she aspired to be a sports reporter. She is an avid reader of fiction. She lives with her husband, daughter, two cats, and one rabbit. She has completed two series of seven books each that take place in the fictional city of Eastboro, Massachusetts, in the 1980s. Watch for more books in the McKinney High and Anomaly series coming soon!

Don't Miss the Next Installment in

The McKinney High Class of 1986 Series

⁓·⁓

Revenge Not So Sweet

Book 6

Turn the page for a sneak peek!

Chapter 1

WHAT HAPPENED OVER THE SUMMER

RHONDA JENKINS COULD FEEL THE eyes on her. It was the first day of eighth grade, and she had developed a lot over the summer. It was hard for her to see her own progress, but it had happened. She had gone from a training bra to a B-cup, and her waist had gotten trim and curvy. Her skin was smooth and free of acne, and she had naturally straight teeth. She had gone shopping with her friend Carol the week before school started, and she was surprised to see that she could now wear some of the same clothes as her brother's classmates in high school. For her first day of school, she had chosen a pair of Gloria Vanderbilt jeans and a halter top. Her back was bare except for the ties around her neck and midriff. She had bought some makeup, and her stepsister helped her figure out what made her hazel eyes stand out. She found a beautiful shade of pinkish-red frosty lipstick, and she enjoyed the feel of the balm against her lips.

She found her homeroom and was grateful to see Carol, who had also been in her homeroom the year before when they were sorted by alphabetical order into seventh grade classes. She and Carol Jasper had been friends since they were in fifth grade at DeMarco Elementary. Rhonda's mother and stepfather had just gotten married and they all moved into her mother's new husband's house south of Carson Lake. Rhonda transferred from Devers Elementary to DeMarco. Carol and her family had moved to Eastboro, Massachusetts, from Illinois the year before, so both of them were very new to the school. Now Carol was sitting at a desk next to Sheila Kenton on one side, and Felicia Iglesias on the other. Sheila and Felicia had been Rhonda's friends at Devers before she left, and now they were reunited at Randall Junior High. When they saw Rhonda, Sheila and Felicia stood up quickly to offer her their seats next to Carol. Rhonda was embarrassed. She didn't expect special treatment from her friends just because she was their unofficial leader. She just had more confidence than they did, and she could talk to people with ease, even back in the days when her chest was still flat.

"Sit back down, you guys," she said, choosing a desk behind Carol where neither of them had been sitting. "I'm fine right here. But thanks."

Carol smiled. "Your new clothes look great on you," she said. "Patrick and Greg J. are both staring at you. Don't look!"

Rhonda slowly turned her head until she was nonchalantly facing the back of the room, as if she just wanted to see what was back there. It was true. Patrick and Greg J. were gawking at her. They smiled and waved when she looked at them, and she smiled back and turned back to her friends. Then she looked to her side. Greg K. and Phil were also glancing in her direction. Rhonda found herself crossing her arms in front of her torso.

"You look amazing, Rhonda," Sheila said with her eyes wide. "What did you do over the summer? Whatever it is, let me know. I want in on it!"

Rhonda laughed. "I didn't do anything!" she said. "Carol and I just hung out while you guys were away, and went to movies and hung out. I guess, well, I just had a growth spurt or something."

Felicia shook her head. "When I get a growth spurt, I just get taller and more awkward. And I usually get more zits. You didn't grow, Rhonda, you developed. There's a difference."

Rhonda felt her face get hot, but she smiled. Her friends were trying to be nice, not make her feel uncomfortable, and she wouldn't make them feel uncomfortable by resisting their efforts.

"Thanks so much, you guys," she said. "You all look great, too. I wish summer could have lasted forever, but it's so good for us to all be back together!"

Mr. Feldman came into the room as the bell rang and introduced himself. He would be their first period science teacher. He handed out their personalized daily schedules. The girls all had their first four core classes—science, math, English, and history—together, and then they split up after lunch for their enhancement classes—art, music, gym, and shop. Rhonda had woodshop for the first half of the year. She thought it looked like fun. And she loved to watch the boys work in shop. They seemed much more motivated in classes like that than in their academic classes. At least the boys that she noticed. She hoped she would see them sometime during the day.

When she met her friends for lunch, Rhonda looked around. Not only were the boys looking at her, but the girls were also staring, and turning to talk to their friends. Then their friends would look. Rhonda looked down at the table. She felt embarrassed, but she also felt something else. A smile came to her face. People were noticing her. People had noticed her before, but it was always because she was nice, friendly, and confident. Now they were looking at her because she was hot, too. She knew she was hot, because before she left for school, her stepfather had tried to get her to change her clothes. He had said it was because he worried that she would get cold.

So she was hot. She always wanted to be pretty, like her stepsister, Sasha, but she had never seen it happening for her. People did things for Sasha. They opened doors and brought things to her. They offered her help. They gave her gifts. This was going to get interesting. She wondered who was the most interested.

John Preston was sitting at the next table. He was one of the most handsome boys in their class. She caught him looking. He was confident. He smiled at her. She turned around and looked at another table. She saw Carl Bishop, Chris Mahoney, Pete Cooper, and Jamie Newell. The boy posse. Carl and Chris were looking. Carl looked away, but Chris returned her stare. He wasn't gawking at her. He was just looking at her in a different way. These were the baddest of the bad boys. There were worse boys, but they weren't "bad" in the same way as the boy posse. The boy posse was a group of boys that got in trouble a lot, but they weren't mean. They weren't bullies. They just didn't care about authority or convention. If it were twenty years earlier, they probably would have been anti-establishment hippies. As it was, they typically wore worn-out blue jeans, T-shirts, and denim or leather jackets.

Rhonda gave Chris a grin, then turned back to pay attention to her friends. They talked about their morning classes and what the afternoon would bring. So far, they didn't hate any of their teachers, which was a good sign. Rhonda hadn't liked Mr. Crisp in the beginning of seventh grade. She could tell he was probably kind of a loner, and he had a thing about popular kids. He didn't seem to think they had substance. But she showed him through her work and behavior that she was a good kid, and eventually he came around. When she saw him in the hall that day, he smiled at her and said hello. She hoped that maybe she could find another teacher this year that challenged her and took her seriously.

After lunch, Rhonda had music, Spanish, and gym. She could see the afternoons would be a breeze. Spanish would be the biggest challenge, but her stepfather could help her. He had spent seven years in Spain after college teaching English and was fluent in Spanish. And it would be great to have gym at the end of the day. She wouldn't have to change out of her gym clothes or take a shower with the other girls. She wouldn't have to worry about her makeup and hair getting messed up for the rest of the day. Chris Mahoney was in gym class, along with Pete Cooper and John Preston. Rhonda considered having cute boys in her class could mean two things: looking sexy to them in her shorts, or getting embarrassed if she was forced to climb up a rope ladder. She shrugged it off. She could probably make struggling up a rope look cute.

It was a warm and sunny day, so Rhonda and Carol decided to walk home from school instead of taking the bus. After dropping Carol off down the block, Rhonda continued to her own house. She tried the knob before inserting the key and found the door unlocked. Her brother Matthew had gotten home before her. She could only hope to escape to her room before he noticed she was home. Matthew was in a bad mood all the time now. His girlfriend had broken up with him over the summer. This was right after their mother and stepfather had revoked his driving privileges for two months after he had gotten a ticket for speeding and running a stop sign. They were making him do extra chores to offset the cost of his fine, and he wanted Rhonda to suffer every minute of his indignity with him. She would rather avoid that.

"Hey, Buttface," Rhonda heard coming from the kitchen. "Don't come in here. I just mopped the floor."

Rhonda sighed. "But I'm starving!!" she protested. "Can't you just throw me a Devil Dog or something?"

She heard a grunt from the kitchen. "Learn how to live with hunger," Matt yelled back.

Rhonda didn't know why Matt was so hostile lately, or why he took it out on her. They had been much closer before Matt had suddenly gotten popular with girls after getting his license. He had never gotten attention like that before, and it had gone straight to his head. Then Lana broke up with him after his ticket, and he decided that she had just been using him for his access to a car. But that wasn't Rhonda's fault. Rhonda would have just dumped him because he was kind of a jerk. She would never use a guy for his car. Well, maybe she would accept rides from a guy if he expected nothing in exchange, but she wouldn't lower herself to be with someone for her own selfish purposes. She would never be able to fake it like that.

"If you don't give me something to eat," she snapped back at her brother, "I'll dump Mom's favorite Ficus plant and all its dirt on the kitchen floor before she gets home, and she won't see all the hard work you did to make it shine like Grandpa Sam's bald head! I'd hate to see what chores she gives you to make up for that."

There was silence from the kitchen. Then a sigh. "Fine," Matt said in a voice of resignation. "You're like one of Cinderella's evil stepsisters."

Seconds later, a plastic-wrapped Hostess Cupcake whizzed by her head and slammed into the wall behind her, falling to the floor. Rhonda picked it up and noticed it was now reduced to crumbs embedded in white cream filling. Matt had a strong pitching arm. She shrugged, then lugged her bookbag to the stairway and went up to her room.

Her stepsister Sasha was lounging on her twin bed in their shared room, reading a novel. "You got home early," Rhonda said, throwing her bag on her bed and ripping the cupcake package open with her teeth.

Sasha looked up and gave her a smile. "I'm a senior now," she said smugly. "I have study hall last period, so I can basically just leave." She rolled over onto her back and put her book face down on her ample chest. "How was the first day of eighth grade? How did the outfit go over? I'm surprised Mrs. Cataldo didn't send you home to change."

Rhonda laughed around chewing on her creamy chocolate crumbs. "No, no one said a thing," she said. "Maybe if I was one of the trouble-makers or something it would have been different. But all the teachers love me. I think I might have actually seen some of the male ones looking at me a little longer than they should have, but I guess they're just human." She got on her bed and laid down, mimicking Sasha. "But there were also some guys my own age checking me out, so that was cool. Maybe a tiny bit creepy. I might have seen some of them drooling." She snickered.

"Any worth giving a second look?" Sasha asked. Sasha had a framed picture of her boyfriend, Danny, on her bedstand, and she was glancing at it now.

Rhonda shrugged. "There was Johnny Preston—oh, I mean John. He goes by John now. He actually smiled at me and didn't look all rattled. It was kind of funny. He never would have given me the time of day last year. I guess boobs do really make you stand out." She laughed. "And Chris Mahoney kept looking at me. He seems so confident. I kind of like that. Most of the guys still trip over their own shoelaces."

"Isn't he the guy that leads that, what did you call it? Posse?" Sasha asked with a grin.

Rhonda smiled. "Yeah, he's kind of a bad boy, but I think he'll grow out of it someday. The bad boys in that posse are all too nice. I don't even see one of them ever dropping out of school or getting hooked on drugs. Well, maybe Carl Bishop. He seems kind of out in left field, but you just never know."

"So are you going to, you know, give either of those guys any of your attention?"

Rhonda closed her eyes. "I don't know yet," she admitted. "I mean, I might look a lot older this year, but I don't know. I still feel like a kid. I mean, I want to go on a date, and I want to kiss a guy for sure, but I just don't know if I'm ready. Maybe I feel confident about some stuff, but there's part of me that remembers that all guys are gross. When is that supposed to change?"

Sasha actually guffawed. "Rhonnie," she said. "It never stops. You just learn to ignore it more. Then, when you get in a relationship, it's easier to ignore. But then when you get serious with a guy, they start letting their grossness out again. I don't think you can get away from it. Just like my dad. He farts in front of your mom all the time. Gross. I'm just glad he holds off when Danny's here. But I'm sure Danny farts, too."

Rhonda shot Sasha a look. She didn't like it when Sasha said negative things about her stepfather. She loved her stepfather. He had come into her life when she was nine, and he had been like an angel swooping down from heaven. They had become close quickly, and Rhonda was his biggest fan. She never even thought about her real father. He had left when she was three, and she barely remembered him. Her mother had pictures of him in a shoebox somewhere in the hall closet, but Rhonda wasn't even interested in seeing them. Her stepfather, Eric, was the only dad she needed.

"Everyone farts, Sasha," she said. "Some of us just do it quietly."

Rhonda heard the door downstairs open, then close, and then Eric's voice calling up the stairs. "Girls," he sang out, "come down and help me bring the groceries in from the car."

Rhonda jumped right up, but Sasha rolled her eyes, set her book aside, and slowly moved her legs closer to the edge of bed. "My dad's not perfect," she told Rhonda knowingly. "Give it a couple of years. I promise you, all dads are nasty and embarrassing. Mine is no different."

Both girls ran downstairs and out the door to retrieve the groceries.